The fiery ~~you see on the cover is created by "laser holography." This~~ *is the revolutionary process in which a powerful laser beam records light waves in diamond-like facets so tiny that 9,000,000 fit in a square inch. No print or photograph can match the vibrant colors and radiant glow of a hologram.*

So look for the Zebra Hologram Heart whenever you buy a historical romance. It is a shimmering reflection of our guarantee that you'll find consistent quality between the covers!

HE HAD TO LOVE HER THEN LEAVE HER

Here was Lisa ... beautiful, precious Lisa, whom he had never stopped loving. He ached, knowing none of it could ever be again. "Lisa," he groaned ....

He pulled her into his arms. "I have never stopped loving you, Lisa," Chaco whispered.

"And I have never stopped loving you," Lisa answered. "Oh, Chaco, I try to forget ... those wonderful days we had together ... and the nights. I try so hard, but I can't."

His lips were kissing her hair, her temple, her cheek. She turned her face to him, and then his lips were searching her own.

Wrong! So wrong it was now, yet so right. How she needed to kiss him again, hold him again. He had so little left. How could she deny him just one last kiss?

ARIZONA ECSTASY

F. Rosanne Bittner

ZEBRA BOOKS
KENSINGTON PUBLISHING CORP.

ZEBRA BOOKS

are published by

Kensington Publishing Corp.
475 Park Avenue South
New York, NY 10016

First printing: November, 1989

Printed in the United States of America

... For all my readers who have waited so patiently for a sequel to Arizona Bride, *and for everyone who loves a good Indian story.*

F. Rosanne Bittner

Introduction

This book takes place in Arizona in the late 1800s, the last days of freedom for the Apache Indians; days when some of their leaders made names for themselves, men like Geronimo and Cochise. As with most other tribes of American Indians, the Apaches trusted the white man and his treaties for too long—until it was too late to fight the inevitable. With a friendly attitude they allowed some whites to come into their land, little knowing it was like letting a crack in a dam go unchecked.

Nearly all events in this novel that involve Cochise and Geronimo—skirmishes with soldiers, massacres, treaties, and reservation life—are historical facts gained from material available to the public. The greatest share of information comes from *Geronimo: The Man, His Time, His Place,* by Angie Debo, University of Oklahoma Press; *The Mescalero Apaches,* by C.L. Sonnichsen, University of Oklahoma Press; and *Bury My Heart at Wounded Knee,* by Dee Brown, Holt, Rinehart & Winston.

The primary characters in this novel are fictitious, as is the basic story; the conversations of my fictitious characters and their involvement with actual episodes and historical characters of the time are products of the author's imagination, designed to fit reasonably with the actual historical events and supposed words of real characters, based on historical record regarding the nature and personality of those characters.

Prologue

There were many battles, treaties, betrayals, and many Apaches on reservations by the year 1863, and it was quite possible that problems with those Apaches who remained rebellious would have calmed from then on—if it were not for the hideous betrayal of one beloved leader, Mangas Coloradas. He was an old man (approximately seventy-three) when he went to soldiers to make peace that year, only to be tricked, arrested, burned, and tortured before finally being shot and decapitated, his body thrown into a sanitation ditch. The old man's murder was uncalled for, and only reactivated Apache uprisings, for Mangas Coloradas was the father-in-law of Cochise, whose name, along with that of Geronimo, would bring fear to the hearts of any white man, woman, or child living in Apache territory.

Cochise and Geronimo were Chiricahua Apaches, who still lived wild and free in the rugged mountains of Arizona. They were soon joined in raiding and revenge by Mescalero Apaches, who had escaped from their hated reservation at Bosque Redondo in New Mexico and were under the leadership of another famous warrior, Victorio. Together this small army of Apaches wreaked havoc on ranchers, miners, soldiers, and townspeople throughout the Southwest and into Mexico. They were called savage murderers, but they only fought for what they felt rightfully belonged to them, and in retaliation for brutal massacres and betrayals by soldiers and the government they had once trusted.

These Apaches were outnumbered a hundred to one by whites, yet they were responsible for a reign of terror that went unchecked for several years, for once the Civil War was over, many soldiers were withdrawn from the Southwest, and some forts had been abandoned. There was simply no money for such things, and the Apaches lived under the white man's general assumption that it was quite all right to murder any Indian they found, even if he was peaceful. No white man was ever convicted or even brought forward for killing, raping, or scalping any Indian, but all Indians were held responsible for any such acts committed against whites, no matter how provoked.

The Apaches' one advantage was the land they knew so well—their ability to hide, their skillful warrior ways, and their endurance. The Apaches could generally outride their pursuers, live much longer without water, survive for days without food, bear the thorns and heat of the Southwest, and disappear into the hills without a trace, leaving their pursuers in constant confusion and exasperation. The Southwest was their domain, and like the wild animals, they knew all the secrets of survival that the white man had to learn the hard way.

Still, the Apache knew his days were numbered, for the white man came to their land is such great numbers it was impossible to fight them all, and the white man's guns and mountain howitzers far outmatched the renegades' tearing, jagged arrow. The Apaches' ability to hide, to strike with surprising quickness, and disappear again, was the only thing that prolonged the inevitable and final demise of their way of life.

There were some who foresaw this sad future very early. One was called Saguaro, and he gave up his life—and gave his son to a white man—to ensure the child would survive. Saguaro's only consolation was that the boy, called Chaco, would be going to live with his real mother . . . a white woman. What the future would hold for his son, Saguaro would never know. That future belonged to his beloved White Flower, known to the white world as Shannon Fitzgerald Edwards, wife of Bryce Edwards, the man who would become Chaco's stepfather, and the man at whose hands Saguaro was killed. Shannon and Bryce's story, and the story of little Chaco's warrior father Saguaro, is told in my novel *Arizona Bride*.

This novel is the story of Chaco, and his white half brother, Troy. It is also a story about the almost impossible choices some people must make in life—choices half-breeds like Chaco had to make during a time when Indians aroused only hatred in the hearts of white men; choices a woman must make when she loves two men but can belong to only one of them; choices brothers must make when they find they are both in love with the same woman. . . .

"... we heard that some white men were measuring land to the south of us. In company with a number of other warriors I went to visit them. We could not understand them very well, for we had no interpreter, but we made our camp near their camp, and they came to trade with us. We gave them buckskin, blankets, and ponies in exchange for shirts and provisions. We also brought them game, for which they gave us some money. We did not know the value of this money, but we kept it and later learned from the Navajo Indians that it was very valuable.

Every day they measured land with curious instruments and put down marks which we could not understand. They were good men, and we were sorry when they had gone on to the west. They were not soldiers. These were the first white men I ever saw."

Geronimo

Chapter One

1890 . . .

Lisa paced nervously along the platform. The train would arrive soon. It didn't seem right that Chaco should be arriving on a train. He should be coming on a horse, a grand stallion perhaps, painted, with feathers tied into its mane and tail.

Chaco! She took a deep breath and squeezed her hands together to keep from trembling. What would he be like, especially after the terrible injury he had suffered? Did he have any feelings left for her? It had been so long ago—that night he had come to her, risking his life for one last moment with her. Perhaps it had been wrong to take him that night, but she did not regret it, nor did she regret the few precious months they had together when they lived and loved in the Apache hideaway of the Dragoon Mountains.

The memory of those golden days when they dared to love, when the Apache were still the rulers of the Arizona wilds, was still so vivid. She still could see his broad, bronze shoulders hovering over her, taste the full lips that covered her mouth. His big but gentle hands had moved over her so gently, while his mouth teased hers in the most bewitching ways.

Oh, how she had loved him—how she still loved him! She

put a hand to her chest, trying to calm her pounding heart. Chaco was coming home. How should she greet him? How would he look at her? So many things had changed, but not their love for each other. Surely not that! It was strange how fate had led them all together—Chaco, herself, Troy. If her father had not left Illinois all those years ago, she would never have known Chaco at all. But the fact remained that she had, and he had been her first man, claiming her virginity for himself, and she had loved him all these years.

But always he had been tormented about his mixed blood, a torment that led him into the pathways of his warrior relatives in a time when the land was still wild and untamed. Chaco's spirit had been Apache, and it had taken him away from her.

Now he was coming back to a different Arizona, a civilized Arizona. He had left on a train, almost three years ago, in a cattle car that carried him to the awful prison in Florida. Now he would return on a train, this time, at least, as a regular passenger. But it would not be the same Chaco who returned. She would need great courage. She would show him how much he was still loved. His injury would not interfere or make him less a man. How could one such as Chaco ever be considered less? Everything about him radiated manliness and courage and power. Perhaps she'd been wrong to give herself to him so long ago, but how could she have said no? She had wanted him more than anything she had ever wanted in her life, and just the thought of his touch still made her feel warm and weak.

If only little Sage could be here to greet him too. Poor little Sage! At least there was Charles, precious, beautiful Charles, the seed of the Apache man who would arrive soon on the train . . . a remnant of the great love she had shared with that man.

She could see the train coming now, and her heart raced.

Her breathing became even more labored. Thank God for his brother Troy. It was Troy who had gone for him—Troy who had tried to convince Chaco that he should come home now that he was free from prison. Was there a man of more conviction and love and dedication than Troy Edwards? She did not think so. And she had loved him, too. But that was another chapter in her life.

"Chaco," she whispered, praying he was finally ready to live in the white man's world. All the events, both joyous and terrible, leading up to this most important moment in her life seemed to flash through her mind at once. How strange that she stood here now, waiting for an Indian man ... this girl from Illinois who had never even seen an Indian until Chaco came along. Her heart soared with love and anticipation, but she knew she must face the very real possibility that he might not be on the train at all. . . .

1873 . . .

Troy Edwards and his brother Chaco raced their horses in friendly competition, red dust flying as they strayed much farther from their father's trading post than they were allowed to go. But in their excitement they paid little heed to where they were, only to kicking and coaxing their horses to ride hard and fast. Chaco rode a red thoroughbred called Indian, a sleek gelding with powerful shoulders and a high spirit, one of his father's finest horses and a gift earlier that spring for Chaco's thirteenth birthday. Troy rode a black mare called Dreamer, one of Bryce Edwards' swiftest mounts, and it was a toss-up which horse was truly the fastest, for each had its share of winning. Indian had won more times than Dreamer, and Troy never stopped trying to change the record.

They headed through a canyon, for the wind was with them today, and both horses seemed eager for the race and not at all tired yet. The sound of the animals' hooves echoed against the canyon walls, making it sound as though there were several horses there instead of just two. In one last strain of kicking and hollering, Chaco managed to reach the distant canyon wall first. Indian reared triumphantly and Chaco let out a war whoop. If anyone had been watching at that moment, they would have seen a young man who was purely Indian, his long black hair flying out behind him, his body nearly naked because of the heat. He wore only a loincloth and apron, moccasins and a headband. Chaco had lately insisted on not only wearing his hair Indian style, but dressing Indian style. Again his mother had reluctantly agreed, feeling helpless to stop the changes that were taking place in her son's soul.

Chaco's yelp came back at him in echoes, and he grinned, for it sounded like there were many Indians hiding in the cliffs above, all shouting war cries. Troy came riding up to him, laughing good-naturedly. "I think Dreamer is just lazy today," he told Chaco. "She was neck-to-neck with Indian and then I felt her slow down on her own."

At ten, Troy was an excellent rider, always determined to keep up with his big brother. But he was sure he would never have the easy way on a horse that Chaco had. There was a grace about Chaco that seemed to come naturally, and when he sat on a horse he and the animal seemed as one. Already Chaco had relinquished a regular saddle for the smaller, padded seat of an Indian saddle, a hand-made contraption that was covered with a blanket. Even without having lived with the Indians, their ways seemed to be inbred in Chaco, so that he did many things their way without even being totally aware of Apache habits and customs. And the boy could do tricks on a horse that were so dangerous they were forbidden by his mother and father, but he practiced them whenever he was away from them.

"I think she loses on purpose sometimes," Chaco answered his brother. "She is a tease, that Dreamer. That's what Father says." He swung a leg over his own horse and jumped down; Troy wished it were that easy for him. He was much shorter

16

than Chaco. It was not that he was too short for his age, only that Chaco was too tall for his. At thirteen, Chaco looked more like sixteen, and even his physique was already looking muscular and manly.

Troy swung his own leg over, sliding down but hanging onto his saddle horn until his feet met the ground. Chaco was standing and staring at the red-rock walls of the canyon, scanning them carefully.

"Is he there?" Troy asked his brother.

Chaco's face was very sober now, and he dropped the reins of his horse, letting the animal stroll at random and rest, nibbling at a few patches of bunch grass. "No," he answered quietly, "but I feel a presence."

A chill moved down Troy's spine. His brother fascinated him, for the older he got, the more he seemed more Indian than white, with the incredible Indian instincts they had heard their father talk about, the ability to sense things others could not, to smell things others could not smell, to see things no one else knew were there. Troy knew about the man Chaco had often seen watching him from the hills, the man he was sure was the spirit of his own father, Saguaro.

"Why don't you ask Father and Mother to tell you more about Saguaro," Troy told his brother. "We're old enough to know, at least you are. Mother is always saying she'll tell you some day. If you plan to come to the mountains alone some day and search for him, you should know all about him first."

Chaco nodded. "I suppose." He faced Troy. "I'll ask them—tonight. Will you help me? I never know how Mother will act. Sometimes she gets so upset when I ask about him, and Father gets that funny look on his face, as though he is guilty of something. I don't understand it."

Troy nodded. "I'll help you."

"Do something to soften Father up first and put him in a good mood. You can do that. He likes you better than me."

Troy frowned. "No he doesn't. He loves you, Chaco."

17

Chaco shrugged. "I'm not his true son. It would only be natural for him to love you more. I understand."

"But he doesn't, Chaco. He treats us both the same."

Chaco shrugged. "I know. I just worry sometimes that he doesn't love me as much. Sometimes he gives me that look, like he's wondering something about me. But I know he does love me in his own way, and would help me just as much as you."

Troy kicked at a stone, his blond curls looking almost white in the hot Arizona sun. "If Father loves me more, then Mother loves you more. She looks at you with different eyes too. It's because of your real father. He is dead and she mourns him still."

Their eyes met again, at first challengingly. Then Chaco managed a smile. "Now I am the one who says you are wrong. Mother loves us both the same. But maybe we're both right." He stepped closer, looking down at his brother. "But we won't let it come between us, will we, Troy? We're brothers. Some day I might be Apache. I mean, maybe I'll live with them and ride with them. But I would still be your brother. Would you still like me if I went to the Apaches?"

"Sure I would. But why would you do that, Chaco? I would miss you."

Chaco turned and walked over to a large, flat rock. He leaped up onto it and carefully studied the canyon walls again. "I know. And I would miss you. But there is this ... this strange feeling inside of me, Troy. Sometimes I want to run away to the hills and never return. I want to sleep on the earth and drink water from a stream and kill my own food and live under the sun and stars. Sometimes our little room in the loft seems like it's smothering me and I feel afraid inside, like I am a captive there and will never be allowed to leave." He turned to face his brother. "And when I sit down to study letters and numbers with you and Mother, my insides get all tight and my chest hurts, and I feel like I can't breathe. Do you think it's the Apache in me, Troy? Do you think perhaps I won't stay forever with you and Father and Mother?"

Troy felt a lump grow in his throat. "I don't know, Chaco. I hope you can stay. I'd be very lonely if you left. Who would ride with me and help me with the chores and talk to me at night about all the things we talk about? Who would teach me things and take supplies to the fort with me?"

A bitter smile passed over Chaco's face. "The fort." He made a face and an odd hissing sound. "Some of those men are not so nice to me when I go there alone. I have been raised by a white man and woman, have always lived the white man's way. I can read and write, and I have a white brother. But to them I am pure Apache, just because my skin is dark and my hair is long. They don't care that I've never even lived among them, at least not since I was old enough to remember. Some of them say bad things to me, when I have done nothing to offend them. I don't tell Father because I know how he is and he can't always be fighting other men over me. I'm getting too big now to run to Father. But some day I'll be so big that I will break their noses myself when they say those things. That will shut them up!"

Troy grinned. "I bet you could break their noses right now! You're big enough, Chaco."

Chaco looked away bashfully. "I don't think so. Not yet." He kept studying the canyon walls, then looked toward the only entrance to the canyon, a good hundred yards away now. "Say, Troy, I wonder where we are. Look at this place. It's a box canyon. There is only one way in and out. I don't think it's very safe here, and I think perhaps we have ridden farther than we are allowed."

Troy stared around at the red walls that seemed to radiate the sun's heat. His fair face was red and his gray eyes showed slight fear now. Chaco was right. This was a perfect place to trap an enemy. He felt goosebumps in spite of the heat, for Chaco had said earlier he felt a presence.

19

"Do you think someone is watching us, Chaco?"

Chaco nodded. "We had better not eat Mother's bisquits here. We should get our horses and start out, but let's not ride fast. Whoever watches might suspect that we know. If we do not act afraid, perhaps they will leave us alone." He walked to Indian, and Troy went to his own horse, deathly afraid that if Chaco was right, it was Apaches who watched. Who else would be lurking in such a place? And wouldn't they just love his blond curls as a trophy? Soldiers had teased him about that for years, some going into graphic descriptions of how a man is scalped. His father had told him many times that scalping was not an Apache practice, but the soldiers loved to fill him with their own stories, including tales of torture.

"Chaco," he spoke up as they mounted up.

"Yes?"

"If . . . if it is Apaches . . . and if they come after us . . . you will tell them I'm your brother, won't you? They won't harm you. You're just like them. But maybe they will take off my hair like the soldiers said."

"You believe too much of what the soldiers say," Chaco answered. "I don't think they are as bad as some men say, and Father says they have good reason to be so angry. But you know they consider our father and mother friends. They wouldn't harm you. I would tell them . . ." He drew up the reins of his horse, staring at the canyon entrance. "Troy, look!"

Troy stared wide-eyed at a small band of Indians who had now lined up at the canyon entrance. His heart pounded furiously and his head ached instantly. Why? Why had they strayed so far from the trading post? Why had they disobeyed? Now what would they do? Would they be taken prisoners and held for ransom, or perhaps adopted as Apaches as other children had been? Or would they be hideously murdered for invading an Apache domain?

One of the Indians rode forward slowly, holding a lance that had a piece of white cloth on it.

"Troy, look! He comes in peace. He wants to talk!" Chaco seemed not the least bit afraid, and his dark, handsome eyes actually lit up with excitement. "That one is someone grand and special, Troy, I can feel it. Look at how he sits his horse. And he is tall, much taller than those others."

"Is he ... is he the one you see watching you sometimes from the hills?"

Chaco studied the man intently as he came closer. "No. No, he is not the same one. I am convinced that one is my father, Troy, because only I can see him. This man is someone else. I wonder what he wants with us? We're not important people."

Troy could not answer. His voice had completely left him. The only sound in the canyon was that of the ghostly clomping of the hooves of the approaching Indian's horse on the hard-rock canyon floor. As he came closer, they could see he was a handsome man, taller than most Apaches, his hair shining clean and brushed out straight and long over bare, bronze shoulders. He was lean and muscular. He wore leggings and moccasins but no shirt. His face looked hard and weathered, and it was difficult to guess his age. Chaco thought perhaps mid-forties, Troy thought perhaps fifty. The man rode directly up to Chaco, while the rest of the Indians stayed behind at the canyon entrance. Neither Chaco nor Troy had any doubt they were Apaches, and Troy felt the skin of his head growing hotter.

Finally the warrior's horse halted, and the man sat staring for a long time at Chaco. He nodded then, a slight smile moving over his lips. "You are Chaco, son of Saguaro."

Chaco was not afraid, for the man's dark eyes looked at him almost lovingly. He nodded.

"I am Cochise," the man said quietly.

A small gasp came from Troy's lips, but Chaco was not surprised. Somehow he already knew who it was on the painted buckskin-colored stallion before him. "You knew my father," Chaco spoke up, more as a statement than a question.

Cochise nodded. "You are his image, Chaco. Many winters

21

I have wondered about you, how you looked, if your heart was as strong and brave as your father's. I see no fear in your eyes, only pride. You are not afraid of the Apache?"

"Why should I be?"

Cochise's dark eyes turned to Troy and moved over him, making the boy feel faint. Cochise looked back at Chaco then. "You have been raised among whites. And so you must think like whites."

"Half of me is Apache. You won't harm me, because I'm Saguaro's son. I only ask that you don't harm my brother. He has a good heart, like his father, whom you also honor."

Cochise held his chin high. "This is so. Bryce Edwards has compassion and understanding for the Apache, which is why he left the white man's army. He once saved my own wife from the hands of white men. For this I owe him, and so I have never brought him harm, nor would I harm his son."

Troy breathed easier, swallowing, drenched in perspiration, but not from the hot sun. His scalp finally stopped tingling.

"How is your mother, the one Saguaro called White Flower?" Cochise was asking Chaco.

"She is well," Chaco answered. "Sometimes there is still sadness in her eyes when anyone speaks of my father."

Cochise scrutinized the boy closely. "And have they told you how your real father died?"

Chaco shook his head no. "They say when I'm old enough, they'll tell me all of it. I don't understand about my mother and Saguaro, for I know of no white woman who would love an Apache man. But there is no hatred in her eyes for him."

Cochise nodded. "It is a story still told among our people, about White Flower and Saguaro, how they came together, how they were parted, and how Bryce Edwards ..." He checked himself. "It is a story your mother and Bryce Edwards must tell you, not Cochise."

"Why have you shown yourself to me then?"

Cochise looked the boy over again. "Your father was an

22

honored and respected warrior who fought at my side many times. I wished only to see his son. Cochise knew where you lived, and sometimes he has watched you from afar. Sons are very important to the Apache, and Cochise was wondering, now that you are growing older and wiser, whose son you are, Chaco—a white man's or an Indian's?"

Chaco's heart tightened with the terrible indecision that had been plaguing him lately. "I . . . I'm not sure. Many times I myself have wondered. I honor my white father, and I love my mother. But sometimes I feel a calling, a need to ride into the hills and be with my real father's people."

Cochise nodded again, smiling more then. "The Apache blood in you is strong then. We need young warriors, Chaco, but more than that, a man must follow his heart."

"My white father has told me this."

Cochise looked pleased. "Bryce Edwards is a wise man." He glanced at Troy again. "And surely his son will follow in his own father's footsteps and be a brave and honorable white man who speaks with a straight tongue."

Troy just stared at the man, tongue-tied and totally in awe of the infamous Apache leader. How many men were allowed to see this man so close these days? Cochise was a hunted warrior, an elusive enemy that thousands of soldiers had been unable to find. Yet here they sat, talking to the man as though he were some kind of long-lost friend. What would his father and mother have to say about this? Cochise looked back at Chaco, eyeing the reddish gelding the boy rode.

"You ride well, both of you," he told Chaco. "It was a fine race."

Chaco beamed. "Sometimes Troy wins. His horse gets lazy sometimes and thinks it is funny to lose at the last minute."

Cochise laughed, a robust, surprising laugh that lit up his otherwise somber face and brought out an amazing handsomeness and kindness that did not always show. "So, you know horses well, do you?"

"I do," Chaco replied. "My brother and I are in charge of all my father's horses, and we help deliver the foals. Sometimes we take them to Fort Bowie all by ourselves to sell or trade with the soldiers."

Cochise's smile faded. "And are you friends with the blue-coats?"

Chaco shrugged. "Not so much. Some of them are good to me. Others are not. They spit on me and call me names because I look Apache, even though they know I live with whites."

A sneer came to Cochise's lips. "The white man has a strange way of judging a man. Does it make you ashamed?"

Chaco sat up straighter. "No. It only makes me angry. Some day I will put my fist into their noses and watch the blood flow."

Cochise laughed again, totally delighted at this son of Saguaro. He was big and strong for his age, and very handsome. He was every bit his father in looks and spirit, and surely it hurt White Flower to look at him, for he must be a constant reminder of Saguaro. Cochise wondered how the boy would feel about Bryce Edwards when he found out Edwards was the man who had killed Saguaro. "It feels good to watch a man's blood flow when that man has been cruel to you. I have seen the blood of many white men flow at my hands."

"Why?" The word came from Troy, who was astonished with himself for even speaking up. But it had come out so easily. "Why do you make war all the time and kill so many white people—women and little children?"

Cochise shot the boy a quick look of surprise and anger. "Why? Because of all the broken treaties," he said calmly but loudly. "Because of all of our women who have been raped and murdered and scalped. Because land that belongs to us by right, through treaties signed by the white man's leader, is being stolen from us by men hungry for gold and a place to call their own. Because all our game is being killed off, our forests stripped, our streams made unclean! Because we have been

24

tricked too many times, lied to too many times, cheated too many times."

The great chief breathed deeply, looking around the canyon. "We said the white man could come to this land if he just took the gold and left. But he was not satisfied with that. More and more came, and now they build cities in Apache country and they herd together the weak ones and push them onto useless land where they are told they must stay and can never leave, never ride free again, never hunt. They force the white man's religion and customs upon us. The Apache trusted the white man's word. But he was a fool to do so. I myself was cruelly tricked, and two of my brothers and a cousin were needlessly hanged, for nothing. Cochise does not forget!"

The man looked back at Troy. "Cochise has been blamed for things he did not do. Whatever happens, the Apaches are accused. If Cochise is to be judged so, then he will commit the crimes for which he is blamed, and perhaps one day the white man will give up and go back where he came from."

Troy looked anxiously at Chaco, speechless after Cochise's long tirade, but Chaco looked as angry as Cochise. The older man looked at Chaco then. "Our hearts were not bad in the beginning," he told the boy. "It was the white man who made them bad. And you, Chaco, are in the middle. One day you must decide which way to go."

"And would I be safe if one day I rode out to be with the Apache, to learn the ways of my father, so that I can better choose?"

Cochise nodded. "Not far to the south and west are the Dragoon Mountains. You have only to ride there alone, and when Apaches find you, say only my name, for they will not understand English. But they will know the name, and they will bring you to me. This is what I came to tell you. I have been counting the years since your birth, and you are thirteen winters now. You are close to being a man in the eyes of Apache. And there are many of my people who would like to see Saguaro's son."

Their eyes held in a deep understanding. "Sometimes I see a man watching me," Chaco told the man. "But no one else can see him. I think it's my father's spirit, watching over me. First I'll speak to my white father and find out the story of my mother and Saguaro; then I'll go into the hills and try to find my father's spirit and learn what it is he wants of me. After that, I'll come to the Dragoons and live with the Apache. I can't say that I will stay. I only wish to learn about my father's people."

"It is enough, son of Saguaro. It is good that you seek Saguaro's wishes. But you must be sure your mother understands that you do not desert her, nor would ever stop loving and honoring her as your mother. It will be hard for White Flower to let you go. But she loved and understood Saguaro, and so will she love and understand his son." His eyes moved to Troy again. "And she has another son, a fine son, the blood of Bryce Edwards, who will always be with her." The dark, all-knowing eyes moved back to Chaco. "I go now. You will tell only Bryce Edwards that you have seen Cochise. No one at the fort must know."

Chaco nodded. "We won't tell them."

The faint smile passed over Cochise's face again. "I believe you. Your word is good." He turned his horse and called out something to the other men. They turned their horses and were suddenly gone. Cochise rode toward the canyon entrance, then turned his horse once, holding up his hand as a farewell. Chaco held his up, but Troy sat frozen and still astounded. Then Cochise rode through the entrance, and all was an unnerving silence so still that Troy's ears hurt. He finally turned to his brother.

"Chaco! It was really him! Cochise!"

Chaco's eyes were watery. "We are honored this day, my brother."

"Chaco, will you really go there, to the Dragoons? Will you really go to live among them?"

"I think perhaps I must. Cochise says I must know both ways, and I think he's right. I'll go and talk to Father and Mother and we'll tell them all that happened here today. I'll ask them to tell me about my real father, and when I know the truth, I'll decide what to do." He turned and faced Troy. "Don't worry. Whatever I do, it won't change how I feel about my brother, and I will come back to see you again. Maybe you could even come and live among the Apache one day. Wouldn't that be a fine thing to tell your children and grandchildren about?"

Troy frowned, then brightened. He had not thought until then just what a privileged situation he might be in, brother to someone highly regarded by Cochise, son of a respected white man. What was there to fear? "Yes, it would, Chaco. Hurry! Let's go tell Pa!" He rode off at a gallop, but Chaco held back. He knew this would not go easy on his mother. And what had Cochise meant by asking if he knew how Saguaro had died? What was it about his mother and Saguaro that they had never told him? Surely he was old enough now. It was time to know the truth, however painful it might be for himself and others.

He rode out behind Troy, looking all around when he got through the canyon entrance. There was no sign of life. Cochise and his men had disappeared like ghosts, making the boy wonder for a moment if they had been there at all. He felt like he was acting out a strange dream, but then Troy called to him and he knew it was real.

Chapter Two

Troy reached the trading post first, jumping off Dreamer and dashing inside to his father, who was setting boots on a shelf.

"Pa! Pa! We saw Cochise! We saw Cochise!"

Bryce Edwards turned to his son, his face showing alarm. Bryce was a big man, still extremely handsome for his forty-three years, most of them spent in hard living in the wilds of Arizona. His hair was still thick, and combed in neat, golden waves that graced the collar of his shirt. His eyes were a gentle gray. He was a hard, strong man, once an army colonel. His beloved wife Shannon came hurriedly through the curtained doorway of a back room, her green eyes wide, her face pale.

"What are you talking about, Troy?" Bryce asked.

"Cochise! Chaco and I saw him! We even talked to him!"

Bryce looked over at his wife, who was visibly shaken. He immediately walked over to her and took her arm, leading her to a bench. "Sit down, Shannon." He squeezed her shoulder and looked at Troy. "Where did this happen? And where is Chaco?"

"He's coming. He was right behind me." They heard horse hooves then, and Shannon grasped her husband's hand anxiously. In spite of her untold hardships since coming to this land, she retained her graceful, southern beauty. Once a wealthy

Virginia-bred young girl, she was now the wife of an ex-colonel who ran a trading post near Fort Bowie, where he had once served. There was an air of mystery around the red-headed, beautiful Shannon Edwards, for everyone knew the half-breed boy called Chaco was her own, and that his father was the once-infamous Saguaro.

"We were riding," Troy was saying excitedly. "And we ..." He stopped, realizing he had to admit they had gone farther than allowed. "We ... we were racing, Pa. Dreamer was winning, and then Indian pulled ahead, so I made Dreamer run faster, and we ... we didn't pay attention to where we were going." He jammed his hands into his pockets, looking down at the floor. "We went too far. We ended up in a canyon ... south of here, I think. It was a box canyon."

"A box canyon? For God's sake, Troy, the only box canyon south of here is Snake Hollow. That must be five miles from here! The both of you know better—"

Chaco came through the doorway, and immediately Bryce saw the change in him, a new maturity about his face, an odd determination in his eyes. Shannon saw it too, and she squeezed Bryce's hand harder, rising from the bench.

"Chaco," she said softy. "What is all this about Cochise?"

Chaco looked straight at her. "I want to know, Mother. I am old enough to know about you and my real father."

Bryce watched him carefully. "And what did Cochise tell you? I would like an explanation of all of this first, Chaco, from the beginning."

Chaco met his stepfather's eyes. "We rode too far."

"So Troy tells me. I will consider what to do about that later. What if it hadn't been Cochise? What if it had been some band of renegades who had no idea who you were? Troy's blond curls would tempt a renegade to grab him for ransom, and you know it. The both of you took a great risk going so far. You don't even carry guns!"

"I am old enough to carry one," Chaco argued. "You should

let me." He held his chin defiantly, with the air Bryce Edwards had so often seen in proud Apache warriors—the same haughty look his own father had carried. "We are sorry, Father. But now I am glad, for I have seen Cochise and I am honored."

Bryce eyed him closely. "What did he tell you? What did he want?" Chaco swallowed, glancing at his mother. "He said he had watched me before, and that he wanted to see me up close—wanted to see how Saguaro's son had grown. He said that I look just like my father, and he . . . he asked if my spirit and heart were like my father's."

Tears filled Shannon's eyes. "And what did you reply?"

Chaco looked from her to Bryce, then back to his mother. "I said I . . . was not sure . . . that sometimes I feel more Apache than white. Cochise told me that some day I would have to decide . . . and he said that if ever I wanted to know what it was like to be Apache, I could ride to the Dragoon Mountains and not be afraid . . . that someone would take me to him and I could live with him as long as I wished."

Bryce felt his wife's hand trembling in his own, and he put an arm around her to support her. "You've hit your mother with all of this too quickly," he told Chaco, upset with Troy also for bursting in with the news so suddenly. "First the two of you ride too far and risk your very lives, then you come running back to tell us you've seen Cochise and he kindly invited you to come and live with him. Do either of you have any idea how all of this affects your mother? You could have been more tactful."

Chaco's dark eyes flashed to his father, and for the first time Bryce saw a hint of rebelliousness, an independence that had not been there before. "Perhaps we would understand better if we knew about my mother and my father. How can we know how she feels about things when no one tells us the truth? Now that I have seen someone who knew my father so well, fought beside him, I want to know more about him. I want to know everything there is to know. And I want to know how he died.

30

Cochise asked me if I knew how he died, as though it were some strange secret."

Bryce paled then, and his mother sank to the bench again, as though she would fall if she didn't sit down. Bryce decided there was no other way than to say it straight out. Chaco was looking for answers, and those answers could not be avoided forever.

"Your father died at my hands," he answered calmly.

Chaco's eyes widened, and he looked Bryce Edwards over as though he had suddenly become an enemy. "You? But ... my father was a great warrior ... a good fighter. You said so yourself. Why? Why did you kill my father, and how? Did you kill him because you wanted to take my mother away from him?"

"He did no such thing!" Shannon rose then, anger in her eyes. "You asked for answers, Chaco. You will get them. But I will not have you blaming Bryce for things he could not help. No one can say now which man would have won. Bryce was an officer in the army, and he and his men ran into renegade Apaches led by Saguaro. They fought, and Bryce found himself in hand-to-hand combat with Saguaro. Bryce is as good a fighter as Saguaro was, but it's possible Saguaro would have killed him. As it turned out ..." Her voice broke and she covered her mouth with her hand. "Saguaro ... wanted to die, Chaco ... because ... because he had given you up ... to me ... and Bryce ... to safety ... knowing there was nothing but death ahead for the Apache. And without his son his heart was broken, and ...."

She could not go on. She sank back onto the bench as Troy watched in wide-eyed wonder.

"Your father fought hard, Chaco," Bryce continued, pain in his own eyes. "I respected him, honored him. As we fought, I sensed he was deliberately missing when he came at me with his tomahawk, only half trying to hurt me. I got him down and he ... he asked me to end his life quickly, honorably. He wanted

31

to die fighting, but he wanted to die, nonetheless. He said his heart was dead already."

Chaco's eyes teared, and he just stared at Bryce, blinking, confused. "Why ... why wasn't I with him? Why wasn't my mother with him? And ... and why did you kill him? You could have let him go."

"He wanted to die, damn it," Bryce said in a louder voice. "If he had lived he'd have ended up suffering the agony of his loneliness even longer, and on top of that he'd have ended up the way they'll all end up one day, Chaco—prisoners on the goddamned worthless reservations, only half men, turned into beggars, humiliated, and stripped of their pride! Saguaro wasn't made for that kind of life. Why do you think so many of them die when they go to reservations? It isn't so much disease that kills them! It's hopelessness, depression, alcoholism! And if you choose to go with Cochise it will be the same for you! Cochise might hold out a little longer—Geronimo, the rest of those who continue to fight—but it will be the same for all of them in the end. Saguaro knew it early on. He didn't want that for you. He had already given your mother over to me because the life they were forced to lead was too hard on her. She would have died. Besides that, she was. . ."

He stopped, unsure how to go on. He began pacing, and the room hung silent while everyone in it waited for him to continue. "Troy, put a closed sign on the door and bolt it," the man finally spoke up.

The boy immediately obeyed, while Chaco watched Bryce Edwards with mixed emotions. The man had killed Saguaro. Bryce Edwards had killed Saguaro!

"This isn't the way I planned on telling you any of this," Bryce spoke up, running a hand through his golden hair. "I was going take you for a ride, someplace where we could be alone, tell you without your mother present. It's very hard on her to have to go over all of it."

Chaco watched his mother. "Why is it so hard? Did you

desert my father? Were you just his captive after all? Did you not love him?"

Her eyes widened, and Bryce marched closer to the boy. "Your mother loved Saguaro and chose to stay with him once when it meant a life of running and terrible danger. It cost her slavery in Mexico! She was captured from Saguaro's village by Utes while Saguaro was gone raiding. The Utes sold her to the Mexicans and I went searching for her and brought her back. Do you know in your young mind what slavery in Mexico means for a white woman? Do you understand what I'm telling you?"

Shannon burst into tears, and some of the animosity left Chaco's eyes. No one needed to explain. Somehow, in spite of his youth, he understood.

"Your mother has been through things that would kill most women—kill most men, for that matter. She is not to blame for one thing that happened. Blame the Civil War if you want to point a finger. That's what started it all."

The man turned and walked behind the counter, taking out a bottle of whiskey and pouring himself a small shot. He slugged it down, then looked lovingly at Shannon, who was still crying. She was still a beautiful woman, in spite of what she had been through. Surely there was not a prettier woman in all the Southwest Territory. But among the Apaches, and even among some whites, her life was food for legend. "Shannon, you can leave if you want," he told her gently.

She shook her head. "No," she said quietly, wiping at her eyes. "I've spent ... years ... trying to pretend it didn't happen ... years avoiding telling my sons. And I'll never be strong enough again ... if I can't sit through this."

Bryce faced Chaco. "You and your brother already know your mother comes from a place back east called Virginia, that she was once very wealthy but that all that wealth was lost because of the Civil War, and that she lost her whole family in that war. We've told you that before."

33

Chaco nodded and Troy choked back tears, feeling sorry for his mother.

"What we didn't tell you is that an enemy of her father's attacked her, tried to rape her. She killed the man with a small pistol she managed to get hold of."

Shannon sat looking at her lap, and both Troy and Chaco just stared at her. She was the gentlest, quietest person they'd ever known. It was difficult to imagine she could kill someone.

"She was desperate," Bryce continued. "Killing him was better than suffering what he had in store for her." Bryce breathed a deep sigh and poured another shot of whiskey. "I'd already met and fallen in love with your mother back then, met her while I was on leave. We were engaged. Shannon was frightened, for it was a time of war and her father had enemies because he spoke like an abolitionist. She thought her father's enemies would have her hanged, so she fled Virginia and tried to get out to me. On the way one of the stage stations where she had stopped was attacked by Apaches—Saguaro and his men. Just before that a stage attendant had told her he'd heard I'd been killed just a few days earlier in a fight with Apaches. His information was only half right. There *had* been a fight and I was badly wounded, but I didn't die. Shannon had no way of knowing that. Thinking I was dead and knowing I was the only one who could help her, she thought all was lost, that she had no place to go, no friends, no one. Saguaro stole her away with him, and she was sure she was doomed to die some horrible death or something ... that to her would have been worse."

Bryce struggled with his own jealousy. It was not easy for him to realize his beloved Shannon had loved another man, innocent as that love was. Shannon sat dabbing at her eyes.

"My father ... he didn't hurt her," Chaco almost groaned. It was more a question than a statement.

Bryce walked to a window and stared at the distant mountains. "No. He felt sorry for her. He saw the goodness in her, the innocence. He intended, I'm sure, to use her as his slave,

34

or perhaps sell her for guns, but instead he fell in love with her. She thought I was dead and she had nowhere to turn. She was afraid if soldiers found her she'd be sent back to Virginia to stand trial for murder. Saguaro became her only friend. He provided for her, protected her ... and eventually her feelings for him deepened. He was good to her. All the while this was going on I was searching for her to no avail. I found out what had happened back in Virginia and knew she must have run to me. After months of searching I gave her up for dead. It wasn't until we came across some Apaches while out on patrol that I found out different. They were fleeing Mexico and heading north. They made it into Arizona, and Saguaro stayed behind while the others went on because ... because your mother was having his baby...." He turned and looked at Chaco. "You. We came along and arrested Saguaro—and I delivered you myself, Chaco. That was when your mother was left with a decision, and it wasn't easy. We'd loved each other very much, thought each other dead. Our joy at finding each other was short-lived. Shannon belonged to Saguaro, was having his baby, and she loved him. And because he was the father of her child, she chose to stay with Saguaro, and I let them both go."

Shannon cried softly, and Chaco stared at her with new fascination. How difficult it must have been for a once-wealthy white woman to end up living in the wilds of Arizona with an Indian. Surely if someone so gentle and proper had given herself to Saguaro, it could only have been out of great love.

"That was the last we saw of each other for months—long, lonely months of worry for me. I knew what life would be like for her," Bryce continued. "Then one day Saguaro came to me to tell me that while he was out raiding Utes had come and raided their camp. Shannon had been stolen and sold to a Mexican. I knew what that meant. So I took a leave and went down to Mexico to find her myself. What I found was not a pretty sight. I killed the man who held her, just as viciously and painfully as I could think of." The words were spoken bitterly, still

35

ringing with deep hatred. "I took Shannon out of there and took her back to the fort with me. She was ... in a bad way mentally, let alone physically. It took her a long time to even speak or recognize anyone. She had suffered greatly, and it's still difficult for her to think of those terrible days."

"Where was I?" Chaco asked.

Bryce turned. "With Saguaro. I got word to Saguaro that I had Shannon. He brought you to me; said I should keep you both. He knew it was impossible for Shannon to go back to a life of running and hiding. She was too weak, too abused. And he felt you belonged with her, hoped your presence would help her get well—and it did. He asked that I keep you—love you as my own—raise you to be strong and honest, and to honor your Apache blood. I think I've done all those things." He signed deeply. "At any rate, Shannon got better and I married her. Later, while out on patrol, I ran into Saguaro again. That's when ... when we fought ... and he all but asked me to kill him." He stepped closer to Chaco. "I've kept my word to him, Chaco. And I do love you as my own. If it could have been any other way, I'd have let it be so. Saguaro chose his own death. I didn't want to kill him. I wept when I killed him. I cursed him for the guilt he'd leave me with. But it's done now, and now you know." He glanced at Troy. "Both of you know. We don't speak to others about it. It's none of their business." His eyes moved back to Chaco. "Now you know why some men whisper about your mother. White men don't hold much respect for white women who have been with Indians. It's a ridiculous attitude, but that's what prejudice does. I knew your mother too well to lose any respect for her, and I understood why she felt as she did about Saguaro. He was an honorable man, Chaco, a brave man, a mighty warrior. He often rode with Cochise. And I couldn't hate him. He had cared for Shannon, probably saved her life. God only knows what would have happened to her if it had been other Apaches who got hold of her. Fate works in strange ways sometimes, Chaco, and you have been left in its wake. You have two bloods, and your mother always knew that some day you would come to this crossroad in your life. She has dreaded it. She loves you dearly."

Chaco studied the man's gray eyes, eyes always true, eyes now filled with pain and sorrow. His parents had suffered greatly. He wanted to hate Bryce Edwards for killing Saguaro. Yet somehow he could not. "I . . . I have to go away and be alone for a while," he said quietly.

Shannon rose, her face pale, her eyes red. "You'll come back?"

Saguaro studied her closely, more closely than he ever had before. His Apache father had loved this white woman. How strange it all was. Most white women taken captive by Apaches were raped, then killed, or kept and sold for ransom. But something about his mother had won Saguaro's heart. And stranger still, she had loved the man in return—a pampered, soft white woman had loved a wild Apache warrior. He suddenly wondered what kind of a woman he would one day love. Did his dark skin and Apache blood mean he would have no choice but to marry an Apache woman? What if he had feelings for a white woman? Would white women look down on him, consider him less than worthy of them? His own mother was rare, with a good heart and compassion for all. She was not like the few other white women he'd met, women who shied away from him as though sure he intended to do something horrible to them.

"I will come back" he answered quietly. "I just . . . need to think about all of this." He turned, and his mother called his name. He looked back at her.

"What did you tell Cochise, when he told you you could come to the mountains and live with the Apache?" She asked the question in a trembling voice.

Chaco sighed deeply, and her heart ached at how very much he resembled Saguaro, realizing that it was not just a physical resemblance, but a spiritual one as well. The eyes. It was all in the eyes.

"I said that I might go." He saw the sorrow in her eyes. "I said that first I would ask you ... about my real father. And that I would go into the hills to be alone and seek my real father's spirit, for I know in my heart that he sometimes watches me. He is dead, but his spirit is alive. I would like to know where he was buried."

Another tear slipped down her cheek. "No one knows. His people came and took away his body. We only know he was buried somewhere in the mountains west of Fort Bowie."

Chaco held his chin up proudly. "Then when I return I will pack, and I will go to those mountains. Perhaps my father will come to me in a vision."

"Chaco, you're too young," his mother groaned in protest.

He shook his head. "I am old enough. Cochise said I am almost a man by Apache standards. I must do it, Mother. Let me go in peace, without the sound of your pleading in my ears. Please don't look at me like I'm a little boy. I can use a rifle and I know the land. I will be all right."

Bryce stepped up behind Shannon, grasping her shoulders. "You have to let him go, Shannon. You can't hold him any more than you can hold the wind, and you know it. You knew it the day he was born."

Shannon mustered a faint smile. She must be strong. She had been forced to be strong since the day she fled Virginia. "I'll ... get some food ready.

She walked toward the door then, standing close to her son, turning to meet his eyes. Already he was taller than she, for she was a tiny woman. "If you should ... go to Cochise, please tell me it wouldn't be ... forever."

The boy blinked back tears. "I can't say for sure, Mother." He put a fist to his heart. "But in here ... I will never leave you."

She put a hand to the side of his face. "So much like him," she whispered. "You are so much like him. My son. My darling

Chaco." She turned and went through the door, and Chaco looked at Bryce.

"I don't want to hurt her."

"I know that, Chaco." Bryce looked at Troy, seeing the lost, confused look on his son's face. The boy had heard more than Bryce would have chosen for his age, but perhaps it was best after all. "You've aged some today, son. I let you listen because I thought you were man enough to know, and if Chaco . . . leaves us for a while, I will need you more than ever."

"Does Mother . . . love me the same as Chaco?"

Bryce stared at him for several long seconds. "If you mean as much, yes. Just as much. But Chaco is special in his own way, just as you are. You are the product of the love your mother and I found when she got well and we could be together again. We spent many years apart, Troy, but we never stopped loving each other. You are the result of that love. And you should feel very special and proud that I let you stay and listen today."

Troy turned his eyes to Chaco. "I don't want you to go away."

Their eyes held in new awakening, affection mixed with a new realization of how very different they really were. "It's only for a few days, Troy, not forever. I haven't decided about Cochise. Besides, I wouldn't leave you forever. We'll always be brothers." He reached out and tousled the boy's golden curls. "Which is why you still have all this hair, huh?"

"I should make both of you work double duty for a few days for riding those horses so hard," Bryce told them. "And especially for going so far. Now you, Troy, get out there and take care of Dreamer and Indian. Rub them down good. I'll send Chaco out to help you in a minute."

"Yes, sir." The boy scurried away and Bryce turned his attention to Chaco.

"I'm sorry about Saguaro, Chaco. Life deals us some cruel

blows sometimes. I always worried ... what you would think of me when you knew."

Chaco's eyes teared again. "You're the only father I've known, and you've been good to me. It's impossible for me to hate you. You kept your promise to my real father." He swallowed. "I'm so confused. I never thought too deeply about my Apache blood until I saw Cochise. I wish you could tell me ... what to do."

"So do I, Chaco, but it's as Cochise told you. A man has to find and follow his own heart. My own opinion is that there is no hope with the Apaches, Chaco. You know that already. And you know your mother would want you to stay with us. But you have a right to investigate that other half of you that you have never really known." He put a hand on the boy's shoulder. "Do what you have to do, Chaco. I won't stop you. And we'll always be here if you leave and want to come back."

Chaco nodded. "Cochise said you are a good white man." He turned quickly away to hide his tears and walked out to help Troy with the horses. Bryce rubbed at his chest, his heart actually aching.

"Shannon," he said softly. He walked out and hurried over to the cabin, going inside to find her preparing some dried beans. She looked up at him when he entered, then rushed to him, bursting into tears. He embraced her tightly. "It will be all right, Shannon. Everything will be all right."

Chapter Three

1874

Word was quickly wired to Tucson, and the town cheered. Chochise was dead. To most whites it was welcome news, and people celebrated in taverns and on farms. In one Tucson establishment the owner offered free drinks and cash prizes for accuracy in throwing darts at a drawing of the great Indian chief. If the contestant hit an eye, he won five dollars; if he hit him in the nose, two dollars, the mouth, one dollar.

"You ought to have a drawing of the whole man," one man shouted. "I know where I'd throw my dart!"

Laughter and drinks were abundant, as were piano playing, gambling, and dancing. With Cochise's early death from an unknown disease, perhaps some of the Indian attacks would subside. None of those who celebrated had ever known Cochise or cared what kind of man he was, or why the Apaches attacked white settlements. They did not understand the terror of losing everything dear to them, of being hunted like a wild animal, shot at for no reason; they did not know the pain of empty stomachs, the horror of having their children torn from their arms to be taken away to faraway schools where they were beaten for speaking their own tongue and for practicing the

41

ancient beliefs they had been taught, the sadness of being told one must forget and abolish all the old ways, worship a different God, abandon sacred rituals, and deny their own free spirits.

From a window of his Tucson office, James Veck watched the celebrating in the streets. A few fights broke out over what should be done now with Cochise's people and the vast land they had been allowed as a reservation. Veck slipped his thumbs into the pockets of his silk vest and turned, facing Stuart Morse, who sat in a chair across from Veck's desk waiting for Veck to say something.

Stuart managed the three supply stores that James Veck owned, and he was Veck's "yes man," for being close to Veck meant having a good life. Veck was fast becoming one of the richest men in Tucson, investing money inherited from a wealthy father in mining interests, real estate, his supply stores, and railroad interests. James Veck saw a future in Arizona Territory, one that would be even more successful once the Apache problems were taken care of. But for the time being, one could take care of those problems and at the same time get rich. Apache wars meant more soldiers in Arizona and more government contracts to be filled by businessmen like himself. Playing both sides was indeed profitable.

"Look at them out there," he finally spoke up, leaning his head in the direction of the window. "Arguing about the Apaches as though there were two sides to the issue." He laughed lightly, taking an expensive cigar from a box on his desk. "There is only one side—our side. Some of those bastards actually think Cochise's people should be allowed to stay on that reservation land." He lit the cigar. "That treaty Cochise signed is a damned farce—letting those Chiricahuas live wherever they choose, letting them keep their old ways and all. The Indian problem won't be cured until they're totally acclimated to our way of living—or all dead—whichever comes first."

Morse watched the end of the man's cigar glow. "You think the peace will last now that Cochise is dead?"

42

"Hell, no. Cochise was all that kept the young restless ones in their place. Caged animals eventually try to break out, and without Cochise to stop them, and Geronimo still out there, they'll start breaking loose."

Morse stood up, shedding a brown suit jacket and going to look out the window himself. Veck liked Morse's business mind, even though the man had no color or personality. It seemed everything about the man was brown. He always wore brown suits, his hair was brown, his eyes were brown, and his skin was brown from the Arizona sun. The man seldom laughed, and he poured most of his waking hours into the three supply stores Veck owned. He didn't even have a family, but that was good. Single employees could concentrate more on their work. Veck wondered why the forty-year-old Morse had never married. Perhaps it was because no woman could stand the man's soft, flabby body. Morse seemed to have no interest in neatness or in looking good.

Veck was himself quite the opposite of Morse—a man who like to gamble and throw elaborate parties. He had several suits of several colors and never wore boots that were not highly polished. He kept up with the latest fashions from the East, and he was an energetic, handsome, trimly built man, with tanned skin, blue eyes, and black hair. He like living in Tucson, where there was little in the way of law and a man could get away with practically anything and build his own little empire. There was plenty of whiskey here, plenty of loose women, and plenty of opportunity for a man like himself. In the business world James Veck was known as a successful man, and one in whom one could place full confidence, especially when dealing in money. Veck had a way of turning hundreds of dollars into thousands. He had turned his inheritance of thousands into hundreds of thousands. He was one of those men who came out west at just the right time, when land could be bought up cheap, to be sold later for a tidy profit. Now he concentrated on buying land that would most likely fall to the railroad.

Veck intended to miss no opportunity to take advantage of the growing territory. Getting rid of the Apaches was one of his primary goals, for they were the only thing slowing progress. His next important goal was to get the Southern Pacific moving on bringing the railroad to Tucson and all the way to Texas. It would increase Veck's ability to keep a large inventory of supplies in his stores, as well as to help mining and bring in even more settlers. The man already had started advertising in newspapers in other parts of the country, telling people what golden opportunities lay waiting for them in beautiful Arizona Territory. But until the Indian threat was truly canceled, there would be those who would be too afraid to come.

He puffed his cigar, turning his chair and chuckling at the sight of dancing in the street. He shook his head. "What peasants," he muttered.

"Indeed," Morse answered. "But then people like that can be used." He turned to Veck. "It's easy to plant ideas in their heads, use them to keep the Indian thing an issue. Somehow we've got to decrease the size of the land the government is letting Cochise's people live on, you know. That's good land— too good for Indians."

"Don't think I don't know it."

Someone knocked at the door, and Veck and Morse both turned. Morse went to the door to open it. Two men stood outside, and Veck recognized them as fellow Tucson businessmen: Cleve Newsome, a young, blond man who ran a hotel, and Howard Smith, older, dark and plain, a barber who also owned two taverns.

"Come in, gentlemen," Veck welcomed.

Both men came inside and Morse closed the door. Veck bade them sit down and they obeyed, young Newsome leaning forward with his elbows on his knees. "We just came to see if you had any ideas how we can do something about the Apaches now that Cochise is dead, Mr. Veck," he spoke up.

Veck grinned, offering them both cigars. Smith took one but

Newsome did not. "My very thoughts, gentlemen," Veck answered. He puffed his own cigar for a moment. "The Apaches are living on a lot of very valuable land. God only knows how much gold is in the Dragoon and Chiricahua mountains. And the whole area is right smack in the middle of land the railroad would go through to get to Texas. We get the railroad on our side and that will help."

"That kind of power is fine," Smith answered, lighting his own cigar. "But what about those who are in sympathy with the Indians? That power can sometimes be stronger."

Veck frowned, studying his cigar. "You can see by looking in the streets how far that kind of sympathy goes. Perhaps in other parts of the country such voices are heard, but not here. It's all really just a matter of time—and of finding the right people to do the right thing."

"What do you mean, Mr. Veck?" Smith asked.

"Well, those young Apache men will get mighty restless now. They'll start raiding again, at least into Mexico. They'll prove they can't be trusted. In the meantime, the Mescaleros are still prowling around, and so is Geronimo and his bunch. They'll keep enough things stirred up to keep the sympathy against the Indian and shrink the reservation land. The government will slowly begin selling off the border land as Indian deprivations continue." He puffed the cigar again. "And there are plenty of Indian haters around who can be bought off to help speed things up." He watched the two men carefully for a moment. "Of course, I could use a little monetary help, if you're so anxious to put the lid on the Apaches. The more you pay a man, the more risks he'll take."

Smith frowned. "What kind of risks?"

Veck shook his head. "Use your head, Howard. Do you really think all raids on settlers are committed by Indians?"

The man thought a moment, then his face lit up like he'd just discovered something wonderful. "White men?"

Veck laughed hard then. "Howard, you amaze me."

45

Cleve Newsome grinned. "And you amaze us, Mr. Veck. Where do you come up with all your ideas?"

"When a man is protecting his investments, he can become very clever," Veck answered. "What you do is, you keep the Indians stirred up, and keep them looking guilty. You support the whiskey peddlers. You kill an innocent Indian here and there, keep their tempers aroused. And you raid a few settlers, disguised as Indians, blame it on the Apaches. And when some other tribe commits some atrocity, you blame it on the Chiricahuas. And of course, reservation agents can be bribed into selling government supplies for a profit and giving the Indians supplies and food that is not quite so . . . expensive."

"Or edible," Newsome added.

All four men laughed then. "Do you get the picture, Howard?" Veck finally asked the man. "Relax. Everything will go our way in due time."

Smith shook his head. "If you say so, Mr. Veck."

Veck's blue eyes took on an icy glaze. "I say so. No stinking Indian is going to cheat me out of damned good land. They shouldn't get one inch of it. What has the Indian ever done to deserve that kind of treatment? They don't understand the value of land." He puffed the cigar again, forcing himself to calm down. It irritated him that uneducated savages should get any kind of humane treatment whatsoever. "That friend of Cochise's, that white man, what's his name . . ?"

"Tom Jeffords," Cleve put in.

"Yes. Jeffords. He's a fool. I'd like to see some Chiricahua lift his scalp, defending them the way he does. Imagine, calling an Indian friend." He laid his cigar in an ashtray and rose, walking to look out a window again. "Personally, the men I found who will do a little dirty work for me have the right attitude. They murdered one Indian family—raped the woman and then killed her. One of them actually uses one of the woman's breasts for a tobacco pouch. Sexiest tobacco pouch I've ever seen."

46

The others looked at each other, feeling little tingles of horror mixed with pleasure move through them. There was little thought given to the right or wrong of it. After all, it was Apaches they were talking about—people whose lives were worth hardly more than that of a coyote or a snake. They would not worry about the Apaches any more, for there were many men like James Veck who would help matters along. Just sitting in Veck's office they could feel the power, the cunning, the wisdom. For every Indian sympathizer, there were ten Vecks. The days of the Apache were numbered.

"Dade Chadwell and Chap Miller," Veck muttered. "That's what they call themselves." He turned. "Oh, don't mention those names to anyone—ever. You're all with me on this just by sitting here the way you are now. With Cochise's death, the timing is perfect for spreading some havoc among the Indians. There is some prime railroad land on that reservation that I intend to get my hands on, and you can too. We kill two birds with one stone here. We keep the Indian problem stirred up, meaning we sell a lot of supplies to the forts that have to be kept active. But we also stir up so much hatred that eventually they will kick the Apaches right out of Arizona all together. As they leave, we buy up the reservation land. We get rich all the way around.

Smith nodded. "We're with you, Mr. Veck."

Stuart Morse rubbed at his chin. "I wonder how Cochise died, anyway. He wasn't that old."

Veck shrugged. "Who knows and who cares? The point is he's dead."

Chaco sat on the massive, flat ridge that overlooked a horizon with no end. Sprawled out before him were endless smatterings of rock formations, scattered about as though God had thrown them down from heaven and let them fall where they may.

How long he had wept when first getting to this place, he didn't know. Now there were no tears left, only a strange emptiness, a heart that was a little harder, and a mind that was confused. Cochise was dead. His one encounter with the man had left a lasting impression, had pierced his soul and body with the keen realization that he was half Apache, that there was a part of him as yet unexplored. Since his chance meeting with the famous Apache leader, Chaco had often dreamed about the man, thought about things Cochise had told him, wondered about his own Apache blood. He had dreamed about going to live with Cochise for a while, to learn more about his real father, about Apache customs and religion.

But he was dead. Dead! It seemed impossible. He was still so young, such a strong, virile man. How could he be dead? The brevity and delicacy of life had never been so evident to him before now.

He picked up a rock and threw it into the yawning expanse below. He didn't feel the hot sun on his back. He didn't feel anything except a great loss. His grief and loneliness were magnified by the land itself. The world here was so quiet, a man could hear the tiniest sounds, even the scratching of lizards. He heard the hard rock hit somewhere below. He thought of the insults some of the soldiers at Fort Bowie continued to heap upon him. More and more he began to wonder where he really belonged. He loved his white parents, and they had been good to him. Bryce Edwards was as good a father as a real father could have been.

But Bryce was not his father. His father had been Apache. Apache. Half of him was Apache. There was a natural restlessness to his spirit that made it impossible to sit still for his mother's lessons in reading and writing. For some reason he could not bring himself to let his mother cut his hair, and he liked nothing better than riding free and alone, sometimes riding off without Troy. He knew it hurt Troy's feelings when he did so, but the older they got, the more different they became, the wider the gap between them, in spite of the love that existed between them.

Troy. Troy was white. He took better to learning. The soldiers liked him. People didn't stare at him and point. White women didn't shy away from him. Everyone tossled his blond curls and commented about his lovely gray eyes. Life would be easy for Troy. Chaco felt no animosity over it. He loved Troy. But he was more and more aware of the differences between himself and his brother—not just outwardly, but inwardly—spiritually.

Chaco was handsome, too, but handsome only for an Indian. That was the way others put it—not just handsome, but a handsome *Indian*, as though the most handsome Indian in the world could still not hold a candle to a white man. To Chaco, a man was just a man. Besides, what did it matter how handsome a man was? It was his spirit, his goodness and wisdom, that counted. But whites didn't seem to judge people that way. The only really good white people he had known in his fourteen years were his own white parents and perhaps one or two of his father's soldier friends. They treated Chaco like a real person, like someone important. They cared about him. But he was old enough to read the eyes of most of the others, to know when he was being silently insulted. The older he got the less he felt he belonged in his parents' white world, yet the thought of leaving his beautiful and kind mother, the thought of how it would break her heart, was the only thing that kept him from going.

He stared out at the lonely land in front of him, wondering where Cochise had been buried. No one knew except the few Apaches who had carried off his body, deliberately keeping the burial site a secret, for the white man had a hideous habit of picking over the remains of famous people and taking precious artifacts for themselves. The Apaches would not allow any white men to pick over Cochise's grave. The whereabouts of Cochise's bones would forever be a mystery, and Chaco was glad.

He stood up, breathing deeply, grasping for some kind of sign, searching for answers. He threw back his head, praying to Usen, the Apache God, hoping that by praying to the Apache God rather than his mother's Christian God, some kind of answer to his confusion would come. He raised his arms and let the sun warm his face for a long, quiet moment.

"Usen," he said softly then. "Great Father of all the Earth, Great Spirit of the Land, guide me. Help me know ... what I am." Tears formed in his eyes and he felt suddenly compelled to stand still and not move a muscle. He waited, eyes closed, sun shining down on him, his heart open to God. Then, unexpectedly, a tingling sensation moved through him, from his fingers down his upstretched arms, through his body.

"You are the earth," a voice spoke softly then. "You are Apache, and that cannot change. Let yourself be Apache, whether in the white man's world or the Indian's. You are what you are. First be Chaco, and be proud. Then go where you will in life."

For a long time he just stood there. He was not afraid, even though he was sure someone had spoken to him from the spirit world. Was this, then, his visitation of the Life Force, the Power that every Apache man waited for, the vision that led him in life? He felt suddenly calm, comforted, and a feeling of wonderful love came over him, more powerful than anything he had ever experienced. He lowered his arms.

"Chaco," someone whispered.

Chaco turned, and there stood a man, but not truly a living being, for he looked hazy and transparent. It was not Cochise. Shivers moved through the young man, his eyes riveted on the tender, dark eyes of the spirit. "Father," Chaco finally spoke aloud.

The form was handsome, tall, and strong. In the face Chaco could see himself. Chaco felt the spirit talking to him, yet it did not truly open its mouth to speak. "You are my life," he heard from somewhere. "For you I died. Use your life proudly. Your

50

mother has raised you into a handsome, healthy young man. Now you must decide. Now you are free to choose . . . white or Apache. When I look at you, I am proud. My heart feels good again."

Chaco just stared, his heart soaring with love. Father! Surely it was Saguaro, his beloved father. He opened his mouth to speak, but nothing came out. He tried to walk to the vision, wanted to hold it, touch it. But it began to fade then. He wanted to cry out for it to stay, but still his voice would not come. And he knew as he watched it fade that it truly was Saguaro. In moments the vision was gone. Chaco stood there feeling strangely comforted, stronger inside, more sure what he must do.

Predictions of restlessness among the Apache began to come true. For two years following Cochise's death, raids multiplied. Settlers, traders, miners, travelers, none were exempt, and all deaths and attacks were blamed in the Tucson newspapers on the Chiricahuas. Rations on the reservation became scarce and always arrived too late, most of them pilfered by middlemen so that what arrived was worthless. The Apaches were hungry and tired of being blamed for things they did not do.

Headlines blazed with new atrocities. Angry whites began ignoring treaty agreements and began moving onto Indian land, mining it, farming it, fencing it. Stray Indians were killed indiscriminately. Villages were burned and Apaches found in small numbers were attacked. Apache tempers were on fire. Without Cochise's presence, the younger men were anxious for war. Promises were broken and raids were conducted just to find food for hungry bellies of the Apache children. Young warriors rode into Mexico to steal gold that unscrupulous whites would take in trade for guns, food, and whiskey, but often the guns were outdated, the food bad, and the whiskey watered down.

The delicate peace Cochise had brought through his own

efforts was being broken. Tom Jeffords could not compete with the confusion broken promises brought to the Apaches. His promises were good, but the government and others would not back him up. He threatened to resign as agent, for neither Washington nor the local government were of any help.

During all the upheaval, school came to the Fort Bowie area. Troy attended, at his mother's insistence, for she was sure a real teacher could be of more benefit than she could in the young man's education. Troy like to read and write, already talked of someday being a writer. Such things were beyond Chaco's dreams. He could think in beautiful words, appreciate the beauty of the world around him, but to put things into words on paper was of little interest to him. Troy liked such things, and at thirteen he seemed almost too intelligent for his age. The two brothers' interests had drifted so far apart that they saw little of each other—Troy attending school and studying evenings—Chaco, now sixteen, preferring to help with the ranch and horses, often off hunting or just riding alone.

For one, life was spelled out clearly, for the other, only confusion and doubt were clear. With the new outbreaks of raiding, Chaco was more aware of hot, angry eyes on him wherever he went in the world of whites. He had grown up with whites, lived around Fort Bowie all his life, and yet they looked at him as though he were as much an enemy as Geronimo. The growing number of children in their area either stared at him or taunted him—or ran away in fear.

All around him Chaco felt the white world closing in, pushing him away, in spite of his parents' kind love. The Southern Pacific was laying track from the west toward Tucson. The Fort Bowie area was growing. Now there was the school, and Troy was making many friends with the growing number of white children in the area. But Chaco made no friends. He retreated more and more into his own lonely world, shut out by those who shunned him simply because he was Apache. His "difference" became more evident the day Troy came home from school with torn, dirty clothes, a black eye and bleeding lips.

"Troy!" Shannon Edwards rushed to her son, making him sit down. "What on earth . . .?"

Chaco got up from where he had been sitting by the fireplace whittling himself a spear. "Hey, little brother, who jumped on you? I hope he looks worse than you do."

Troy looked up at him strangely, his mouth pouted, his eyes somewhat resentful. Chaco stepped back, losing his smile. He suddenly felt even lonelier, even more foreign. Bryce came inside then, his good mood quickly changing when he saw his battered son. Shannon quickly wet a cloth and began gently washing dirt and blood from Troy's face.

"What's going on here?" Bryce asked, pulling out a chair and sitting down near his son.

"I got in a fight," Troy answered.

"That is very obvious. What were you fighting about, and with whom?"

Troy remained silent while Shannon smoothed some of the blond curls back with the cool cloth. Chaco watched silently, knowing immediately what was wrong when Troy looked at him again. Their eyes held and Chaco stepped closer again.

"It was me, wasn't it?" he said angrily. "You had a fight over me!"

Troy swallowed and looked away. He loved this wild, brave brother of his; admired his daring, his strength, his riding skills. But having an Indian half brother made life difficult for a white boy in Arizona. "I don't want to talk about it," he answered quietly.

Shannon looked at Bryce, then at her Indian son. How she loved him! How she hated the hurt she saw in his dark eyes now. Such a handsome, smart, wonderful son he was, but so terribly lonely inside—a loneliness she could not help. She looked back at Troy. "Did someone say something about Chaco?" she asked.

53

Troy sighed. "They always say things, and they make fun of me—call me an Indian lover—call you and father Indian lovers."

Bryce's gray eyes sparked with anger. "We *are* Indian lovers," he grumbled. "Don't you ever be ashamed of it, Troy, or of Chaco. I quit the army because of orders to shoot Indians on sight and because I got tired of broken promises and treaties."

Troy stared at his lap. "I'm not ashamed. I just ... get tired of listening to it all the time. Today I just decided not to. I clobbered Jimmy Neals."

Shannon looked at Chaco again, who was just staring at his younger brother. She saw in Chaco's eyes a hurt so deep that it tore at her heart. Troy looked at his brother again, blinking, trying to hide the resentment Chaco had already seen in his brother's gray eyes.

"I'm sorry, Chaco,' he said.

Chaco frowned. "Sorry? For what? For sticking up for your Indian brother?" Chaco's fists clenched. "I am the one who is sorry, sorry for making life bad for you, for making you have to get into fights and be ashamed."

"No one is ashamed of anyone," Bryce put in. He rose from the table. "Damned stupid ..." He looked at Chaco, then walked up to him while Shannon washed Troy's face a little more. "It was just one kid, Chaco. It's nothing to be concerned about."

"He hurt my brother, made him feel bad."

"It's all right, Chaco," Troy assured him. "He didn't hurt me much."

Chaco's dark eyes glittered with anger. "No! It's *not* all right. It's bad!" He stormed out, slamming the screen door of the small cabin, jumping onto the back of his horse that grazed loose nearby, and riding off.

Bryce looked at Shannon and saw the terror along with resignation in her eyes, the dreaded fear all mothers face with their sons. She was losing her Chaco, her little Indian boy. It would not be so bad if he were simply getting married or had a new job. She would lose him to that world she had once known as the woman of Saguaro, but that world was not safe for anyone now, especially not for the hot-tempered young Apache men.

"Oh, Bryce, I'm losing him," she said in a near whisper. "All my fears of his Apache blood taking him from me . . ."

"Shannon, don't."

"Why can't they just leave us alone? Why do they have to judge people the way they do? Chaco wants and needs friends as much as any boy."

Bryce studied her lovingly. She had suffered so much. "His friends might have to be Apache, Shannon. You can't shelter him forever, and it's getting harder and harder for him to live here with us, around the soldiers and all. Perhaps our love for him isn't as important as his happiness. Saguaro asked us to keep him until he was man enough to make his own decisions. Now he's got some deciding to do. He's been different ever since Cochise died and he stayed alone in the mountains for so many days. Something happened to him there, Shannon, I'm sure of it. His Indian blood is pulling at him."

Shannon sat down wearily beside Troy, rubbing his shoulders. "Are you hurt badly, Troy?"

The boy shook his head. "I hurt Chaco's feelings, didn't I?"

She leaned over and kissed his cheek. "No. Not you, Troy. The others did that. And you're a good boy for sticking up for him."

Troy sniffed. "Chaco and I used to be so close. We did everything together. Now it's all different. It's like we don't know each other any more. But . . . I still love him."

"Of course you do."

He licked at a sore lip. "I wish we were still little. We were good friends then. We promised each other we always would be good friends."

"And you always will be," Bryce told his son, gently stroking

55

the blond curls. "No matter what happens, Troy, you and Chaco will always be friends. Blood is important. You share the same blood—your mother's. Be proud of it, and be proud of your brother, no matter what others say. Chaco has a good heart, but he is judged for his looks. I'm sorry for what happened today, Troy, but I'm glad you stuck up for Chaco. You sure you aren't hurt bad?"

Troy shook his head, then met his father's eyes. "I'm scared, Pa. I'm scared of what will happen to everybody, especially Chaco. Everybody says such bad things about the Apaches, I don't know what to think."

"You remember the things your mother has told you about them, and the things I've told you from my army days, like how Saguaro saved my life. They aren't bad, Troy. They're just desperate. And for the time being you're going to have to be very strong, like your mother. She bears a lot of insults and strange looks, knowing what they are thinking. But they don't understand the beautiful side of the Apache, and they don't want to understand. They just want to force the Apaches away so they can take over Apache land. But the battle will not be easily won, Troy. You and I will help see to that."

Troy studied his father's steady eyes. "You and I?"

"We're going to stand up for what is right, Troy—always—not what is popular but what is right. And some day you'll use that education you're getting to help. You're a very smart young man, and you love your brother. I've never mentioned it before, but I see you doing great things some day. You remember what happened today, remember how those people talk, remember prejudice and hatred. You say you like to write. Maybe some day you can use that writing to help people like the Apaches."

Troy shrugged. "How?"

"I don't know yet. That will be up to you."

Troy looked at the doorway. "He'll go to the Apaches, won't he?"

"Your brother is a very confused young man, Troy," Bryce

56

answered, his heart aching at the desolation on Shannon's face. "I'm afraid that's what he's thinking of doing, and it will only mean disaster for him. I'm doing my best to make him understand he's better off here, but the way he's treated, it makes my argument pretty weak."

"He'll go to them," Shannon said quietly. "There is too much of Saguaro in him. I see it more every day." She walked to the door just in time to see him riding off again. Always it seemed he was riding away from them. When would the day come that he did not come back?

Chapter Four

Bryce Edwards looked up from sweeping off the wide boards of the porch that graced the front of his trading post, watching the approaching carriage. It seemed too fancy for these parts, and it seemed almost a shame to see the dust rolling from under its wheels and covering its fine, black finish with a layer of grit.

Two men were inside the carriage, one driving, the other, looking very important, sitting in a cushioned seat behind the driver, shaded by a fringed canopy from the hot Arizona sun. The carriage came to a halt in front of the trading post, and the well-suited man in the cushioned seat disembarked, grabbing hold of a briefcase and walking briskly up the two steps to the porch where Bryce stood.

"Good day to you, sir," he spoke up confidently.

Bryce studied the medium-built man who he knew instinctively was fresh from the East. He nodded. "Good afternoon. What can I do for you?"

The man put out his hand. "I am Vincent Colyer, here on government business, and on behalf of the Society of Friends. You have heard of the Society?"

Bryce shook the man's hand and studied him carefully. "Some. Mostly Quakers, I believe."

The man nodded. "Yes, sir. And I am one, if that is what

you are wondering. I have been sent out here by the government to investigate the Indian problem, the reservations, how they can be improved, that sort of thing. Might you be Bryce Edwards?"

Bryce grinned a little. "I might be. Why do you ask?"

Colyer laughed lightly. "I was directed here by the commander at Fort Bowie. He tells me you once served as an officer in the army—a very good one, I might add. He also tells me that part of the reason you left was that you did not agree with some of the army's tactics regarding the Indian."

Bryce folded his arms and leaned against a support post. "Seems to me he told you a great deal about me. Anything else you can fill me in on, like why you care anything about what I do with my life?"

The man reddened a little, setting down his briefcase and removing his hat. "I'm sorry, Mr. Edwards. Perhaps I approached this wrong. It is just that I am looking for men like you, that is, if it's true you have compassion for the Indians as well as a better understanding of them than most. Part of my mission out here is to find men like you, men who have lived out here a long time and understand the land and its people. I am told you are a stepfather to a half-breed son. Is this true?"

Bryce's eyes clouded warily. "It's true. And I hope that whoever you spoke to at the fort explained that in the right way. I'll not have my wife insulted."

"Oh, be assured, nothing detrimental was said about your wife. I was simply told you were good to the boy and had a marvelous capacity for understanding the Indian."

Bryce moved away from the post and took a paper and tobacco from a pouch he wore on his belt. "May I ask your reason for investigating my personal life?"

"Oh, yes. Yes. As I told you, I'm looking for men who understand the Indians and are experienced at living in this land. I've been appointed by the government to come out here and see what I can do to improve the deplorable conditions between whites and Indians. I need to find men who can help me. From all things I have heard about you, you are perfect."

Bryce finished rolling a cigarette and lit it, blowing smoke from his mouth and studying the man with his gentle but somewhat defensive gray eyes. "Perfect for what?"

"Mr. Edwards, I would like you to consider being an Indian agent, probably at San Carlos."

Bryce frowned, taking another puff on the cigarette. "San Carlos? That's north of here. I have a business to run, Mr. Colyer."

"Oh, but you would be well paid, and living quarters would be free." The man turned and paced. "Mr. Edwards ..." He stopped when he saw a handsome young Indian riding toward the house, his muscular chest bare except for a string of turquoise beads that graced it. His long, black hair blew in the wind, and he sat on the horse with a natural grace. He came closer, halting his horse and eyeing Colyer warily.

"Chaco, this is Mr. Colyer. He's a representative of the government, here to offer me a job as agent at San Carlos. Mr. Colyer, this is the Apache son you heard about—Chaco."

Chaco nodded but did not dismount.

"Well, I am very glad to meet you, Chaco. How old are you now? Nineteen? Twenty?" He studied the boy curiously. Chaco was extremely handsome, a magnificent specimen of young manhood, and seemingly all Apache. How strange that he lived here with these white people.

Chaco tossed his head proudly. "I am sixteen summers."

Bryce grinned. "Chaco's father was tall for an Indian. Chaco is built like Saguaro, who was a big man. He has always looked older than he is." The familiar pain moved through his heart again at the memory of Saguaro, the lingering jealousy of knowing the man fathered a son by Shannon, the sorrow of being the one who killed Saguaro. Chaco moved his dark eyes to Bryce.

"You will go to San Carlos?"

"I doubt it, Chaco," Their eyes held. Chaco would hate it there, Bryce was certain, for even though he would be among the Apache, they were reservation Apaches—people who had lost their spirit, people living in a virtual prison.

"But you could be such a help," Colyer argued. "You're probably aware of how bad living conditions are on the reservations, and how unscrupulous some of the agents are. Cheating, whiskey peddling, rotten food, never enough supplies—all these things are rampant on the reservations, and mostly because of agents who cheat the government, selling the good supplies for their own profit and leaving only useless material and rotten food for the Indian. With all that goes on—disease, lack of sanitation, living quarters with leaking roofs and dirt floors, well. . . ."

The man sighed deeply again, and Chaco listened with a growing hatred in his own heart for what the whites were doing to the Indians. "It's a pitiful mess, Mr. Edwards," Colyer continued. "We must have more adept men running the reservations, men who care about the Indians. Being an agent has to be more than just a job. It has to be thought of as a public service, a commitment to narrowing the gap between white men and Indian. We Quakers don't believe in racial division. All men are equal in our eyes, and deprivations against America's original citizens must be stopped. We have taken their land from them, and now we let them starve and freeze and die of white man's diseases. We have taken away their principal means of survival but have given them nothing to replace it. They are lost and running and afraid, and I can't help but believe that most of what they do is simply for survival—stealing food and supplies from local citizens because they no longer have any means of fending for themselves."

Bryce took another drag on his cigarette, then threw it down and crushed it out with his foot. "You're close, Mr. Colyer. I appreciate the fact that you care. Not many men the government sends out here do. And thank you for the offer. But I can't just give up everything I have built up here. And I have to consider my wife and my sons. They would be a part of the decision."

"Well, I wish you would definitely think about it, Mr. Edwards. I . . ."

Shannon came to the door then, her plain blue cotton dress doing little to detract from her lovely form. At first Colyer just stared, for she was much more beautiful than he had imagined, and there was still the hint of wealthy elegance about her, in spite of all she had been through. Colyer did not know all the details and his curiosity was enormous, but he knew better than to pry. "You must be Mrs. Edwards."

Shannon looked from the man to her husband, and Bryce reached out and drew her to him. "She is," he replied. "Shannon, this is Vincent Colyer. The government sent him out here to investigate Indian matters and reservation life."

Shannon nodded to the man and put out her hand. "Hello, Mr. Colyer. I hope your intentions are better than those of most men who are sent out here."

Colyer took her hand, looking at her with admiration. "I belong to the Society of Friends, Mrs. Edwards, and our intentions are fully Christian and compassionate, I assure you."

"Mr. Colyer has asked me to consider being agent at San Carlos," Bryce put in. His wife looked up at him in surprise.

"San Carlos?" Her eyes moved to Chaco. She saw the dread on his face. She already worried that the boy would leave her and go to the Apaches who still rode free. If they went to San Carlos, Chaco would hate it. He would surely leave them then. "Oh, Bryce . . ." She looked back at her husband.

The man patted her shoulder. "Relax, love. I already told him no. It's just something to think about, and something we have both considered more than once."

"And there is the business to consider—and Troy."

Bryce gave her a squeeze. "And you. I'm not sure it would be best for you. Mr. Colyer is just looking for good men, that's all. For once the government is taking a keener interest in the Apaches and realizes they need help." He looked at Colyer. "As long as you're out here investigating things, Colyer, I suggest you look into some of the mindless massacres of peaceful Indians. If such things continue, there will never be peace."

"Massacres?"

"I doubt any soldier would tell you about it. The soldiers, and I'm sure General Crook, are not extremely fond of men like you, men of peace, men who think the Indian should be treated fairly. Most people's attitude is simply kill every Indian in sight, exterminate them all if possible. Some citizens have chosen to do just that, taking the law into their own hands and attacking peaceful Indians, raiding their camps, murdering, raping, burning. As long as those things go on, and treaties continue to be broken, there will never be peace. Besides that, there are the whiskey peddlers to contend with. A drunk Indian is easier to cheat, and the Indian loves whiskey. It's one of the few things left that gives him pleasure, takes him away from reality, makes him feel powerful and closer to the spirit world. But it's their worst enemy. They drink themselves into oblivion, to the point that they care about nothing else. It only feeds their feeling of hopelessness in the end. The whiskey peddlers have got to be stopped. But the Indians won't help you. They cover for them, hide them, protect them, because they want the whiskey. So it's a hell of a struggle."

"There would not be a problem if the white man would leave the Indian alone," Chaco spoke up. "And if the white man kept his promises." He stepped up onto the porch, towering over Colyer, making the man wonder just how "tame" this young Apache was. His curiosity was overwhelming when Chaco stepped up to his mother. Could the beautiful, red-haired, green-eyed woman really be this young man's mother? It seemed impossible.

"I could never live there," he told Shannon, then shifting

63

his gaze to Bryce. "But it is true a good white man like you is needed there. Don't let me stop you, Father."

Bryce shook his head. "You are more important, Chaco."

Their eyes held. Chaco could see that his name, which his father had given him and which stood for Chaco canyon because of the wide difference between his two bloods, was more fitting than ever. He stared at Bryce Edwards, the white man he loved dearly, and then his mother, the beautiful woman from another world Chaco had never known, but who had loved an Apache man.

"I don't think I will be with you much longer," Chaco told them. "I feel torn in half inside. I must decide whether to stay or go." He turned to go inside the store and Shannon grasped his arm.

"Chaco . . ."

He stopped, turning and eyeing her with a strange sorrow. "I have decided." He went inside then, and Shannon looked at Colyer with tears in her eyes. "Excuse me, Mr. Colyer." She went inside and Colyer looked at Bryce.

"I have apparently come at a bad time."

Bryce sighed, taking a last drag on his cigarette and stepping it out. "It's all right. Chaco has been going through a bad time, growing up trying to decide what he should be—do. I'm afraid some of the whites around here don't treat him very well, even though he's grown up with us. He looks Apache, and that is all that matters to them. It's been hard on the boy."

"Of course." Colyer folded his arms. "Mr. Edwards, I can see in your eyes you are a man of compassion. Truly you are perfect for the job of agent at San Carlos. I wish I could get you to agree to go. I'll leave you an address. If you change your mind, please do write to me."

Bryce nodded. "I'll do that. Thank you for your interest."

The two men shook hands. "I would stay and talk more, but there is no sense in doing so until you decide you want the job," Colyer told Bryce. "And I hope things work out with Chaco."

"Yes, so do I—mainly for Shannon's sake. It's very hard for her. No mother likes the thought of her son riding off to a life that could get him killed."

Colyer nodded. "Of course, even if the boy goes to Geronimo or some other Apache tribe that still runs free, it is only a matter of time before he ends up at a place like San Carlos."

Bryce's gray eyes saddened, and he glanced at the doorway. "I know that. His own father wanted us to raise him so he would be safe. But there is a spirit in the Indian, Mr. Colyer, that no other kind of upbringing can kill. It's there, and it makes an Indian an Indian no matter how he's raised. Chaco has a longing, a need that we can't fill for him." He looked back at Colyer, his face brightening some. "I'm sorry you couldn't meet our son Troy. He's at school. He has dreams of being a writer, a journalist of some sort."

Colyer smiled. "Well, I hope he achieves his goals, Mr. Edwards." He handed Bryce a piece of paper from his inner pocket. "Here is where you can write me. Thank you for your time. I have several places to go yet. God be with you and your family."

"Thank you. I'd invite you inside for a cool drink, but I have a feeling my wife is a little upset right now."

"I understand."

They shook hands once more and Colyer walked back to his carriage, smiling and waving as the carriage drove away. Bryce watched after him—an example of those many men and women from the East who knew nothing about Indians but whose intentions were good. He supposed the average white would never truly understand the soul of the Indian. He'd been around them all his life, and Shannon had even lived with them. And still there was some part of the Indian spirit they could not quite grasp. It was that part that Shannon feared the most, that special pull that had taken hold of Chaco and that would probably take him away from his white mother. Shannon would try to understand, but she never really would. She would simply patiently abide by it, quietly allow her son to be Indian, just as she had done with his father.

Chaco. It seemed only a year or two since Saguaro sent his baby son to Bryce and Shannon to be raised. Chaco had been a happy, plump, lively child, innocent of all the prejudices that would some day plague him. If only they could have that Chaco back. But he was gone now, perhaps never to return.

Chaco heated the sopapillias on a rock he'd placed in the fire. The little pillows of fried dough an Indian woman had cooked for him to take along on his return journey smelled good, and he wondered if they would taste as good as his mother's. Shannon Edwards had learned many of the recipes of the Indians while living with them, and she was just as adept at preparing those foods as any Apache or Navaho woman. He picked up one of the sopapillias and tossed it back and forth from hand to hand to cool it, then took a bite. It was pleasing to the tongue, but not quite as good as his mother's, perhaps because it had been reheated and was not fresh.

He sat down cross-legged by the fire then to eat the rest of them. He realized he missed his mother more than he thought he would, and his brother and stepfather. It would be good to see them all again, and he would have much to tell them, for he had actually lived among the Apaches on the old reservation Cochise had been given. He had ridden in alone and with what little Apache he knew he had explained his presence to one of the old ones. He wanted to see how they lived, wanted to hunt with them, wanted to learn all that he could.

To his pride and joy he had been readily accepted, for he was the son of the famous Saguaro, who had ridden with Cochise many years ago. He was the boy given to the white woman but who now was returning to his father's people. He had spent many weeks with the Apaches. Now he returned to his white mother, but only because he had promised her he would. But he would go again. He knew it. He liked this life too much, and he had to learn more, know more, give it more time before he made his final decision. Yet he was already sure what it would be, for his world among the whites was becoming more and more lonely. He wished that he could stay with his mother, for her eyes were so sad when he had left. But he was learning to hate most whites, and to love the wild, free life among the Apache, who accepted and befriended him readily because his father had been Saguaro. He had found them to be loving, gentle, and devoted to their children, a struggling people fighting to keep what was rightfully theirs.

He smiled at the thought of how Troy would be all wide-eyed and excited, asking him a hundred questions. Chaco felt older now, wiser, more manly. He had watched and listened to council discussions, where the younger warriors had argued for all-out war, claimed they must follow Geronimo and ride against the whites again, for there was never quite enough food and they needed more horses. They wanted only to remain free, to keep fighting, to never give up. Chaco could not blame those who wanted to keep running and hiding and raiding. The anger in them was great, for treaties had been broken over and over again, and the Apache was hunted like a wild animal. Whenever they did anything in self-defense or for survival, it was deemed savage, and the Indians were called bloodthirsty and vicious. But when atrocities were committed against the Apaches by whites, they were overlooked, for the motto among most whites was that the only good Indians were dead ones. He bit into another sopapillia, thinking of Little Deer, how pretty she was, how brave she'd been at the Sunrise ceremony. He had not thought much about girls until Little Deer caught his eyes. He was forbidden to speak to her or touch her, but when she could get away with it, she had looked at him in a way that brought uncomfortable but pleasing stirrings in his loins. She was very young, but old enough to have her first flowing and be honored in the ceremony for the coming of womanhood. She was beautiful, and Chaco wondered what it would be like to lie next to her the way his mother and Bryce lay together. He had heard them sometimes in the night making love. Now his curiosity was keen about such things.

Little Deer. They were both too young for him to make her his wife. It frustrated him. He sighed deeply, picking up a stick and poking at the coals of the fire, so lost in thought he didn't hear anything behind him. It was a lesson he would not forget, and after that day he determined always to be more cautious, to allow his Indian instincts to guide him, never to be so careless when traveling this land alone. A shot rang out, and a hot pain pierced the top of his right shoulder, knocking him forward. He managed to put out his arm and roll sideways, avoiding falling directly into his campfire.

As first he was stunned and confused. He rolled toward his horse, where his rifle still rested in its boot. But several more shots rang out, hitting the dirt around him and preventing him from getting to Indian. He heard war whoops and laughter then, the sound of horses' hooves coming toward him, down the rocky hill below which he had camped, little rocks tumbling as his attackers descended.

Chaco shook his head, trying to gather his thoughts, then scrambled again for his rifle, but another shot rang out, and this time pain ripped through the calf of his left leg. The boy could not help crying out then, as his leg crumpled under him. By then two men were right beside him, their horses almost stepping on Chaco.

"Well, lookee here," one of them snickered. "I believe it's a young Apache boy, all alone. What you doin' out here all alone, boy? You lookin' for some kind of vision or somethin'? Maybe a little pain will help you contact the spirits."

Both men laughed and dismounted. Chaco could not even see them clearly, because of his pain and the particles of dust and sand that had gotten in his eyes. The only thing he knew for certain was that they were white.

"He looks kind of familiar, Dade," the second man spoke up then.

"Just looks like a plain ole' Apache renegade to me," the one called Dade replied. "You know what the rule is for Apaches. We can shoot them on sight and nobody gives a damn." He kicked at Chaco's ribs and the boy grunted, trying to get to his knees. "Only thing is, shootin' is too good for 'em. They ought to suffer, that's what. The secret is to beat the hell out of them and let them live so's they remember and know they'd better be good."

"I say we hang him. Apaches hate hangin'. Somethin' about it they think is humiliatin'—they won't go to Apache heaven or some dumb thing like that."

Chaco was kicked again and rolled onto his back. A heavily booted foot pressed on his throat so that he began to suffocate. He wiggled and kicked out violently, trying to get to his knife, but he felt someone remove it from its sheath.

"Oh, no you don't," came the second man's voice. "Nothin' more dangerous than an Apache with a knife in his hand."

Chaco grabbed the ankle of the man who was choking him, and with a strength that surprised them both for his youth, he yanked the man's leg, making him fall. He started to scramble away.

"Get him, Chap," the one called Dade yelled. "Don't let the little son of a bitch get away! I'll kill him!"

Someone tackled Chaco, and the boy fought wildly, punching, scratching, kicking, an almost equal match for the one called Chap. "Come and help me, you bastard," the man yelled. "The kid's strong as the devil!"

Chaco felt himself being pulled off Chap. The names sounded vaguely familiar to him, but he couldn't quite place them. Now the one called Dade held his arms behind him, and Chap dealt him several blows to the midsection, then kicked the boy in the groin. Chaco had caught only a glimpse of Chap through blurred vision, noticing a red neck scarf around the man's neck. That too seemed familiar. But there was no time to think about that now. He felt himself pushed down then, the hard rocky earth scratching at the skin of his back while someone heavy sat on top of him, grasping his hair tightly and yanking on it painfully.

"I'm gonna' teach you a lesson, boy, about how Apaches is hated around here and had best stay out of sight," came Dade's voice. "You want a vision, boy? I'll give you one." The man looked up at Chap. "Go get me a bottle of whiskey." He looked back at Chaco, jerking at his hair again. "What did you have in mind, boy, out here all alone? You was careless, boy—makin' a campfire so's a man could see the smoke from afar. Out here we don't go easy on Apaches. You fixin' to maybe raid some innocent farmer, maybe grab you a white girl to get yourself into, huh? How old are you, boy? You old enough to know what to do with a girl?" A big fist came across Chaco's face. "I expect so. Apaches learn them things early."

Chaco tasted blood. Then the one called Chap returned.

"Stand on his wrists," he heard Dade tell the man. Chaco started to fight again, but he was too weakened by the surprise attack. Someone grabbed his arms and pulled them up. Then he felt the painful weight of a man standing and pressing down on both wrists, smashing them into the earth. Chaco cried out, and the moment he opened his mouth a liquid was poured into it. He coughed and choked, but Dade grasped his jaw and yanked down, pouring more down his throat. Chaco had to swallow or choke.

"There you go, boy, the favorite drink of the Apache—some nice, strong firewater. You should love it, boy. All Apaches love this stuff. You ever get drunk, boy? Oh, my, you can have a hell of a vision if you get drunk." He yanked painfully on Chaco's jaw again, and again came the whiskey. Chaco had tasted whiskey only once, out of curiosity, when Bryce was out of the supply store. He didn't like it, and he was well aware of what it had done to some Apaches. He had vowed to stay away from it, and Bryce and Shannon had both warned him more than once that it would be wise of him to never touch it. Now Dade continued forcing the strong, burning liquid down his throat so fast that Chaco felt like he would vomit. He struggled to turn his face away, but it was impossible. Soon all feeling began to leave him. He was no longer aware of his pain, or even what was happening to him. The world around him began to float strangely, and the voices of the men called Dade and Chap seemed miles away.

"That's just about the whole bottle, Dade," Chap was saying. "Hell, that will kill the boy."

"So? What's the loss?"

Both men laughed, and Chaco sensed the great weight on his body and wrists suddenly left him. "Let him lie there," Dade mumbled. "If the whiskey don't kill him, the sun will— or maybe he'll bleed to death."

"Yeah, well you'd better hope there's none of his friends or family around."

"Don't worry about it. We haven't seen an Apache for miles. I wonder what the little bastard was doing here all by himself? Check out his horse. It's probably stole from someplace."

There was a moment of silence, and Chaco rolled onto his stomach but was unable to get up at all. It seemed everything in his body had gone to sleep, and his mind swirled with thoughts of his white family, Cochise, Little Deer.

"Look here, Dade. The saddle bag on this horse was hand-made—Edwards Trading Post it says here—carved right into the bag."

"What?" Another moment of silence. "Hey, there's a brand on the horse—B.E."

"Shit! Bryce Edwards."

"Who?"

"You know. The man that owns that trading post not far from Fort Bowie, where we tried to trade them hides last fall

71

and he wouldn't take them because he claimed they wasn't properly cleaned. Don't you remember? He was livin' with a white woman folks claimed once lived with the Apaches. The whore had a half-breed son. I think this is the same kid."

"Damn! We can't take the horse. It might be recognized. Edwards was once in the Army and has a lot of friends at Fort Bowie. I don't want a pack of damned soldiers after us. Let's get out of here."

"What about the kid?"

"Leave him. He'll never last anyway. Even if he does, he don't know who we are. He only saw us that one time, and we never even talked to him. It was his pa we dealt with. Come on. Let's go. We've had our fun for the day. I only wish we could run onto a lone Apache more often. It's been a right pleasurable experience."

Both men laughed, and then there was the fading sound of horses riding off, then only silence. It was only minutes before shadows began circling around Chaco, waiting, watching ... buzzards ... just another part of nature, of the violent land in which man and beast lived according to the law of survival. Now it was the buzzards' turn.

When Chaco awoke the sun seemed to be in the wrong place for the time of day. Hadn't it been setting when he made camp here? At first he could not remember what had happened, and when he moved he was consumed with pain, not just from his wounds, but also pain in his head and eyes. He groaned and managed to get to his knees, but then was hit with instant, wretched vomiting. It seemed every muscle, every nerve in his body screamed with pain and agony, and his stomach lurched and tightened of its own accord. A terrible thirst engulfed him, and he crawled to Indian, who stood faithfully nearby, nibbling on dry grass.

Chaco managed to grasp the horse's leg and pull himself up

to the bridle, grasping that and getting to his feet. He loosened his canteen and slumped to the ground again, shaking violently, his head swirling in pain and confusion. He opened the canteen and took a swallow of water, but it only made him sick again, and he vomited until miserable pains engulfed his abdomen, which had nothing left to give but which continued its convulsive heaving anyway.

After several minutes his stomach finally relaxed. The young man held up the canteen with a shaking hand and poured some water over his face, which seemed to help. He decided he would not drink any more for the moment. He recapped the canteen, lying back and trying to gather his thoughts.

Slowly it all began to come back to him—the men, the beating, the gunshots, the whiskey—the smelly, hot whiskey. Why? Why had they done that to him? He'd done nothing to them. They could at least have asked him why he was there. And surely they had left him for dead. It was only then he realized that buzzards were circling overhead.

"Get away," he tried to shout, but his voice was weak. He picked up a rock to throw at them, but it didn't go far. "You won't . . . be feasting on me."

He looked up. The sun was in the east. It was morning. Had he lain here all night then? It had been late afternoon when he was attacked. He wondered why they had not killed him, why they had not taken his horse. He closed his eyes and struggled to remember. Names, they had called each other by name. What were the names? Maybe Bryce would recognize them, if he could only remember. And he and Bryce would go together and find them and kill them!

Never before had he been so full of vengeance and hatred. Now he understood. Now he knew how other Apaches felt. Now he truly understood hatred and prejudice. How well he understood! Up until now he had always lived with Bryce Edwards, been under the man's protective wing. As long as Bryce was nearby, no one dared go too far in insulting Chaco. But once alone, once away from the loving protection of his parents, he would have to be constantly on guard.

Think, he told himself. Names. ... Dade! Dade was one of the names. And the other name—it was something like what men wore when chasing down wild mustangs and cattle. Chaps! Chap. That was it! Chap and Dade. They were unusual names, and because of that perhaps Bryce would recognize them.

He got to his knees again, his whole body trembling and weak. He vowed he would never be caught off guard like this again, and by God, no white men would ever again touch him, humiliate him as those two had done! The only good thing about it was the wretched sickness from the whiskey. Now he would hate it for the rest of his life. He never wanted to touch it again. Just the thought of it made him feel sicker.

He managed to gaze around the canyon, the rising sun making his head ache more. He saw no signs of life. It was only then that he became aware of the wound in his left calf. It gaped, and was packed with dried blood. His right shoulder ached, but he knew it wasn't badly wounded. It was the leg wound that worried him. If if became infected he could lose his leg. It had happened to more than one man in this wild country where any wound was dangerous.

"I've got to get ... home," he mumbled, half crawling to Indian. "My mother ... she'll help me ... Troy ... Father." He managed to again get to his feet, clinging to Indian, and with extreme effort he pulled himself up onto the animal's back. By the time he got on the animal he was sweating and panting. It would not be easy to stay mounted, but he must get home or he could die. There would be time for vengeance later—once he was healed.

"Come on, Indian, you know the way. Take me home, boy." He urged the horse into motion, and Indian obeyed. Chaco headed the animal northeast. He knew he was already out of the Dragoon Mountains and perhaps only a couple of days from home. He had to hang on for those couple of days, keep his senses. It he passed out he could die. And on top of that he had to keep watch for enemies that might be lurking about, more men like those who had attacked him. He rode blindly, the hot sun burning into his dark skin, his head reeling, wondering how long it would take to get all the hated whiskey out of his system.

Never would he forget! Never! It wasn't the beating, or being shot at from behind that angered him nearly as much as the humiliation of being held down while the whiskey was poured down his throat. That was the worst. That had injured his pride, listening to their words about Indians and whiskey. He would get them! Somehow he would get them both! He was Apache now. The Apache desire for vengeance was great inside of him!

Chapter Five

Chaco awoke to the familiar smell of oatmeal cooking. He lay still a moment, hoping he was really where he thought he was and that he was not just imagining it. He stirred slightly, feeling pain in his leg but enjoying the feather mattress and quilts of his parents' bed. He looked around the room, gathering his thoughts, some of the joy leaving him as he began to remember what had happened, how he had come to be here. Rage began to move through him. Never had he been so keenly aware of his Apache blood and what it could mean for him as he grew into a man.

Bryce Edwards appeared in the doorway then, and Chaco raised his yes to meet his stepfather's. "Chaco," Bryce said softly. "Are you fully awake this time?" The man moved closer to the bed, bending over the boy.

"I am awake," Chaco replied sullenly.

Bryce studied him intently, seeing a new look there, something he did not like—hatred, bitterness, revenge. He sat down on the edge of the bed. "What happened? Who did this to you?"

"White men!" The words were sneered, as full of venom as any the most warlike Apache could utter. "Stinking white men!"

In only a moment Shannon was coming into the room, for Chaco had said the words loudly in his anger. "Chaco!" She moved closer, coming around the other side of the bed. "Oh, Chaco, you're awake. Are you in much pain?"

Just looking at her gentle, beautiful face removed some of his anger temporarily. "A little."

"Well, I know we've told you never to touch whiskey, but it's all right for medicinal purposes, Chaco. I'll get you some and you can swallow just a little . . ."

"No!" The word was shouted so heatedly that Shannon jumped. She stared at him wide-eyed, and Bryce stood up and walked around to the foot of the bed.

"Don't shout at your mother, Chaco."

Chaco put a hand to his head. "I am sorry. But I never want . . . any whiskey . . . ever . . . not even for pain. Those men . . . they made me drink whiskey. . . . I don't know how much—a whole bottle maybe. They said . . . ugly things about Apaches . . . and whiskey . . . and after they shot and beat me, they held me down . . . forced me to drink their stinking, rot-gut whiskey." His body shuddered and he began to sweat.

'My God," Shannon whimpered. She turned away. "I wondered . . . when something like this would happen."

Chaco met Bryce's eyes. "I lay there . . . all night. When I woke up I was so sick I thought perhaps I would die . . . and my insides would come out through my mouth. Them making me drink that whiskey—that was what made me hate them—more even than for hurting me. I will kill them!"

Shannon sniffed and turned to meet Bryce's eyes, and he saw all the pain and fear there. He leaned on the brass rail at the foot of the bed, meeting Chaco's eyes again. "We'll have no such talk. If there's any killing to do, or justice to be had, it will be done the right way, or at my hands, not yours."

"You do not need to do my fighting for me! Those men are mine! Mine!"

77

"Calm down, Chaco," Bryce said with authority. "Tell us from the beginning what happened."

Chaco licked at dry lips. "I was camped, bothering no one." The boy rubbed at his forehead with a shaking hand. "I . . . need some water."

Shannon hurried to a bucket beside the bed and dipped a ladle into it, then raised it to her son's mouth. Chaco sat up slightly and took a sip. Their eyes met, and he saw the terror in his mother's. "You cannot shelter me forever, Mother. I have been with the Apache a long time. I know many truths now. And I must face whatever I must face." He looked back at Bryce, then shifted again, wincing with pain, not just from his leg. His ribs and abdomen and neck ached from being so violently ill. "They snuck up on me . . . shot at me from behind. The first shot grazed my shoulder and knocked me senseless, just long enough for them to keep shooting at me so that I could not get to my horse. I took another shot in my leg, and then they were upon me . . . beating me . . . calling me dirty names and saying . . . bad things about the Apache. Then they held me down . . . and forced me to drink the whiskey." His eyes teared from being so angry. "I will never forget! Never!"

Bryce sighed deeply, taking a prerolled cigarette from his shirt pocket while Shannon moved to a wash bowl near the bed and wet a cloth. "Did you get a good look at them, get their names? Were they familiar to you?" Bryce asked.

Chaco clenched his fists. "They hurt me so bad right away, I could not see them very good. But I remember one wore a red neck scarf . . . and they called each other by name."

Shannon leaned over and sponged perspiration from Chaco's face.

"I don't like this fever," she said with concern. "I'm worried about infection."

"I am fine. It is just hot in here," Chaco assured her. He looked back at Bryce. "I heard them call each other Chap . . . and Dade. I will not soon forget the names."

Bryce frowned, lighting the cigarette and taking a drag.

"Those names sound familiar," Shannon spoke up, rinsing out the cloth.

Bryce's normally gentle gray eyes were suddenly cold. "Very familiar. I've met them," he said, his voice cool. "They'll not get away with this." He started for the door.

"Father, where are you going," Chaco asked, pushing his blankets aside.

"You stay right in that bed. I'm going to Fort Bowie to report this, and to contact Jeffords. I know who those two men are. I'll have the soldiers keep a lookout."

"No! They are mine!" Chaco managed to move his legs over the side of the bed and stood up, but he grasped a dresser, nearly falling.

"Chaco, get back in bed," Shannon pleaded.

"They are mine," he told Bryce angrily. "You will go after them yourself, or send the soldiers. I want to kill them myself!"

"Don't talk stupid," Bryce interrupted, stepping closer to the boy. "You're seventeen years old. But it isn't so much your age as your race! They're white men, Chaco! White men! And you, I must remind you, are Apache. Or at least that's how others look at you. Don't you understand what that means? You can't go after those men. You can't go after *any* white men. If you do, you'll hang for it, no matter how right you are!"

Shannon watched with a breaking heart, and Chaco just stared, meeting his stepfather's eyes angrily. "It is not fair! They can go around killing Apaches or doing to them what they did to me—two men against one who is injured—and they can get away with it?"

"No. I'm going to do my best to see that they do not get away with it," Bryce assured him. "I'll try it the right way first, and if that doesn't work, I'll go after them myself."

"If you go after them yourself, then let me go with you,"

Chaco pleaded. "Please, Father. My heart will never be happy if I do not at least see vengeance taken."

Bryce took another drag on the cigarette. "I don't know. We'll talk more when I get back from the fort. For now you get back in that bed and off that leg. We had a hell of a time cleaning it up and closing the wound. You'll break everything open again."

Chaco stood there breathing heavily, blinking back tears. "I ... cannot forget, Father. What those men did. I am so ashamed." His jaw flexed in anger. "They kept ... pouring that filthy whiskey ... down my throat. I tried not to swallow, but I had no choice." His teeth gritted. "I tell you again I will get those men myself. I will go to Geronimo!"

Bryce stepped closer to him, grasping the boy's shoulders. "You can always stay here. We'll work something out."

Chaco shook his head. "It is not that. It is me—inside. I was full of joy—and Apache pride—the day I met and spoke with Cochise. Now I know what being Apache means to men of this world—your world." His body began to tremble, and more perspiration appeared on his forehead. Bryce urged him back to the bed.

"You'll be able to think more clearly when you're healed. Don't worry about any of it now, Chaco. Please just get off that leg, and don't be a worry to your mother while I'm gone. Get some rest."

Chaco sat down on the bed, breathing heavily. "Make me a bed ... in the other room ... on the floor. I should not take this bed."

"It's all right for a couple of days. Your mother will sleep in the loft with Troy and I can bed down in the main room so you won't be disturbed. Right now just concentrate on getting well, Chaco." He helped the boy swing his legs back into the bed. "We're just glad you're here for now, Chaco. We were getting worried. Where were you when all of this happened?"

"Southwest of here, just coming out of the Dragoons. It was . . . about a mile south of Thorn Creek." He sank into the bed. "I will get them myself," he mumbled.

"You'll do nothing of the kind," Shannon told him, covering him with a light blanket and leaving the quilts off. "And right now you will rest." She met her husband's eyes and saw the worry there. Bryce turned and walked through the door, and Shannon quickly followed him all the way outside. "You know who they are, don't you," she said, once they were out of hearing distance.

Bryce sighed deeply. "They were here a few months ago trying to sell some worthless buffalo hides. Dade Chadwell and John Miller—called Chap by most. I think the commander at the fort will know them, too. They're buffalo hunters—some of the worst kind. I remember them because I remember how they looked at Chaco, and at you. I wanted to remember their faces and names in case they ever came back."

"Bryce, be careful. What would I do if anything happened to you?"

He smiled softly and kissed her cheek quickly. "All I'm going to do right now is go to the fort and talk to Jeffords and report what happened to Chaco. Those men are probably long gone for the moment." He turned away and threw down his cigarette, his face hardening. "Bastards! It's the goddamned white men like them that keep things stirred up. And they wonder why in hell the Apaches keep fighting!"

She put a hand to her stomach. "You're worried about him, aren't you? You're worried about what this will do to Chaco."

He ran a hand through his thick, blond hair. "Yes, I'm worried. That look in his eyes . . . God, I've seen it before, Shannon—the way Saguaro looked so many times. Those sons of bitches hurt his pride badly—the worst thing you can do to an Indian. And they damned well knew it! If I do find them, I'll rip them apart limb from limb!"

As he moved off the porch and headed for the horse shed

Shannon watched with an aching heart. It wasn't just the Indians who had to make terrible choices. It was white men like Bryce Edwards, men who thought the Apaches deserved fair treatment and so were often just as hated as the Indians. Bryce had already left the army because he could no longer follow orders to shoot Apaches on sight. She turned wearily back into the house. Would there ever really be any peace between whites and Indians? It seemed everyone had been at war ever since the first arguments and skirmishes started back in Virginia before the Civil War broke out. Forever she had been involved in wars and her heart felt ravaged and torn. Now there was Chaco to worry about, the hatred in his eyes, the determination to have his vengeance. She knew this day might come, yet somehow she had hoped it wouldn't.

Bryce rode into Fort Bowie, feeling the old attachment, remembering the days when he was the commander here. Some of those years were bleak and left a lingering sorrow on his heart, for he had spent many years in this place wondering what had happened to Shannon Fitzgerald, thinking she was dead then discovering she was living among the Apaches. There was a time when he thought perhaps she would never belong to him again.

But that was over now, as were his Army days. Now both he and Shannon had lived in Arizona too long to leave it and go back east. There were too many attachments. And there was Chaco. Shannon had not wanted to take him back east, where people would stare and ask questions, where he would feel like a foreigner. Here he was in the land that suited him, but so many whites had come since Chaco was born that Bryce feared the boy would still feel like a foreigner, for Arizona was changing rapidly. It was rumored a railroad would be coming through this very area within a year or two, meaning an influx of even more whites. This land was not anything like it had been when Bryce first came here, when all Apaches rode free.

He waved to a sergeant, then headed for the commander's headquarters. Most of them were gone now, those men who had served under him many years ago, fighting hand to hand with Apaches, fighting with him against Cochise at Apache Pass.

He wasn't sure just when it was he made up his mind he could no longer follow Army orders on how to handle the Indians. Perhaps it was when he'd seen the look in Saguaro's eyes the day he handed Chaco over to him to keep. He'd never fully realized until then how "human" the Apaches were. Or perhaps it was when Cochise was tricked at a peace conference and his family was arrested, his brother and two cousins hanged for nothing. But the most influential event was most likely the day Bryce killed Saguaro, realizing the man actually wanted to die. The sorrow he felt over that day still plagued him, and that was when he knew for certain his army days were over.

He had ridden Dreamer today. He dismounted and tied the fine black mare to a hitching post and walked inside. Colonel Henry Blazer, fairly new at the fort, looked up from where he stood with a cup of coffee, studying a map. He was a tall man, slender, with a heavy mustache and sideburns, thick eyebrows that shrouded rather beady, dark eyes. His dark hair was graying at the temples, and as always he was neatly attired in an immaculate uniform. Bryce never failed to wonder how he kept his boots so shiny in the Arizona dust.

Their eyes met, and Bryce felt the tinge of animosity he always felt with this man. He'd never had problems with any other commanding officer here, but he suspected Blazer did not hold the same sympathies for the Apache that Bryce did, and that he could not understand how Bryce Edwards could live with a woman who had been married to an Apache man, or take the woman's half-breed son as his own. None of these things were voiced, they were only suspicions in Bryce's mind, vibrations he felt whenever he spoke to Blazer. And Bryce did not doubt the man was a little jealous that Bryce was so well liked around the fort and had once been a commander here himself, or forgive the fact that Bryce had actually resigned from the army while still a young man. To men like Blazer, that was a dreadful sin.

"Edwards," he said now, nodding to Bryce and walking to his desk. "To what do I owe this honor? You haven't been around much lately." He put out his hand, but there was no firmness in the handshake. "Haven't seen much of your boys lately either."

He motioned for Bryce to sit down, and Bryce took the man up on his offer, taking a chair directly across the desk from Blazer. "You haven't seen me much because I don't like to leave Shannon alone. Used to be both boys would be there when I was gone, and they can both shoot straight. But Chaco's been gone the last few weeks and Troy goes to school, so I stayed close by."

"Well, those boys are growing, Edwards. You'll have to hire yourself someone to help you watch over the place. Your sons will both be heading out on their own before you know it." His eyes narrowed slightly. "Of course, we all know you needn't fear too much from the Apaches, seeing as how you're such good friends with most of them."

Bryce ignored the slight sneer in the remark. "There are some kinds of white men out there who are more dangerous than the Apaches, Colonel. I worry about them more than I do Indians."

The colonel laughed lightly. "I hardly think there is a white man alive who can compare to an Apache when it comes to sneaking and lying and stealing," he answered, "let alone rape and murder. And where, may I ask, has Chaco been?"

"That's part of the reason I'm here—that and the kind of white men I was just talking about. Chaco was attacked while camping alone, Colonel, by two white men—I know who they

84

were. Chaco heard them call each other by name, and you've probably seen them around the fort."

The colonel frowned. "Attacked? Why? Did he do something to them, steal something from them?"

Bryce bristled, holding his temper. "Chaco is a good boy, Colonel, a little wild, I'll admit, but I've raised him to never steal or bring harm to anyone. I would trust him to the limit. He did nothing to those men. They attacked him from behind, snuck up on him and shot at him, deliberately wounding him in a way that wouldn't kill him. They wanted him to suffer. Two grown men attacking a seventeen-year-old boy. They beat on him and then forced whiskey down his throat, practically a whole bottle. They left him for dead. It's a miracle he made it home. We had a hell of a time fixing up his leg. They shot him through his left calf."

The colonel frowned, leaning forward on his desk. "Well, we both know that Chaco hardly looks like a boy. He's as big and strong as any man and was probably taken for one. Maybe they thought he was some renegade planning an attack on some innocent homestead."

"There are no maybes, Colonel," Bryce replied in a louder voice. "Chaco did nothing to provoke the attack. Boy or man, he was camped alone, minding his own business. You know how many incidents we've had like this one! These white vigilantes have got to be stopped! If they don't stop murdering innocent Apaches we'll never have peace. It's time the white man was punished for atrocities against the Apaches. If we don't show the Apaches we understand justice, that men are punished equally, there will never be a complete surrender."

The colonel met Bryce's fiery, gray eyes. "Probably not. But prejudice cannot be changed overnight, Edwards, especially prejudice born out of personal loss—white men whose wives have been raped, children murdered, homes burned. . . ."

"The Apaches don't know how else to try to hang on to what

85

they feel is rightfully theirs!" Bryce stood up, sighing deeply and walking to a window. The room hung silent for several minutes. "I didn't come here to argue about the Apaches, Colonel Blazer. I came here to talk about my son—a boy who is half white, and was raised white—a boy who was beaten and shamed by two cowardly white men who will continue to make trouble if they aren't stopped. They were at my trading post last year. I remember them, a couple of buffalo hunters—Dade Chadwell and John Miller. Some call Miller Chap."

"Ah, yes, I know those two. They were here at the fort not long ago, headed south, I believe."

Bryce turned. "I want a wire sent to other forts to be on the lookout for them. I want them arrested and tried for what they did."

The colonel smiled as though it were a funny joke. "Mr. Edwards, how far do you think I'd get with a request like that? You know it's useless to try to arrest white men for doing anything to an Indian. No white jury in this territory would convict them. Besides, they'd twist their story to make your son look bad, say he stole from them or something. You know how readily people would believe it." He leaned back in his chair. "You have those two arrested and they'll end up going free. Your son will be left with a bad reputation, and you'll be worse off than when you started. My suggestion is to let it lie. Your son is all right, I take it. You said he was home and mending. Just be glad he wasn't killed."

Bryce just stared at the man, fighting an urge to jump over the desk and land a fist into the colonel's face. His jaw flexed in anger. "Do you have a son, Colonel?"

The man nodded. "William. He's in college right now."

"And how would you feel if some ruffians came along and beat the hell out of him, shamed him in the worst way they could, ambushed him from behind for no reason."

The colonel shook his head. "There's no comparison, Edwards. You're talking about white men brutalizing white men.

There have always been laws for that. But it's impossible to apply white man's laws to Indians."

"Why? They're just humans like everyone else. Those men attacked Chaco just because he was an Indian, just for the evil fun of it! They didn't even steal any of his belongings or his horse. They wanted nothing more than to beat up a helpless Indian boy. I can't let that go, Colonel. And we continually tell the Apaches our laws and justice apply to both sides."

"Of course we tell them that. But you go actually arresting white men and trying and punishing them for what they do to Indians, and you'll be the one who gets hanged, not them. We have to go along with the citizens right now, Edwards. You know that. And what would Washington say?"

"I don't give a damn what Washington says!" Bryce stepped closer. "But I'll tell you what I say. I am registering an official complaint against these two men and requesting they be arrested. And since I'm sure you'll do nothing about it, I am going to find them myself and deal my own form of justice! I'll not let this go, Colonel. Chaco has been too hurt. If he doesn't see justice done, he's going to just get more rebellious—maybe even join the Apaches. I don't want to see that happen, not just for my sake, but mostly for my wife's. It would break her heart to see Chaco join the Apaches."

The colonel took a pipe from a drawer and lit it. "That is a matter for you, your wife and Chaco."

Their eyes held, and Bryce hated the man more than ever. "There really isn't much I can do about it," the man added. "And I would advise you not to take the law into your own hands."

"Out here a man has little choice, when not even the United States Army will help him," Bryce hissed. "There's only one law out here, Colonel—the law of survival—and a man has to reap his own justice. I reported the incident. That's all I can do for now. And I don't intend to go home and tell my son that no one is interested in prosecuting these men. I'll tell him the army will do everything they can. If he thinks otherwise, he'll run off to find them himself. I feel it in my bones. I don't intend to lose him over this, Colonel. I'll take care of Dade Chadwell and Chap Miller my own way."

Bryce headed for the door. "Edwards," the colonel called out. Bryce turned. "You aren't an army officer any more. You can't make your own orders."

Bryce held the man's eyes challengingly. "When it comes to my sons, I'll make up the rules as I damned well please!"

The night was still, that stillness familiar to a desolate land. The distant mountains loomed black against the backdrop of a full moon. Chaco limped out onto the porch of the small Edwards cabin. The last few days had been a living hell for him, as he struggled through an infection from the bullet wound, screaming as his mother and stepfather cauterized the wound, begging them not to cut off his leg. Now he was healing, but only on the outside.

Bryce was sitting on the steps with Troy, and they both turned to see Chaco approaching.

"You should still be off that leg," Bryce spoke up, rising to grasp Chaco's muscular arm and help him to a porch post. Chaco grasped it and looked from Bryce to Troy and back to Bryce.

"I wanted to talk," he told his stepfather.

Bryce frowned. "Do you want Troy to leave?"

Chaco shook his head. "He is my brother. You and he . . . and my mother are among the few whites who are special in my heart." He swallowed. Bryce noticed that since living among the Apaches his speech tended to be patterned after the way a true Apache would speak after learning English. The Apaches had quickly made an impression on him, even on the way he spoke. For weeks it was the only way of speaking Chaco had heard, and now it was his own, making him seem even more Indian. "But I cannot stay here just for the three of you, Father," he went on. "I have thought long about it, and I knew from your eyes the day you returned from the fort that the soldiers will do nothing about those men who attacked me. That says it all, Father. I do not belong here now. They will not let me belong. I am going to Geronimo."

Bryce's heart tightened. "You don't have to do that, Chaco. It will all work out."

Chaco shook his head. "No. It will never work out. In a couple of days I will ride into the Dragoons and I will seek out Geronimo and ride with the Apache. Perhaps it is my Apache blood, but my heart is so full of hatred and revenge I cannot sleep. I will never know that revenge in this world. I can only know it in another."

"But Chaco, what will I do without you?" Troy spoke up, rising from the porch. "You're my best friend."

Chaco's eyes teared slightly. "You have new friends now, white friends at school. That is as it should be. This is your world, but not mine. It does not mean we cannot continue to be friends. If I should ever see you, I would never harm you."

Bryce eyed him closely. "And you would harm others?"

Chaco held his chin up, meeting the man's eyes squarely. "I would be Apache, whatever it will mean. If riding with Geronimo means raiding whites, then I will do it."

"Then you will become a hunted man, just like the rest of the renegades, Chaco," Bryce answered, his voice almost choking in his sorrow. "Your mother and I did not raise you to do this."

"You raised me as best you could, Father. But only part of me has white blood. All of your teachings could not change the other side of me, the side I have never fully explored or known. My real father would want me to know it, now that I am a man."

Bryce looked away. "Once you go, you can never come back and live freely again. You know that."

There was a long silence while Chaco struggled not to cry himself. "I know," he answered quietly. "But something inside of me will not let me change my mind. I . . . I have already spoken to Mother. She is inside weeping. You should go to her. You are her strength. I am grateful for the love you have had for her over the years, for your generosity in taking me in when my real father asked it of you, for loving me because I am Shannon Edwards' son. You have done well, Bryce Edwards. This has nothing to do with you or my mother. It has to do with being Apache. I can no longer live among a people who judge me for my skin. Half of me is white, but nothing about me looks white, and so it has already been determined I do not belong here."

Bryce whirled, his eyes red and watery. "Damn it, Chaco, there is nothing out there for you, nothing but starvation, perhaps imprisonment and death!"

Chaco swallowed again. "I know that. I go anyway. I ask your blessing."

Bryce studied the dark eyes and slowly nodded. "All right. You're old enough to decide, I suppose." He put out his hand, but the moment Chaco took it the two embraced and wept together.

Troy watched his older half brother, who had always remained somewhat elusive and mysterious. He determined that some day, somehow, he would do as his father had once imagined and find a way to be the voice of those like Chaco, those who still rode free, clinging to the refuge of the wild mountains, hoping against hope for some kind of freedom to live their own way, hoping for a place to call their own.

He thought about their carefree days, when Chaco was still young enough not to understand the prejudice or to think much of his Apache blood. He thought about the day they met Cochise, the impact it had had on Chaco. That emotional event had never left him. Nor had it left Troy, who would never forget the compassion and sorrow in the eyes of Cochise, who died only a year later. He wondered now that once Chaco rode away, as Cochise had that day, if he would ever see his brother alive again. His heart hurt and his throat constricted so that it was hard to breathe without shuddering in an unwanted sob. Chaco would go away. They had been so close, and yet it seemed to Troy that he hardly knew his brother at all.

Chapter Six

Chaco had not forgotten the vision. He must first be Chaco. To him, that meant exploring all that made him what he was, and he was convinced in his own heart that his father was surely trying to warn him not to love a white woman.

He wanted nothing more now than to be Apache—all Apache—and he captured four wild horses on his way south, presenting them to Naiche, son of Cochise, and asking the man to appoint someone to teach him all the ways of the Apache, someone with whom he could live and ride and hunt and even raid, someone who would sponsor him in the test of manhood and make sure that his white parents were informed if he should die. To this person he would present two of the wild horses. Because Cochise had been good friends with Chaco, Naiche agreed to Chaco's request. He was given to Coyotero, a proven warrior, aged twenty-two and unmarried.

Coyotero was not kind, not because he disliked Chaco, he liked him very much. But Chaco still had much to learn about being a true Apache, and Coyotero worked Chaco hard. Food was scarce, since raiding had started again and the government had cut off supplies. And so Chaco got even less than the others. Sometimes if he didn't do something right, Coyotero would hit him, sometimes knock him down. Chaco was not allowed to strike back. He was learning patience, learning that there were superiors who must be minded, all the way to the moment of raiding. Once the battle began, it would often be every man for himself.

But Chaco did not participate in raids. He was not allowed to. He did, however, accompany Coyotero, tending the man's horse and weapons. But as he watched, he felt the thrill, the excitement. He had seen what some Mexicans did to Apaches, and he understood Apache vengeance. He knew raiding had started again against the whites also, but he felt the anger of Apache hearts, knew their frustration at all the broken promises, at raids faked by white men for which Apaches were blamed, and at rumors that the Chiricahuas would have to go to San Carlos. And he still carried his own bitterness and hatred over the beating and humiliation suffered under Dade Chadwell and Chap Miller. He would never forget, and he prayed that some day he would find them both. He knew now the Apache techniques for making a man suffer, and they would suffer, of that he was certain!

After several weeks of being toughened the Apache way, Chaco was forced to starve himself for four days, after which he underwent the test of manhood. First he would be made to run through two lines of warriors, who beat him and poked at him with spears. If he made it to the end of the lines, he was to walk over hot rocks. And then came the ultimate test, hanging by the skin on skewers until the skin tore away, a ritual adopted from Plains Indians farther to the north.

The day of Chaco's test was a day of celebrating and festivities. There were other young men who would also be undergoing the brutal test. Chaco was not afraid. He was Apache now, and he would stay Apache as long as possible. Already the great Victorio was raiding all over the Southwest Territory, making new headlines in the Tucson newspapers. And in only a few days the band with which he lived would head south to Mexico again, there to join up with Geronimo, fleeing the ru-

93

mors that they would have to go to San Carlos. Chaco had not yet met Geronimo, but he looked forward to the day.

The ritual began, and the lines of men with clubs and sticks and spears was a blur before Chaco's eyes. He put aside all thoughts of his mother, of Troy and Bryce. He thought only of Saguaro, and how proud his Apache father would be if he passed this test. And he thought about Little Deer. She was among this tribe and would be watching. He had paid little attention to her when he first arrived. He wanted to concentrate on becoming fully Apache. But she had grown prettier than ever and was still not married. Her father expected great gifts before he would give her to anyone. Perhaps one day he would buy her himself. But Chaco could not think about such things now. He ducked down and started running, feeling the blows and fiery stings as he drew on all his strength and his Apache spirit to survive this first test.

Chaco awoke to soft singing. Everything hurt, or so it seemed, and when he started to move he grunted with the pain. In the next moment someone was bending over him, gently washing him with a cool cloth.

"Lie still, young warrior," a woman's voice spoke. "You made Coyotero proud this day. You are an Apache now, and can go out with the war parties. Soon Naiche will join Geronimo, and between Geronimo and Victorio, all the white men will flee our land, and you, Chaco, will be another warrior feared by the whites."

He blinked, focusing his eyes on a young woman he'd seen before. His heart beat a little faster, for he recognized Nina, a beautiful young Apache woman who was widowed and who was said to have entertained several young men since the loss of her husband. What was she doing here beside him, and where was he?

"I need water," he told her.

She obeyed, quickly taking a gourd and dipping it into a bucket of water nearby. She bent over, the strings of her tunic untied so that a generous portion of her full breasts showed as she gave him the water.

"Rest, Chaco," she said softly. "I will prepare you something to eat, and soon you will be strong again."

"I . . . passed the test?"

She smiled with white, even teeth. "Yes. And watching you stirred great desires in Nina. To truly be a man now, you must know woman. I told this to Coyotero, and he agreed you should mend in my wickiup, and that I should teach you the other things a man should know. You are pleased?"

In spite of his pain and weak condition, what she was telling him stirred desires he'd purposely buried when watching Little Deer, for she was forbidden to him for now. But Nina was right. He must know about woman, must know how to touch Little Deer without frightening her. And some day it would surely be Little Deer.

"I am pleased," he told Nina.

She smiled more and leaned over him, bending down and touching his cheek, running a hand lightly over his thighs and what lay between them. "Get well quickly, Chaco. Nina has bathed you. You are as fine as a young stallion and your body is beautiful and strong. Nina is anxious to please you."

Chaco closed his eyes. She smelled of sage and cedar, and he knew instinctively that there was nothing this young woman would not teach him.

The days stretched into a week, and Chaco grew stronger. He was presented with a new bow and arrows from Coyotero, who pronounced him part of the tribe now, free to ride with the other warriors. Never had Chaco felt more like he belonged, more at home. He fit here. And it seemed more and more evident that this was the only life for him, that he had made the right decision.

Now, living with Nina, Little Deer had momentarily become less important. He was not ready for virgins. He must first learn, and Nina was teasing him, building his curiosity and desire so cruelly that she was all that was on his mind. He had not touched her yet, for he had been too weak, and she had not given any signal that she was ready.

But every night she peeled off her tunic and stood naked in front of him before going to bed on her own mat. He watched her eagerly, studying her gentle form, her silky skin, the roundness of her hips, the patch of hair that surely hid the place where a man puts himself inside a woman. Her breasts were full and firm, and he wanted to suckle them like a child. As he grew stronger, he kept waiting for her to come to him, give him some kind of signal that he could make love to her, but still she made no moves in that way, and he felt tortured.

He finally was strong enough to hunt for her, and he began bringing home meat, sure that his gifts would make her come to him. But still to no avail. Finally one cool evening he followed her to the river, where she had gone to fetch water. She wore a light blanket around her shoulders, for it was unusually chilly. He had meant all day to talk to her, to ask if he could sleep with her, but he could not get up the courage. Perhaps outside the wickiup it would be easier.

He lagged behind, studying the sway of her walk, wanting her. She went to the river and dipped the bucket, filling it, then set it on the bank. She sat down then, sighing deeply as though sad. Chaco watched in wonder then when she lay back and pulled up her tunic. She placed her fingers over the dark patch of hair that hid secret places and soon was making little whimpering sounds. "Oh, Chaco," she whispered.

Chaco's eyes widened. Was she fantasizing about him? Was she wishing it was he who touched her that way? Had she been waiting for him to come to her all this time, when he thought she would come to him? He swallowed for courage and moved from behind the bushes where he had been watching. She gasped and sat up, pulling down her dress. "Chaco!"

"What were you doing?"

"I ... it's ..." She covered her face. "You saw!"

He came closer, kneeling down next to her. "You spoke my name. What were you doing?"

"I was ... wishing that you ... desired me."

He carefully reached out and touched her hair. "Don't you know that I do?"

She slowly raised dark eyes to meet his own. "But you do not come to me in the night."

He grinned a little. "I was afraid. I thought ... I thought you would come to me."

Their eyes held, and in the next moment he covered her mouth, kissing her the white man's way, realizing that even in his innocence this was one thing he could teach her about making love. She responded with wild, whimpering kisses, falling back onto the grass, the blanket beneath her.

Chaco's desires knew no bounds then. They both moved in a wild frenzy of touching, quickly removing her tunic, hastily removing Chaco's leggings and loincloth. At first nothing seemed more important than getting inside of her. She opened slender thighs, and he moved between them while his lips found the full breasts he had so wanted to taste. He sucked at them in heated ecstasy, while he fumbled with himself, poking and pushing until he found the right place.

He moved inside of her almost violently, for never had he known this kind of pleasure. She pulled him into her soft moistness, panting his name, crying out with pleasure. He knew he was pleasing her, and it brought forth feelings of manliness that no hunt, no raid, no test of manhood had ever made him feel. He moved in heated rhythm, and she met him with equal timing and with such precision that in moments he felt the wonderful explosion that made him cry out. He grasped her hips from

97

beneath and pushed hard, while over and over the throbbing continued until at last he was spent.

He lay limp on top of her then, and she stroked his hair, whispering sweet words in Apache. " 'Now you are a real man," she told him. "You came and took your woman. That is how it is supposed to be, Chaco."

He raised up a little, studying her beautiful face. "I want to do it again."

She laughed lightly. "Of course you do. But we will go back to the wickiup first. There are other things we can do, Chaco." She reached down and lightly fingered his manpart, reawakening him. He was young and this was all new to him. He would take her many times this night, she was certain. "Do all that you will, Chaco. Touch me, taste me, learn about woman. You will learn to go slower, learn to be more gentle, learn to keep you life inside for a long time before letting it go. I will help you learn."

He wondered if there was anything more wonderful than being with a woman, and as he stood up and quickly dressed, he already ached to have her again. But watching her naked body before she pulled on her tunic made him wonder how a white girl must look naked. Surely she would be like white velvet, her nipples pink fruits. He shook away the thought. It was wrong. It could never be. Nina smiled at him, and her tunic hung open, revealing one breast just before she pulled the blanket around herself. For now there was only Nina, and much to learn. He would not mind the lessons.

There followed four years of raiding, during which time the Edwards had no contact with their son. Headlines were filled with new Indian atrocities. Slowly the name Chaco began to be linked with Geronimo, Naiche, Victorio. Shannon Edwards prayed every night for her son's safety, not believing some of the tales that were told in the Tucson papers. She knew that no

98

matter how Apache he became, Chaco would not harm white women. She was sure of it. It hurt deeply to imagine that he could raid and kill and steal, yet he was only doing what he thought was right to help his own people. They had been brutalized, cheated, scattered, left homeless. There were never any headlines about what was being done to the Apache, only to the whites. There was never an explanation for Apache retaliation. It was all designed to make the Apaches out to be nothing more than vicious killers with no feelings, no heart. To kill them was no worse than killing a skunk.

Troy was eighteen and had finished his schooling. He had talked about his love of writing and a desire to go east to learn more about journalism.

"I hope you can do something about the one-sided reporting that is done here about the Apaches," Shannon told him one night at the super table. "It seems the newspapers are doing their best to discredit the Apaches at every turn. Why aren't stories printed about things like what happened to Chaco when those white men attacked him? Why doesn't anyone explain why young men like Chaco ... do what they do?"

Her voice broke and Bryce took her hand. "Some day something will be done, Shannon," he promised her. "I don't know just what yet. But the truth will be told.'

"I'll tell it," Troy spoke up. It hurt him to see his mother so upset, and he missed Chaco terribly, although he wondered now if there could ever be a closeness between them again. Did Chaco still remember the old days? "I remember how Chaco looked after that happened to him ... how he felt. And I see the faces of those Indians who turn themselves in at Fort Bowie to go to San Carlos. I'm not sure how I'll do it, but somehow through my writing I'll help tell their side. I promise you, Mother."

She smiled through her tears. "Thank God for my Troy," she spoke up, wiping at her eyes. "You're so much like your father—brave, handsome."

He reddened a little and shook his head, poking at a piece of meat. "You just say that because you're my mother."

Bryce laughed lightly, squeezing his wife's hand. "Well, if you're just like me, you're a lucky boy."

Troy looked at him and they all managed a light laugh then, but the pain was still there, all of them thinking about Chaco.

Troy truly was like his father, in nature, in strength, and in the same golden handsomeness, the same gray eyes. He excused himself from the table and went out onto the porch, the determination to help his brother through his writing growing inside of him. He was tired of headlines that screamed of new atrocities by the Apaches, always naming Geronimo as the primary instigator, even when they knew otherwise. The aim seemed to be to accuse Geronimo of every outrage in the Territory, including those committed by white men, outlaws who had a free hand in stealing and murdering because they knew the Indians would be blamed. Bryce was sure such things were going on but could not prove it. Troy wished he could find a way.

It was a lawless time, a time of confusion and false accusations. Forts were gradually replenished with more soldiers in response to an outcry of Arizona citizens for better protection, and they all lived in constant fear that Chaco would one day be caught and imprisoned, perhaps for something he did not even do. Surely now there could never be a day when he could again live peacefully with his brother. "Little" Chaco was gone. He was big now, grown into the man his real father was, a young man who could not ignore the heated passions of his Apache blood.

Troy stared up at the black sky dotted with a million stars, wondering where Chaco was this night, how he was. He had no idea that soon, very soon, a young white woman was destined to bring his brother back to him, and destined to awaken Troy Edwards' heart to realities of life he had not yet known . . . and to awaken it to love . . . love for a white woman who could never belong to anyone but Chaco.

Lisette Powers took out a handkerchief and pushed it up under the rim of her bonnet, wiping perspiration from her hair and forehead. She wondered if they would ever again see a place where there was green grass and water—or even people. The constant jostling of the wagon made her head ache, but she said nothing. Her father kept promising her things would get better.

Father. John Powers was always jumping from job to job. Now he had sold their small farm in Illinois and was carting them west with stories about finding gold. She hated this place and so did her mother. She longed to go back home and wondered why her mother always went along with whatever her husband wanted. Was that the way love was? Was a woman supposed to give up everything dear to her just to follow her man's dream?

Lisa was frightened of this lonely trail. It was supposed to be a "shortcut" to Tucson, or so some men in the last town they passed through told them. They had left the Butterfield route, and there was no one to help them if they should have trouble. Why had her father done this? She was terrified of marauding Indians, who were said to attack wagons and do hideous things to whites, especially to the women.

She missed her friends and Illinois. What was there out here for a seventeen-year-old girl? She could not quite forgive her father for taking the risk bringing her out here. The men who had given them these directions had teased her about her blond hair and blue eyes and how the Indians would like to get their hands on her. She had quickly run away from them, but it seemed she could still feel their eyes on her.

Her mother rode on the seat beside her father, while Lisa rode in back, the heat almost overwhelming her. Her mother had grown silent and distant, and Lisa knew she was hurting inside. If only they could go back! Go back! Surely there was no Tucson ahead, no civilization, no people.

"Father," she called. "Someone is coming."

The man pulled the wagon to a halt, wondering how on earth anyone had found them here and what they could want. Lisa watched from the back, her heart beginning to race. Three of them were the men who had teased her! It suddenly all made sense, even in her young, innocent mind. They had advised them to take this "shortcut" only to steer them from the main road so that they could ambush the wagon. She crawled under some blankets in a corner, her breathing coming in short gasps as the men came closer and surrounded the wagon.

"It's you," she heard her father speak up. "What's wrong?"

A shot was fired and she heard her mother scream. Lisa whimpered and hunkered down, praying she would not be found, already sure why these men had come. Her mother screamed more, and her blood ran cold. The wagon bounced then and someone was inside.

"Come on, missy. I know you're in here."

Lisa froze as someone rummaged through the wagon, then screamed when he ripped the clothes and blankets from over her head.

"Well, well. Thought you could hide, did you?" He grinned through yellow teeth. "Come on, you pretty thing. Somethin' tells me you ain't never been touched by man. We're gonna' have a real good time with you."

She screamed and fought as he yanked her toward the back of the wagon. A big hand slapped her hard, knocking her right out of the wagon. Someone else picked her up by the hair of the head and dragged her over to her mother, who already lay naked and beaten on the ground, men surrounding her.

Chapter Seven

"I do not understand this, a white man abusing his own kind," Coyotero said softly to Chaco in the Apache tongue. From a rocky ridge above they watched four white men rape a woman one after the other, while a young girl, apparently the woman's daughter, watched in horror, held back by two more men who awaited their turn.

"I understand it," Chaco sneered. He had not forgotten how wicked white men could be. The worst evil was to be cruel to your own people. He had never found the men who had attacked him, but he would not stop searching. In the meantime, he rode proudly with those Apaches who still held out in the hills and created havoc for the settlers. Why these particular settlers had strayed from the Butterfield route through Arizona he could not imagine, but it was a stupid decision. Outlaws had quickly seized upon them, and Chaco had no doubt the girl would be raped but her life spared so that she could be sold, to Apaches or Comanches or Mexicans. He had never participated in the abuse of a white woman, for always he could see his mother. But neither had he stopped his Apache brothers from their own abuses. He could not fully blame them. Many of them had seen their own wives and daughters raped and murdered by soldiers and raiding settlers, had seen their babies smashed and mutilated. They had been the brunt of broken promise after broken promise, and everything they held dear was being stolen from them. Their hatred was great, their blood hot, their vengeance hungry.

"I think we could get us some food and clothes, and some whiskey. That kind of white man always carries whiskey," Coyotero said with a grin.

Chaco's dark eyes studied the young girl, who was weeping bitterly. Her hair was golden like the sun, her skin fair and reddening from exposure. "I will never again have a thirst for whiskey," he muttered. "But I, too, would like a piece of those bastards who hurt their own kind." He moved his eyes to a man who lay farther off and who appeared to be dead. "We will be blamed for all of this," he told Coyotero. "We might as well do what they will accuse of us doing."

"That white girl might be untouched. She would be a good prize, perhaps bring much ransom money from the whites, or maybe make some Apache man a new young wife."

"Do not touch her," Chaco warned.

Coyotero frowned. "You are too soft with the white women. How else can we give their men a lesson to leave our own women alone? How else can we threaten them to leave our territory? The worst thing we can do is abuse their women."

"My father spared my mother. I owe it to his memory to spare the white women I find. And I owe it to my mother, who weeps for me."

"Then spare them. It does not mean I have to," Coyotero hissed.

Chaco turned dark eyes to him. They lay sprawled on the ledge looking down at the horror below, preparing to move in with seven other braves and murder the outlaws and loot their gear, as well as the wagon. "I have never asked you to spare anyone, never stopped you from doing whatever you wish. Every warrior makes his own war. But this one time I ask you, let me have that girl. I will take her to where it is safe."

"And get caught? Get hanged? She is a worthless white squaw who will not appreciate your kindness!"

"It does not matter."

"Why?"

Chaco sighed, turning his eyes back to the golden hair. "I do not even know why. It is just . . . a feeling. In her I see my mother—begging for her life, being carried away by my father, who protected her. I dreamed a few nights ago about a young girl with golden hair, as though I was to find such a girl. I have no idea what it meant. I only know I cannot let this girl be harmed. Let me have her, Coyotero." He looked at the young man again. Coyotero had become a close friend.

"You are not the leader of this raid. I am," Coyotero told him.

"I have led many of my own raids. If I were the leader of this one, and you wanted the girl for yourself, I would have to say no. But there would be other times when you might ask the same, and I would say yes. Now I ask you—spare her for me. Tell the others not to harm her. If they do, I will kill them!"

Chaco's eyes smouldered threateningly. Coyotero knew he meant exactly what he said. There was an air of authority about the young man, seemingly passed down from his infamous warrior father, Saguaro. Coyotero sighed. "All right."

They crept down from the ledge to join the others. "We go," Coyotero told them. "There is a young girl left. She is Chaco's."

One of them grinned. "She is anyone's," he muttered. "I enjoy the look of terror in the eyes of the pale-faced women. I like their white skin."

Chaco leaped onto the back of his horse, an Appaloosa gelding. He whirled the painted horse, riding up close to the Apache man. "I have asked that she be spared. Coyotero has spoken."

"And what will you do with her? Be nice to her?" The man laughed.

Chaco whipped out a huge knife before the man could say

105

anything more. He held it against the warrior's cheek, startling the man with the swift movement. The warrior sat rigid and waiting.

"Perhaps I will be nice to her. But I will not be nice to you if you touch her," Chaco growled. He whipped the knife away, allowing its tip to pierce the man's cheek lightly. He whirled around again, joining Coyotero, and all seven of them rode in a line around the ridge and down a rocky descent toward the wagons below.

Lisa knew there was evil in the world, but never had she known or suspected anyone could be as cruel as the six who had attacked her father's wagon. She felt herself weakening from her struggles, and she squeezed her eyes shut against the humiliation being visited upon her mother, a humiliation that would soon undoubtedly be visited upon herself. Her screams had turned to quiet weeping, and her mother made no sound at all now.

Why? Why had they come here? Her father. How she hated him now for bringing them here to this lawless land! Now he lay dead, her mother being raped and beaten—out here in the middle of a desolate land Lisette hated. If only her father had stayed with the Butterfield route they would have been safer. And if he had truly loved them, he'd have let them take a stagecoach to Tucson and followed behind in the wagon rather than force them to travel in the bumpy, hot wagon through dangerous country.

What did any of it matter now? She would never see Illinois and green and trees again. She would never see her old friends again. She would die today, or perhaps even worse, they would keep her alive. Now someone was pushing her down. She could hear laughter and a tearing at her clothes. Again she struggled, vainly, so vainly. It seemed in the distance she heard a new sound, thundering horses, strange yips and cries. Hands let go of her.

"Goddamned Apaches," someone cried.

Apaches? Apache Indians? An even greater horror moved through her. She had heard stories of hideous tortures by Apaches, the slow methods by which they killed their captives, the slavery of white women used like whores. Was any of it true?

She got to her knees. Horses were circling, stirring up dust. Through it she saw one young Indian thrust a lance through one of the outlaws, excitement in the Indian's eyes, a grin on his face. He shoved hard, jerking the outlaw off the lance. He turned then, his eyes on her. He was a big Indian, but she guessed he was not much older than she. She stood transfixed, unsure what to do now. Surely these Apaches would have something worse in mind for her than did the outlaws.

He rode closer and she backed up. She looked around for an escape, but there were several other warriors encircling her, a couple of them fighting hand to hand with two surviving outlaws as though enjoying the fight, the others ransacking the wagon, throwing out clothing, food, utensils; laughing and shouting in their strange tongue. They were dark, so dark. And they were nearly naked. Her terror grew until she felt she was choking on it.

The first Indian dismounted, swinging a leg over and sliding off the horse with graceful ease. Lisette's legs ached from a desire to run, yet she was too terrified to move at all. The young man knelt over her mother.

"Leave her alone," Lisette screamed, the tears coming again. "Can't you see . . . what they did to her? Leave her alone!"

Chaco looked up at the girl. "You do not have to be afraid of me."

Her eyes widened. English! He spoke English! And it wasn't even broken as though he'd just learned it. It was spoken as well as any white man. He was leaning closer to her mother

107

again. Her mother's lips were moving. What was happening? Her mother lay partly scalped, cuts all over her body. The outlaws had apparently intended that her rape and murder be blamed on the Indians. Lisette had heard them joking about it.

Suddenly, to Lisette's horror, the young Indian pulled out a huge knife and plunged it into her mother's heart.

"Mama," Lisette screamed. "Mama! Mama!" She crumpled to the ground.

Chaco rose, putting his knife back into its sheath and turning to Coyotero. "Let it not be said that Chaco has never killed a white woman," he told the man in the Apache tongue.

Lisette understood nothing of what was said. She only knew that the young Apache man she had hoped for a tiny moment might be good, just because he spoke English, had just killed her mother.

"You filthy beast," she screamed at him. Where she got her courage, she wasn't sure. Perhaps it was pure anger and hopelessness. She charged at him, scratching at him wildly, beating on him, trying to scratch at his eyes.

Chaco was amazed at her strength and fury. He wrestled her to the ground while some of the others laughed, several of them shouting teasing remarks about what he should do with her.

"Hey, Chaco, you got a wild one, huh?"

"You will have to tame her, Chaco."

"We thought you were going to save her, Chaco. It looks like you are the one who needs saving."

"She is no good. She will never thank you for saving her, Chaco. Let us have her."

None of it was understood by Lisette, but she could guess at their remarks. At the same time, none of the other Indians could understand anything Chaco said in English to Lisette.

Chaco struggled until he finally had her hands behind her. "Lie still, you stupid girl," he growled. "I am here to help you."

"You killed my mother! You killed my mother! You stinking

savage!'' Her words were screamed in bitter hatred. Chaco pushed her over and sat on her hips, holding her wrists tightly behind her and binding them.

"I did not want to have to do this, but you will not listen to me, so I must. I will take you to safety."

"I don't care what you do with me. You're lying anyway. You killed my mother. I know what you'll do to me. I've read about you dirty Indians!"

His own anger rose then. He grasped the blond hair and jerked her head back. "Perhaps you should not believe everything you read, white woman! And do not insult me again, or I might change my mind about not hurting you! You are lucky it is I who has claimed you. The others would not be kind."

"Kind! You call this kind?" She broke into renewed tears, going limp as he got off her and pulled her to her feet. He turned her to face him.

"Look at me," he demanded.

She turned deep blue eyes up to meet his dark ones, eyeing him defiantly. Then she spat at him. He jerked as though startled, then grinned faintly, shaking his head.

"I told you I would not hurt you," he told her, suddenly wondering how his own mother had reacted when Saguaro first captured her. "I will take you to a place where there are whites who. . . ."

His words were interrupted by the sound of a bugle. Now his own eyes showed fear. "Soldiers," he muttered. Lisette screamed as he grabbed her about the waist and dragged her to his horse. He shouted something to the others, mounting up and hoisting her onto the horse in front of him as though she weighed nothing at all. He plunked her in front of him, and Lisette was too weak now to fight him. Surely he was taking her to slavery and death.

The others also mounted up, some carrying some of the supplies they had looted. They rode off, hard and fast. Behind them they left her own murdered parents and the mutilated bodies of the outlaws. Lisette could hear more horses in the distance, another bugle call. Soldiers! Perhaps they would catch up with these Apaches and save her! She could only hope they would. But she vaguely remembered stories of how good the Apaches were at eluding their pursuers, how difficult it was for the soldiers to find Apaches once they got into the hills and mountains, how fast Apache horses could run. This one was running now, thundering, panting. She'd ridden only a few times. Now she bounded along at an excruciating pace, a powerful arm around her to keep her from falling. Where was this Apache who spoke English taking her?

In the distance a troop of soldiers stopped at the massacre site, while a few rode on after the Apaches. But they would not catch the Indians. Not today. Those who stayed behind to investigate the massacre saw all they needed to see. The wagon looted, a man and woman lying murdered, the woman obviously repeatedly raped. The other dead men were surely some men who had perhaps offered to help the settlers get safely to their destination. But they had failed. They had all been attacked by Apaches, the woman scalped and mutilated, murdered. All of them murdered.

"This one is still alive," one of the soldiers shouted to a sergeant. The sergeant walked over to the private, who was bent over one of the outlaws. The outlaw knew he was dying, but he was not about to do so without making sure the Apaches took the blame for what happened here. Even to his death he took his hatred and prejudice.

"Who did this," the sergeant asked, bending over the dying outlaw.

"Apaches," the man muttered. "Tried ... to help these ... people. Apaches came ... Chaco ... heard the name ... Chaco. Took the girl."

"Girl? They took a white girl?"

"Pretty girl ... their daughter ... seventeen ... eighteen. I don't know. Chaco ... he took her. He ... he killed the woman."

110

The sergeant gritted his teeth. "So," he sneered. "He's gotten just like the rest of the bastards!" He turned to the private. "We'll get him some day, Johnson. I just hope the others can catch up to him and save that poor girl! That damned Chaco has gone too far this time!"

He gazed off into the distant hills, where Indians and soldiers had both disappeared. He ordered more men to follow. "Keep tracking them," he shouted. "I'll send for more help!"

Chapter Eight

They rode hard, winding through rocks and squeezing through several deep crevasses; moving almost silently through pine forests, clattering through canyons. By nightfall the soldiers had given up and Lisette had no idea where they were. The country was wild and mountainous. Here and there small, round cacti and scrubby brush managed to cling to life, seemingly growing right out of rocks. The cacti bloomed pink and yellow and white, and Lisette thought it strange that there could be anything of beauty in this land. To her it was wild and barren and evil, just as the man who had stolen her was wild and evil. It made her shudder to think that the arm around her belonged to the young Indian man who had killed her mother, yet he would occasionally give her a hug that was almost reassuring.

Finally they stopped, shouting back and forth at each other in words she did not understand.

"Have we lost them?" Coyotero asked Chaco.

"I think so. We had better stop. It is bad medicine to ride at night. We will disturb the spirits. Let us make camp, but light no fires. We can be back in our village by tomorrow afternoon."

Another laughed. "Those soldiers cannot keep up with Apaches. They will not find us now."

Chaco dismounted, pulling Lisette off the horse with him. He spread out a blanket, working by the light of a full moon, then pushed her down onto the blanket. He pulled out his knife and she whimpered.

"Do not worry," he told her. "I am only going to cut the cords of your wrists. It is foolish of you to fight, and I do not think you have the strength left anyway. And there is no place for you to run now. For one such as you to go out in the country alone is certain death."

He knelt down behind her and slit the cords, then put his knife in its sheath and sat down beside her but facing her, pulling her arms around in front of her and gently rubbing her wrists.

"I did not want to hurt you," he told her, putting a hand to the side of her face. "Are you all right?"

She jerked her face away. "Don't touch me, you filthy murderer!"

His dark eyes flashed with anger again, but when she tried to jerk her arms away he kept hold of them, still rubbing at her wrists. "She asked me to kill her," he said quietly.

The others threw down blankets and laughed and talked among themselves, sharing stories of how they killed the bad white men, discussing the clothing, food, and utensils they had managed to steal and how their wives and mothers would appreciate the loot.

Lisette faced Chaco in the moonlight. There was a gentleness to his touch, and an odd regret to his voice.

"I have never killed a white woman before," he told her. "The others tease me about it, and some get angry. I made them think I killed her just for the sport of it. But when I leaned over her, she begged me to kill her. She did not want to live after what those men had done to her. So I killed her—out of mercy. And she asked me not to hurt you, to help you."

113

Lisette grinned in almost a sneer. "My mother asked a wild Apache man to watch after her daughter?"

"I do not think she even realized I was an Indian. She did not know who she was talking to."

"And did you tell her you would take care of me?"

"I did."

"A fine lie that was!"

He studied her in the moonlight. As uppity as she was, he felt like throwing her down and showing her a thing or two. Her hair shined gold in the moonlight, and the suspicion that she was still untouched by man made him want her more. He had learned much from Nina, enough to make him wonder about this beautiful young white girl whose breasts were nearly exposed from her torn dress.

"Apaches do not lie," he answered. "And she did not need to ask me. I intended to help you, to take you near a fort and drop you off. But then the soldiers came and we had to run. Now we are deep in the Dragoons and near my people. I cannot take you back right now. I would be caught." He sighed. "I am sure they think I stole you away deliberately—to torture and rape." He let go of her and rose. "Bastards," he muttered. "We will be blamed for all of it."

She watched him take more blankets from his horse. He came over and put one around her shoulders. "Here. It gets cold here at night. I will sleep beside you to help keep you warm, but you do not have to be afraid. It is only because two bodies under a blanket are warmer than one." He brushed the side of her face with the back of his hand where her face was swollen from when the first outlaw hit her and threw her out of the wagon. "Does it hurt much?"

She met the dark eyes again, astonished that he truly did seem to care. "Not much. The hurt inside is worse." She suddenly burst into tears. "My God, what am I going to do! My father, my mother! Our wagon! Everything is gone, and here I

114

am in some wild country at the mercy of an Apache Indian!"
She curled up and wept, pulling the blanket over her head.

Chaco sighed, reaching out and squeezing her shoulder. He
leaned closer. "I will get you out of this somehow, but for now
you must go to my village with me. You must not be afraid.
But do not insult the others and anger them. They might decide
you should be shared. I have claimed you. Be obedient, at least
in their eyes. Do you understand?"

Her reply was more weeping. Chaco rose, imagining what it
must have been like for his mother all those years ago. What
did Saguaro do? How did he handle her? He retrieved his rifle
and another blanket, then tethered his horse and went back to
lie down beside her. The other braves were also bedding down.

"You could have a good time tonight, Chaco," Coyotero told
him. "The ones who have never had a man are the best. It is
too dangerous to take her back now. You might as well keep
her and claim her."

"I will think about it," Chaco answered, covering himself
and moving in beside her.

"Your white mother gave you a heart too soft," one of the
others spoke up.

Chaco sat up slightly. "Take up your knife and say it again.
I will show you how soft my heart is," he spat back. "It is yours
that will show soft, when my knife slices into it!"

The other Indian only laughed. "When she becomes too
much bother, we will take her off your hands," he told Chaco.

"Your three wives would not care for you to add a white
woman to their wickiup," Chaco answered.

There was more laughter, and then Chaco settled in beside
Lisette again, reaching around her and feeling her stiffen. She
still shook with sobs, muttering "Mama." Chaco breathed
deeply of the soapy scent of the soft, golden hair that caressed
his face. How tempting it was to feel for the full breasts, to
taste the full lips, to push up her dress and force her to submit.
But he did not want her that way. And he knew her grief and

terror were great. He had promised to help her, and he would—somehow.

They woke to singing birds and bright sunshine. Lisette stirred and blinked, and it took a moment for all the horror to come back to her. When it did, she sat upright, her heart quickening, her blue eyes darting around the camp. The others were gone, but the young man who had captured her was stirring a fire and cooking something.

"Well, you are finally awake," he told her.

She looked around again. "Where are the others?"

"They left for the village. I told them I would follow. The soldiers no longer hunt for us. It is safe to wait here awhile. I did not want to wake you. It is good that you slept so long. You will be stronger."

She frowned. He had let her sleep, and now he was making something to eat. Why? In spite of her grief and the horrible ache throughout her body, whatever he was cooking smelled good. He picked up a canteen and held it out to her.

"Here. Are you thirsty?"

She nodded, taking the canteen from him and noticing it had U.S. ARMY stenciled on it—stolen from a soldier, no doubt. Who was this strange Apache man who was actually being kind to her and who spoke English? She sipped some water, then capped the canteen and set it aside.

"I . . . I have to go to the outhouse."

Chaco grinned. "Here the rocks and brush are the outhouses. Pick one and go behind it."

She swallowed, slowly rising, watching him carefully as she backed toward a large rock. Chaco looked at her again. "Do not worry. I will not attack you or watch you." He laughed lightly and shook his head. Lisette quickly darted behind the rock and relieved herself, coming back to see he was still bent over the fire.

"These are little biscuits fried in animal fat and mixed with beans. It is not much, but it is food. For a while you will have to get used to Apache food, until I can get you to a fort, or perhaps to my parents. They would help you."

She frowned, walking closer. "Your parents?"

Chaco put some of the food on a tin plate. "My white mother and white stepfather. They are good people. I have a brother, too. He is eighteen now. I have not seen any of them in over four years."

She sat down on the blanket. "You . . . you used to live with them?"

"All my life. My real father was Saguaro, an Apache warrior. He helped my mother once, much as I am helping you now. She soon learned not to hate him. Instead they fell in love." He met her eyes. "I am the result."

Lisette reddened, looking down at her plate. "I see."

"My Apache father was . . . killed." He decided not to bother with all the details. "Before he died, he asked a white soldier friend to raise his son for him, for even then the Apaches were hunted and murdered constantly. The white soldier was also in love with my white mother, and Saguaro knew her life would be better with the white man. Since I was her son, he knew I would be loved. So my mother and the soldier married, and they kept me."

Lisette swallowed a bite of biscuit. It tasted better than she thought it would. "Why aren't you still with them?"

Chaco sat down, stuffing a biscuit into his mouth. "Because I look all Apache," he told her with his mouth full. He chewed and swallowed. "In the white world that is like being a snake. They treated me bad, not my parents—they are good people— but the others. I cannot live in the white world. Two white men attacked me and almost killed me. That was when I knew I had to leave that world and join the Apaches." He swallowed another bite. "Besides, there is something inside of me that makes me want to live in these mountains, to ride free and not live by

117

all the rules white men have for themselves. I like it out here—free, wild, close to Usen."

"Usen?"

"That is our God. I know all about yours, through my mother. As far as I can see, there is little difference."

She took another bite and set her plate aside. Her stomach, upset by all the turmoil, already felt full. "What is your name?"

"Chaco. What is yours?"

"Lisette. Most call me Lisa."

He nodded. "It is a pretty name."

She studied him more closely. He was hard-muscled and tall. If he were not Apache and threatening, he would be most handsome and appealing. He was nearly as dark as the other Apaches she had seen, and had the dark eyes and long, straight hair. But his white blood had smoothed out the harsh Indian look and had made him taller than most Apaches. His mixed blood had created a young man of extreme handsomeness, with high cheekbones and even, white teeth. "Did my mother really ask you to kill her?"

He met her eyes. 'Yes. I saw the pleading in her eyes. She died quickly." He looked at his plate. "I am sorry."

"But ... you wanted your friends to think you killed her gladly. Why?"

He shrugged. "I told you why. We are to show no mercy. To the Apache, the only way to make the white man leave is to be as cruel as we can be. Many times the Apaches are attacked by white men, massacred, their women raped and murdered, their babies smashed or shot. So we do the same back to them. But because of my white mother, I cannot bring myself to kill white women. The others sometimes speak against me for it, but I have fought and killed enough of them that they seldom speak against me any more. I have proven my manhood and taken the test of manhood. But yesterday, it was good that they saw me kill her. They do not have to know I did it out of mercy. I

118

would have done the same to my own mother if she had asked me."

The talk of her mother's death brought sudden new tears. Lisette turned away and cried quietly. "I can't even ... give her a decent burial," she sobbed.

"The soldiers will do that. Do not worry about it." He frowned. "Do you not cry for your father also?"

Her shoulders shook. "It's all his fault. He ... brought us ... out here ... looking for gold. If we had stayed in Illinois, none of this ... would have happened."

Chaco took a swallow of water. "White men. They are always looking for riches. The only good white man I know is my own stepfather. He was once a great soldier, but he saw how wrong it was the way the Apaches were treated, and he quit being a soldier. I have a white half brother—Troy. He is also good. But I have no use for most white men. I know how evil their hearts are. So do the men who ride with me. Many have lost wives and daughters, fathers and sons."

Lisette sniffed and wipes at her eyes. "What am I going to do now?"

"Stay with me. Perhaps somehow I can get you to my mother and father. They would help you. My mother would understand. She lost her whole family during the Civil War. Many bad things happened to my mother. She is a strong woman, a good woman."

He began cleaning up camp. "We must go soon."

She nodded resignedly. What choice did she have? She rose on weary legs and began rolling the blankets, wondering if she would ever feel clean and pretty again, wondering if she would ever get over what had happened, seeing her mother lying under those men. No man would ever touch her that way—not ever. And why had they half-scalped her—white men? She looked at Chaco.

"The soldiers will think you did all of it, won't they?"

He met her eyes, walking closer. "Now you understand. Many times white men murder their own kind, then try to make it

119

look like the Indians did it. It happens all the time. Everything is blamed on the Apache, so the outlaws have free rein." He bent down to clean the plates with sand. "They will say the white men there were good—perhaps leading you settlers. They will say all were attacked by Apaches, your mother scalped and raped, then murdered. Yes, we will be blamed." He shoved the plates into his parfleche. "It is interesting that these white men always scalp the victims to blame the Indian. If the soldiers had any sense, they would understand that it could not be Apaches. Apaches do not scalp their victims like some other tribes do."

Lisette swallowed. "I . . . I'm sorry. If I ever get back to the soldiers, I'll tell them the truth, Chaco. I'll tell them about the outlaws—and how you killed my mother out of mercy and helped me."

He smiled bitterly. "Tell them what you want. They will choose not to believe you. They will say you are just hysterical and do not remember it the right way."

"But it's the truth! They would have to believe me!"

"They believe what they want to believe and no more."

He loaded the blankets and parfleche onto his horse, hanging the canteen around the horse's neck. He moved onto the animal's back in one graceful, swift motion, then offered his hand. "We must go."

She glanced up into even rockier hills. "You won't let them hurt me?" She looked back up into dark, steady eyes.

"I won't let them hurt you."

She swallowed, her heart tightening with wonder at what lay ahead for her. She was completely at the mercy of this one man. If she made him angry in some way, perhaps he would choose not to be so kind and would turn her over to some of the others. Indians! She had never even seen one so close up, not wild ones. Was he part of those who rode for the infamous Geronimo? It seemed incredible that she was suddenly a part of these wild, hunted people who were talked and written about so much.

She reached up and he took hold of her arm, then reached down and grabbed her about the waist and hoisted her up. She winced when she straddled the horse. "I'm so sore," she muttered.

"I know. It will not be much longer." He took something from another bag. "Here. It is a deerskin shirt. It is soft and will protect you from the sun. Your skin is fair, and your arms and shoulders are exposed from your torn dress." He placed the shirt over her head and she reached her arms into the sleeves.

"Thank you," she said quietly, grateful that he had still not touched her wrongly, had not torn her dress further and forced himself upon her as she was sure at first he would do. Still, they were not back at his village yet. What would happen then? She would be helpless, among only Apaches. She knew nothing about them or their language. This young half-breed was her only hope.

"I don't believe it," Bryce said sternly, pacing before the hearth.

"Believe it," Colonel Blazer told him.

Shannon looked away. She did not like Colonel Blazer, nor most of the soldiers. These were new ones. They had no memories of the old days, and no respect for what she had been through. To them she was simply the white woman who had "slept" with an Apache man twenty years ago and had borne a half-breed son—a wild boy who now rode with the Apaches and murdered white people, or so he was accused.

"Chaco would not deliberately kill a white woman. And he would not steal away a young white girl and defile her," Bryce argued.

"Well, he has," Blazer growled. "If you two had seen what my men saw, a white woman scalped and brutalized, lying dead

121

from a stab wound to her heart. The only man who lived long enough to talk told us who did it. Chaco, he said. Chaco."

Shannon closed her eyes, trembling.

"Apaches don't scalp their victims!"

"Apaches are what my men saw, and the woman was scalped! Maybe they've decided to start scalping for the fun of it!"

"I say white men did it! What were six men doing there with a wagon of settlers? You know as well as I do what could have happened, Colonel. This territory is full of outlaws out marauding and blaming everything on the Indians. I'm telling you Chaco would not have done that. I know him too well! And if he rode off with that girl it was to help her. If your soldiers hadn't chased them, he might have brought her in for help. Now he'll be afraid to bring her in. He isn't stupid, Blazer! He knows what everyone will think! If these things were handled right . . ."

"You are no longer in charge, Edwards! Don't tell me how to run my business! I'm simply telling you the facts. You can interpret them as you wish, but Chaco is a hunted man now. You should know that! I'm warning you."

"And I am warning you that if someone shoots my son down on sight, he'll answer to me!"

Blazer's eyebrows arched. *"Your* son?"

Shannon let out a light whimper and Bryce's gray eyes blazed. "Get out of my house, Blazer," he growled.

The colonel grinned. "If you're so worried about your Apache friends, Edwards, you should take that agency job they offered you—or rejoin the army. I'll keep you informed."

"You do that," Bryce told him, opening the door and holding it for the man.

Their eyes held challengingly, and then Blazer left. Bryce turned to Shannon. "Somehow this will work out, Shannon."

She shook her head. "They'll hunt him down and hang him. His only hope is that girl. But if she's . . . if she's like so many others, she'll do everything she can to make Chaco look guilty.

God only knows what she saw—what it did to her mind." She turned to look at him, the horrible grief in her eyes breaking his heart. "He wouldn't do it, Bryce."

He walked up to her, pulling her into his arms. It seemed that ever since he had known her there had been some reason for her to grieve. "I know that. We both know it." He glanced at Troy, who had stood silently in his bedroom doorway through the entire incident. "All three of us know it."

"Do you think we'll ever see Chaco again, Pa?" the young man asked.

Bryce held Shannon closer. "God only knows, Troy. God only knows."

Lisa rubbed her dress on the rock to clean it, watching how the other Apache women washed their clothes. But she only watched out of the corner of her eye. She was afraid of them, and Chaco had warned her to be careful. Apache women were known to be unkind to white women prisoners, which was how they looked at Lisa. It was a defensive reaction, retribution for all the hurt and disease and loss the Apache women had suffered. They thought white women weak, and abusing white women captives was just another way of showing the whites they did not belong in this land and should get out.

Most respected Chaco's warnings not to harm Lisa, but there was one Lisa feared the most. She was called Nina, and her looks were threatening indeed.

"I live with her off and on," Chaco explained. "She thinks she owns me but she does not."

"You mean . . . you sleep with her?" she had asked in astonishment.

Chaco only laughed. "I am not the only one. But I have no real wife, not yet, anyway. Some day perhaps. There is one called Little Deer I have been watching. Four summers ago she celebrated the coming of womanhood but her father has not let her marry. She is now only fourteen. I know by how she looks at me that she would like to be my wife."

"Fourteen! She's ... she's a child!"

"Not by Apache standards."

Why had the words brought the odd jealousy to Lisa's heart? She knew it was ridiculous, and she ignored the fact that she had been having feelings for Chaco that no white girl should feel for any Indian man. Perhaps it was only because she had become so dependent on Chaco for protection and shelter. They shared the same wickiup, shelter woven from branches that was surprisingly big and cool. Yet Chaco had not touched her wrongly. She was learning how to cook the Apache way, how to make use of wild meat and plants. She sometimes wore deerskin tunics Chaco had bought from other women, for all she had was her torn dress and one other that the men had taken from her wagon. Getting used to this new but temporary way of living had helped her sorrow, for she was very busy and very tired most of the time. This was not a life to which she was accustomed, even though she had always been taught to work hard. She doubted now that the hardest-working white woman could hold a candle to the daily toils of Indian women.

Now Chaco had become more like a good friend. Lisa felt stronger. She kept to herself, talking only to Chaco, hiding inside the wickiup at night when fires glowed and drums beat and warriors danced while women sang and chanted. Outside the wickiup was a wild people she did not understand. Inside it was safe. She tried to keep from thinking of how Chaco looked at night when he stripped to his loincloth before going to sleep. She'd never seen a man quite so exposed, and again his words about the one called Little Deer brought an odd ache to her heart.

She sighed. What difference did it make? Soon he would take her to safety and this nightmare would be over. He would marry Little Deer, and she would be among her own kind again. Somehow she would forget about all of this, get over the horror of it. But sometimes she wondered if she would ever really forget the one called Chaco.

"Need more sand," a young girl spoke up.

Lisa looked up into the face of a tiny, slender girl of perhaps fifteen. She was quite pretty, and she smiled at Lisa. "I Little Deer."

Lisa was not even aware that her mouth had dropped open. This was the one Chaco had talked about! Again a prick of jealousy annoyed her, but she pushed it aside. The girl was trying to be nice. "More sand?"

"Ai." The girl bent down and rubbed a little more into a spot on the dress caused by animal fat. "See? Rub it hard. How do white women wash clothes?"

Lisa continued to stare at her. "They ... they have wash tubs and scrub boards ... and soap."

"We do not have much. When people are always hunted and running, it is hard to have nice things."

Lisa frowned. "Yes. I suppose." She watched the girl scrub away the spot. "I didn't know anyone else around here spoke English."

"There are a few. My family was captured and taken to San Carlos a few years ago. There I learn English from a white lady. But we all run away again. Soon Geronimo will rejoin us."

The girl handed the dress to Lisa. "Thank you," Lisa told her. She studied the dark eyes. "Why do they always run away?"

Little Deer shrugged. "Reservation bad place. Much disease. Many die. Some die of broken hearts. It is hard for an Indian to stay in one place. It is not natural. And the food is bad—very bad—rotten meat. The agents cheat us, the white suppliers cheat us, they all cheat us. We come back to the mountains we love—live the way we choose."

"But ... it can't last forever, Little Deer."

"I know. We will live this way as long as we can. Even Chaco,

125

who grew up among the whites, knows we cannot live in that world."

Lisa watched her carefully. "Are you and Chaco . . . I mean . . . he's told me about you."

The girl seemed to actually redden. "Even though he has white blood, I think Chaco is the finest Apache man in this camp. One day I think he will ask my father to give me to him."

Lisa looked down at her dress, hiding her jealousy, furious with herself for feeling anything at all. "I hope it will be soon, Little Deer."

"Yes. So do I."

Lisa fingered the vanished spot on her dress. "Why are you befriending me, Little Deer?"

"You are Chaco's captive. He has said to be kind to you. A woman respects her man's wishes. He is not really my man, but I think of him that way."

Lisa smiled softly. "Thank you, Little Deer. I need a friend. I'm so scared here. I don't know anything about your people."

Little Deer looked around the village. "You know all you need to know. If you ever get back to your own people, tell them how we weep. Tell them how we starve. Tell them how our little children cry for food that is not there, and how they die of white man's diseases. It is bad. But we hate the reservation and we are afraid to turn ourselves in, afraid the soldiers will shoot us down. It has happened before."

"Hey, Little Deer, you stupid girl," someone spoke up in Apache. "Get away from the white whore. Why do you speak to the white bitch with whom your intended sleeps at night?"

Little Deer and Lisa both looked over at Nina, who stood across the creek, her tunic hanging loose, her long hair flying in several directions. Lisa had not understood the words, but she understood the attitude. Her blood chilled.

"You leave her alone," Little Deer replied in the Apache tongue. "Chaco has said to leave her alone. Go away, Nina!"

The woman sneered. "I will go away, for now. Tell the white woman in her tongue to watch the shadows, though. Since Chaco brought her here, he has not come to my bed. I miss him. I do not mind giving him up to an Apache wife, but not to this white bitch! You tell her that! Chaco makes me feel good at night. I want him back!" The woman whirled and marched off.

"What did she say," Lisa asked.

Little Deer watched after her. "It is not important," she said bitterly. "She is a bad one. She took care of Chaco after the test of manhood and he started sleeping with her. Now she thinks she owns him. She likes men. She is only practice for the young braves, but she also makes trouble whenever she can."

Lisa shivered. "She frightens me. Let's go back. Chaco might have returned by now with some fresh meat."

"You go back. I should not look upon Chaco or talk too freely with him. It is forbidden." She rose. "Good-bye, Lisa." She hurried off and Lisa watched after her. Her jealousy was made more painful by the fact that Little Deer was a nice girl, the only Apache woman who had been kind to her so far. She rinsed and wrung out her dress, then headed back for the wick-iup.

What a strange life this was. Who would ever dream these things would happen to her when she headed west with her mother and father? Once time healed the wounds, what tales she would have to tell her grandchildren! Already she was feeling sorry for these people. Perhaps she was destined to stay in this wild land. Perhaps there was some reason for all that was happening. But what it was she could not imagine. All that mattered was getting back to her own people—somehow. Yet that would mean probably never seeing Chaco again, and she was beginning to value his friendship, appreciate his kindness, but to also admire his utter handsomeness and gentle ways. Yes, it was time to get back to civilization, before her passions became as wild as this land and its people.

She hurried back to the wickiup, and from behind thick brush Nina watched. She didn't like this white woman. Chaco was too good to her. She was too pretty, with her golden hair and full bosom and blue eyes. Surely Chaco was fascinated with her, wanted her. He should not be so kind to her. She was bad medicine. Nina knew the story of Chaco's father, Saguaro, who had come to his death for loving a white woman. This woman would mean the same for Chaco. Perhaps there was a way to make the white woman leave, to run away into the wilds where she would die. Nina would see to it.

Chapter Nine

Lisa handed Chaco a plate of roast rabbit. The bones held little meat. He looked at the food and shook his head. "We have over-hunted this area. We will have to move on soon. Besides, too long in one place and the soldiers finally find you."

Lisa watched him pick at the meat. "Why don't they just give up, Chaco? They're all starving. You're starving."

His dark eyes quickly moved to meet hers. "Pride. Pride and what is right. That is why we do not give up."

"But . . . you had a good life. You've traded it for this."

"Someday you will understand why. A man has to be a man, Lisa. And he has to help his own kind. I help my people however I can, and I live where I am accepted."

"You will also die out here."

He shrugged. "Perhaps. What do you care?" He deliberately hid the feelings that had grown to almost painful proportions during his many nights of sleeping in the same wickiup with the golden-haired white girl. He had come to know her well, to see the good in her. He did not like the way he was feeling. It was bad.

Now their eyes held and she suddenly reddened. "I care very much," she said quietly. "You've . . . become a good friend.

129

You helped me. I've seen the starving children. How can I not care?"

He wanted to ask if she had special feelings for him, but he did not. It would be a foolish and useless question. Even if she did, it was a path to nowhere. "I will take you back soon. It won't matter then."

She raised watery eyes to meet his. "It will always matter." She swallowed, moving back to her mat and stirring the fire. "Those people out there, to me they're wild and different and frightening. Some are cruel, vicious. But I never understood before why. You have taught me many things, Chaco, about the beliefs and feelings of the Apache. You have taught me to feel their desperation, their sorrows, their fierce pride, their love for this land they feel belongs to them. When I go back, I can never be the same person I was when you brought me here. Nothing will ever be the same for me again."

Their eyes met again. "Nor for me," he told her. He set his plate aside and cautiously moved closer, crouching in front of her. "Sometimes ... sometimes I do not want to take you back. Yet I know I must."

A tear slipped down her cheek. "And sometimes I don't want you to take me back ... yet I know it must be done."

She swallowed and did not move away when he leaned closer. How often had she wondered what it was like to kiss him? She'd been kissed before—a few boys who stole them teasingly, one who had been special. But not so special that she could not bear leaving him behind.

Chaco's lips touched her own and fire swept through her. It was not the feeling she had expected. She'd had nightmares about what had happened to her mother. She had not got over the terror and horror of it. She wanted nothing to do with men, or at least so she thought. But now, with Chaco's lips on hers. ...
Why didn't she stop him? Why did she want this Indian man to kiss her?

He parted her lips gently, touching her hair with his hand

130

and lightly stroking it. She felt herself shaking, felt her cheeks flushing as he left her mouth and moved his lips to her eyes, lightly kissing each one. To her surprise, when he moved back, his own eyes were watery.

"We are good friends now," he told her. "It is best that is all we ever are. Our worlds are far apart, Lisa, just as it was for my mother and my Indian father. They knew happiness for just a little while."

"Perhaps that little while was worth it," she said softly, wondering how she ever found the courage to speak the words.

He smiled lightly but sadly. "Perhaps. But I have seen mostly pain in my mother's eyes all her life. I would not want to see it begin in the eyes of another young woman who is good like my mother. I have learned from her what can and cannot be." He rose. "In a week, perhaps, I will take you back. I will risk it. It is not good that you stay here any longer. Until then I will not stay here at night."

Her eyes widened. "But ... where will you stay?"

He looked at her briefly, then turned. "I will stay with Nina. It is the best way to be sure I leave you alone."

He ducked outside and her heart raged with jealousy. She wanted to call out to him but knew better. He was doing what was best for both of them. But why did it hurt so bad? She would rather see him run to Little Deer and marry her than to go to that wicked Nina!

She touched her lips, savoring the lingering flavor of his wonderful kiss, wondering how she could ever go back now and live like a normal white woman, fall in love with a white man. Nothing would ever be the same, not ever again.

Little Deer came back from the shadows where she had gone to relieve herself. It was late and a few fires flickered. Everyone slept. Soon they would break camp and go to Mexico to join Geronimo, who had again fled after breaking away from San

Carlos. It seemed the reservation could never hold their rene-gade leader for long. Time and again Geronimo had either been captured or had voluntarily given himself up to the reservation agents and soldiers, only to flee again. Little Deer was sure that this time he would not go back, for he feared for his very life. There were many white people who wanted him hanged.

Little Deer made her way back toward her father's tipi when she noticed someone else darting about as though sneaking around trying not to be seen. Little Deer ducked down and watched. Someone with long hair was heading toward Chaco's wickiup, the one in which he had left the white girl alone. The whole camp knew he had been sleeping with Nina. Some of the men did not like Lisa being left free and alone. She was surely worth much to the white men who might pay ransom for her, or to the Mexicans who would pay gold for her, gold that could in turn be traded to unscrupulous white men for guns and am-munition.

Chaco had caused much talk and arguments in camp, and many warned him how his own father's concern for a white woman had in the end brought him great sorrow and finally death. Little Deer's own heart ached with sorrow at the thought of it. Everyone said Chaco was falling in love with the white girl, that she was bad medicine for him. Little Deer did not know if it was true or not, but perhaps her dream of becoming Chaco's chosen would always be just that now. Perhaps the white woman would even get him to go back to his white world and leave the Apaches for good. How she prayed that would not happen. For now, all she could do was silently love the young man who had come to them from the cruel white world seeking refuge among his own kind.

She watched quietly as the figure approached the wickiup where the white woman slept. She was sure it was the figure of a woman, not a man. Who could it be? Many of the women had threatened to cast out the white woman, but the most dangerous threats had come from Nina.

Nina! Was it she? Little Deer darted toward Nina's wickiup, daringly throwing aside the blanket over the door and ducking inside. Chaco sat up, grasping the Colt revolver his white stepfather had given him and pointing it at her.

"It is I, Chaco," the girl whispered. "Do not shoot."

His eyes widened. What on earth was Little Deer doing here in his wickiup in the middle of the night? It was a daring thing to do and could cost her her reputation and bring possible disfigurement for being so brazen.

"Get out of here," he ordered gruffly. "You should not be in here."

"I only want to help you. Where is Nina?"

He looked around, setting the gun aside. He frowned, looking back at Little Deer over the dim light of a fire. "I do not know."

"I was going to the woods to . . ." The girl reddened. "I saw someone . . . sneaking toward the wickiup where the white woman sleeps. Perhaps it is Nina. She has threatened to harm the white woman."

The girl ducked out then, running, hoping no one saw her enter Chaco's wickiup.

Lisa stirred at a touch on her shoulder. "Chaco?"

Suddenly a strong hand grasped her about the throat, pushing hard, choking off her air. "It is not your precious Chaco, white one! It is I! Nina!" The Indian woman pulled out a small knife and held it over Lisa, who was struggling to grab at the woman, reaching up to scratch her eyes. But it was to no avail. Nina was very strong, her arm longer than Lisa's arms, her hatred very great. She kept pushing, and Lisa felt herself going black from lack of air.

"You are bad, bad medicine," Nina sneered. "Soon we go to join Geronimo. We do not need bad medicine like you along.

133

Chaco's mother destroyed his father. You will not destroy Chaco!"

The woman stabbed at her, but Lisa managed to duck her head sideways just enough that the knife caught her outer ear. Lisa could not scream when she felt the blade pierce the entire ear, for her voice and most of her breath were gone now. She was only vaguely aware of the wound, and saw Nina raise her hand again, saw the knife hovering over her, ready to come down, perhaps in her eye.

Suddenly someone grabbed Nina's wrist. Lisa was only somewhat aware that the woman had been thrown across the wickiup. She heard slashing sounds then, unaware that Chaco was there hitting at Nina with his quirt. In his rage he could not stop himself. Over and over again he hit Nina as she cowered under him, whipping at her until she finally managed to crawl out of the wickiup. Outside a few had come out of their own dwellings to see what all the commotion was about, watching Nina stumble toward her own tipi, bruised and crying. A few nodded their heads. So, there had finally been a confrontation between Nina and Chaco over the white woman. Yes, the white woman was bad medicine. Chaco should never have kept her. But woman trouble was a man's personal problem. They returned to their own dwellings.

Inside the wickiup Chaco knelt over Lisa, who still struggled for breath. Her ear bled profusely, the blood running into her hair. Chaco grabbed a cloth and wet it, holding it to her ear, pressing it tightly.

"Ch . . . Chaco," she managed to choke out.

"It is all right. She will not bother you again," he told her. "I am sorry, Lisa."

"Stay . . ."

"I will stay." He pulled her head into his lap and kept pressing the cloth. "Lie very still, Lisa. She cut your ear badly. It will take a while for the bleeding to slow. Once it scabs over good, we will clean you up."

134

Lisa pressed her head back against his arm, opening her mouth wide and gasping for breath, at first terrified that her throat would not open again.

"Relax, Lisa. Try to relax."

"Why ... why ..."

"She is bad ... and jealous ... that is why."

"Jealous ... why ... jealous ..."

He reached under her head, bringing her up to cradle her head in his arm, still holding the cloth to her ear. "You know why," he said quietly. "Perhaps because I am a fool like my father was."

She closed her eyes, snuggling against his strength, feeling safe and protected now. What was he telling her? That he loved her?

"How ... did you ... catch her?" she asked, feeling her consciousness fading.

"Little Deer was outside. She saw Nina heading this way and warned me."

"Little Deer," Lisa whispered. "You ... should marry ... she ... loves you."

Chaco sighed. "I know." He bent down and kissed her hair. "But tonight I know that is not enough. When I saw Nina's hand raised, and thought perhaps she had already stabbed you to death...." He said nothing more. He rocked her, holding the cloth to her ear and letting her relax in his arm until she fell into a fitful sleep.

For five days Lisa lay in pain, her ear throbbing almost constantly, swelling slightly from infection. Her only consolation was Chaco, who stayed with her as much as possible, often holding her. In her pain and the memory of Nina's attack, she was terrified whenever Chaco left her. She clung to him like a child when he returned. She managed to drink large quantities of tizwin, a form of liquor Apaches made from corn, which

135

helped the pain but which also left her light-headed and feeling warm. Chaco made her drink a lot of it just before he would apply a special salve to her ear, a salve made from plants and used by the Indians to treat wounds. To let him touch her ear was excruciating, but when she drank the tizwin it did not hurt nearly as bad. But it also made her want to reach out to Chaco, her friend, her dear, sweet friend, to touch him, kiss him. She told herself it was just the liquor, that she must be careful to think and to be careful of the silly feelings the liquor gave her.

Sometimes Little Deer came to help Chaco, or to sit with Lisa when Chaco had to be away. By the sixth day the pain began to subside and Lisa's earlobe began to shrink back to its normal size. She watched Little Deer carefully brush one of Chaco's deerskin shirts. The girl held it almost lovingly, unaware Lisa was watching her. A fire crackled nearby, and Lisa could see with clarity how it all should be—Little Deer and Chaco, together in this wickiup, man and wife. Little Deer was pretty and devoted. She would be a perfect wife, a loving wife, an obedient wife. And this was the life she knew. In spite of all Lisa had learned, the fact remained she was as different from Chaco and his way of life as night was from day.

Little Deer turned, seeing Lisa's eyes on her. She smiled. "How are you feeling?"

"Better," Lisa replied. She sat up, running a hand through her hair. "I must be a mess. Is there still blood in my hair?"

Little Deer nodded. "I will help you wash it if you wish."

Lisa studied her closely. "Chaco said you warned him Nina was coming to my wickiup. Why? She would have killed me. Why did you care?"

Little Deer shrugged. "I could not have slept at night, knowing I could have stopped her. Chaco would have been very sad if you had been killed. And I know the white soldiers would say Chaco killed you. Chaco is going to take you back alive and well. That will be good. Then they will believe he did not take you against your will. You will tell them?"

Lisa nodded, her heart heavy at the thought of leaving. "I will tell them."

Their eyes held. "You have feelings for Chaco?" Little Deer showed no jealousy, only sadness.

Lisa looked down. "How could I not? But it doesn't matter. I'll be leaving soon. I hope . . . I hope Chaco marries you soon, Little Deer. You will be a good wife for him."

Little Deer set Chaco's shirt aside. "I will be like a second wife in his heart."

Lisa frowned. "What do you mean?"

"I watched him when you were suffering. I saw the look in his eyes. He was not frightened because he would be blamed for your death. He was frightened of losing you. He loves you." She looked at her lap. "Chaco does not have the nature to hit a woman. Yet he beat Nina badly for hurting you. If she did not get away, I think he would have killed her."

Lisa chilled. "I have caused Chaco much trouble, haven't I? Are the others angry with him?"

"Some of them. We all leave soon for Mexico. They say Chaco can come only if he leaves you behind so that the soldiers know you are all right and do not keep hunting us. We will be safer when they know the truth."

Lisa put a hand to her disheveled hair. "Yes," she said quietly. "It will be better all around when I go." She closed her eyes against tears. He loved her. Little Deer had seen it. Surely Nina knew it or she would not have tried to hurt her. Surely they all considered it a weakness on Chaco's part to love her. She was causing him a bad time. The thought that he loved her sent shivers of desire through her, for she knew deep inside that she loved him in return. But it was very important that neither of them express that love or let it go any further. How strange her world had become. Perhaps once she got back in her own world, the pain of leaving Chaco would not seem so bad. But he had become everything to her. She had no one now. She didn't want to go into a world of strangers, to answer all the questions they would throw at her, to be away from the safety of Chaco's arms and wickiup. "I'd like to wash my hair and put on a clean tunic," she told Little Deer aloud.

Little Deer rose. "I will help you." She hesitated a moment. "Do you love Chaco?"

Lisa sighed. "I . . . I don't know. I think I'm just mixed up, being in a place so strange to me, around people I don't understand and who hate me."

"They do not hate you. They just do not trust anyone who is white. The whites bring us disease and bad times." She came closer. "I think I will miss you when you go, Lisa, even though my Chaco loves you. In another time and place, we could be good friends."

Lisa smiled sadly. "Yes. How sad that we can't all get along and learn to understand each other."

Little Deer nodded. "I will heat some water and help you wash."

Chaco hesitated when he entered the wickiup, seeing Lisa bent over a fire, her sun-gold hair clean and shining, the tunic she wore draped enticingly about her lovely figure. He could see the curve of her hips, studied the velvety white skin of her arm. He breathed deeply for control.

"Well, you are looking better."

Lisa turned to look up at him. "I was, until I brushed my hair and accidentally scraped my ear." She swallowed, her eyes teared. "I'm afraid I've spoiled everything. It hurt bad, Chaco."

He frowned and walked closer, pushing back her hair to study the ear. His touch made her feel weak. How she wanted to shout that she loved him, that she did not want to leave this place ever, in spite of its dangers and hardships. He wore only leggings, and his broad chest was close. She could see the hard muscles of his arms and wanted to kiss them. In her young life she had never felt the intense passion she was lately feeling for

138

this young man, the butterflies in her stomach, the shortness of breath, the feel of hot blood flowing to her cheeks.

"It is redder again but not bleeding. It will probably take a little while for it to calm down. Drink a little of the tizwin." He moved to a hook inside the wickiup where an animal skin pouch holding the tizwin hung. He brought it to her, ignoring the thrill he'd felt at the feel of her lustrous hair in his fingers, ignoring the way her full breasts filled out the tunic, her nipples forming little points at the ends. "Here," he told her. "Swallow a little."

She smiled slightly. "Isn't it a sin in my world to drink whiskey?"

He frowned. How he hated the word whiskey. But it was a fact that the liquor did help ease pain. "It is not whiskey. It is tizwin. That makes it all right."

She laughed lightly. "I like your reasoning." She sipped a little. "I have to be careful. A person could get to like this stuff. If my mother saw me ..." She stopped, a stabbing pain of sorrow wiping the smile from her face. How easy it was to think of her parents still alive. Surely she would go back to her world and find them waiting for her.

Pain and regret moved through Chaco's eyes. "I am sorry," he told her.

Lisa suddenly wanted more tizwin, wanted to kill the pain not just of her ear, but her heart. She drank more.

"It's all right," she told him then, kneeling down to turn a piece of meat hanging over the fire. "You didn't really kill her. Those men did. This land did. My father did by bringing her out here in the first place. He never should have done that." She closed her eyes and sighed. "Sometimes I wonder if I'll ever forget what they did," she groaned. She swallowed more tizwin and looked up at him with eyes so sad and blue and beautiful that he could not resist kneeling beside her and putting an arm around her.

"You will never forget. It will ease with time, that's all."

She met his eyes, so close to her now, so dark, so beautiful. The tizwin, drunk too fast, made her feel heady, melancholy, alive with love. "Chaco," she whispered. A little voice warned her not to say it, not to let the tizwin cause her to be foolish. But he was so close, and her pain was going away. No, not just the pain. She was going away. Away! Away from Chaco! "I don't want to leave you," she blurted out, tears coming to her eyes. She threw her arms around his neck. "I don't want to leave you, Chaco. I love you. My God, I love you."

He closed his eyes, moving both arms around her, bending his head and breathing deeply of the smell of her clean hair. He let his hand roam over her back, down over her hips. "And I do not want you to go," he whispered. He moved his hand under her legs, lifting her like a child and carrying her to the now familiar bed of robes. He laid her down on it and moved beside her. "Perhaps there is some way you could stay. . . ."

"It's wrong," she whimpered. "It's impossible. And there's Little Deer to think about."

He touched her lips, his eyes watery. "Little Deer knows. She understands. I care for Little Deer, but not like I care for you."

"I . . . I don't know why I told you," she protested. "I . . . let me up, Chaco. I feel . . . I feel weak. It's the tizwin."

"My white father always said that a man speaks his true heart when he is full of whiskey. Why should it be any different for a woman?" He met her lips, teasingly biting at them, parting them, moving one leg on top of her. "I want you, Lisa. I have never wanted anything as much as I want you," he whispered, kissing her lips, her chin, her cheeks, her eyes, her throat. "I want to be inside of you, to be your first man." He met her lips again, his great hunger and passion pulling the same emotions from Lisa.

Her mind reeled with love, her body with desire. She wanted to know that this could be beautiful, that it did not have to be like the outlaws with her mother. She needed to know in order to forget the horror of that day. And suddenly it didn't seem

140

right that it should be anyone but Chaco, sweet, beautiful, wonderful Chaco. The tizwin made her feel so relaxed, so alive, so passionate, so unafraid. She knew she was being bold, even sinful. Yet it didn't seem to matter at the moment. This was Chaco drawing out these beautiful passions. This was Chaco unlacing her tunic, kissing her wildly now, moving his lips to her throat, down ... down ... to her breasts ... breasts never seen or touched before by man.

She heard a strange cry. Had it come from her own throat? Chaco! He was gently tasting her breasts, sending flames through her body, his hand moving under her tunic and stroking her bare hips. Now he was slipping the tunic the rest of the way off and she didn't even care. Why? Why did she not stop him? What was this thing the tizwin did to her? Now that she was healed it did more than make her feel better. It made her feel wild and alive and on fire—brazen and willing. She was offering herself to Chaco and she could not stop now. He seemed to be everywhere, kissing, touching, stroking, groaning in his own excited desires. He was seeing and touching places she never dreamed she would let any man see and touch. But he made it all so easy, so beautiful.

No. This was wrong. Not the physical act, but the notion that they could stay together. Of course they couldn't stay together. She must stop him. But her body would not obey her mind. Never had she felt this way before. The thrill of his touch was unresistable, the extent of her love for him too powerful. She wanted to please him, to belong to him, to be one with him, even if it could not last. She ignored the terrible pain she knew she would suffer when they faced the fact that they must part. It was easier to pretend that they could always be together.

His fingers moved in a circular motion, touching her secret place, making her breathing come in short gasps, making her want to give him everything, making her cry out his name and tell him she wanted him. A wonderful explosion ripped through her, making her arch up to him. He left her for just a moment,

141

and she watched through eyes blurred from love and passion and tizwin—watched him remove his leggings and loincloth, exposing that part of man she thought she would always hate. But he was beautiful. It did not frighten her.

Then he was on top of her again. She felt the weight of him, knew what he would do. She waited, glorying in the fact that they lay naked, skin touching skin, her light skin against his dark skin. Suddenly there came the pain, lessened from the tizwin, but still there. They were one, united in body. The thrill of it, the absolute glory of it, overshadowed the pain, the wrong. They moved rythmically.

"Now you can forget," he groaned into her ear. "It is good. It is beautiful. It is not like with those bad men."

His hands moved under her hips, pushing up, bringing out womanly passions awakened for the first time.

"I love you, Lisa," he moaned. "It is wrong, but I love you."

"Chaco," she groaned. His life poured into her and he whispered her name in return, then lay limp beside her. "I love you too," she whispered.

Chapter Ten

A bird perched on a branch of the wickiup, just outside where Lisa and Chaco lay sleeping. It chirped loudly and Lisa stirred, then snuggled against the warmth behind her—a body—Chaco's body. It took only seconds for her to realize what that meant, to remember, hazily, what had taken place the night before.

Guilt and uncertainty swept through her. The tizwin. He had tricked her with it! She had drunk so much of it she couldn't even remember all of it. Was it two or three times that he took her? Had she really let him do the hazy things she was remembering now, let him explore every inch of her as though she were some new object he'd never seen before? Was he laughing at her?

She let out a whimper and moved slightly away, curling up. His hand began to gently rub her bare back then.

"Don't," she whispered.

"What is wrong?" he asked, rubbing at his eyes and stretching a moment before moving closer to her.

She curled up as though she preferred he not touch her. "You tricked me," she whimpered. "My God, what have I done?"

He sighed, sitting up slightly. "Loved me. That is all. And I

143

have loved you. I did not trick you, and we did nothing wrong. You are my wife now, according to Indian custom."

She sniffed. "Not according to the white man's."

He carefully stroked the golden hair. "No difference. Our God smiles on all love; the only difference is a piece of paper. I do not know what will happen to us, or how we can truly stay together. I only know that I love you, Lisa, and whatever happens, in my heart you will forever be my wife. I took what no other man has taken, and it is mine now. You are mine." He pulled her around, forcing her to look at him. His dark eyes were true, so honest. He was not lying. He was not laughing at her.

"Are you all right?" he asked.

She swallowed, settling against him then. He folded his arms around her. "I don't know," she answered. "I think so."

"I will take you to a waterfall where we can bathe," he told her.

She felt strange, different, afraid. She was a woman now, made one by this Apache man who, three weeks ago, she did not even know. "Chaco, I'm scared. What will happen now?" she asked softly. "It's too late to turn off my feelings, to ignore them. It's too late to pretend I don't love you. But we can't be together like this forever ... and yet now I can't bear the thought of being apart from you."

He pulled up her chin with a gentle hand, then met her lips softly. In the next moment she was wrapped around him, melted against him, on fire with the morning sun. He made no reply to her statement other than to burn her mouth with his own. Everything about him was wild: desert, mountain, and cactus. He was the land, the animals, the forbidden. And all those things only made her love and want him more.

Again they made love, his every touch awakening the wonderful things she had discovered the night before, only with a keener awareness, for now she was not dulled from tizwin. Now she was more alive than ever, more on fire, more passionate, more in love. Her relaxed state, the sweet morning air, the singing of the bird, all combined to make the moment more beautiful, yet more painful, for she knew already that moments like this could not last long. He apparently did not want to face that yet, so she wouldn't either.

She was lost in his power and beauty, only vaguely aware of her own slender thighs parting to welcome him, catching through her misty eyes the contrast of his dark hand moving gently over the satiny white of her skin. She gasped as he reached under her, grasping her bottom to make her meet him more fully, bringing out every ounce of glorious ecstasy, his rhythmic, rotating movements removing the last remnants of pain left from her first intercourse. She was a woman now. He had made sure of that. They belonged to each other and he loved her. Surely it was not so wrong to give this young man his pleasure and to take pleasure in return.

Perhaps in her own world she could have resisted. But that world seemed far away and unreal now. So much had changed in her life in the last few weeks. Sometimes she wondered if she was the same Lisa. She had no family left, no friends. There was only Chaco. Had anyone from her world looked for her at all? Did anyone know she even existed any more? Did anyone care? Chaco cared. Chaco was her friend. Chaco loved her. Chaco had protected her from the outlaws, from the other Indian men, from Nina. She was becoming totally dependent on him, but it didn't matter. She loved him. He was so easy to love, so good inside, in spite of his wild outer nature, so utterly beautiful to look at, so sweet and gentle when he touched her.

Again his life poured into her and her name exited his lips in a quiet groan. He moved away from her then, turning over, then standing up to tie on a loincloth. "I will take you to a place where we can bathe," he told her again, "Then we will talk." He picked up her tunic, then went to her carpetbag and

145

took out a bar of her soap and a washcloth. He took down a piece of deerskin, treated to be amazingly soft, which was cut to be tied and knotted into another loincloth. It would be his clean one. He came over to her then. "Wrap the robe around yourself."

She obeyed. He handed her the things he had gathered, then bent down and picked her up in his arms. He carried her outside, now strangely quiet. She sensed he did not want to talk yet, perhaps did not want to face what they must face. He carried her through a quiet village in which most still slept, carried her beyond the wickiups and around the bend of a mass of rocks to the waterfall, setting her on her feet. He pulled off the robe and she stood there naked. He untied his loincloth and threw it aside, then stepped back slightly, his hands resting on her milky-white shoulders, his eyes taking in her beauty in the full sunlight.

Lisa stood there feeling self-conscious, clutching the soap and cloth and dress to her chest, her face turning crimson.

"I wanted to see you this way," he told her, brushing lightly at her hair. "You are more beautiful in the light of day than you are by the light of a fire. It is usually the other way."

She hung her head bashfully, yet could not resist taking in his own masculinity, studying her Apache stallion in all his glory, moving her eyes from the muscled thighs to his striking manhood, over the flat stomach to the broad chest and up to his own handsome face and dark eyes.

"It's the same for you," she told him. "But there is one great difference, Chaco."

Pain moved through his eyes. "What is that?"

She stepped back, setting aside the things she held. "Look at me, my skin against this land. If I stood here long, I would burn so badly I would die." Her eyes moved over him. "And look at you, so brown and strong. From a distance one could hardly spot you. You blend with the rocks and the earth. You

146

belong here as much as the wolves and the cactus. I don't fit at all." She met his eyes, her own tearing. "Chaco, what are we going to do?"

He looked at her for a long time. "We will do as my mother and my real father," he told her then. "We will keep and hold what time we have, treasure every moment, hope that it lasts for a long, long time. We will endure for as long as we can, and if the day comes that we must part, we will be together forever—in heart and in spirit. Time and separation cannot erase or change what happened between us last night and this morning, cannot change our love for each other. It is done, Lisa. It cannot be changed, ever."

Their eyes held for a seemingly endless, quiet moment. Lisa felt suspended in time and space, unreal, wild and free. Yes. They would simply have each other for as long as possible. Something wild and wonderful and memorable was happening to her here in this desolate land. Only God could know the reason for any of it. If and when she would return to her old world, she could not know. She only knew that now she wanted to stay in this world with Chaco, with the Apache. She wanted to endure in this land for as long as possible. Maybe by some miracle it could last forever. It was too painful to face the fact that it could not. The Apache were a hunted people. Surely it was only a matter of time. Precious time.

She stepped closer, reaching out to him. He folded her into his arms then and they stood there together, clinging to the precious present, which was all they had. There was no tomorrow. There could never be a tomorrow.

Coyotero's dark eyes moved from Lisa to Chaco. "The white woman cannot go. Our people think she is bad luck," Coyotero told Chaco in the Apache tongue. Lisa could not understand him, but she didn't need to. She knew from Coyotero's threatening countenance what was being said. But she did not fear for herself. She feared only for Chaco. He was losing his place among the Apache because of her. These people were all he had.

"She stays with me," Chaco replied. Although he, too, spoke in Apache, it was obvious he was defending her. His voice was angry and raised, and he rose when he spoke, going to stand beside her. "She is not bad luck."

"She made you beat Nina," Coyotero answered, rising now himself. "She has bewitched you so that you do not treat her the way other white prisoners are treated. She is worthless, for you do not trade her for things we truly need! We could get guns for her—horses, food! The Comancheros would pay much for her and you know it! And because of her the soldiers hound us so that we must go into Mexico. Either kill her, trade her, or give her back to her own people, Chaco!"

"She is mine, and I am keeping her. Since when do you tell another Apache man what to do with his own prisoner?"

"Prisoner?" Coyotero spit. "She is no prisoner! *You* are the prisoner!"

"I am no one's prisoner!"

"You are the prisoner of mixed blood. And now your white blood makes you be kind to this woman! You must decide, Chaco! Are you white or are you Apache?"

Chaco jerked as though struck. He pulled out his hunting knife and Lisa gasped as he held it threateningly toward Coyotero. "Do you doubt my skills as a warrior, or my love for my people? If you do, I will cut out your gizzard!"

The words were growled, and Coyotero watched him carefully, swallowing, remembering the stories of this young man's warrior father and how honored he was. Yet even Saguaro had fallen under the spell of a white woman.

"I do not doubt those things" he answered carefully. He breathed deeply to dispel his anger. "We are friends, Chaco. Do not let this come between us."

"It is not I who lets it come between us. It is you."

148

Coyotero shook his head. "Not I, Chaco. It is the others. They believe she is bad and they do not want her with us. If you keep her, then you must stay behind when we go."

Chaco nodded. "Then I will stay behind."

Coyotero frowned in surprise. "It would be a great risk, Chaco."

"I will take the risk"

Their eyes held and Coyotero's eyes saddened. "You are a fool, Chaco. The soldiers will find you. When they do, it will not matter what she tells them. They will not believe her. You will be a dead man. Your own father died because of a white woman."

Chaco's heart pained him. How he wished he could have known his father better. If only he were here now to talk to. The great Saguaro! He straightened himself even taller and held Coyotero's eyes boldly. "If my father was willing to risk his life for a white woman, there is no dishonor in my doing the same." He threw his knife so that it landed in the ground near Coyotero's feet. "I have spoken. The rest of you go. If the time comes I can no longer keep the white woman, or if she dies, I will rejoin you."

Coyotero's eyes moved again to Lisa, and she felt a chill. He looked her over as though she were naked. He looked back at Chaco. "What is this magic she holds over you?"

"She is a good woman, as good as any here."

Coyotero smiled bitterly. "As good as Little Deer?"

The words stung, and Coyotero saw his only hope of changing Chaco's mind. "Little Deer is better," the man told Chaco. "Better because she is our kind. She can survive here. This white one will not. And since you have chosen to throw her away, perhaps now I will speak for Little Deer myself."

Pinpricks of jealousy stabbed at Chaco. For many long months he had watched Little Deer, considered her worth as a wife, loved her quietly. But not the way he loved Lisa. Not in

149

the terrible passion and desire he felt for the white woman who had so unexpectedly come into his life. He had no rights now to Little Deer. He was giving up much for his Lisa, including the close friendship he had developed for Coyotero.

"You have that right," Chaco answered. "But if you are cruel to her, I will cut out your heart, even though you are my friend," he warned.

Coyotero held up his hand. "I bear a scar on the palm of my hand, from the day we cut ourselves and mixed our blood. In my heart I am sure you will not last long alone with this white woman. You will come back to us, Chaco. We need you, your fighting skills, your hunting skills. Soon you will see the foolishness of your ways. I will not speak for Little Deer—yet. I will wait awhile, for soon you will come and claim her for yourself." He turned then, ducking out of the wickiup.

Chaco moved his eyes to Lisa. She saw a sadness there that tore at her heart. "Chaco, what is happening?"

"They say we cannot go with them to Mexico. They think you are bad luck."

He walked over and pulled his knife from the ground. "I told them to go on without me," he added quietly. He turned and looked back at her. "We will find a way to survive."

She frowned, her heart pounding. "Chaco—out here? Alone? It will be so hard for you."

His eyebrows arched. "For me? What about you?"

Again she felt the darkness of separation closing in around her. How long could any of this last? She closed her eyes and turned away. "What am I doing to you?" She shook her head. "You should take me back, Chaco."

He stepped closer. "Is that what you want?"

Her shoulders shook slightly and she turned then, burying her face against his chest. "God forgive me. It's not what I want at all. I want to stay with you forever."

He held her close and kissed her hair. "Then we will stay together. I am a good hunter and I know how to hide from the

150

soldiers. We can do it, Lisa. It will be hard for you at first, for you are not used to this life. Perhaps once we have hidden here in these mountains long enough for the soldiers to stop looking for us, we can make our way north—far north—where neither Indian nor white man knows who we are. Perhaps we will find some settlement in which to live where it is civilized enough for you but not too civilized for me."

She looked up at him with tear-filled eyes. "Oh, Chaco, do you think that's possible?"

"We must try. But we cannot leave here yet."

She watched him carefully. "But ... what about your own people? What about the Apache? Can you truly leave them forever, Chaco?"

She saw the loneliness there, knew what he was giving up for her. "I can do whatever I must to stay with you. Here we can go neither to the Apache nor to the whites."

She embraced him again, allowing her youthful trust to let her believe they could really make it work. Both of them would be sacrificing much, yet to be apart now seemed unbearable. She would be strong for him. She must.

The weeks that followed were a chapter in Lisa's life that nothing else would ever match. The living was hard, yet beautiful. It was as though the Dragoon Mountains and everything in them belonged only to Chaco and Lisa. This was their world. It began to be easy to imagine that nothing and no one else existed outside of the vast expanse of rocks and hills in which they now lived.

Lisa's skin darkened to an enticing milky brown, and her eyes seemed even bluer against her tanned face and blond eyelashes. The sun bleached her hair even lighter, and her new way of living firmed her already nicely rounded hips and muscles so that to Chaco she was becoming more beautiful than ever. Each buried the heartache they sometimes felt over lost

151

loved ones. Chaco had lost his Apache friends and could never go back to his real mother and the white world he had once known. Lisa had lost her parents in the ugly attack by the outlaws. But the pain of it was lessening, and the world she had once known was fading in her mind.

At times it seemed she had never lived as a white woman at all. She began to enjoy the newfound freedom that came with living the wild, Apache way. There were no rules here, no clocks, no stiff, uncomfortable clothing. There was only sun and freedom, animals and mountains. She learned to ride, learned to shoot a bow and arrow, not well, but good enough to help ensure survival in a brutal land.

Lisa did not listen to the little voices that asked her what she would do if she got sick or wounded, or if she got pregnant and had to have a baby all alone out here. She ignored the tiny ache that sometimes came to have another white woman to talk to, to wear a pretty dress and dance to fiddle music, to sit in a hot tub, set a table with fine china, go to church. This land was church, a campfire and tin plates their table setting. The tunic she wore was more comfortable than any white woman's dress, and sometimes Chaco took her to a hot, bubbling spring he had found, where they would splash and enjoy the luxury of the warm water.

Often Lisa wondered if the way they lived was anything like the Garden of Eden. She felt like Eve, and surely Chaco was Adam, the perfect man.

The weeks turned into three months of wonder and discovery—not just discovery of the art of survival, but a discovery of bodies and the wonder of making love in all the ways there were for a man and a woman to express themselves. They had the freedom to share each other any time of day, for there was nothing but the animals and the mountains to watch. Sometimes she would be bent over a stream, washing clothes or utensils, and Chaco would be there, grabbing her from behind, pulling her down, tickling her until she could bear it no longer, then touching her in other ways, hands and lips making her abandon all modesty.

Sometimes she was the conqueror, touching him in ways she knew he enjoyed, moving on top of him and teasing him with her gentle movements until his ecstasy was almost painful.

They knew each other intimately now—every curve and dip, every tiny mark and crease, every method of arousal, every wonderful way there was to express their love, to give and take, to enjoy and be enjoyed. Life was hard yet beautiful.

The nights began to get cooler, and Chaco suggested they find a place to settle permanently for the winter, a place where they could begin stacking wood and buffalo chips for winter fires.

"Much of this land is warm in winter," he told her. "But we cannot stay where it is warm, in the lower regions. We must keep to the mountains. It will get cold."

Day after day was spent gathering necessary supplies, smoking meat, digging roots and picking wild berries. It would be the most settled either had been in a long time, and Lisa was actually looking forward to a long winter buried in the mountains with Chaco. In the winter no one would bother searching for them. They would surely have many months of peace.

Lisa prided herself in what she had learned. For winter moccasins she sewed skins from the shaggiest part of an elk Chaco had killed. He taught her how parts of the animal were used. There were several other animal skins that would be used to cover them heavily in the night, and they would lie warmly together in the shelter of their strongly built wickiup, away from the world below, away from the fighting and prejudice, away from the strict rules of the white man's world, away from reality. . . .

* * *

Lisa put one more piece of wood on the fire. "I think it's going to be very cold tonight," she told Chaco, who watched her from their bed of robes.

"I smell snow in the air," Chaco answered. "It is nearing the white man's October, I think, from the feel of the air, the colors and shapes of the plants."

She turned and smiled, then moved over to him. "I've lost all track of time. It seems strange for it not to matter." She bent closer and kissed him. "We will have to stay very close to keep warm.'

He opened the robes to reveal his naked body. "Then you had better come to bed," he said with a wink.

She laughed lightly, unlacing her tunic and letting it fall. He drank in her beauty as she slithered in beside him and he folded the robes over her, kissing at her neck.

"Chaco," she whispered, stroking his hair. "I think I should tell you."

"Tell me what?" He moved down and savored the full, pink nipples of her young breasts.

"I think I'm going to have a baby."

He stiffened, moving up to meet her eyes. "You are not sure?"

Her eyes danced with happiness. "Sure enough."

He frowned, moving a hand over her stomach. "When?"

"In the spring."

He signed, laying his head against her breasts. "How can I let you have a baby all alone out here? Sometimes white women have trouble having babies."

"I am just as capable of giving birth in the wilds as your Apache women."

He met her eyes again, seeing the fear she was trying to hide. He sighed deeply, pulling her close. "I am not so sure, and neither are you. I will have to think about this."

"There is nothing to think about. I can't possibly go to a doctor. The moment I reenter the white man's world I'll never be able to come back to you again. I won't go, Chaco, and you can't make me."

He kissed her hair. "Our child will be more important than even our being together."

Her heart began to race with fear at his words. "We'll all be together, all three of us," she said louder, her voice trembling. "Don't talk like that, Chaco. I'll be all right. Maybe we can find another band of Apaches to live with and the women can help me."

He sighed deeply. "Maybe." He kissed her eyes, her cheeks. "We have the winter to think about it. I just do not want to lose you because of the seed I planted in you. It is my seed, Lisa, my child. I want him or her to live, just as my own father wanted to be sure that my mother and I would survive. He made a great sacrifice for that. If I must do the same . . ."

She put her fingers to his lips. "Chaco, don't. I don't want to think about it." Her eyes teared. "Make love to me, Chaco. Please make love to me. I get so scared sometimes. This is all we have—right now, tonight, this moment. I don't want to think about what will happen in the spring."

He kissed her lightly. "I am so happy you carry my child. I only wish I knew we could all stay together." His own eyes teared, and then he met her lips more hungrily, suddenly feeling the desperateness of the situation, wanting her, wanting her so.

He drank in her mouth, savoring its sweetness, moving his hand down to the warm moistness that waited for his gentle fingers. He liked the power he felt when he touched her in ways that made her weaken and come alive. She belonged to him— only to him—this velvety white beauty. And now she carried his child. It made him love her all the more, made him ache for her, drown in her. He kissed and licked at her, moving down to her breasts, feeling somehow stronger and more secure when he savored them while he teased other places with his fingers until she whimpered his name.

His powerful body moved on top of her, in full command of her every movement, yet at her mercy himself, for there was no way to stop the painful urges she brought out of him other than to invade her totally. He pushed and she pulled, arching up to him, both of them feeling a keen fear now that these could be their last days together. Surely they at least had the rest of the winter. But what would come after that? Both knew this could not go on forever, but neither could face it.

He moved rhythmically, his desire and ecstasy mixed with an odd sorrow so that as he pushed into her deepest recesses his love for her made him want to cry. He groaned her name over and over, and she lay there with her eyes closed, her golden hair spread out on the robes, her slender body reaching for him, her sweet lips whispering his name in return until he shuddered and released himself. He came down on her then, wrapping her in his arms, unable to control his tears.

The wind howled, suggesting a coming storm. The little wickiup sat nestled in a hollow. Inside were two people who slept in each other's arms, the wind blowing so hard they could hear nothing outside, where a vengeful Nina pointed.

"There," she said to the handful of soldiers who had accompanied her. "I told your leader I would find him. Nina knows these mountains. Nina knows Chaco. There is where he keeps the white woman prisoner tied so that he can use her as he wishes. He killed her mother. He is bad. You can catch him now."

The sergeant in charge grinned at her. This Nina was a wild one, and he did not doubt he was not the only one who had enjoyed the pleasure of her body in his sleeping bag at night. Now she had led him to the infamous Chaco. He would probably get a promotion if he captured the notorious renegade.

"It's gettin' too dark to go in tonight," he told her. "Mornin' is soon enough."

Nina stared at the wickiup with dark, jealous eyes. Chaco would regret beating her, regret choosing the white whore over Nina. Now he would be caught, and he would hang!

Chapter Eleven

Lisa awoke first. Everything seemed too still ... different somehow. She shivered with the chill of the morning, then wondered if that was all it was ... the chill of the morning or some kind of danger. She crawled away from the bed of robes and slipped on her tunic, then hesitated before going outside, some sixth sense telling her to be careful. She pushed aside the hide door covering just slightly, peeking out.

Her blood froze. Soldiers! They were moving among the rocks.

She ducked back inside, a little whimper of horror exiting her lips. Chaco! They were after Chaco! No! It couldn't end this quickly. It couldn't! It wasn't fair. Why couldn't they let them alone? Everything had been so perfect, so wonderful. Only the night before they had made love. Now there would be no choice but to part, for his life was all that was important now. She hurried over to his side.

'Chaco! Chaco, you've got to go! You've got to run!" She shook at him and he groaned and sat up.

"What?"

"Run, Chaco! There are soldiers outside!"

He leaped to his feet, grabbing up his loincloth and quickly tying it. "How many?"

"I don't know. I peeked out of the door and saw them. I thought it was best they didn't know I had spotted then." She grasped her stomach. "Oh, Chaco, you've got to get out of here!"

He froze momentarily, their eyes holding. "Not without you," he whispered.

"You can't take me! I'd be a burden. They're close, Chaco! You've got to ride as only you can ride, and you can't do it with me along. Alone you can get away. You know the land, the places to hide. Hurry, Chaco! They'll kill you!"

His breathing quickened and his eyes teared. "I cannot leave you."

She choked in a sob, stepping closer and hugging him. "I love you, Chaco. But you have to go. You have to! Maybe somehow God will let us be together again! But you can't take me with you now. I'm pregnant, and you have to ride hard." She pulled away. "Hurry!"

Their eyes held for only a moment. "Lisa," he groaned.

She turned away. "Go," she whispered. She moved to his parfleche and threw in what clothing she could gather quickly while Chaco grabbed his pistol and rifle, throwing a quiver of arrows over his shoulder and taking up his bow. Lisa shoved the parfleche at him. He quickly kissed her and turned. "Wait," she spoke up. "Let me go first. I'll act like I see nothing. I'll untie your horse and bring him closer, then you come out and ride hard."

So little time! So much to say ... If only they could make love one more time! Surely this was not really happening. Lisa moved to the door again and peered out, seeing no one. She walked casually outside and to Chaco's horse, untying it and leading it to some green grass near the wickiup. "Now," she said softly.

In an instant, Chaco was out. He leaped on his horse and kicked the animal hard, letting out a war whoop and heading away from the wickiup at a hard gallop.

Surprised soldiers began firing. Bullets flew around Chaco while Lisa screamed his name, yelling for him to hurry. She ducked down. It seemed bullets were coming from every direction. She shook with fear for Chaco, screaming his name again when it appeared a bullet wounded him. His horse stumbled slightly and Chaco fell forward, but in a moment he seemed to be in control again, ducking around and behind great rock formations, zigzagging in a way that confused the soldiers, who were shouting orders back and forth.

"Get the son of a bitch! Don't let him get away," someone yelled.

"I told you we should have come in last night," someone else shouted. "We could have caught them off guard."

"Goddamn it! He's getting away!"

"I think I wounded him. Somebody try to track him. Maybe there's blood you can follow."

"Nobody can track an Apache through the mountains. You might as well try to trap the wind!"

"At least we saved the girl!"

Lisa watched Chaco disappear into a crevasse that seemed to swallow him up. She knew the place, a great crack in a huge slab of rock that was invisible from where she stood. It was just wide enough for one horse, and on the other side was wide open country—and freedom.

"Ride hard, Chaco," she whispered, her heart screaming with love and pain. Chaco! How suddenly it all had ended. How quickly and cruelly reality had come to slap them in the face. It was all like a strange dream, these past weeks with the Indian man who had captured her.

"Ma'am? You all right?" came a voice behind her.

Lisa whirled, her body jerking in sobs of grief that the man mistook for tears of joy at being found.

"Everything's okay now, ma'am. We'll take you back to your own folk." He looked her over curiously, as though to wonder if she was somehow to be considered a loose woman now for having been the captive of an Apache warrior. It was strange how whites thought of such women. They pitied them, yet they shunned them. "You're Lisette Powers? We found some papers on some butchered white people left behind when Indians rode off with you. Found a birth certificate with your name on it."

Lisa looked back in the direction in which Chaco had ridden. "Yes," she answered quietly. "I am Lisette." She put her face in her hands and wept. More soldiers came then, and Lisa heard a woman's voice.

"Too bad soldiers not catch that bad Apache man who rape you and kill your mother," the woman said.

Lisa looked up quickly into Nina's face. Her heart filled with both fear and hatred. The hatred won out, and Lisa got to her feet, glaring at Nina. "You," she hissed. "I might have known! You brought them! You knew the good hiding places and you brought them to catch Chaco!" Tears began streaming down her face. "You're filth! You're filth and a liar and a traitor!" She lunged at Nina but a soldier grabbed her.

"Hold on there, little girl. This Apache woman only wants what's best for her people, and she just saved you. What's wrong with you?"

Lisa jerked away. "Saved me?" She moved her blue eyes to meet the soldier's eyes. "Maybe I didn't *want* to be saved!" She looked back at Nina, while the soldiers all eyed her strangely, wondering at how wild and loose this pretty white girl might be now. The Indians had a way of seemingly hypnotizing their white captives so that often when they were rescued they wanted to stay with the Indians rather than go back to their own people. Apparently that had happened to this one.

Lisa wondered at the fact that now Nina spoke English. She had apparently deliberately spoken only Apache around Lisa when in camp so that Lisa could never understand what she was saying, surely just another effort at making Lisa feel less welcome. "*She* is the bad one," Lisa shouted. "She was jealous because Chaco cast her out. She even tried to kill me!" She pushed back her hair and showed the closest soldier her scarred ear, then tossed her head and looked at Nina again. "If not for Chaco, she would have succeeded."

"She crazy woman now," Nina said flatly. "She wounded by Chaco. She suffer much, not know what she talk. Chaco even kill her mother, yet she shows no regret. Her mind no good."

"Chaco did not kill my mother," Lisa answered defensively. She had to convince them of that. If she told the truth, they would never understand, even if she explained her mother's pitiful state, that her mother wanted to die. Chaco's only possible salvation was to convince them that he did not kill her mother and that he had not harmed her own person in any way. Surely that was why they searched for him, thinking they could hang him for murdering a white woman and for taking a white girl captive. She turned to the soldier. "One of the other Apaches killed my mother, after the outlaws raped and beat her and killed my father! The Apaches didn't do any of it! They came to help us. Then soldiers came, and Chaco was afraid, so he rode off with me. He was going to take me to help, but soldiers were right on us and Chaco was afraid to take me back and try to explain."

The man's eyes narrowed. "You defendin' that filthy bastard?"

She held up her chin, meeting his eyes squarely. "He is not a filthy bastard. Chaco is good. And he didn't do any of the things they say he did. You have to believe me."

His eyes moved over her as though she were naked. "I believe he filled you with some kind of Apache firewater and raped you till you don't know your own mind any more," he answered. "Now we're taken' you back, sister, and you'd best remember how white folks feel about their own kind defendin' murderin' savages! It could be bad for somethin' as young and pretty as you. Now you come with us. Soon as you're back with your own kind and rested, you'll begin to get some sense back

162

in that head." He took her arm. "Come on, young lady, if I can still call you a lady."

She jerked her arm away, almost sick with his words, and with the thought that it was suddenly over. Over! Chaco! He had ridden into the hills and disappeared like the wind. Would she ever see him again? She turned to a grinning Nina. "Chaco's Apaches will get you for this," she warned, so angry more tears came. How she wished she could be as vicious as Nina. It was only the gentleness of her upbringing that kept her from clawing out the young woman's eyes.

"I good Apache now," Nina sneered. "I help soldiers find poor white girl who is captured."

Lisa stepped closer. "You are a bad Apache," she told her, wiping at her eyes. "You have shown the soldiers a secret Apache hiding place. When I see Chaco again, I will tell him what you have done."

Nina tossed her head. "You never see Chaco again," she sneered. "How you find him, hmmm? Can you travel alone in this country? And how he come to you? Turn himself in to soldiers?" She laughed. "He never turn himself in and live in prison like dog! Or maybe he hang!"

Lisa struggled not to let the awful truth of the woman's words make her break into wretched sobbing. But holding back the tears only made her feel even sicker. She looked back at the soldier who had grabbed her arm. The way he looked at her made her more afraid of the soldiers than of the Apaches. His eyes were hardly different from the eyes of the outlaws who had intended to rape her until Chaco came along.

"I have to get my things," she told him. "I still have my carpetbag and some clothes."

He nodded. "Go ahead. We have to get started."

Lisa quickly ducked inside the wickiup, feeling instantly surrounded by all that was Chaco, instantly engulfed in his love, in the memories of the hard but sweet times they had spent here, the nights in each other's arms, shutting out the rest of the cruel world.

Chaco! She went to her knees, sobbing uncontrolled tears, rocking in her sorrow. How could she leave this place? If only they would leave her here. Then Chaco could come for her. But they would never leave her, and if they did, they would only set a trap for Chaco. What was she to do now? Where was she to go? Someone came inside then.

"Let's get goin', girl" came the voice.

She jumped up, afraid of being alone inside the wickiup with him. Chaco had told her stories of what was done to some Apache women when captured by soldiers or marauding white men. She quickly gathered her things, sniffing and wiping at her eyes, struggling to gain control of herself. She had to think. She didn't want to go to some strange fort full of strange, curious men.

"Where are you taking me?" she asked.

"Fort Bowie for now. You got kin someplace?"

She thought of her mother and father and swallowed back the renewed sorrow. "No." She met the man's eyes. "Chaco spoke often of his white mother." She thought of the story, of how his mother had been a captive of his Apache father and had fallen in love with him. The woman would surely understand her own predicament. "He said she lives near Fort Bowie with her husband and Chaco's half brother. I would like to go to her. She . . . she would want to know that Chaco is all right."

The man scowled. "What is it them Apache men do to make their captives go soft on them?" he sneered.

She swallowed. "They don't all treat their white captives the way soldiers treat Apache captives," she answered boldly. "I have learned a lot in my days here, mister. Mostly I have learned a whole different side to the story, have seen it with my own eyes. The Apaches have done some terrible things, but they're frightened and desperate. They don't know how else to make the white people leave but to try to scare you out."

He grinned, his teeth slightly brown from tobacco juice. "Well, we don't scare easy, now, do we? And you sure talk strange for bein' took against your will."

"It was against my will. But I realized later Chaco only took me away and attacked our camp to save me from the outlaws. I'm telling you the Apaches didn't do any of what you found. My father and mother and I were attacked by outlaws. They killed my father, then beat and raped my mother. They were going to do the same to me until Chaco and his friends came along. My . . . my mother was crazy from what happened to her . . . sure the Apaches had come to do even worse. So she begged them to kill her. They were confused by her actions and screaming. One of them . . . one of them killed her . . . but she was already as good as dead." She hung her head at the memory. Mother! How unreal it all was.

"And the one who stabbed her was Chaco. Right?"

"No," she lied. She would never tell them it was. "It was not Chaco."

She met his eyes again. "To a dying man I am sure all Apaches look alike."

He nodded. "Perhaps. Can you identify the one that did it?"

She shook her head. "I was too confused myself . . . too frightened. That day they all looked alike to me, too."

"The Apache woman out there says Chaco did it."

"She would say anything to get him in trouble. She hated him."

"Why?"

Lisa reddened. "None of your business. I don't have to answer any of your questions. Take me to your commander and let him ask the questions. But first I want to go to Shannon Edwards. That's Chaco's mother."

"I know who she is. Everybody knows Shannon and Bryce Edwards—and everybody knows the woman was laid by an Apache man."

Lisa picked up her things and walked out. It was no use

talking to such a man, no use trying to make him understand. None of them would ever understand. She didn't dare tell him she was pregnant or that she loved Chaco. They would use her like a dog if she did. Until she was within the safety of Chaco's mother and stepfather, she must show a little gratitude for her "rescue" or her very person was in danger.

A few men were riding back when she went outside. "We lost the bastard," one of them shouted.

Lisa breathed a sigh of relief. Thank God he got away! But how could she ever be with him again now?

"That the girl?"

"She's the one," the sergeant answered. "For all her gratefulness we might as well have set the wickiup on fire like we talked about doin'. I didn't want to for fear of hurtin' the girl, but she don't seem so anxious to be saved." He shoved Lisa toward his horse.

"Happens sometimes," another replied. "Soon as she's back where she belongs and bathed and dressed right, she'll come around."

"We could bathe and dress her ourselves," one of them commented with a grin.

Lisa felt her blood chilling. The sergeant tied her things onto his horse. "We won't have none of that. Colonel Blazer would have our asses. Just remember, even though she's been with an Apache man she's still one of us. She's still a victim of Apache brutality and trickery. She's just a kid. She don't know her own mind and she's scared to death."

Lisa felt a small bit of gratitude to the man, even though she did not like him. Her safety apparently hung on the mere fact that she was white and supposedly a victim. She would keep her defense of Chaco quiet until she was safely away from these men. No matter what she said, they would all think what they wanted. She knew now Chaco was right. No matter how hard she tried to make them believe the truth, he would probably be hanged if he was caught.

The sergeant helped her up onto his horse behind him. No! They were leaving! They were leaving this secret, wonderful place that belonged only to her and Chaco. She glanced back at the wickiup to see one of the men setting fire to it. She wanted to shout for him to stop but knew it would be misinterpreted. Chaco! Oh, God, how was she to bear this? He had become her whole world. Now that world was being destroyed before her eyes.

She turned away, but as they made their way through rocks and cacti, the smoke from the burning wickiup burned in her nostrils. It was done—over. But not completely. Not completely. She carried Chaco's life in her belly, and no one would take it from her. No one!

"I told you . . . Chaco did not kill my mother," Lisa repeated for what seemed the hundredth time. "Please . . . I'm so tired. I just want to be taken to Chaco's mother."

Colonel Blazer studied her scathingly. Lisa wiped at more tears, wondering where they continued to come from. She was sick of burning eyes and ugly, suggestive remarks and intimate questions. They had made it all ugly—all of it. They were making Chaco out to be a rapist and murderer. The journey back to Fort Bowie had been long and tiring, with few stops for rest. She didn't dare tell them she was pregnant, and she desperately feared losing the baby. She had to hang on to it. It might be all she had left of Chaco now. But how would she manage, single and alone, walking around with a big belly and no husband, the brunt of ugly remarks from whites? How had Chaco's mother handled it all those years ago. What a remarkable woman she must be.

"Why would a dying man name Chaco as your mother's murderer?" Blazer asked again.

Lisa sighed and sniffed. "I don't know. I told your sergeant . . . a man can get confused when he's badly wounded. Surely to that man all the Indians that day looked alike." She met the man's eyes with her blue ones, still pretty in spite of being bloodshot from lack of sleep and from crying. "Why would I defend an Apache Indian who killed my mother?"

Blazer looked her over—her sun-darkened skin, her tangled hair, her common tunic. "I don't know. Why don't you tell me," he answered. "It's been known to happen before, white women captives coming back unwillingly, speaking in defense of the very men who captured and tortured them."

"I was never tortured."

"Not even at first?"

A couple of the soldiers standing in the room shuffled, and Lisa could tell they wanted to snicker. So, surely they thought she'd been somehow raped into submission, turned into a common whore. Her eyes narrowed into slits of hatred.

"You would never understand and I don't have to explain anything to you. The only thing you need to know is that Chaco was kind to me. He never harmed me or forced me in any way. And he did not kill my mother. The outlaws killed my father and beat and raped my mother. They would have done the same to me if Chaco hadn't come along. I'm glad he came. Glad!"

Her lower lip quivered and she turned away. "You're all trying to find something to accuse Chaco of. You won't get it from me." She faced Blazer again. "Why don't you just try to understand the Apache? Why won't anybody try to understand ... to talk to them ... to be fair with them?"

Blazer's own eyes darkened. "Little girl, we're beyond being fair with the likes of Geronimo and his renegades. And if Chaco has gone to be with them, it is only a matter of time before all of them are captured. General Sheridan is on his way here right now to confer with General Crook. Crook is one of the best Indian fighters in the army. A campaign is planned that will root out all Apache renegades once and for all. And I guarantee that the next time you see Chaco, it will be at the end of a noose or behind prison bars, no matter how much you defend him. Now I suggest to you that you get a grasp of yourself and what you are saying. You are a very pretty girl with many happy years ahead of you. We can understand the terror and confusion of being an Apache prisoner. Perhaps you're afraid that if you accuse Chaco of something bad, he will come and kill you. But you're safe now and you don't have to be afraid. You don't have to defend him out of fear."

"But I'm not," she cried.

"Think of you're reputation, girl," Blazer shouted at her. "Why don't you tell us the truth!"

On his last word Lisa burst into more crying, and the door to Blazer's office opened. Lisa was hardly aware at first that two men had stepped inside, while someone behind them shouted to them that they were not to go in. The room fell silent for a moment and Blazer's chair scooted back. The man rose.

"No one gave you permission to be here, Edwards," he growled.

Edwards. Lisa look up, captured immediately by kind, gray eyes set in a marvelously handsome face. Could this be the stepfather Chaco had told her about—the man who was so amazingly understanding of the Apache and who had loved and remained devoted to Chaco's mother, even after she was captured by Indians and bore a half-breed son? The man called Edwards looked at Blazer.

"What the hell are you doing to this girl? She looks ready to drop."

"We're simply trying to get the truth out of her," Blazer replied angrily. "She insists she was not harmed and that Chaco did not kill her mother. You know what happens to some white women. . . ."

The man stopped. Bryce Edwards' tanned face darkened even more at the words.

"Yes. I know full well what happens to some white women. Maybe this one is telling the truth. Did you ever consider that?"

169

Blazer folded his arms in front of himself. "All I know is I have the dying words of a white man murdered and mutilated by Indians that Chaco killed the white woman. No one is going to believe the frantic defense of a helpless, terrified white girl who was captured by Apaches and forced to submit to them through their damned rituals and drugs."

"You stupid son of a bitch," Edwards growled, lunging for Blazer.

"Pa!" A well-built young man who stood beside Edwards and who greatly resembled the man grabbed Bryce's arm. "Don't, Pa! They'll arrest you."

Two of the soldiers in the room had already trained their rifles on Bryce. Blazer grinned. "Go ahead, Edwards. I'd love to put you in our little jail cell."

Lisa watched in wide-eyed wonder. Yes. This man surely did love Chaco. And the younger man with him must be Chaco's half brother, Troy. He was nearly as tall as his father and filling out like a man, he bore his father's handsome looks.

Bryce straightened. "The men you sent for me said the girl wants to come home to us. I'm taking her out of here. Right now."

"I haven't finished questioning her," Blazer answered.

"There is nothing left to ask. It's obvious you've been harassing her for hours! I'm taking her out of here right now or the newspapers are going to be printing stories about how the colonel at Fort Bowie treats returned women prisoners!"

Blazer's face reddened slightly. "All right, Edwards. Take her. I'm sure she and your wife will have plenty to talk about!"

Lisa could see the terrible hurt in the man's eyes, and her heart went out to him. She saw the same hurt in Troy's eyes, as well as deep affection for his father.

"Come on, Pa. Don't let him get to you. He just wants to put you in jail. We've got to get back to Mother.'

Bryce continued to eye Blazer. "Our day is coming, Blazer."

Blazer snickered. "Your day is over, Edwards. You had your

chance at this post. You commanded this fort once. But you gave that up because of your stupid sympathy for the Apaches. Just remember that you have no power here now. Take the girl and get out. And plan on seeing your cherished stepson soon. Crook will find the renegades, and life will not be easy for them when he does!"

Bryce turned away from the men, resting his eyes on Lisa. He stepped closer, kneeling down in front of her. The moment her eyes rested on his she was comforted. He understood. "Is it true you want to come with us?" he asked her.

She sniffed and nodded. Bryce could see through the dirt and the tired eyes that she was a beautiful young girl. Surely Chaco had been extremely attracted to her, but he could not be sure just what had happened between them. He would not ask questions here.

"Do you have family back east?" he asked.

"No," she said quietly. "I . . . have no one." She pressed her lips together, wanting to say she had no one but Chaco, but afraid to say it in front of the soldiers.

Bryce took her hand. "You have us," he told her. "For as long as you need us. We'll take care of you until you decide what you want to do."

She nodded, new tears coming. Bryce rose, helping her out of her chair. He led her out, saying nothing more to Blazer. She walked on legs so tired she wondered how she would ever go another step. She wanted nothing more than a soft bed in which to sleep, hoping she could sleep hard and long and deep enough to temporarily forget the awful sorrow of losing Chaco and the sweet life they had made together.

A soldier handed Bryce the girl's carpetbag and Bryce kept an arm around her as he led her out. Troy followed, feeling sorry for the girl called Lisa Powers, and also seeing the beauty behind the dirt and tears. He thought it almost too bad that perhaps his brother considered this girl his own. There were few pretty girls around Fort Bowie. They seldom came to this desolate land. Most went on to Tucson, or were passing through to California. This was about the prettiest one he'd ever seen. She created strange urgings deep inside, a feeling of protectiveness, for she had been his brother's captive and perhaps was special to Chaco. Surely she cared for Chaco or she wouldn't have defended him so against the questions and stares of the soldiers.

Troy mounted up, taking the carpetbag from his father, who lifted Lisa onto his own horse, then mounted up behind her. They rode out of the fort and away from prying eyes. Lisa's fears began to dissipate as Bryce Edwards' arm wrapped around her reassuringly. She was going to Chaco's mother, the one woman who would understand it all. Only then would she tell the truth about her mother, and finally admit that she was carrying Chaco's child.

Chapter Twelve

The ride to the Edwards' trading post and ranch was not as far as Lisa thought it might be. Bryce Edwards headed his horse toward a small cabin, around which red roses managed to bloom in spite of the arid climate. Lisa knew only a woman who adored flowers could have kept such beauty alive in a land that seemed to sprout only cacti and scrubby pine. She could not help wondering at Chaco's tale of his mother once being a rich southern belle, before the Civil War, engaged to the handsome soldier, Bryce Edwards, then being stolen away by Apaches when she headed west to be with her intended husband.

Already she had sensed the closeness of the family, just by watching Troy Edwards trying to keep his father out of trouble at the fort and by listening to their conversation as they rode home.

"Is Chaco all right?" Bryce had asked her.

"I think so. The soldiers shot at him. He might be wounded. One of them claimed to have hit him, but I couldn't tell."

"Damn," Bryce had whispered.

"Pa, maybe we should try to find him," Troy had put in.

"You know your brother is as good at hiding as the rest of them. We'd never find him," Bryce had answered. "Some other Apaches might find you and not know who you are, and that would be the end of you. I've lost one son. I intend to keep you."

Troy had shrugged. "It might be worth the risk."

"For what? What would you do if you found him, Troy? He won't come back and right now it's best he doesn't. There is nothing we can do right now. Chaco knows how we feel. He knows he's loved."

They rode silently for a little while. "I miss him," Troy spoke up then. "Do you think we can ever all be a family again?"

Bryce sighed deeply. "I don't think so, Troy."

Troy said nothing after that, riding ahead of them as though he didn't want anyone to see his face.

"We'll all have a lot of questions," Bryce told Lisa then. "But only because we love Chaco, not to upset you. And when we first get home I want you to bathe and go to bed. There will be plenty of time later for talking. It seems obvious, Lisa, but I'd feel better hearing from your own lips that Chaco didn't mistreat you. I like to think he's still the Chaco I raised."

She turned her head slightly. "He was very good to me, Mr. Edwards. He never hurt me."

Bryce had said nothing more. Now a woman made her appearance, coming out of the cabin to stand on the porch. She wore a soft green cotton dress, and as they came closer Lisa could see the remaining beauty of what once had very obviously been a ravishing young girl, someone who still carried that beauty in womanhood. There was just a hint of gray in the auburn hair, and her green eyes were still large and bright, her skin surprisingly fair for living in this land, making Lisa wonder how fair she must have been when first she came here.

The woman stepped down, eagerness on her face, her eyes moving from her son to Lisa, to Bryce and Lisa again, then to Bryce. "Chaco?"

"He's all right, as far as we know," Bryce told her. He dis-

174

mounted, lifting Lisa down. "This is Lisa Powers. She was with Chaco when they found him. She's the girl he rode off with a few months back." He put a hand on Lisa's shoulder. "Lisa, this is Shannon, Chaco's mother."

Lisa just stared. Their eyes held, and Lisa's began to flood with tears. Instantly she knew this woman understood it—all of it. Here was someone, finally, to whom she could talk about all she had been through, a woman to whom she could openly tell how much she loved Chaco, a woman who would understand when she told her she was pregnant by an Indian. Shannon stepped closer.

"You were . . . good friends?"

Lisa shook, breaking into sobs then. "I love him," she squeaked.

Shannon closed her eyes, coming closer and taking the girl into her arms. Oh, the pain of it, to remember Saguaro and how it had been for her, to remember the sorrow that had never left her when he died, to remember her own months with an Apache warrior whom she had loved. She held Lisa tightly.

"We'll talk about it later, after you've rested," she told the girl. "I want to hear all about it, why Chaco rode off with you and kept you, exactly what happened." She patted Lisa's shoulder. "Come on in the house. I'll help you wash and you go right to bed."

The woman led her inside. Bryce watched after them a moment, realizing how difficult this was for his wife. He looked over at Troy, who watched until the women disappeared inside.

"She's pretty," he said quietly.

Bryce grinned a little. "A man would be a fool not to see that."

Troy looked over at him and reddened some. "I'll take care of the horses." He handed Lisa's carpetbag to Bryce and led the horses away. Bryce headed for the trading post, noticing a couple of his hired hands staring at the house as the two women

175

went through the doorway. He decided to hold a meeting with all his help. They would understand that Lisa Powers was a nice, respectable girl, and anyone who treated her otherwise would be fired.

Inside the cabin Shannon poured hot water into a large wash-tub, then got out soap and some towels. "No one will come inside until I tell them to," she told Lisa. "You take a bath. I'll get you a flannel gown. When you're through, I want you to sleep." She set the soap and towel on a chair beside the tub. "Are you hungry? Thirsty? Would you like some lemonade?"

Lisa just stared at her, circles under her tired eyes. "What ... what am I going to do?" she sniffled.

"Right now you are going to bathe and sleep. You have a home here, Lisa. If there is someplace you would like to go back east, Bryce will arrange it for you."

The girl shook her head. "I could never leave now," she said in a near whisper.

Shannon felt a lump in her throat. How well she understood! She nodded. "Then you don't have to leave. I don't want you to worry about it for now, Lisa."

"But I'm ..." She put a hand to her stomach. She barely knew this woman. How could she tell her? Yet how could she not? This was Chaco's mother. And it was so hard to keep it all inside. "I'm pregnant," she said quietly, hanging her head.

The room hung silent. "Dear God," Shannon finally whispered. She sighed as though very weary and stepped closer to the girl. "It's all right, Lisa. I understand. We'll work it out. Don't you worry about a thing. I'll tell Bryce, and we'll all talk together when you've rested. Come now. Get undressed and get into the tub. I'm going out for just a moment. I'll be right back."

She leaned forward and kissed Lisa's hair. Lisa met her eyes and saw the pain in them in spite of Shannon Edwards' gentle smile.

"I'm ... sorry," she sniffed.

176

Shannon put a hand to the side of the girl's face. "Don't ever be sorry for loving someone, Lisa. I have never been sorry for loving Chaco's father. I make no excuses for it, and I do not hang my head over it. Surely you gave my son a few months of peace and happiness. That is all that matters. Now the important thing is to keep the baby. You do want it, don't you?"

More tears came. "More than anything, Mrs. Edwards."

Shannon smiled. "Then you should start by taking your bath and getting some rest. Now do as I say and I'll be right back."

She turned and left, and Lisa quickly removed her tunic, stepping into the warm, soapy water and moving down into it. She closed her eyes, thinking of her last night with Chaco. Chaco! How was life to go on? Thank God she would have his child, but none of it would be easy. She could only thank God she had found these kind people who understood so well what she was going through.

Outside, Shannon approached her husband, who stood on the porch of the trading post. He saw her pleading look and walked closer to her, out of hearing distance of a hired hand who stood nearby.

"She all right?" he asked.

Her eyes teared. "Oh, Bryce!"

He put a hand on her shoulder. "What is it?"

She swallowed. "She's ... she says she's pregnant."

He frowned, then closed his eyes. "My God."

"Bryce, I had you to fall back on. She has no one. We have to protect her, Bryce. She wants the baby, but around here ... a girl everyone knows was a captive of Apaches walking around with a big stomach ..."

"I know. We'll work it out somehow." He put an arm around her, sighing deeply. It was happening all over again.

Never had the wind sounded so lonely to Chaco as it did now, moaning through the canyon below. He looked over the

177

edge. A drying river ran below, perhaps five hundred feet down, maybe more. He had never seen Chaco canyon, for which he had been named, named for a canyon because its two sides would never meet. Never had he felt so torn in loyalties, yet the danger of returning to the white world must end up making his decision for him now. He could never go to Lisa.

The wind whipped up sand that stung at his bare skin. His heart ached fiercely as he stared down into the lonely canyon. The howling wind seemed to move right through his bones as well, crying out for him.

Lisa! How empty and wrong everything seemed without her. If only he had taken the chance and had taken her back right away he never would have got so involved. She was his woman now. His! Chaco's woman! She even carried his child, a child he might never see. His only consolation was that she was safe now, that she would be where she could get help when the baby came. Surely she was with his mother and father now, and he had no doubt they would show her love and understanding and give her a home.

But that did not relieve his present loneliness, or the torture of wanting a woman he could not have. It had all ended so quickly and cruelly. One moment she was in his arms, and in the next she was gone. He was in a kind of shock, as though Lisa had been killed and was suddenly gone from his life. For him she might as well be dead now. How could they ever be together again?

He hung his head and wept quietly, then breathed deeply for control. He must be strong. He was Apache. He must face the fact that it was over, that even if he could get her back it would be wrong to bring her back to such a life. She was better off, and so was their child. It was done. If he had any sense he would go to join Geronimo in the south. Yet he could not bear the thought of being so far away from her. If only he could catch glimpses of her now and then. But that would only prolong the agony. No. He must go south.

178

He stood up, glancing down again at his side where the soldier's bullet had passed through the skin, harming no vital organs. There did not seem to be any infection from it. He straightened, facing the sun.

"Forgive my weakness over the white woman," he prayed. "It is something that cannot be. Help me to be the Apache I must be, for there is no longer any choice. Guard my Lisa. Keep the wind at her back and let the sun warm her. Protect her from the evils of the white man's world, for she will suffer, carrying the child of an Indian. Do not let them harm her and call her names. And bring forth from her womb a healthy child she can love and who will love her in return."

A great heaviness filled him. Not only would he not see Lisa again, he would not see his child. It was overwhelming to realize what he must give up now. He had never dreamed this could happen to him. It would all have been so simple if he had simply married Little Deer and gone on south with the others.

Little Deer. Had Coyotero claimed her? Or had he saved her, sure Chaco could never last with Lisa, sure his friend would also come south. It would be hard to admit Coyotero was right. But he was. That was the awful truth. Lisa was gone, gone to a world Chaco could never reenter. He groaned Lisa's name, walking to his horse and grasping it around the neck. He cried quietly against the mane of the horse.

He stood there, the hot sun burning into his shoulders, alone. So alone. The quiet emptiness of the land that he usually enjoyed now seemed like an enemy, more lonely than he had ever felt it before. He realized then it was not the land and surroundings that made a man feel empty and lonely, it was the man himself and the mistakes he made along the way of life, as well as what man did to one another. Because of the white man's prejudice, he could never go home, and never be with Lisa.

He slowly climbed onto his horse. He headed south.

* * *

"My father foolishly thought he could take a shortcut," Lisa said quietly at the supper table. She wore a blue cotton dress that matched her lovely blue eyes. Her clean, golden hair hung in soft waves past her shoulders, and Troy could hardly take his eyes from her, nor could he stop the pity he felt for her. "Then the outlaws came."

She poked at her meat aimlessly. "It was ... terrible. They killed my father and made me ..." She swallowed and shuddered.

"You don't have to talk about it, Lisa. We understand," Shannon told her.

Lisa stared at the meat, studying the holes in it. "They did bad things to my mother ... and would have done the same to me. Then the Apaches came." She met the woman's eyes. "Chaco *did* kill my mother, but it wasn't like they think," she blurted out.

Shannon's eyes widened and she glanced at Bryce.

"What do you mean?" Bryce asked.

"He ... he leaned over her. I didn't know until later what really happened. When he stabbed her, I hated him, and I was terrified. He grabbed me, and then the soldiers came and he rode off with me. When he first grabbed me he said not to be afraid, that he would bring me here—to safety. But the soldiers were close on us and he was afraid, so he rode into the hills where he knew he could lose them. They swarmed through the hills so much that he had to stay in hiding at the village ... so that's how we ended up there. And before we knew it ... we became ... friends."

She blushed and blinked back tears.

"What about your mother?" Shannon asked.

Lisa swallowed some coffee before continuing. "Chaco told me she asked him to kill her. I think she was probably delirious, sure Chaco was going to do to her what the outlaws had already done. My mother ... was delicate. She could never have lived with what happened to her, and she was so badly beaten that she could never have survived.

"He killed her then . . . hoping the others would think he did it purposely to show he was not afraid to kill a white woman. He told me later the others often made fun of him because he wouldn't hurt white women. What he did . . . he did to help my mother. He wanted the others to think he was showing he had no mercy for white women. It took me a long time to understand it all, but there was something about him . . . his eyes . . . the sincerity there. I believed him." She met Shannon's eyes. "He wouldn't have killed her if he hadn't seen the insane look to her, heard her pleadings. I'm sure of it. The outlaws had even half scalped her. I don't think she would have lived."

Shannon sighed, closing her eyes. "That won't matter to the courts."

"Oh, I know," Lisa answered, looking from her to Bryce and then Troy. "That's why I won't ever tell them the truth," she went on, looking back at Shannon. "I'll never tell them, I swear! I love Chaco. I love him so. . . ."

She blushed deeply, again looking at her plate. "I don't know how it all happened. It just . . . did. We were friends, and then . . . somehow . . ." She swallowed. "An Apache woman who hated me attacked me. She said I was bad luck and bad for Chaco. She would have killed me if Chaco hadn't caught her. He beat her and chased her away. She nearly cut off my ear. Chaco stayed with me while I healed. I grew so dependent on him. I was so scared, and he was so good to me. Being together just seemed so . . . so right and good. And inside, I'm his wife. He said as much. In the eyes of the Apache, we're married. And in our hearts. I don't care what the white people say about it."

Shannon reached over and took her hand. "Of course you're married—in God's eyes. I understand all of it, Lisa."

"I should probably go away. I'll just be a burden to all of you."

"Nonsense," Shannon answered. "We are responsible for you now, and we will care for you because you're a lovely girl and because my Chaco loved you."

Bryce rolled a cigarette, fighting his own painful memories. He had accepted what had happened to Shannon long ago, loved her in spite of it. But it did not erase the pain of knowing she'd been with another man, even though she could not be blamed for it. If not for Saguaro she probably would have died. But they had lived with the pain of those days for years, and probably always would. Now here was another girl in the same predicament, only worse. She had no Bryce to whom she could turn. She was alone. He lit his cigarette and took a puff.

"Don't worry about what other people say. I'll knock their teeth out," Troy spoke up. "If my brother loves you, that's all that matters. You can live with us. My mother would like having another female around. And it's her grandchild—my nephew. You have to stay with us. You can't go running off someplace. You're carrying my brother's kid."

Lisa only blushed more, putting a hand self-consciously to her stomach. Bryce scooted back his chair and got up. Everyone had finished their meal but Lisa, who could not find her appetite. Bryce paced, holding the cigarette between his lips.

"All right," he spoke up. "We all know it won't be easy." He faced Shannon. "But then nothing ever has been easy living out here. We could move to someplace new, but we all know we can't do that, either—not with Chaco out there with the renegades. If he does get caught and is brought in, he'll need our support. And for various reasons ..." he walked closer to his wife, putting his hands on her shoulders from behind, "we have learned to love this godforsaken land—and the Apaches— and my trading post is doing well. We stay, and that is that." He moved over to Lisa, patting her head. "Now we have an addition to our family, and soon there will be yet another. And nothing anyone does or says outside this family can hurt us or take away the joy of having Chaco's son or daughter in this household. The problem we are left with is that Lisa will soon be showing, and in the eyes of the whites, she is an unmarried girl. I don't like the idea of how men will look at her, what they'll say. If we could leave here, we could make up any story we wanted to keep her and the child from cruel remarks and stares and torment. But we can't leave, so we're in a kind of predicament."

Troy swallowed, then took a deep breath. He could not forget the way the soldiers were looking at Lisa back at the fort. How much worse would it be for her when they found out she was pregnant? His love for his brother and his soft heart combined to give him courage.

"I could marry her," he spoke up.

All three looked at him in surprise. Lisa reddened deeply, as did Troy. He bashfully avoided her eyes and looked at his father.

"Why not? I'm almost nineteen. That's old enough. I wouldn't . . . I wouldn't touch her or anything. It would just be for looks. After the baby is born we could work something out— an annulment or something. Nobody has to know. And around here, who would blame me for marrying the first pretty girl that comes along? She's got no place to go, so it makes sense she'd get married so she'd have a man to take care of her. Next year I'm going east to school to study journalism, so I won't even be around."

"I . . . I couldn't," Lisa spoke up. "I can't just marry somebody I don't love . . . I mean . . . you're very nice, but. . . ."

"You wouldn't have to love me. I'd never expect you to really be my wife." He got up himself then, while Bryce glanced at Shannon, exchanging a look of near shock, both of them turning their eyes back to Troy. He'd just met this girl yesterday and had barely talked to her. Lisa had fallen asleep and slept all the day before and part of this day. Troy never saw her until he came in from chores to eat supper. And now he was offering to be her husband. Now Troy met his father's eyes.

"Tell her, Pa. Tell her she can trust me. I wouldn't do anything to her. She belongs to Chaco. It would be my way of helping Chaco protect her. All she needs is a husband—for looks. That's what I'd be. Nobody would think much of it, and it would stop people from gossip and stares. They don't know what really went on between her and Chaco. They're just guessing."

"You would be taking a wedding vow, Troy," Shannon spoke up. "Swearing before God to love and cherish her for the rest of your life."

He shrugged. "So? That's what I'll do. What's wrong with loving and cherishing your brother's wife? It doesn't mean you have to go to bed ..." He stopped, reddening again. "You know what I mean. Don't the Indians do that? Don't brothers take care of each other's wives? God knows who loves whom, who's really the husband and wife. But all anybody on the outside would understand is a husband and a wedding band. I can give her both."

"I ... I hardly know you," Lisa spoke up, wringing her hands nervously. Troy glanced at her, then looked at the floor. "You don't have to. I mean ... it's not like I'm taking you away someplace. We'd be right here." He looked at his father. "Don't you see? It's the only answer. She needs a husband. Who else could you trust to marry her just for looks?"

Bryce looked carefully from his son to Lisa, who sat quietly staring at her plate, then back to his son. "And what if your own feelings for her grow deeper than you anticipated? The fact that she is your wife could create feelings in you you don't expect. And she *would* be your wife—legally."

Troy met his eyes boldly. "She belongs to my brother. You know better than to ask that, Pa. You know *me* better."

"And what if another girl comes along you really do care for enough to want to marry?"

Troy hesitated, turning away. "Out here? There isn't a lot to pick from, Pa."

"And when you go east? What if you find someone there? You going to say 'sorry, but I'm married to my brother's wife'? I'm sure an eastern girl would understand that."

"Please, stop," Lisa spoke up. She broke into tears. Shannon put a hand on her arm, and Bryce took a long drag on his cigarette. Troy met his eyes squarely.

"Pa, it's the only answer for now. It has to be done quick, before she shows. You know you can trust me. And if anything happens that somehow she and Chaco can be together, we'll dissolve the marriage. Or if . . . if I should find somebody else. I'd just explain it. If some girl I love can't understand it, then she's not worth marrying anyway."

For a moment the room was silent, except for the soft crying of Lisa. Bryce studied this son he had raised, proud of the young man's love for his half brother and his chivalrous attitude, but worried about how easily his own affection could grow for Lisa once she was his wife. The boy had only been with a woman a couple of times, when groups of prostitutes would ride into the fort in wagons to make money off the soldiers. But that kind of sex, Bryce well knew himself, was not satisfying, not like having sex with a good woman that you love deeply. Troy was at an age when most young men had strong desires that were hard to control. But Troy was also an extremely good and trustworthy young man. Bryce took a long drag on his cigarette and then put it out.

"We're forgetting one thing," he said then. "It's Lisa's decision, not ours."

The girl looked at Shannon first.

"Troy is a good son," the woman told her. "I'm sure he's sincere, Lisa. And if he says he would never touch you, he means it. You can stay right here with us, sleep in the loft. Troy usually sleeps over at the trading post anyway."

The girl looked at up the loft. "Did Chaco use to sleep up there?"

Shannon nodded. "Chaco and Troy use to sleep up there

185

together when they were small boys." She blinked back tears. "So many times I've wished it could be that way again."

Lisa looked up at Bryce. "It's up to you," he told her. "I know you're all confused right now, Lisa. Troy's right that it has to be soon, but it doesn't have to be tomorrow. You take a few days to think about it. Talk to Troy. I want you both to think very hard about it. Then you make up your minds. Whatever you decide, we'll support you."

Lisa slowly rose. "I think I'd like to lie down. I'm still tired. And I'm all mixed up."

"Of course you are." Shannon rose and put an arm around her. "You go on up to the loft and I'll bring you some blankets. We're all still like strangers to you, and here we are talking about letting you marry Troy. It all must be so frightening for you."

Lisa faced her. "It isn't that. I feel good here—safe. I already feel like you're my family. I know so much about you, through Chaco. It's mostly, mostly that I can't get used to the thought I might never see him again." Her voice broke and she turned away.

Troy met his father's eyes. "It would work, Pa. I know it would. We'd be all right."

"You're asking a lot of yourself, Troy."

"Maybe. But I've never had to put up with all the hell Chaco has. If I can help him a little, I've got to do it. He wouldn't want people looking at her and whispering about her like they will when she starts showing. They might still talk, but not like they would if she doesn't have a husband. And strangers who don't know us at all would never know the difference." He glanced at Lisa again, then walked to the door. "I'm going for a ride. Maybe tomorrow Mother could fix us kind of a picnic lunch and I could take Lisa down by the river where we could talk."

Bryce nodded. "All right. I think that's a good idea."

Troy went out, stopping for a moment to scan the surrounding hills. His brother was out there alone somewhere, probably more alone than he had ever been, suffering the same loneliness his own father, Saguaro, must have suffered when he had to give up Shannon and their son. If he could help his brother by marrying Lisa, he would do it. There didn't have to be any feelings involved.

Chapter Thirteen

Lisa wore a soft yellow dress that had been Shannon's when Shannon was young, but womanly roundness had made the dress too tight for her now. Many of Lisa's clothes had been lost with her raided wagon, and Shannon was already busy making her new dresses, some with no waist, in preparation for her pregnancy.

Troy carried a basket of food, walking beside Lisa to a river that flowed about a half mile from the trading post but that was a mere trickle now.

"In the spring the river is pretty wide," he explained as they walked. "But this time of year there's not much there. There's lots of wildflowers along the banks, though. I can pick you some if you want. They'll die out soon. Winter's coming."

Lisa glanced at the distant mountains. Chaco had talked of winter, too, and how cold it would be in the mountains. Was he up there? What would winter be like for him? She was in the valley. She would be warm, other than a few chilly days and perhaps one or two snowfalls. How would Chaco spend the lonely winter? Would he have enough to eat?

She moved her eyes to Troy, who was watching her. "You think about him all the time, don't you?"

She reddened and looked ahead again, continuing the walk. "Yes," she answered quietly. "I'm sorry."

Troy shrugged. "Why should you be sorry? He's the father of your baby. You must have loved him a lot. I mean ... you seem like a nice girl. You wouldn't ... I mean ... you know what I mean."

She stopped and looked up at him. "You don't think I'm bad?"

He studied the blue eyes. At times her face seemed like just a child's. She was caught in the "in-between" years of girl and woman, and womanly desires had betrayed the little girl.

"If I thought you were bad, I wouldn't marry you."

In spite of her love for Chaco, she couldn't help but be impressed by Troy Edwards' manly attitude and extreme good looks. He was such an opposite of his brother, with thick, blond hair and soft, gray eyes. She felt led by hands of fate that would leave her no choice in life anymore. First there had been Chaco. Now there was this brother called Troy, offering her security and respect. What would Chaco think of all of this? She felt so trapped, yet she was not afraid, for there was something about Troy Edwards that made her trust him implicitly.

"You're asking a lot of yourself, Troy. We don't even know each other."

"I know my brother loved you and that you're carrying his baby. That's all there is to know. And you know I care about Chaco and want to make sure his woman is respected and watched after."

She reddened and turned away again. "Tell me about yourself, Troy. Have you gone to school? Do they have a school out here?"

"Sure. Near Fort Bowie. I went there till last year. Pa's been saving up to send me east to a special school where I'll learn journalism. I want to be a writer, a reporter."

She smiled. "That sounds exciting. Would you stay and work in the East then?"

They reached a grassy spot near the river and he stopped and spread out a blanket, then set the basket on it. "Here. Sit down." He patted his hand beside him where he had already sat down. She obeyed, but did not sit close. Troy folded his legs and leaned forward, resting his elbows on his knees. "I wouldn't stay in the East," he told her. "I want to come back here and do some honest reporting on the Apaches. Everything you see in the newspapers out here is biased."

Lisa frowned, meeting his eyes again. "Wouldn't that be dangerous?"

He shrugged. "Maybe. But I figure I can give a first-hand account of the Indians' grievances, having lived with Chaco and all. And my mother and father know a lot about them of course, speak their language even. Pa has fought hand to hand with them. He was a colonel out here for a lot of years at Fort Bowie. He knows a lot about the Apaches. He quit the army because he couldn't obey the orders to shoot Indians on sight."

The thought gave Lisa a chill. Poor Chaco! He was in so much constant danger. What a terrible way to live. She looked down at the blanket and picked at a piece of lint. "Wouldn't it be hard to find a newspaper that would print articles in favor of the Indians?"

"Probably. But there's always somebody willing to stick his neck out. If not, I'll start a newspaper of my own."

She met his eyes again. "So you've lived here all your life."

He nodded. "Grew up helping Pa with the trading post and ranch. Used to be just me and Chaco. But when Chaco left, Pa hired a couple of hands." He sobered and stared out at the trickling river. "I miss Chaco a lot. We were close when we were young. We used to lay and talk till all hours of the morning, used to race our horses and wrestle. Chaco was just like the rest of us for a while. But as he got older ... I don't know ... I guess no matter how an Indian is brought up there's just something there that's different, something about the Indian spirit, I guess. He wouldn't let my mother cut his hair and he wouldn't go to school. The other kids made fun of him, and the older he got the worse it got, the harder it got for him to live among whites. Then a couple of white men attacked him when he was camping alone—beat him pretty bad, shot him twice and forced a whole bottle of whiskey down his throat so the next day when he came to he was awful sick. He almost died, first from the whiskey and then from an infection from a leg wound. I think that was the turning point, when he knew he couldn't live with us any more. So he left. It about broke my mother's heart, but she understood."

Lisa toyed with the lint again. "She seems like a wonderful woman, so warm and understanding."

"She is. But she's sure been to hell and back."

Lisa's heart tightened. Already she was beginning to understand that kind of hell. "Your father must also be wonderful—accepting her, marrying her."

"My pa can give a man a pretty bad time when he's angry. He's a good fighter and a brave man. But when it comes to my mother, he's like pudding. He's real good to her, tries to protect her from bad things people still say about her because of Chaco and all, treats her like the respectable lady she is. She comes from a fine family in the South, but they're all dead now and she lost all her property back there."

He swallowed, picking a weed and toying with it. "Lisa, I guess ... I guess that's partly why I offered to marry you. I didn't say anything in front of my mother because it's hard for her to think about those things. But I know the hell she's been through, and how bad it would have been for her if she hadn't had my pa to marry her and be by her side." He twirled the weed in his hand. "I know it's not quite the same with us. I mean ... my mother and Pa, they love each other, knew each other before Saguaro captured my mother. We don't know each other at all. But that doesn't mean we can't pretend in public, that I can't give your baby a name. And he or she would have the right name—Edwards." He shrugged. "Chaco never took

191

a white name, but if he did, it would sure be Edwards. My mother talked once about calling him Charles Edwards if he ever had to take a white name for some kind of registration, or if it would keep him from being put on a reservation. At any rate, you'd have a father for your baby."

"But ... what about later, after the baby. Two years from now? Three years from now?" She pulled off the piece of lint and met his eyes.

He could not help appreciating her beauty. His look gave her an odd warmth. "We can't worry about that now. We can only take a day at a time, Lisa. Maybe something will happen that you can be with Chaco."

"But if I can't ... Troy, you can't go your whole life married to someone who doesn't love you that way—and I can't either. And you'll need a—" She blushed and turned away. "You'll need and want a woman of your own some day, someone who can be a real wife to you. It's only natural."

He studied the golden hair, telling himself to be careful, warning himself that this would be a strictly benevolent act. "We'll worry about that if and when it happens. It's better to be married and divorced than to never have been married at all, isn't it?"

She met his eyes again. "You would have certain rights. I would belong to you."

He shook his head slowly. "You already belong to Chaco. He's my brother, Lisa. I wouldn't take something from my brother, and he wouldn't take from me. And I'd never touch you against your will. I could never do that. You have to trust me. Think of the baby. Besides, like I said, I'll be going off to school in a few months, not long after the baby is born. It will be easier then. When I come back, we can decide what we're going to do. That will give us both lots of time to think it out. In the meantime, you'll have a wedding band and a husband."

A light breeze blew her golden hair over her face. She pushed it back. "What if Chaco should come for me?"

Troy glanced at the surrounding hills. "I know my brother. He won't come."

Lisa's heart tightened with the dread of never seeing Chaco again. "Why? He loves me."

He met the blue eyes. "That's why he won't come. It will be like his Indian father and my mother. Saguaro gave my mother over to my pa because he knew it was best for her. It about killed him to do it, but he loved her enough to know she could never live his way. And now that you're pregnant, and you've been returned to us, Chaco will leave it that way. He knows my folks will take care of you and the baby. It doesn't mean he doesn't love you. It means he loves you very much, enough to give you up."

She blinked back tears, putting a hand to her stomach. "It can't just end . . . just like that. It's like it's all just some strange dream. I don't understand all these things that are happening to me. It's like I can't control my own life any more. All I want is Chaco, and to be able to live in peace someplace where everyone will leave us alone."

She put a hand over her mouth and sniffed, and Troy reached out and touched her arm. "Don't cry, Lisa." He shifted and moved closer. "Listen, I bet somehow, some day, you'll get to see him again, maybe even be together. But the way things are right now, it just can't be. And soon you'll be showing. We've got to decide. I promise I'll be no more than a very good friend. We can be that much, can't we?"

She sniffed and nodded.

"We can worry about all the other later. All we can do is take a day at a time." He squeezed her arm. "Come on. Don't cry. I know you love him and miss him, but you have to think about the baby. You have to eat and stay healthy and not be getting all upset all the time. The baby is the most important thing, right?"

She nodded, taking a handkerchief from the pocket of her dress and blowing her nose. Chaco! Had it all really happened?

She'd given him her virginity, her love, her soul. Now it seemed she walked in a vacuum, caring about nothing, unsure where to turn.

"Tell me about yourself," he told her. "You're from Illinois?"

She nodded again. "A little town called Sweetwater. My father heard talk of gold. He's had so many different jobs. He was the kind of man who could never sit still. My mother didn't want to come out here. If only he'd listened to her." The tears came again and he moved an arm around her shoulder. "My poor mother," she wept. "All that suffering. What a horrible way to spend your last few minutes of life."

Troy squeezed her shoulders. "She's in no pain now, Lisa. She's someplace where it's real pretty and peaceful. And her last prayer was answered when God sent Chaco to keep those men from hurting you. Come on. Talk about something else. What was Sweetwater like? Did you go to school there?"

She wiped at her eyes. "Seventh and eight grade. That's all most people think girls need. I read and write well, but sometimes I wondered about going on to higher learning. But my father, he could never hold a job, and I ended up working to help pay the bills. My mother and I took in sewing and such. Then my father got the wild idea of coming to Arizona. Mother and I wanted to stay behind and wait for him, but he insisted we come too, said he'd be lonely." She sighed deeply. "My life back in Illinois seems a hundred years ago now—a different Lisa Powers. It seems impossible that I should be sitting here, pregnant by an Apache Indian and thinking about marrying his white half brother, whom I barely know." She sniffed and blew her nose again. "It's all so incredible."

"Well, you'll sure have lots to tell your grandchildren about, right?"

She couldn't help but smile, then turned to face him. She was close, so close. He was tempted to kiss her yet knew he dared not, and again he reminded himself he was to have no such feelings for this young woman.

"You have such a wonderful outlook on life, Troy," she told him.

He shrugged, giving her a light squeeze before letting go of her and moving back a little. "So, see what a good friend I can be? You need anything, Lisa, anything at all, and I'll help you. You just name it."

She thought of Chaco. Chaco was what she needed. She studied him for a moment as he lay back. He was lean and muscular, a beautiful young man, a young man she might have been very attracted to if she hadn't already been made a woman by the darker and equally handsome Chaco. It was Chaco who owned her heart now. It could never belong to anyone else.

"Do you really think he'll never come, Troy?"

He looked at her silently for several long seconds. "He won't come, Lisa."

Her eyes teared again. It was too much to bear, all these changes in her life. She opened the picnic basket, staring at the checkered cloth inside. "What if I lose the baby, Troy? It would all have been for nothing."

He raised upon one elbow. "It would never be for nothing. Either way, it would look best if you married me. Even without the baby, people will talk. I told you, Lisa, just take one day at a time. Don't think about the maybes. This is here and now. You're pregnant and I'm willing to marry you. I'm the only one you can trust to marry you and not offend you."

She closed her eyes and sighed. "It's all so crazy. Maybe . . . maybe your father could take me back to Chaco. . ."

Troy let out a long sigh before she finished, laying his head back. "He'd never do that, and Chaco wouldn't want him to."

"But . . . what if Chaco comes himself and takes me away, sneaks in at night when he wouldn't be caught?"

This time Troy closed his eyes. "I've told you over and over. He won't come, Lisa."

195

Her heart pounded with the dread of truth. "But it's only been six days since I was last with him. I ... I can't get it all right in my head, Troy, and I can't comprehend never seeing him again. Surely it can't all be over so quickly. A few days ago I slept beside him." She looked away, swallowing back tears. "Just a few days ago. We were so happy. We were going to spend the winter alone in the mountains. Chaco couldn't take me south with the others because they thought I was bad luck. So we stayed behind. He actually ... deserted his people ... for me. I've ... given myself to him ... and now he's gone ... like he was a ghost or something."

Her words broke. She wondered if she would ever get over the shock of it all, ever be able to accept not being able to be with Chaco. She'd known all along it could probably never last, yet the reality of it was so painful. In the next moment Troy was beside her again, and she leaned back against his chest, hoping to somehow find some little comfort in the arms of Chaco's brother.

"He *is* like a ghost, Lisa," he said quietly. "He always has been. They all are, the Apaches, I mean. You can't find them any easier than you can see and find the wind. Look at Geronimo. They're talking about sending thousands of soldiers to search for him, and he's just got a handful of people with him. Most of the Apaches are already at San Carlos. You have to face what he is, Lisa, and the fact that the most he can ever hope for now is to be found innocent of any crimes if he's caught, which isn't likely. And if he is, they'll probably still put him in prison for a while, just for being a renegade. After that it will be the reservation, unless my folks can pull some strings. You could never live like that. And even if my folks could get him freed, which is very unlikely, he couldn't live like we do any more. He's been wild for too long, he can't stand the way he's treated in our world. And he'd not want you living forever the way he needs to live. Any way you look at it, you can't be with my brother. The reality is you can't be together again, but

196

you're carrying his baby and that's that. At least you have that much."

She covered her face with her hands and wept. "I . . . don't think I can stand it," she sobbed. "I've lost too much . . . too fast."

He hesitantly petted her hair. "You can stand it. You're strong like my mother. I can see it. She's been through things a whole lot worse, Lisa. I don't know how much Chaco told you about her, but she can help you. She's been through all of it and more."

"But . . . she had your father to help her."

"I know. And I can help you—not quite the same way—but I can be your friend and love you like part of the family, which is what you are. And you have my mother, and my father, and soon you'll have Chaco's baby. It will all seem better then. You'll see."

She pulled away then, surprised she had leaned against him and had found it so easy to do. "I bet you're tired of me bawling all the time," she told him, her voice shaking. "I'll try not to the rest of the day." She quickly wiped at her eyes and nose as he watched with sympathetic gray eyes. "I bet you'd like to eat some of the chicken your mother cooked for us."

He smiled softly. "Sounds good to me. Are you a good cook?"

She dabbed at her eyes once more. "Pretty good." She met his eyes then, begging him with her look to be patient with her. "You're quite a person, Troy. I already have great affection for you just because I can see how much you love Chaco. I realize you're giving up some of your own freedom for him."

He scooted over to his original spot and took a pipe from his pocket, as well as some tobacco with which to stuff it. "Chaco was always special to me," he told her. "I always looked up to him, admired his freedom and courage. We were together the day he met Cochise for the first time."

"Cochise! I've heard all kinds of stories about him back east before we ever came out here."

197

Troy lit the pipe. "He died about seven or eight years ago. It was real hard on Chaco. He was only about thirteen or fourteen at the time, and he all but worshiped the man after he'd met him. I guess it was Cochise who first planted ideas in Chaco's head about living with the Apache. He had quite an effect on Chaco. Chaco was never quite the same after that. He was harder to reach, harder to reason with, rode off alone a lot. I think he's always wished he could have known his real father. He told me he saw him once—Saguaro's spirit spoke to him."

He puffed his pipe a moment while Lisa put a piece of chicken onto a tin plate for him. "I wish I could grasp that, that Indian spirit. It's like they know things we whites will never know, like they can talk to the earth and the animals and the sun. They're as much a part of the land as the wild things. People like us, we're foreigners here." He puffed the pipe again. "That's one of the things I'd like to write about. What gives us the right to come here and claim this is our land and the Indians have to give it up? They were here first. If somebody else came along and tried to take away what we have, we'd fight tooth and nail for it. But when the Indians do it, we say they're bad and should be imprisoned. Just because they have something we want, we make them the bad guys and say everything they do is wrong."

He looked at her to see she was studying him intently. "You're very brave to want to point out those things, Troy." She swallowed, suddenly captured by his gray eyes and his sympathy for the Apaches. She finally tore her eyes from his and took out another piece of chicken. "I will marry you, next Sunday," she told him then. "And even though ... even though we won't be man and wife in the full sense, I will be proud to call you my husband in public."

She felt her cheeks turning crimson as she casually tried to bite into a piece of chicken.

"And I'll be proud to call you my wife," he answered quietly. He set his pipe aside and picked up his own plate of chicken.

"You're learning the real truth about the West, Lisa. Nothing out here is like back east. Strange things happen, and they happen fast. Out here the first word is survival. You have to be practical about things, and old rules and manners don't always hold. First comes survival—above all other things. My mother was a survivor and so are you."

He set his plate down a moment again, reaching out and touching her arm, and she turned to meet his eyes. "And you'll never regret marrying me, Lisa. I swear to God I'll never offend you or make demands on you. We'll just take a day at a time and see what happens. And if we end up continuing on together, I'll be a good father to your baby."

He let go of her arm and picked up his plate, then met her eyes again, giving her a brilliant smile and a wink. Again she thought how wonderful he would have been to meet, if there had been no Chaco. But there had been a Chaco and he would be her first love for the rest of her life. She picked up her own chicken, but again she could find no appetite. All she could think of was the quick words she and Chaco had had that morning they parted—no time to make love once more, no time for the right words, just running and shooting and a burning wickiup. Burning! Burning up their love, their memories, their sweet life together, burning in her nostrils until she wanted to die.

But she could not die. She was carrying Chaco's child, and she would have that child, even if it meant having to marry a near stranger to make it legitimate.

Chapter Fourteen

Shannon walked out onto the porch, where Lisa stood staring out at the mountains to the south. Troy headed for the barn to brush down some horses. Lisa watched him a moment, then turned when Shannon touched her shoulder. Shannon moved her own eyes to the southern mountains then, putting an arm around Lisa's waist.

"It does no good to yearn for him, Lisa," she spoke up. "Men like Chaco are always just beyond your reach. You will have to learn what I taught myself, to be grateful for the special memories I have, to know I loved a man who was lonely and needed loving, and that I wanted and tried to stay with him, but that it was impossible. I don't regret any of it. It was so hard to accept at first, but I had my Chaco, and you'll have your own baby."

Lisa put a hand to her stomach again. "What if it's a boy and he ends up wanting to be Apache like Chaco. I could never watch my son ride out of my life."

"All mothers have that to face, Indian or white. A man must go his own way. But as far as being Indian, your son will be more white than Indian, and by the time he grows up the Apache way of life will be no more. Their days are numbered. At least you will have more of a chance keeping your son than I had keeping mine. But there will always be a certain spirit about him that will separate him from you, even if he's right under your own roof. You'll just have to accept that, too."

Lisa watched Troy come out of the barn leading a horse. "I've had to accept so many changes in my life so quickly. I feel so tired, so lost."

Shannon gave her a hug. "I know that feeling. But you're so young, Lisa. You will learn to live with all of it. Things have a way of working out, and time heals many things. You just have to believe me when I tell you that if you are patient, the hurt will heal. It's all a matter of time. There are moments when I wanted to die, even though I had Bryce. I know you don't have that, but you do have Troy, and me and my husband. We will see you through all of this." She shook her head. "I just wish Chaco had used better sense in the first place. He must have known it could never last."

Lisa watched a hawk flying in the distance. "He knew. We both knew. It just didn't seem to matter."

Shannon smiled sadly. "We tend to ignore reality when it comes to love. Love and common sense just don't seem to go together."

Lisa nodded. "Sometimes it hurts so bad, Mrs. Edwards."

Shannon patted her side. "No more 'Mrs. Edwards.' It's Shannon. And Bryce is Bryce. We will soon be your in-laws."

Lisa turned and met her eyes again. "Aren't you a little resentful? I mean ... it isn't an easy thing Troy is doing. He's your son, too. It just doesn't seem fair to him."

Shannon studied the pretty face. Yes, it would be easy for her Indian son to fall for such a beauty. "Troy is almost nineteen, still young but man enough to make his own decisions. If he wants to do this for his brother, I won't stop him. You and the baby are all that is important for now. Troy knows that. I just hope..." Her eyes turned almost to pleading. "Be careful, Lisa. I don't want him to get hurt. Don't feel ... obligated sometime in the future ... to be a wife to him sexually, unless you really care for him. If you ever give yourself to him out of some kind of gratefulness, it would be a mistake. He has such a soft heart. He would fall in love with you, and when a man is in love he likes to think he is first in the woman's heart. I have always made sure Bryce knows he is first in my heart, even though I loved Saguaro dearly. It is possible to love two men, but you must be so very careful."

Lisa had blushed at the words, but she understood why the woman spoke them. She was trying to protect her son. She turned away. "I could never give myself to another man without loving him," she answered. "I wouldn't hurt Troy. I don't want anyone else unless it's Chaco."

Shannon folded her arms then, sitting on the porch railing. "You feel that way now because your love for Chaco is still so fresh. But you are very young, and eventually certain needs will awaken inside and you will look at Troy differently. He is a wonderful young man, and extremely handsome. Just make sure that if you ever consummate your marriage, it is out of love and devotion, something permanent, not gratefulness or a moment of just needing a man. I know my words seem bold, but I've been through it all, Lisa. There was a time when I had to make a choice, between Saguaro and Bryce. I chose Saguaro, even though I already loved Bryce and had promised once to marry him. I've never told anyone this, but back in Virginia, before I ever came out here, Bryce and I made love. We were very young and we weren't married yet. But we knew we were going to be separated for a while and passion won out."

Lisa looked at her in surprise, realizing it was almost an honor that this woman was confiding something so personal.

"Then all the rest happened. At the time Saguaro captured me, I had been led to believe Bryce was dead. I thought Saguaro was all I had. I got pregnant, and then Saguaro and his band were captured by soldiers. Bryce was in command. I found out he was still alive and I had to make a choice. I had just had Saguaro's baby, and I couldn't bear taking the child from

202

his father. So I chose Saguaro, knowing it could not last much longer and wanting his last days to be happy ones. Bryce let us go."

Tears formed in her eyes, and she looked down. "For the rest of my life I will never forget the look on Bryce's face as we rode away. I have never seen such hurt, such loneliness." She looked back at Lisa. "I would hate to see that kind of hurt on Troy's face. Both of my sons have suffered in their own ways. I hope that both of them will find happiness eventually."

Lisa held her eyes. "I won't hurt him, Mrs.—I mean, Shannon."

Shannon smiled sadly, taking her hands. "The circuit preacher will be by here Sunday. I have the prettiest blue material. I'd like to make you a new dress. And we'll make a cake."

They went inside, two women who had known the pain of loving men they could not have; two women who well knew the hardships of living in an untamed and lawless land.

Lisa clung to Troy's arm to keep from falling. Would her shaking legs last? What was she doing? How had she come to this? She repeated the marriage vows almost absently, able only to envision Chaco—their last night together, the wonder of being his woman. But this was Troy slipping a ring on her finger, now saying the vows to her in return, so sincerely that one would think he really meant it. Was it a sin to make these vows before God just for appearances? Would she go to hell for it?

Troy squeezed her hand, bringing her back to reality. She met the soft gray eyes.

"You may kiss the bride," the preacher was saying.

Their eyes held almost in surprise. Troy winked, as though to remind her they had better make this look real. His face became blurred as he bent down and met her lips gently, surprising her with a wonderful kiss that was more pleasant that she would have liked. He embraced her then.

"It's all right," he whispered in her ear.

Now the preacher was congratulating them. Shannon hugged her. Then Bryce hugged her. Cake and coffee were served. The hired hands were invited to share in the eating, and they all congratulated them both. If any of them had insulting thoughts about any of it, none of them showed it. Lisa suspected that was due to Bryce Edwards, who would probably fire them on the spot if they made one bad remark. There was considerable visiting, and the day passed quickly.

Then they all were gone. Lisa and Shannon changed into simpler dresses and made supper while the men went back to their chores. But several minutes later Troy was back inside looking sheepishly at his mother, then moving his eyes to Lisa.

"The men are making fun, about tonight and my new bride and all."

Lisa reddened and set some plates on the table.

"That's to be expected, Troy," Shannon told him.

"I know, but . . . I just realized . . . if this is going to look real . . . I mean . . . maybe for a night or two you and Pa should sleep in the back room at the trading post and leave me and Lisa alone in the house."

Lisa turned away, her heart beating more quickly. Could she trust him? Could she truly trust him?

Shannon sighed, wiping her hands on an apron. "I see what you mean. Yes, I suppose you're right. It would be only natural for us to leave our newlywed son alone on his wedding night. Did you say anything to Bryce?"

"We already talked about it. He said he doesn't mind sleeping over at the post." He looked at Lisa, whose back was turned. "Is it all right, Lisa?"

She fidgeted with a loaf of bread, slowly slicing it. "Of course," she answered quietly. "We're supposed to be married, aren't we? If we don't stay alone together, they'll talk, maybe start figuring it all out." She sniffed. "It's all so silly, isn't it? One could almost . . . laugh." Her voice choked. "This certainly isn't what I used to dream . . . about the day I got married."

Shannon shook her head. "If Chaco were here, I would thrash him good."

The room hung silent for a moment, and Troy shoved his hands in his pockets, feeling awkward, wishing there were some way to comfort Lisa, already feeling protective and responsible. Then Lisa laughed lightly, surprising both of them. She sniffed and wiped at her eyes, turning to look at Shannon.

"I just tried to picture you thrashing a twenty-one-year-old wild Apache man. He's not exactly a little boy any more."

She covered her mouth and laughed again, and Shannon's sober face also broke into a grin, as did Troy's.

"Mother still thinks she can turn us over her knee," Troy spoke up, laughing louder. "Imagine! Mother going after Chaco with a stick."

The two women broke into even harder laughter and Bryce walked in, totally surprised by the frivolity, fully expecting just the opposite. "What did I miss?" he asked.

Troy ran a hand through his hair. "Mother is going to give Chaco a licking the next time she sees him," he answered. "He's been a bad boy."

He sat down and laughed harder, as did Lisa, who wiped tears that were a mixture of leftover weeping and now laughing from her eyes. Bryce chuckled at the picture of his small wife chastising her grown Indian son. He looked at Troy then. "I take it the matter of who will sleep where is settled?"

Troy nodded, trying to control his laughter. "It's all settled, Pa. Lisa and I will stay alone in the house for a couple of nights."

The mood of the evening remained a little lighter, and soon after supper Bryce and Shannon left, Bryce giving his son a rather warning look before leaving. The house was suddenly quieter, an awkward silence penetrating every corner. Lisa

205

walked to a rocker beside the hearth and picked up some knitting. How strange this all was.

Troy came over and sat down across from her, taking out a pipe. "Normally I'd go out and do more chores after supper, but they'll be expecting me to stay in with my new bride," he spoke up. He lit the pipe.

Lisa stared at the knitting. "All my life I dreamed about the day I married, about how wonderful it would be, a church wedding with all my friends and family. I tried to imagine what my wedding night would be like."

Her cheeks flushed, and Troy struggled to ignore how pleasant it would be to truly make her his bride. But he had vowed that he would remain simply her friend, someone to protect her and the baby from the cruelty of the outside world.

"Lots of things don't work out like we picture them."

He puffed the pipe and she met his eyes. "Oh, Troy, I'm being so selfish," she told him. "Surely you've thought the same things, thought about finding just the right girl and making her wedding night nice for her. I'm sorry to always be talking about my own misfortune in this."

He smiled obligingly. "Well, it won't be easy for either one of us. But we'll manage." He picked up a pad of paper that he always kept nearby, then dipped a quill pen into some ink and began writing. Lisa began knitting, and for nearly an hour the only sound was the ticking of a clock on the mantle of the fireplace. Finally Troy looked over at her. "What are you making?"

"A sweater and stockings for the baby. Then I'll make a blanket, if we can find the right yarn. Bryce ordered some."

He sat back a moment. "I could take you to the fort tomorrow, show you off, buy a few supplies. Might as well start setting people straight."

She bit her lip "I don't know. It frightens me to go there. Those men, they were so cruel. I wouldn't want to see that Colonel Blazer again."

"I'll be with you. You don't have to be afraid."

She met the gray eyes again, stirred by his strength and determination. She smiled. "All right. Maybe we should go at that." She swallowed. "They can't make me answer any more questions, can they?"

"I won't let them near you."

She blinked back tears. "Thanks, Troy." She sighed and set aside her knitting. "What are you writing?"

He shrugged. "Oh, I'm just fiddling with some thoughts."

"Can I see?"

"I suppose. It won't make a lot of sense." He handed over the tablet and she scanned the writing.

"Apaches people, too," she read. "Feel pain, love, hate, revenge, fear. Have right to love, right to protect their own. Spiritual. White man could learn much from Indian." The writing moved to a short poem. "Feel the wind, rising, falling, rising again. It is the heart of the Indian. Feal the raindrops, wet and warm. They are the tears of the Indian. Hear the wolf, howling its sorrow. It is the voice of the Indian. Touch the earth, the plants. They are the body of the Indian. Feel the sun on your skin. It is the spirit of the Indian. There is nothing separate between nature and the Indian. All are one. It is a special oneness the white man cannot know without forgetting his own pride and selfishness and letting go so that he is like a child, new and innocent. That is what the Indian is like, in spite of how he appears to the white man in all his savageness. He is just a child, open to what is true and important in his life, ignoring the frivolous lust and greed of the white man."

She moved her eyes to meet his, realizing he'd been watching her carefully and that he felt self-conscious about the writing. "Troy, that's beautiful. Chaco would love it."

"You think so?"

"I know so." She smiled. "You're going to be a famous journalist some day, perhaps write books, too."

He smiled bashfully, taking back the tablet. "First I have to go east. There are places and things I've never even seen. I've spent my whole life right here. I've never even seen a big city. But I'm going to."

It suddenly hurt to think of him leaving, but she knew he must, and she also knew she had no right to ever ask him to stay, even though he was her husband. He had done enough just by giving her his name.

"You might get away from here and never come back," she told him then.

He shook his head. "I don't think so." He rose from the chair, setting his pipe aside. "Thanks for what you said about the writing. Maybe I'll let you read more of my stuff."

"Oh, I would like that very much." She rose also, and their eyes held a moment.

"Well, I guess we might as well get some sleep. It's been a long day."

She nodded, turning away and going to the loft ladder. "Good night, Troy," she said quietly.

"Night." He watched her climb the ladder, then walked into his parents' bedroom and undressed. He cursed the stupid urgings he felt for her just because she was now his wife and decided that as soon as a new wagonful of prostitutes came to Fort Bowie, he'd pay them a visit, if he could do it without anyone knowing. He lay back on the bed, staring up at the ceiling, above which she lay in the loft. Did she sleep with nothing on under her gown? He rolled over, feeling guilty for the thought. Perhaps it would not have been so bad if he hadn't been forced to kiss her in front of the preacher. It had been a much nicer kiss than he had anticipated. Her lips were full and beautiful, and they had known man. How much would it take to reawaken the womanly needs his brother had awakened in her?

He made a fist and pounded it into the pillow. That was a stupid, crude thought! She was a nice girl and she belonged to Chaco. She was his brother's woman. Once he got used to living this way and got over the newness of the marriage, he would be all right. Tomorrow he would take her to the fort and they would have a good time putting on a show for everyone of being the happy newlyweds. That would shut their mouths!

In the loft Lisa climbed into her own bed. She liked this place because Chaco had once slept here. She curled up, listening to the ticking clock. Downstairs Troy cleared his throat, and her heart tightened. Could she truly go to sleep, alone in the house with a man who was rightfully her husband? Would she wake up in the middle of the night to find him clawing at her and making demands? No. Surely not Troy. She closed her eyes, and pure exhaustion brought the much-needed sleep. When she awoke it was morning and there was movement downstairs. She quickly rose, pulling on a robe and looking down from the loft. Troy turned with a pot of coffee and caught her watching him.

"Good morning," he told her, raising the coffeepot. "Is this any way to treat your new husband—making him get breakfast?"

Her eyes widened. "Oh! I'll be right down." He wore only pants and no shirt, and she could not help noticing the magnificent physique. He was truly a beautiful young man, both in looks and in spirit. She turned to dress and could hear him laughing lightly. She breathed a sigh of relief. He would keep his promise, and she was beginning to love him like a brother and a friend. Thank God Chaco had this wonderful family to whom she could turn. She would do like Troy had said and take one day at a time now. That was all she could do.

The days turned into weeks, then months. A Christmas dance was held at the home of a neighboring rancher, and Troy insisted on attending, even though Lisa's stomach was large with child.

"You're sitting around too much," he told her. "You need to get out and so do I. It will be fun."

Lisa had to agree it would be nice to see some other people, and Bryce and Shannon were also going. In spite of stares and gossip from many, there were others who were kind and friendly to Shannon and with whom she had made friends and exchanged visiting and recipes.

"It will be fun," Bryce assured Lisa. "They always bring in a big pine tree from the mountains and decorate it."

"But I can't dance in this condition."

"Sure you can." Troy immediately pulled her out of her chair and put an arm around her, taking her other hand and whirling her around the room as he hummed. Everyone laughed, including, finally, Lisa herself.

"I feel like a cow," she told Troy.

"Well, you're a very pretty cow then."

Their eyes held for a moment, a flicker of more than just friendship there. He wondered if she realized the agony he suffered keeping his promise to her. It had been harder than he thought it would be. She in turn was feeling more and more guilty for keeping him from leading the life of a normal young man. Surely there would be a few other young girls at the dance. Maybe they weren't all beautiful, but his natural instincts must be to savor a little of each of them and perhaps steal a kiss behind a tree.

A couple of times he had visited the fort and was gone all night with no explanation. She did not ask questions. But one of those times she'd heard one of the hired hands talking about the prostitutes who were camped outside Fort Bowie. Why the thought had brought a painful jealousy, she could not explain. She had no right to be jealous or expect him to be true to her in any way. He was a man with needs, and her heart was still so full of Chaco. Yet because of Troy Edwards' goodness and attention, she could not help having feelings for him. She wondered how many people married without love then fell in love later. Was such a thing possible? And yet everything about Chaco was still so uncertain. They had not heard from him, and

210

she knew she could never be with him again. Still, she could not help the faint hope that somehow she could.

"You are going, and that is that," Troy told her. "Your husband has spoken."

She bowed slightly. "As you wish."

As they laughed together, out in the hills a group of renegades gathered, having come down from the mountains because of an early snowstorm. They shivered in their too-light clothing, and their stomachs ached from hunger.

"It is too dangerous," Coyotero spoke up to Chaco.

"We have no choice. The women and children are starving. All the food is down here in the valley where the white men are. They have it all! The bastards! Their stomachs are full and ours are empty! They kill our game, cut our trees for warmth, they even steal from the reservation Indians, giving them bad meat and keeping the good! Now our people starve. We have to raid some of the settlements, find some food and take it back into the mountains."

"Soldiers are everywhere now."

"I am not afraid of a few soldiers. Geronimo is counting on us. The people are counting on us. Just do not go near my father's trading post." He walked away from the light of their campfire, and Coyotero followed.

"What about the white girl?" he asked. "Will you go down and try to find her?"

Chaco turned to face him in the moonlight. "No. Even if I found her, I would leave her there. She is where she belongs, and I am where I belong. It is over."

"Is it?"

"I told you it was! Why do you always ask about it!"

"Because you are not the same Chaco. You are more full of hatred than ever before, and I know your heart is heavy for the white girl. She burns in you like the hot sun."

211

"I have no more interest in her."

"Then prove it by marrying Little Deer. If you do not speak for her by the next full moon, I will! I am tired of waiting to see what you will do, and I do not need to. I only do so because we are friends."

Chaco stiffened, glad Coyotero could not see the tears in his eyes. "I will ask for her when we return. She will be my wife and that will be the end of it."

Coyotero nodded. "Good." He headed back to the others, and Chaco turned away again, his chest heaving in deep breathing to stay in control. Lisa! How he still loved her! How he missed her! But that moment in his life was over forever. The worst part was he might never see his child. Where was she now? Was she with his parents? Was she all right? Did she still carry the baby? How he longed to go down and see her, but it would be wrong to do so. It would only make everything harder on both of them. It was done. There was no going back and no going forward. There was only existence and survival. He would marry Little Deer, who still faithfully waited for him. She would be a good wife, and perhaps by relieving himself in the night with her he could rid his soul of the fiery desire he still carried for Lisette Powers.

Chapter Fifteen

"Do you really think it's his baby?" one woman asked another.

"They certainly act as though it is. But it was an awfully sudden marriage, right after the girl was returned from captivity."

'Oh, but we've seen quick marriages out here before. She was homeless. I'm sure Troy Edwards would never have married her if she was pregnant by an Indian, even if it was his own brother! No man would do that. He's such a pleasant young man, so handsome and intelligent. He would have better sense than that."

"Surely he would. I could understand the mother letting the girl live with them if it was Chaco's child, but they certainly would not have let their white son marry her."

"They do look happy."

Troy danced slowly to the fiddled waltz. "You all right?"

"I'm having more fun than I thought I would," Lisa answered. "Thank you for bringing me."

"My pleasure," he said with a wink. "Besides, I enjoy watching the ladies talk behind their punch."

Lisa laughed lightly. "I noticed, too. They haven't seen me

for a while. I'm awfully big for supposedly only being five months along, Troy. How do we explain the early birth?''

"Simple. An early birth.''

She smiled. "You know what I mean.''

"As long as we stick to our stories all the way through, there will be no problem.''

"And if the baby looks Indian?''

He frowned. "My father's mother was quite dark, so he tells me. His father was the blond one. Somehow the dark blood finally came through.''

The school teacher, Thomas Greggory, approached Shannon and Bryce, who stood at the side watching the dancers. He grinned, greeting them by raising a glass of punch. "Good evening.''

Bryce watched him carefully. "Hello, Tom.''

"I was just wondering when and if Troy will go on to school in the East. He's very bright, you know. I thought he would have gone by now.''

"Well, with a new wife and all, and with Lisa expecting, he's waiting until the baby comes.''

Greggory's eyebrows raised. "Of course.'' He glanced over at the couple. "Looks as though the two of them wasted no time.'' He looked at Bryce challengingly, and Bryce's gray eyes narrowed.

"You know youthful passion, or didn't you ever experience it yourself?''

Greggory reddened slightly, quelling an urge to make a remark about Lisa. "I seem to remember something of that.'' His eyes moved to Shannon, then back to Bryce, and both knew what the man was thinking. "But then it's been years for all of us, hasn't it?''

Bryce put an arm around Shannon. "For some of us it never ends,'' he answered.

"Bryce!'' Shannon reddened, but Bryce held Tom Greggory's eyes.

214

"Troy is a very happily married man, Tom, and all your fine teaching will pay off when he goes to college. You'll see. He'll return an accomplished journalist. He might even make a name for himself some day.'

"I'm sure he will. You've brought him up well. It's too bad your other son didn't stay and get his eduction. He'd be much better off."

"Maybe," Bryce answered. "He was, and is, also a fine young man, in his own way. He tried to do it right, Tom. People around here wouldn't let him."

"Well, there doesn't seem to be much future for him, does there? It's too bad. You know Crook is preparing a campaign to get Geronimo, don't you?"

"Of course I know. I would appreciate you covering a different subject in front of my wife. Or you can take your conversation someplace else."

Greggory reddened and moved his eyes to Shannon. "My apologies, Mrs. Edwards. I . . ."

His words were interrupted by the sound of gunfire and the yipping and calling of Indians outside. Horses began circling the huge barn where the dance was being held, their hooves thundering in a terrifying warning. Everyone knew only one kind of people could make the noises they were hearing now.

"Apaches!" A man came running inside. "They're all over the place!"

The music stopped and a few women screamed. Lisa's heart jumped with a combination of fear and anticipation. Would they be those Apaches who knew Chaco? Would they remember her? What on earth were they doing here at all?

They were supposed to be in hiding in the mountains. Troy pulled her back with others as already some warriors charged right into the barn on horseback before the men could get the doors closed. Most of the whites inside didn't even have weapons on them, and those who did didn't have time to show them before several young Apaches scattered among the crowd, bran-

215

dishing rifles and forcing the crowd to move back by riding up next to them. Most did not understand the shouted Apache words, but they did understand the threatening gestures and they all obeyed, wanting to get as far away and be as inconspicuous as possible. Were they here to kidnap someone for ransom? A few little children began to cry.

Outside several warriors were already riding off with stolen horses, Inside, while certain ones moved their horses around the circle of people, others began grabbing food from the tables—biscuits, bread, tubs of butter, pies—throwing most of the food into parfleches.

"Filthy, thieving heathens," someone from the crowd growled.

Shannon only watched in pity. She could see they were hungry, most of them lean, too lean, in spite of their hard-muscled bodies. Their faces were gaunt. Their ribs showed. They were starving, and she knew already they had only come for food and fresh horses to continue their hiding.

Two more Apaches came inside then, and Shannon gasped. "Chaco," she whispered. She started forward and Bryce grabbed her tightly.

"Don't make a move, damn it! The others don't know you. And don't say his name!"

Her heart raced. Her son! Her son! So long it had been since she had seen him. If only she could go to him! Hold him! Yet it seemed incredible it was he at all. He wore buckskin leggings and a leather vest, his chest adorned with shell and turquoise beads, copper bands on his arms. His hair hung nearly to his waist, and was brightly decorated with feathers and beads. His face was painted with red and black stripes as though for war. He was as fierce looking as the others, perhaps more so. And in him she saw Saguaro. Never had the likeness been so evident as it was now, and it tore at her heart.

Chaco's dark eyes stared at her in surprise at first. He had not expected to run into his own family here. But what was

216

done was done. He looked almost sorry, and he longed to go to her as she did to go to him. He dismounted, leading his horse near them. His eyes darted to Bryce. "Keep her still," he said quietly in English so his Apache friends would not understand. "Do nothing. They will kill you if you do. They are hungry—and angry."

He whirled then, grabbing some of the food, while some of the others moved among the crowd, stealing shawls, hats, a few jackets. So much had happened at once that it was only then that Lisa noticed Chaco. Her heart nearly stopped, as she stared wide-eyed at him. Chaco! Troy noticed him at the same time and squeezed her arm.

"Don't do it," he told her quietly. "Don't you dare say a word, especially not his name."

One of the other warriors came closer, looking Lisa over. She was pretty—and pregnant. As such, perhaps she was worth something—guns, gold, food. If not, her baby could be adopted into the tribe and the woman could be sold to Mexicans or made into a fine slave for himself. He suddenly grasped her hair and yanked her forward.

Lisa screamed and Troy lunged at the young Indian.

"Keep your hands off my wife, you son of a bitch," he shouted, forcing the Indian to let go of Lisa and knocking him to the ground. They rolled for a moment, then got to their feet, and people gasped as the young warrior pulled a knife, grinning with the thought of killing this white man. In the next moment Chaco was there, standing between them. He tossed his head toward Troy.

"Shik'isn!" He growled the word, meaning "brother" in Apache.

The other Indian glowered at Troy for a moment, then pointed to Lisa. Chaco turned and their eyes held. Lisa wondered if she would faint. He was beautiful, but he looked so tired and hungry. Oh, how she longed to run to him, but she could do nothing. Not here. And he must leave quickly. There was too much danger. His eyes moved to her stomach, then to Troy who moved to stand protectively beside her. Troy had called her his wife. He glanced at her hand. A wedding band. He struggled to show no emotion. Never had the air been so tense as the three of them felt it that moment.

The other Indian started for Lisa and Chaco's arm shot out hard against his chest before he could get close. His dark eyes drilled into the other Indian's eyes. "Shiyee," Chaco spat at him. "Shiyee!"

Bryce and Shannon recognized the Apache word for "mine." Shannon's heart raced. What would Chaco do? What was he thinking? The second Indian man backed up and turned away, going back to the table and collecting more food, while the other Indians continued to guard the crowd. Women whimpered and cowered and men were sweating. No one wanted to be an Apache captive.

Chaco turned his dark eyes back to Lisa, who was now beginning to cry. His chest hurt with the longing for her, the sight of her swollen belly. Wife. Troy had called her wife. Of course. What else could they do? But how much of a wife was she to him? He glanced at Troy and Lisa's eyes suddenly filled with sadness. He had lost so much. Oh, how she still loved him! How she longed to tell him so!

For a moment Troy wondered what he would do. Then Chaco nodded, his now watery eyes moving to Lisa once more before he whirled and shouted something to the others. The warriors began backing out of the barn then, their bags filled with food and clothing. Suddenly there was a commotion on Chaco's right, and he turned to see Bryce struggling with a man who held a gun. Bryce wrested the gun from the man and shoved him aside, then looked straight at Chaco.

"Get going," he shouted.

Chaco hesitated, realizing his stepfather had just saved his life. A million childhood memories passed through his mind in a flash, and he looked at Bryce lovingly and apologetically, then at his mother once more.

"Shimaa. Doo baa shil gozhqq da." He turned and quickly left, and Shannon closed her eyes against the tears. "My mother," he had said. "I am sorry."

Everyone stood almost frozen in place as they listened to the fading sound then of thundering horses. The Apaches were leaving, disappearing into the darkness like the ghosts they were.

"What's the idea stopping me like that?" the man with the gun shouted to Bryce then. "I could have got one of them!"

"It was his stepson, I'll bet," someone else spoke up. "The half-breed Chaco. He's a renegade and he slipped right out from under us!"

"If anyone had shot one of them we'd have all been slaughtered," Bryce shouted back angrily. "It would have been very foolish!"

"You're just an Indian lover," someone yelled.

Lisa covered her face and turned to Troy, who took her into his arms soothingly. Chaco! Chaco! It was all reawakened. All the love and desire. All the memories. But he'd looked and acted so wild. It had never been more clear to her that they could never live together forever. Troy, Bryce, Shannon, and Chaco himself—they had all been right. But the truth was devastating. Troy felt her weakening in his arms.

"Come on. I'll take you home," he told her.

Men were running around, shouting orders to get the women to their homes and form a posse. "Maybe we can catch a few of the bastards," someone yelled.

"They're just hungry," Shannon told one woman, grabbing her as she went by. "Couldn't you see that?"

"Good! They can starve to death as far as I'm concerned," the woman answered. "I'm sorry one of them is your son, Mrs. Edwards. He must have been, the way he looked at you. But that doesn't erase what they've done! We can't even hold a

Christmas dance without the threat of those savages coming in here and murdering and stealing!"

"But they didn't murder anyone!"

The woman looked at her scathingly and hurried on with the others. Everything was bedlam, women carrying on, children crying, men shouting orders. Shannon and Bryce hurried over to Lisa and Troy.

"Oh, dear God, poor Lisa," Shannon spoke up. "Let's get her home."

Thomas Greggory came up to Bryce. "If I were you, I'd take that job you were offered up at San Carlos," he told the man. "If you're so fond of the Apaches, go live with them!"

The man moved on and Bryce put an arm around Shannon. "Maybe I'll do just that," he said quietly.

They walked out into the darkness. Their own wagon and horses were still intact. Troy lifted Lisa into the back of it and sat down beside her, while Bryce and Shannon climbed into the seat and Bryce got the horses into motion.

"It's a godsend we came," Shannon spoke up to Bryce in a shaky voice. "If we hadn't been there, Chaco might have been shot."

Lisa clung to Troy. He had never held her this tightly since marrying her. He knew her heart and mind were whirling with having seen Chaco again and with the renewed agony of remembering their love. His own heart was full of his brother. But it had made room for one more, and the feelings were becoming intense. He took advantage of the situation, holding her tightly. He could not resist kissing her hair lovingly and she only snuggled closer, crying against his neck. Seeing Chaco had had a strange effect on both of them, somehow drawing them closer.

They all sat around the hearth, Lisa just beginning to compose herself, Shannon struggling to be strong. Seeing Chaco

220

had not been easy for any of them, especially to see him and not touch him.

"He looked so hungry," Shannon said in a near whisper. "If he were with us, he wouldn't have to be hungry."

"He made his choice, Shannon," Bryce answered. "It isn't your fault or mine. It's a mixture of society and his own spirit."

The woman dabbed at her eyes. "But what will happen now?"

"God only knows. I. . ." Bryce stopped when he heard a shuffling at the door. He immediately jumped out of his seat and grabbed his rifle, and Troy walked to the corner and got his own. If there were bands of Indians out scavenging this night, they could not count on being exempt from a raid. Bryce walked to the door, standing aside from it. He heard nothing for a moment, then someone knocked lightly.

"Who is it," he spoke up.

"Chaco," came the reply faintly.

"Chaco!" Shannon stood up, as did Lisa, but Bryce waved them back.

"Any of them could use his name," he whispered. He turned back to the door. "How do I know it's you?"

"My mother was born in Virginia, and I am telling you this in English. And you bear a scar on your chest put there by my own father."

Bryce grinned a little and opened the door. Instantly the room seemed filled with him—tall, dark, wild.

"Chaco," Lisa cried.

He went to her first, sweeping her into his arms. They clung together and he whispered her name. Troy turned away. After several long moments Chaco pulled away from her, looking down at her, smoothing back her hair lovingly. "Are you all right? You are well?"

She nodded through tears. "I only have about six weeks left."

He studied her with tear-filled eyes, brushing her face with the back of his hand, then moving his hand to her swollen stomach. "You will love him?"

"Of course I will. Oh, Chaco, take me away with you. Take me someplace where . . ."

He put his fingers to her lips. "Hush. It cannot be. I have only come to tell you that I love you, that I will love you forever, to touch you once more. I should not be here. There are men everywhere searching for us. I must leave in a moment."

"You can't!" She hugged him again and wept.

Shannon stepped up to him and he reached out and hugged her also. "My mother," he whispered. "I am so sorry."

Shannon could say nothing. She put her arm around Lisa and the three of them hugged. Troy turned to face them, holding Chaco's eyes then. Chaco read them well.

"You married her because of the child?"

Troy nodded. "We aren't . . . we aren't husband and wife in the true sense."

A shadow of jealousy moved through Chaco's eyes, yet he knew he had no rights to her and never had. He swallowed back his feeling of possessiveness, seeing a kind of pleading in Troy's eyes. "If you should become husband and wife in the true sense, I would be happy for you," he said. "It would be best. You are my brother. You would be good to her."

Lisa looked up at him in surprise. "Chaco!" Tears ran down her face. "Chaco, what are you saying!"

"You know what I am saying. I should never have allowed my feelings for you to take control. I am sorry, Lisa. We both know it cannot be, just as it could not be for my mother and Saguaro."

Shannon wept harder and Chaco gently pulled away from her. He looked at Bryce. "I thank you, both of you, for taking Lisa in. I hoped that you would when you heard she had been taken by the soldiers. I was afraid for her. Now I know she is well and cared for. It is all I need to know."

"Chaco . . ." Lisa reached out for him but he stepped back.

"Wait!" Shannon hurried to the cupboard, grabbing a gunny sack filled with potatoes. She shoved in a sack of flour and one of sugar, a few onions and two loaves of bread. "Take this with you."

Their eyes held as she handed it to him. "Thank you, my mother," he told her. His eyes moved around the room then. "Thank all of you, for being my family and loving me. I am sorry to worry and hurt you." He looked at Lisa. "I love you, Lisa."

Her sorrow knew no bounds as he turned and disappeared through the door. Troy quickly went to Lisa, holding her as her feet seemed to go out from under her. They could hear a horse galloping away in the night. Gone. This time for good. There was no more wishing it could be any other way. Lisa turned to Troy, weeping against his chest, for the moment hardly considering his remark to Chaco that he loved her. She could not think about that now. Not now. She could only let him hold her, and pray for Chaco.

Chapter Sixteen

Chaco came inside the wickiup to find Little Deer stirring a fire. She was wrapped in a heavy robe; outside the wind howled. Chaco carried a rabbit inside.

"Look what I got. We will feast tonight. Coyotero will come and eat with us."

She looked up at him with eyes watery with tears. Chaco frowned. "What is wrong, Little Deer?" He set the rabbit down and knelt down beside her.

"I have just been thinking," she said softly. "About you, my husband."

He smiled a little. "What about me?"

"About how your heart is full of that white woman . . . and when you hold me . . ." She sniffed and puckered her lips, stirring the fire again. "I am a bad wife, wanting to own you."

He took her chin and forced her to look at him. "What are you saying, Little Deer?"

"I am saying that at first I did not mind, when you made me your woman. It was . . . so beautiful. And I have loved you for so long, since you first came to us and I was just a girl. I thought . . . as long as I can belong to Chaco and give him pleasure in the night, it is all I need. But when you make love to Little Deer, still, after all this time, it is not Little Deer that you hold. It is her, the white one."

The hurt in her dark eyes tore at his heart. "You have always felt this?"

She nodded. "The longer it goes on—the more it hurts. I do so love you, Chaco. I wish ... when you touch me ... it was truly me that you wanted."

He studied the young, lovely face; reached up and petted the long, flowing hair. "I make you a promise, Little Deer. From this moment on, it will be you I touch, you I love, you I want. It is true my heart is still full of her. It always will be. But you are a good wife, and you give me much pleasure and comfort. I have been unfair to you, and I beg your forgiveness. I did not know you felt this way, or that it showed."

He met her lips. It had been several weeks since he had said a last good-bye to his family. Once winter ended, it was probably only a matter of time before he would be caught. For the time that was left, Little Deer deserved the love she so desired. Their wedding night had been passionate indeed, but his own passion was for a woman he could not have, and he had taken it out on poor Little Deer, who had not complained about his eagerness as he stole her virginity almost recklessly.

He kissed her gently, moving a hand under her robe and dress, stroking her bare hips, probing between her legs as his kiss burned into her. He would show her it was she he wanted and none other. He must think only of Little Deer—her goodness, her patience, her acceptance of his love for another. If not for Little Deer, Lisa might be dead at Nina's hands. He owed this girl much, for she had waited so long for him, and she was a devoted, uncomplaining wife.

She began to cry with relief, fearing that if she spoke up to him he would become angry with her. But he picked her up instead and carried her to their bed.

"What about the rabbit? And Coyotero?" she asked.

"They will both wait. Coming into this warm wickiup with my pretty woman waiting for me takes away my appetite for food."

He pushed up her tunic, pulling another robe over them for warmth.

"Chaco, the fire."

"My own fire is burning." He met her lips again, searching, trying to prove to her that she was loved as much as Lisa had been, even though it was not true. Yes, she was loved, but in a different way. He could never love her like Lisa, but this was all he had now, and she was beautiful and good. A man needed a woman. He got up and removed his moccasins and leggings, trying desperately to ignore the burning jealousy he felt at the thought of Lisa doing this with Troy. Surely it would happen. They were husband and wife, and she knew he was never coming back. Troy was good, handsome, her own kind, just as Little Deer was Chaco's own kind. He had to face it and face his own marriage and the fact that he was hurting poor Little Deer.

He pulled the covers from her for a moment, exposing her nakedness from the waist down. "It is too cold to remove my shirt and your tunic and lie naked," he told her. "But I can still enjoy my woman."

He bent down, kissing her belly, moving downward until she gasped with the pleasure of his touch. He forced himself to concentrate only on Little Deer. He moved up and pulled the robe back over them, moving between her legs and kissing her neck.

"I love you, Little Deer. I dearly love you. And I make love only to you. Do not ever cry over such a thing again."

His lips moved over her eyes, her cheeks, her neck, meeting her mouth hungrily then as he invaded her tiny body with his magnificent manliness so that she cried out with the glory of it, arching up to his rhythmic movements until the wonderful pulsations came that made her totally abandon herself to him. She cried out his name, in total ecstasy at the joy of knowing and feeling inside that this time he truly was making love only to her, only to Little Deer.

His life poured into her and he lay still beside her then, while outside the winds howled, echoing the loneliness of his heart. He did love her. He supposed he had ever since coming to be with the Apache and watching her celebrate her coming into womanhood. He was two men, each loving a different woman. There was one he loved more, but he would never tell Little Deer.

Lisa felt all the terror and heartache she had suffered since coming to this land was epitomized in the pain of childbirth. Now a new terror filled her, the unknown wonder of giving birth to a child, and the fear that the pain that raked through her now would last for hours. How could she stand it if it did? Already the claws of labor had dug through her abdomen for six hours. How much longer was it to go on?

She clung to the posts of the headboard, breathing in pants, dreading the next pain, wondering where Chaco was. It was early April. The baby was late, but that was good as far as explaining to others. But the joy of bearing it was marred by the realization that he or she might never know its father. And perhaps Little Deer was pregnant by now. Would Chaco learn to love her more? Would he love their children more? Surely not! He had promised she was first, would always be first in his heart.

Chaco! With every new pain she groaned his name. He should be here to celebrate his child. Did he know? Did he feel it happening through his intense spirit?

Shannon stayed by her side constantly, encouraging her, assuring her everything seemed all right. But what if she lost this baby? How terrible that would be! She must have this baby! It was Chaco's child! Chaco's! It was all she had left of him. She must be brave, as brave as any Apache woman.

But it was not Chaco who waited outside the bedroom as anxiously as any father. It was Troy. Sweet Troy. He had never mentioned what he'd told Chaco that night, but she had remembered. He'd said he loved her. And she supposed in her own way she loved Troy Edwards. Was it possible to love two men? Did Chaco love Little Deer?

Again came the pain, this time deeper, more deliberate, totally beyond her own control. For two more hours this deeper pain pulled at her relentlessly until the blessed words "it's coming" were spoken by Shannon. The baby took over then, determined to make its way into the cruel, cruel world. Lisa's screams chilled Troy's blood, who was scared to death she was dying and who knew in that moment how much he cared for her. Minutes later Shannon shouted from the bedroom. "It's a boy!"

Troy looked at his father, and Bryce caught the tears in his eyes. "I wish Chaco could know," was the first thing Troy said.

Bryce walked over and squeezed his shoulder. "You've grown to care very much for her, haven't you?"

Troy nodded. "I don't know what to do, Pa. I don't know how to approach her. I . . . I made her that promise that I never would. But it all looks so hopeless as far as Chaco. Now here she is with a kid. I can't leave her on her own. I mean . . . I don't feel trapped as far as having to stay with her. I feel trapped because I care more than I thought I would, and I'm not sure how she feels about me."

Bryce sighed, sitting down across from him.

"In a few minutes you can see the baby," Shannon shouted from the room.

"Hurry up, " Bryce answered. "We're going crazy out here. Lisa all right?"

"Lisa is fine."

Bryce took out tobacco and paper and began rolling a cigarette. "Why don't you just tell her how you feel," he said to Troy. "Maybe she has feelings she's afraid to talk about, too.

It can't hurt to tell her, Troy. You don't have to go jumping into her bed. Just tell her and see what happens."

The young man shrugged. "Maybe I will ... after she's healed and all."

"Tell her right now. She's just had a baby, your brother's baby. She must be feeling pretty lost herself."

Troy got up and paced, shoving his hands into his pockets. "Maybe I should." He glanced at the bedroom door. Bryce lit his cigarette and smoked quietly. Troy felt his heart tighten when he heard Lisa crying, wondering if he should go in to her.

Finally the crying quieted and Shannon came out of the bedroom. "I think I got all the afterbirth, but I'll have to try for more later. She's so worn out, poor thing."

"Why was she crying?" Troy asked anxiously.

Shannon poured some water into a bowl to wash her hands. "She's pretty down, Troy. The child is beautiful—healthy and strong. But considering the circumstances of this birth and the fact that a woman sometimes gets depressed after giving birth, it's all pretty hard on her." She looked up at him and smiled. "She'll be all right." Her eyes moved to Bryce and she could not hide the joy in them. "Oh, Bryce, he's wonderful! I have a grandson! A grandson!" Her eyes teared then. "If only Chaco..." Her voice broke then. It had been a long, trying day for her. Bryce got up and walked over to take her into his arms.

"Can I go and see her?" Troy asked.

"It's all right," his mother answered between tears.

Troy stared at the doorway for a moment, then hesitantly walked through it. Lisa lay with her golden hair spread out on the pillow, wearing a clean gown and cuddling a dark baby close beside her. She raised her eyes to meet Troy's. There were circles under her eyes and she looked so small. Troy walked over beside her, sitting down carefully on the edge of the bed and leaning over her.

"You okay?"

One tear slipped down the side of her face. "I guess so. I'm just so tired. And everything hurts."

He smiled the sweet, unnerving smile that belonged only to Troy Edwards, reaching out and touching her cheek with the back of his hand. "Sure it hurts. But it will get better. Just think, some women have eight or ten of these little things."

"Oh, Troy!" She rolled her eyes as though the thought at the moment was horrible. He grinned more and studied the baby, pulling a blanket away from its face and touching the velvety skin.

"He's beautiful, Lisa. Just beautiful."

"Isn't he, though? Chaco would be so proud!" The words brought a lump to her throat and her eyes teared more.

Troy leaned closer, and to her surprise he kissed her cheek. "I love you, Lisa. I might as well tell you now as any other time."

She watched his eyes, so sincere, and her emotions raced in confusion. "Perhaps it isn't really love, Troy. Perhaps it's only sympathy, your feeling of responsibility. You haven't even been east to school yet, Troy. I'm all you've ever known."

"It doesn't matter. I'll take care of you forever, and I . . . some day I want you to be my real wife . . . if you'll have me."

The baby squirmed and she hugged it closer. Chaco's baby. But it was Troy who was here with her now, Troy who loved and protected her, Troy who had married her just to keep her respectable. He was so beautiful in his own way, and every bit a man.

"I . . . don't know," she whispered. "I can't think about it now."

"You don't have to. I just feel better saying it." He grinned. "How about that, a man proposing to his own wife?"

She smiled herself at the thought of it, reaching over and taking his hand. "You've been so patient, Troy."

"It's all right. But pretty soon, now that the baby is here

and I'll be going east, we have to decide what we're going to do. We can't hang in nothingness forever, Lisa."

"I know." She squeezed his hand. "Give me a couple of weeks, till I'm healed."

The words stirred deeper needs inside of him. Did she mean she'd let him make love to her? He leaned closer, meeting her lips gently, a kiss much more wonderful than she had anticipated. Yes. Perhaps it was time to live for the future with a man who could offer her security and who would love her baby much more than some stranger ever would, for the child was a part of Troy, too. He left her lips, and the look in his eyes stirred her own deeper, long-neglected needs. He straightened then, touching her face again. "What are you calling my nephew?"

"Charles. Your mother said if she ever gave Chaco a white name, it would be Charles. So I'll name his son that. Charles Bryce Edwards."

Troy nodded. "I like it. So will Pa." He moved his hand to touch the baby's tiny fist. "You know, among the Indians the father seldom brings up the son. It's usually an uncle that does it. So I guess we're doing the right thing by Chaco anyway."

A pain stabbed at her heart. "Yes. I suppose we are." Their eyes met again, and he read her thoughts.

"I know you'll always love him, Lisa. I'd be crazy to think you'd stop. But you can't be together. All I'd ask is that you love me for me, let me be a good husband to you."

She reached up and took his hand, turning her face to kiss his palm. "I love you, too, Troy," she said quietly. "I can't help but love you. I guess there are all kinds of love, aren't there?"

He squeezed her hand again. "Sure there are." He leaned down and kissed her once more, moving his lips to her ear. "Get well soon," he whispered.

The words brought a blush to her face. The baby started

crying and he rose to leave. "Wait," she told him. "Stay with me while I feed him."

She was crimson, but he knew she wanted it to be a beginning. He sat back down and she opened her gown, exposing one breast. Charles quickly found his mark and the crying ceased. Troy watched in love and desire, studying the reddish baby's skin against the milky white of its mother's breast. He wanted to taste of it himself, and he felt more protective and in love at the lovely sight of the baby sucking away in peaceful delight.

Their eyes met and hers teared. "Help me, Troy."

He smiled, leaning down and kissing her hair. "I'm right here and I always will be."

Charles was a month old when the news came. Bryce entered the house, his face pale, and Shannon quickly read his eyes. "Bryce, what's wrong? Is it Chaco?"

Bryce glanced at the chair where Lisa sat nursing Charles, a blanket covering the baby and her exposed breast. Lisa swallowed, holding Charles closer, and Troy walked in behind Bryce, also looking concerned.

Bryce breathed deeply, walking closer to Shannon. "He's all right—for now. A man was just here who had come from Fort Bowie. Chaco, Geronimo, the whole bunch turned themselves in at San Carlos, on the promise from the agent there that there would be no charges brought against them if they gave up peacefully and remained on the reservation where they belonged. But the man who told me said Colonel Blazer is doing all he can between himself and Washington to get permission to arrest some of them, including Chaco, for murder, theft, you name it. He'd love to see Geronimo and some of the others hang, including Chaco. We all know that. All we can do is pray it won't happen."

Lisa closed her eyes and rocked quietly.

"Oh, Bryce, what can we do?"

"They'll escape," Troy spoke up. "You know Geronimo. He gives himself up, and then he takes off again. They won't keep him there long. They're hungry right now, but as soon as they're strong again, they'll escape, especially when Geronimo hears they're trying to get him hanged. And Chaco will go with Geronimo the minute the man breaks again."

"That's all possible," Bryce answered. "But in the meantime, they're at San Carlos, and every time they're caught again or give up again, that's where they'll be taken. We have to be glad Chaco and some of the leaders weren't taken to Fort Bowie, or it might have been bad for them." He looked at Troy. "I know it wouldn't be easy on you two to go there, to be around Chaco. But right now I have to think of your mother. If worse comes to worst, she should be with her son, see him again, be able to talk to him. I'm thinking of taking a job at the agency as interpreter, assistant, whatever help I can be. That man Colyer who was here a while back is still after me to be agent there, but I'd like to just go there and feel things out first, mostly just be near Chaco. You and Lisa would probably have to go with us, since you'll be leaving for college this fall and then Lisa would be alone. I can find someone to watch the trading post. We'll come back here eventually, but right now I'm not sure how soon."

Troy looked at Lisa. They had been closer since the baby's birth and since he told her he loved her. But their marriage still had not been consummated. She was just beginning to get her strength back. What would this do to their delicate marriage? Would his own waiting continue?

"We have no choice," Lisa told him. "We should be near Chaco. And we need to know if. . ." She turned away, her heart burning with jealousy. "If he married Little Deer. Perhaps she needs our help. Perhaps she is with child." She looked back at Troy. "Your mother deserves to know if she has another grandchild on the way."

235

Troy looked at his father. "It would be best for Mother. Besides, I'll be leaving soon." He turned and walked out, and Lisa watched sadly. His voice had been full of disappointment. Charles had fallen asleep, and she pulled him away from her breast and closed her dress, getting up then and handing the baby to Shannon.

"Could you put him down for me? I want to go and talk to Troy."

Shannon nodded, taking the baby, feeling closer to Chaco whenever she held the infant. Lisa hurried out, calling to Troy as he approached a corral. He turned, waiting as she walked closer to him.

Their eyes held, and he could not resist the words. "Lisa, it's either over with you and Chaco, or it isn't. I thought I could live like this, but I can't."

"Oh, Troy, don't hate Chaco because of me!"

"I don't hate him. I could never hate my brother. But at the same time I love and want you. I thought we ... sort of had an agreement. Now if we go to the reservation, and you see Chaco again ..."

"Troy, he'll be a prisoner there. And he's probably taken a wife by now. It's all changed now, don't you see? Yes, I love Chaco. But I love you, too, and I know what I must do to protect my own future, and my son's. There is no future with Chaco. I have come to understand that."

He shook his head. "I'm not so sure. And I don't want to be second choice, Lisa, kind of like taking what you can get if you can't have the best."

Her eyes teared. "That isn't fair, Troy. You're wonderful. You are the best, and so is Chaco, both of you wonderful in your own ways, but so different. I love you, Troy. I've learned to love you. It's a different kind of love than what I had for Chaco, maybe a better love, because we've been forced to know each other, to be wonderful friends first and lovers second."

236

"Lovers?" His eyes glittered suddenly with desire. "When were we ever lovers?"

She blushed but held the lovely gray eyes with her own blue ones. "A lot of times—in our minds and hearts—the couple of times you kissed me. You know that. We've both just been afraid of offending each other, of breaking promises, of loving someone that maybe we can't keep. But you are my husband, Troy, and sometimes when I think about that, about what that should mean, I feel things I didn't think I would."

He reached out and drew her close. "Prove it to me, Lisa. Prove to me there will be no more Chaco in your life, that you love me and want to be a real wife to me."

His lips met hers and fire ripped through her. She wanted it to be totally for Troy Edwards, for he was as fine and strong a man as any woman would want. She ignored the fact that it was a mixture of womanly need and urgent desires for the man she could never have again. She set her mind on Troy Edwards alone. He was here and he loved her, and she could not ask for a better husband. Neither of them wanted to face the fact that any part of this could be based on too many wrongs—that she loved someone else more, that he had not even been out in the world enough to know the true meaning of love, that each felt great obligations toward the other. It was enough that they truly did love each other in their own way, and that they were great friends, and that they each had needs and desires that must be satisfied.

Oh, how wonderful it felt to her to be held, loved, appreciated as a woman—protected, claimed! And how good it felt to him to press a woman close, taste her mouth, know that finally she would allow him the intimate pleasures a man had a right to enjoy with his wife.

Suddenly, finally, they melted into oneness, feeling a desire only for each other. She returned his kiss with great passion, wanting him. Yes, she truly wanted him. And he was her legitimate husband. There was nothing wrong in this. She forced Chaco out of her mind. She had suffered with the pain of it for too long. She convinced herself while her lips melted into Troy's that she could put Chaco out of her life forever now, for here lay her future, here in the arms of her beautiful Troy.

Now he left her mouth. He kissed her eyes, her cheek, her neck. "God, Lisa, I want you," he groaned.

She broke into tears of joy, desire, sorrow. "And I want you," she answered. "Help me, Troy. Help me be a woman again. Help me start over."

"We'll be okay. You'll see. I love you, Lisa."

"And I love you."

"Are you healed? Are you well enough?"

"I think so."

She kept her face against his chest, her own embarrassment making him want her even more.

"You stay here," he told her. "I'll get Pa outside and have a talk with him, see if I can get them to sleep in the back room of the post tonight so we can be alone."

"Oh, Troy, I'll be so embarrassed."

"They'll understand."

"Maybe they'll be angry. I mean, we assured them this wouldn't lead to anything truly serious." She leaned back and met his eyes. Yes. Troy Edwards would be easy to love. And yes, it was dangerous to allow this. She hadn't actually seen Chaco yet. But she must forget him, for her sake, for her son's. Chaco could hang. If not, he would run away again, of that she was as certain as Troy.

"We have a right to let it be as serious as we want," he answered. His warm, gray eyes were filled with love for her. "I'll take good care of you, Lisa. Maybe ... maybe I won't go east after all. Maybe ..."

"No! You must go, Troy. You've planned it so long and you're such a good writer. Don't pass up the chance to be even better."

"Then you and Charles could come with me."

She reached up and touched his face. "It's taking everything your father has to send you alone, and you won't be working so that you can support the three of us. In the East, the cost of living would be much higher for a family. It won't be for long, Troy. I'll be all right. I'll be with your parents. When you come back, maybe you can get a job in Tucson, and we can move there together."

He smiled. "Sure." He kissed her lips gently then. "I'll be right back."

The rest of the evening seemed to move swiftly. Bryce and Shannon said nothing, but Shannon looked worried. Lisa was sure it was because of Chaco and had nothing to do with her and Troy. It seemed almost too soon that they were alone together and Troy was behind her, wrapping his arms around her, carefully unbuttoning her dress down the front from behind, telling her sweet things, kissing her neck, her bared shoulder, letting her fall back so that he could bend over and kiss at the full breasts that became more exposed as he opened her dress.

Yes. She would stop hoping she could ever again be with Chaco this way. Here was her future, in this man's arms. He carried her to the bed, and when he was himself naked there was no denying he was as much a man as his brother. His broad, tanned shoulders hovered over her then. His body was hard muscled and beautiful, his kisses sweet and gentle, his desire great and his intentions true.

The newness of it all after having a baby brought temporary pain, but soon all the joy and wonder of being with a man returned. For a moment she could not help thinking of Chaco, of how beautiful this had been with him, how glorious and fulfilling.

Yet it was just as beautiful with Troy, who came at her hungrily but gently, his hands traveling over her in just the right ways, hands trained by the whores who had taught him these things. Soon the vague thoughts of Chaco left her. This was

239

Troy touching her, entering her, Troy moving rhythmically, groaning with the want of her, her husband, her *real* husband. Little pains of remembering Chaco calling her his wife, his first and only true wife, stabbed at her here and there, until another kiss from Troy, another thrust of his hard body into her own, erased the pain. She was a woman again. She had a home now, a real, solid home, the first one she had had since leaving Illinois and losing her parents. And she had a husband and a son.

At the trading post Shannon lay wide awake, staring at stars through a window. "I can't help feeling Lisa is just trying to prove she can forget Chaco, Bryce. I'm worried one of them will be badly hurt. What will happen if she sees Chaco again?"

"You can't live their lives for them, Shannon. You've been through enough yourself. We've just got to hope for the best. They looked happy enough to me."

"But why now, right before going to the reservation and possibly seeing Chaco?"

"I think the decision was made before this. They've just waited because of the baby. It has nothing to do with learning Chaco is at San Carlos."

"I hope you're right." She sighed deeply, then wiped at tears Bryce could not see in the dark. "Oh, Bryce, what will happen to Chaco?"

"That's part of the reason we're going to the reservation. I want to protect him, make sure he gets his rights."

Shannon suddenly shook with sobs. "He's my son. He's my little Chaco. He's always been . . . so special."

"I know that." He rolled over and pulled her into his arms. "God, don't cry, Shannon. You've cried too much since I've known you. I don't know how you have any tears left."

"Hold me, Bryce," she whispered, clinging to him like a child. "What would I have done all these years without my Bryce?"

"You'd have survived, because you're a strong woman, Shannon Edwards."

"Oh, no. You've been my strength. My sweet, wonderful Bryce. I've put you through so much."

He kissed her neck. "It's all been worth it." He held her tightly, wanting her, but knowing her heart was too full of sorrow. There would be a better time. Their love had survived so many trials and sorrows. It would survive whatever was to happen to Chaco—and to Troy and Lisa.

Chapter Seventeen

It was not a long journey but neither was it an easy one. The strain of what could happen to Chaco was on all their minds, as was the added strain of wondering how Lisa would feel once she saw him. And Shannon worried about Bryce. She knew it was not easy for him to leave the trading post. He had worked hard to build it up. But he knew time might be short for Chaco, and until things were settled with the Apaches, neither Bryce nor Shannon could in good conscience ignore the needs the Indians might have. They had stayed in the West and around Fort Bowie because of the Apaches and their concern for them. Now if there was any way to help, they would do so, especially when Chaco was among them.

Years earlier, a good friend of Cochise, a white man named Tom Jeffords, had been agent at San Carlos, and had sincerely tried to make life good for the Apaches there and to live up to the promises of the Great White Father in Washington. But those promises had been made to Cochise, and upon his death Washington seemed to feel it was all right to ignore those promises. Agents had moved in and out of San Carlos since then, most of them useless, most of them totally ignorant of Indian customs, religion, likes or dislikes, and most of them perfectly willing to cheat the Indians if they could benefit by doing so.

By the time Bryce arrived, another agent had resigned. No one was in charge except the few whites who had business there, mostly suppliers and a few missionaries, all of whom immediately expressed a hope that Bryce, with his experience with Apaches, would consider the job. Bryce suggested telegrams be sent to Washington and to Vincent Colyer, which was immediately done. But Bryce could see that if he accepted his job would not be easy, considering the attitude of the general public toward the Apaches. One famous Tucson newspaper voiced those feelings when it printed: "The kind of war needed for the Chiricahua Apaches is steady, unrelenting, hopeless, and undiscriminating war, slaying men, women, and children, until every valley and crest and crag and fastness shall send to high heaven the grateful incense of festering and rotting Chiricahuas."

There were roughly five thousand Apaches living on the reservation. As soon as the Edwards took note of the living conditions there, they knew the word for the Apaches was *existing*, not living. It tore at their hearts to think that Chaco was living among these people whose faces showed their loneliness—caged animals, mountain Apaches forced to live in a desert area where it was not uncommon for the temperatures to soar to a hundred and ten degrees. They had arrived in the midst of a sandstorm, which were frequent in the San Carlos area, as were centipedes and snakes. Bryce's first instinct was to turn right around and take the women back home, but neither of them would hear of it.

"We're here to help, and we'll stay," Shannon told him sternly. "Ask them where we can find Chaco."

They were led to a group of buildings and to an empty, airless little log cabin, which Bryce was told would be his headquarters if he chose to stay on. Lisa struggled to keep her composure, never dreaming they would find the kind of conditions that existed here. The cabin would offer little, if any, privacy, and would be crowded. Troy immediately told her he would build them a cabin of their own, giving her a reassuring hug.

She clung tightly to Charles, as though afraid some unseen thing would come and grab him from her.

After some water and a few moments of rest, a missionary preacher named Mark Hammond led the four of them through the main part of the reservation, where dark, listless eyes watched them all warily, and men and women alike sat about looking bored.

"The disease and death rate is high," Hammond told them as they walked. "Tuberculosis is the worst. And what disease doesn't take, alcohol does, along with malnutrition. We don't get our food supply shipped in often enough, and often when it gets here, it's rotten. Somebody is scraping the best off the top somewhere, Mr. Edwards. Maybe you can figure out what is happening. So far there's been no one who cared to find out, probably because they're a part of the payoff, if you know what I mean. Jeffords cared, a long time ago. But he gave up trying to do anything about it."

Bryce was immediately consumed with a desire to right the wrongs, but he hated subjecting Shannon and Lisa to the kind of life they would lead in this desolate place. But now that they were here and he saw how bad it really was, he knew he could not leave for a while, and that the women would not want to leave either.

"I'll do my best, if Washington wants me," Bryce told Hammond.

"I've heard of you, Mr. Edwards. I think you'll do a good job." He led them toward a corral-type enclosure, where several Indian men sat with sullen faces. Several soldiers were stationed around the corral. "I must tell you that our biggest problem is cheating by suppliers and, of course, the ever-present whiskey peddlers. If we could get rid of the thieves who keep the Indians stirred up for their own profit, we would go far in winning the battle to civilize the Apaches." He halted, nodding toward the corral and looking sympathetically at Shannon, then to Bryce.

"Your son is with these men," Hammond told them, "under special guard."

"Dear God," Shannon whispered, noting the wide-open, shadeless area. Food sat around in pans, the way dogs would be fed.

"Geronimo is in a special hold, a windowless cabin. That's via the orders of a Colonel Blazer at Fort Bowie, who'll be here in a couple more days to take Geronomo and a few of the others back to Fort Bowie. I think he's planning to take Chaco, too. I've argued about the conditions under which these men are being held, but to no avail."

Lisa put a hand to her stomach. The baby had been left behind with a missionary woman, since it was so hot and it was his nap time. Lisa halted, afraid to go any closer. Troy kept an arm around her, while Bryce walked up to the fencing, gazing around at the prisoners. "Chaco," he called out.

A young man sitting at a corner post raised his head. They stared at each other, and then the young man slowly rose.

"Chaco," Shannon called out then. "Chaco, is it you?" She clung to the fence tightly, her throat constricting. He was so thin and bruised. Someone had beaten him. His hair was stringy and he was dirty, caked blood covered parts of his body. She knew he always kept himself clean and handsome. This condition could only be from the way he was being treated in this squalid little square where he was held like a wild animal.

Chaco slowly walked closer, astonishment on his face. Troy kept an arm around Lisa, leading her toward the fence, and two soldiers approached.

"What's going on here? Who are you people?" one of them barked.

"I am his mother," Shannon snapped, whirling on the man and startling him. "I have come to talk with my son, and you, sir, will walk away from here and let me talk to my son in private!"

The soldier's eyes shifted to Bryce. "You always let your woman give the orders?"

In a flash Bryce yanked the rifle right out of the startled soldier's hands. "Usually," he answered, "especially when I agree with her. I was a colonel once myself at Fort Bowie, mister. Don't ever wave a gun toward my woman again. And you'll see more of me. I intend to stay on, as the new agent."

The soldier's eyebrows raised. He looked Bryce over, noting the man's size and stance of authority. Then he shrugged. "No matter. We'll be heading out soon with this bunch of renegades."

Bryce threw the man's rifle to the ground. "Who beat him?"

The soldier shrugged. "Damned if I know. Why don't you ask him?"

"A hell of a lot of good that would do. The word of an Apache against a white soldier." He backed away. "Pick your rifle up and get out of here."

The man just grinned and nodded, bending down and picking up the gun. Bryce turned angry eyes to the second soldier, who also turned and left. Mark Hammond walked a few feet away to wait while Shannon Edwards turned to her son. Chaco stared at them with dark eyes that had changed from surprise to sullen hatred by the soldier's words.

"He is the one," he hissed.

"The one who beat you?" Bryce asked.

Chaco nodded.

"I'll do something about it."

"So will I," Troy spoke up. "The bastard!"

Chaco's attention had been so riveted on his mother and the soldier that he had not even realized Troy and Lisa were there, partly because he had not expected Lisa ever to come to such a place. He caught her eyes then, and his own widened.

"Lisa!" He backed away. "She should not be here! She is done with this, all of it! Take her away from here!"

"Chaco. Oh, Chaco, let us help you," Lisa spoke up, rushing

246

toward the fence then. But he turned away, moving to an opposite corner.

"Take her away!" he shouted.

"Chaco, I have ... we have a son ... a boy," Lisa called out to him. "He's healthy and beautiful. I call him Charles."

He turned away, hanging his head. A son. How he longed to see him. How he longed to be able to be free and see the son or daughter Little Deer would give him. He was shaken by the sight of Lisa. He had truly thought he had forgotten her, put her out of his mind and heart forever. Now here she was, so beautiful! It shamed him for her to see him this way.

"Take her back to the main headquarters," Bryce told Troy. "I'll talk to Chaco. Maybe she can come back tomorrow morning, after I've talked to him. Seeing him like this is a blow to his pride."

Lisa broke into tears and Troy led her away. Bryce put a hand on Shannon's arm. "Wait here." He walked around the fencing, unable to climb through the wooden posts because chicken wire had been nailed over it and barbed wire wrapped around the top post. He walked up to a gate, where the soldier he'd had the confrontation with stood guard. "I'm going inside," he told the man.

The soldier looked as though he was thinking of telling him no, but a look in Bryce's eyes told the man he'd better not object. He gave Bryce a sneering look and stepped aside. Bryce pushed open the gate and walked inside, quickly walking over to Chaco.

"Chaco." He reached out and squeezed the young man's arm reassuringly. "When we heard you were here we had to come, Chaco. Now that I'm here, I'm going to be the agent here, if Washington approves."

Chaco looked at him with eyes showing faint hope. "You?" He nodded slowly. "Ai. That would be good, Father." His face fell again. "But it will not help me. Soon soldiers will come for me. They will hang me. They will not even ask Lisa to testify.

It will be without a proper trial, the way it always is for us." He nodded toward a small, hot-looking building not far away. "He is in there—Geronimo. It is not right. They made promises, told us we would not be imprisoned or accused of any crimes. I should have known they did not intend to keep such promises."

"I'll make sure they're kept."

Chaco smiled bitterly. "You will not be able to stop it." He looked toward Lisa, who was walking away with Troy. His eyes filled with tears. "She is well? And my son?"

"She is fine. Your son is very handsome and healthy, Chaco. He's a grand mixture of Indian and white."

Chaco closed his eyes, breathing deeply. "I wish that I could see him."

"I'll bring him to you if you want me to."

Chaco nodded. "I would like that." He met his father's eyes. "She is still Troy's wife?"

Their eyes held. "Yes, in every way now, Chaco. Troy takes good care of her. He loves her."

Chaco swallowed, struggling to show no emotion. "Good. That is good. I took a wife also—Little Deer. She is with child. She is here on the reservation, but I do not know where. They will not let her come and see me. Please find her and take care of her for me, and the child when she delivers."

"You know we will."

Chaco looked around at the others. "Look at them—once-proud warriors." He met his father's eyes again. "It is not so much the land we fight for. It is ourselves, Father, all the things that make us Indian. They want to take all that away, cut our hair, destroy our religion, take the children from the parents and send them to white man's schools far away. So many of the children die there, Father, die of loneliness and despair. Do not let them take my children there."

"I won't."

Chaco looked over at his mother. "She should not be here.

It is best she does not come back to this place. And do not bring Lisa back."

"Lisa I can keep away, I think. But not your mother, Chaco. I know what goes on in her mind and heart. You are her son. Go and talk to her. Just let her touch you, see you. Give her that much, Chaco. She weeps for you constantly."

Chaco sighed resignedly, walking back to where Shannon stood. They could not touch because of the fencing. "May the spirits guide you," Chaco said quietly. "Thank you for coming, Mother. It is good to see you again. You bring back many happy memories."

She came as close as possible, studying her beloved son. "My poor Chaco."

Bryce moved back through the gate and came around to his wife, putting a hand on her shoulder. "Shannon, come back and rest awhile. It's been a long, hot journey. Rest and come back in the morning. You can talk then."

"Yes, Mother, you should rest," Chaco added. "Please. Do it for me."

"Are you all right? Are you injured?" she asked, paying no heed.

Chaco's eyes moved menacingly to the soldier with whom Bryce had had the confrontation. "I am all right. Perhaps I will even get away," he sneered.

"Chaco, don't do anything foolish," Bryce told him. "I might be able to get you out of all this. You are half white, you know."

Chaco looked at him with near hatred in his eyes. "I will not leave my friends because I happen to have white blood. And it does not matter to the whites. A half-breed is even worse than a full blood. You know that. It will not save me."

"I can pull strings. I have a lot of old connections from my army days."

Chaco shook his head. "No. Do not pull strings for me, Father. I will die with honor alongside Geronimo."

"It isn't necessary. And you know that if you die it will be by hanging. That is the most humiliating way for an Indian to die."

"Then I will find another way to die before they hang me," he said curtly, raising his chin. "I will fight and they will have to shoot me." There was an air about him that was all Apache now, fully wild, unreachable. There was nothing left but to tell him they loved him. It was good that Lisa had trained herself to give up ever leading a normal life with Chaco.

They left with promises to find Little Deer and to come back the next morning with her so she could see him, and to bring his son by Lisa. He asked again that they not bring Lisa along. He wanted her last memories to be good ones, of their days alone together before the soldiers found them.

"Tell Lisa that Nina is dead," he added with a sneer. "She was my friend once, but she betrayed us. She is the one who tried to kill Lisa and cut off part of her ear. And she is the one who led soldiers to me and Lisa. She tried to come back to the tribe. I told them she was a traitor who led soldiers to her own people. The other women beat her and forced her over a cliff." His eyes sparked. "I was glad to see her die."

Bryce and Shannon both watched him with a realization that this young man was not the Chaco who had lived with them as a little boy. All the torment and ridicule as a youngster among whites had made him exceedingly bitter, and his life with the Apache had made him equally wild. Still, there was something left of the little boy in the way his eyes softened then.

"You never change, my mother. You still carry the beauty that captured my father once. Lisa and I are like you and Saguaro, are we not? It can only end in sorrow."

Tears ran down her face and she nodded. "I know, my darling son." She forced a smile for him. "I will be back in the morning."

"Bring Troy with you. I would like to speak with him."

Bryce put a hand to Shannon's waist. "We'll bring him." He urged Shannon to leave, stopping to glare at the soldier.

"My son had better be well treated while I'm away from here. And give them all some decent food!"

The soldier's eyes moved over Shannon, then to Bryce. "*Your* son?"

Bryce left Shannon and stepped closer, looking down at the man who was much shorter than he. "That's right, soldier. And you'd better be careful. You're walking a thin line. There are too many ways of taking care of scum like you, and as far as I'm concerned, the army is getting pretty shoddy when it lets in your kind. Now if there is something more you want to settle, you come and see me when you're off duty. I'd be glad to oblige, overjoyed, in fact."

The soldier glowered at him, then backed off, turning and walking away. Chaco watched sadly as his mother had walked away. She was a proud, strong white woman. Now Lisa would also have to be proud and strong. If only life could have been different—for his mother, for Lisa. He cursed himself for having allowed himself to love someone he should have known he could not have. He turned, needing to look away from his mother. He walked back to where he had been sitting, realizing too late that someone was behind him. He felt a vicious blow to the middle of his back, a blow that made his knees buckle. He fell face down, and the soldier Bryce had had words with stood over him.

"Nobody tells me what to do with an Indian," the man sneered. "I don't do any Indian any favors, and your father, as he calls himself, can't do a damned thing about it any more!" He turned away, laughing then at the sight of the fallen Chaco. "Great warrior, they call him." He laughed again. "Not much of a warrior now."

The night was quiet and warm—too warm. Lisa and Troy had chosen to sleep in their covered wagon, which was cooler than the tiny cabin. But Lisa lay wide awake, listening to the

251

occasional wail of an Indian woman, the cry of a baby, envisioning poor Chaco corralled like a mustang, beaten with no chance to fight back. She could not help thinking of their days and nights together. Chaco. The father of her son. Such a proud warrior he was then. Her chest heaved in an unwanted sob. Troy drew her close.

"He'll be all right. Somehow Pa will make it right, Lisa."

She cried into his shoulder. "He can't, Troy. Oh, this is such a terrible place. He shouldn't be here! He shouldn't!"

Troy sighed deeply. "I know." He sat up, then began moving around in the dark.

"What are you doing?" Lisa asked.

"Be quiet," he whispered.

She waited, afraid to talk much more for fear of waking the baby, who lay sleeping on the other side of her. The heat interrupted schedule of the journey had made Charles cranky, and it was a great relief to have him sleeping. Finally Troy bent down close to her.

"I'll be back in a while," he whispered.

She grasped at him, feeling a shirt and realizing he was dressed. "Where are you going?"

He kissed her cheek, keeping his lips close to her ear. "Don't ask. And whatever happens, go along with me. Never tell anyone I left this wagon, understand?"

"Troy! Troy, what are you doing," she whispered in a near whimper.

"Hush, woman." He put fingers to her lips. "No more questions."

"Troy, I don't want anything to happen to you, or Chaco. I'm . . . I'm taking Charles to him tomorrow. . . ."

"No more talk, I told you. Blazer could get here any day, even tomorrow. Once Chaco is in his hands, there is no hope of rescuing him. Blazer will put him in chains, I'm sure of it. He won't get my brother."

He disappeared, and her heart pounded wildly. What was he

252

doing! Chaco! Troy! She loved them both. Should she go to Bryce? No. She was Troy's wife. He had given her instructions and she must follow them or he could be killed, and so could Chaco. She suddenly wondered which would be the most unbearable loss for her, and she turned over and wept into her pillow. How could a woman love two men? Yet she did.

Troy sank to the ground, recalling the days when he and Chaco played "Indian" and practiced how to sneak up on people, how to keep hidden and be very, very quiet. Chaco was always better at it, and Troy prayed now that he could do better than he had ever done before.

He made his way through the shadows of campfires, slinking along until he was near the corral where Chaco and the others were kept. It was heavily guarded, with lanterns sitting all around, a campfire in the center of the corral and several outside of it so that it was well lit. Most of the Indians inside slept, but Troy was sure they would sleep lightly, for their danger was great and their bellies hungry.

Troy gave out a trill whistle, one he and Chaco had used as young boys at play. He prayed Chaco would remember the call. A couple of soldiers looked around, and one of the Indians sat up straighter. It was Chaco. He lay back down then, and Troy was sure he recognized the call but didn't want to draw attention to himself. Troy called out again to assure Chaco he was close by and should be prepared. He saw Chaco nudge a few of the men who lay near him, waking them. He grunted something to them in the Apache tongue. One soldier shouted for them to shut up and they quieted.

Troy dredged up all the old daring and wildness he and Chaco shared as boys. It was now or never. He had thought about this ever since seeing Chaco penned up, thought about how it would feel to see his brother hauled off, perhaps hanged, and most of all what it would do to Lisa. He let out an Indian war cry as real and chilling as any Apache could do on his own.

The soldiers were in instant alarm, shouting, running. Troy

moved quickly in the shadows to another spot and yipped and called.

"They're comin' for Geronimo," one of the soldiers yelled.

Someone fired into the darkness.

Troy yelled again, and the Indians inside the corral were fully awake, all of them confused except Chaco, who quickly urged the men with him to start creating their own confusion. They yipped and called, running around inside the corral while the soldiers shouted back and forth at each other, frightened to death they would be killed.

One soldier tripped and fell and others kept firing into the darkness toward the sound of the calls.

"Nanlyeed! Nanlyeed!" Chaco shouted the order to the Apaches to run. He darted for the gate, hitting the ground when the guard there turned to fire. He rose again quickly as soon as the gun went off and, pushing through the gate, knocked the soldier down. He grabbed the man's rifle. Several more warriors followed him through, darting around in the shadows, startling other soldiers as they moved in quickly, hitting them with rocks and anything else they could find, stealing more rifles. Two soldiers were shot as Chaco headed for the little cabin where Geronimo was held. The soldier guarding it lay sprawled on the ground unconscious, and the door to the cabin was open. Chaco quickly darted into the darkness. Gunfire played all around him and he hoped the others had got away.

"Chaco," he heard someone call. Then came the familiar war cry he and his brother used to share as children, and a gun fired in the darkness. As Chaco headed in the direction of the gunfire someone grabbed him and they fell into a ditch. Chaco grabbed at his abductor's throat.

"Chaco, it's me! Troy!"

Chaco released his hold. Both of them were breathless. "I have ... a horse for you," Troy told him, breathing deeply in order to talk. "Don't know whose ... it is. Just grabbed him. Get the hell out of here, Chaco."

Both men struggled to their feet, and Troy shoved another gun and a box of ammunition into Chaco's hands.

Chaco struggled to see him in the darkness. "What can I say, my brother?"

"Nothing. Just go! Blazer might be here tomorrow. He'll hang you!"

They both stood there panting a moment, while around them shouts and gunfire continued. Now it seemed the entire camp was awake.

"Lisa," Chaco breathed, agony in his voice.

"She'll be all right. I'm taking good care of her, Chaco, and Charles. He's a fine boy."

Chaco could see him a little better now. "Father said ... she is truly your wife now."

There was a moment of tense quiet between them, while all around them total confusion reigned.

"It was time, Chaco. She had to start living again. I love her, Chaco." He wondered for a moment if his brother would shoot him for taking Lisa, but then Chaco only reached out and pressed his arm.

"It is good. Thank you, my brother, for tonight. Tell Lisa I ..." He hesitated. "Take care of my Little Deer."

"We will, Chaco."

Chaco suddenly embraced him. "I wish it could be like the old days, shik'isn."

A lump rose in Troy's throat. "So do I, Chaco. Some day I'm going to help, through my writing." He forced himself to pull away. "Get going. Here." He left a moment, returning with a horse that was bridled but had no saddle. "I let Geronimo out. I don't know where he went. Just don't ever mention my name in this. I'm hoping they'll think it was just other Apaches who did this. Now get going!"

Chaco mounted up and rode off and Troy ran back to his wagon, a good half mile away. He hoped he'd get there in time before anyone started asking questions. It was only then the pain began to hit him. He'd been shot. He knew it but had to ignore it until Chaco got away. His guess was the bullet had passed through his side. He could only pray the wound was not dangerous, and he wondered how he would explain it if soldiers or reservation people spotted him.

Things began to get dimmer as he ran. He prayed he would make it to the wagon, or he would be found out and would probably be hanged for helping Geronimo and the others get away. As he approached the pitiful headquarters cabin, he could see Bryce standing outside with a rifle. Mark Hammond was beside him, both of them staring toward the place where all the noise and confusion had taken place.

"I think I should go over there," he heard Bryce saying. "Something could have happened to Chaco."

"I wouldn't just yet," Hammond answered. "Someone might accuse you of helping your son escape. I doubt that is what is happening anyway. Probably some Indians got drunk and started a ruckus."

"All the same . . ."

"You aren't in charge yet, Mr. Edwards. You'd better stay out of it," Hammond advised.

Troy moved through the darkness, approaching his wagon from the other side then moving quickly, climbing inside.

"Troy!" It was Lisa. She quickly lit a lantern.

"Oh, my God, he's wounded," came another voice. It was his mother. Troy's eyes widened.

"What are you doing here?" he whispered.

"I came over to check on you and Lisa when all the noise started. Your father yelled to keep all of you in the wagon. When Lisa told me you weren't here I knew. I didn't tell Bryce you were gone."

Their eyes held. Troy was sweating and dirty, and a huge bloodstain was spreading on the side of his shirt. "They can't know," he finally spoke up.

"Oh, Troy," Lisa whimpered.

"Don't let on." He collapsed onto the feather mattress, his frame seeming to fill the entire bed of the wagon. "The bullet ... went clean through. Just pour some whiskey in the wound ... and wrap it good. Get rid of the shirt. Burn it. I'll ... feign sickness tomorrow ... be up and around by the next day. Nobody ... will ever know."

Lisa and Shannon looked at each other. Never had Lisa loved him more, but it hurt to realize Chaco had not had a chance to see his son. Shannon leaned closer. "Did he get away?" she whispered.

"I ... think so. I gave him a gun ... and a horse."

She kissed his forehead. "My darling Troy. Such a chance you took."

The two women quickly got off his shirt then, and suddenly Bryce was at the back of the wagon. "I think I should go ..." He stopped, seeing the bloodstained shirt, the pale look on his son's perspiration-soaked face. "My God! My God, Troy, what have you done!"

Lisa put fingers to her lips. "He's wounded," she whispered, tears on her cheeks. "Just tell the others he's sick."

Bryce stared at him a moment, his eyes watering. He looked then at Shannon. "Troy says he got away," she told him quietly.

Bryce closed his eyes a moment, then got down, closing the back canvas flap so the women could tend to Troy's wound.

Sheer bedlam broke loose throughout the reservation then, amid soldiers cursing, running horses, and sporadic gunfire. By the next morning over half the Indians at San Carlos had fled, inspired by the sudden break of their leader. The corral where the prisoners had been held was empty, as was the shack that had been a prison for Geronimo.

Miles away, as the sun rose, Chaco gazed toward the reservation from a high plateau, his heart heavy, his throat aching with sorrow. It was only in the morning, when it got light, that he noticed the blood all over the front of his clothing. It was not his own. He had touched only one person—Troy. His brother had been wounded setting him free. He was not sure which was the biggest reason the tears came then, that Troy had been wounded or that the woman he loved belonged to his brother now. He had left everyone behind, his son, the precious son he would never see, and Little Deer, heavy with child. How long would it last this time, his freedom? And what of his brother? How badly was he hurt?

"Chaco! We go," someone yelled to him. He turned to Coyotero and nodded.

"Ai. We go," he said quietly.

Chapter Eighteen

It was two days before Colonel Blazer showed up, already angry from the news he had heard from scouts who rode out to meet him. He and his men thundered into the reservation and rode directly to the small cabin where Bryce waited expectantly with Mark Hammond and Troy. Troy mustered all his strength to pretend to be fine, showing no sign of weakness from loss of blood or the pain that stabbed at his ribs.

Sabers rattled and dust rolled as the soldiers approached the cabin. Bryce stepped forward to meet them, and Blazer glared at him.

"I cannot believe what I have heard," Blazer spoke up loudly. "Not only am I told that Geronimo and practically half the Apaches at this reservation have broken loose, but to top it off I am told you are here, in hopes of becoming the next agent here. I don't suppose, Edwards, that your arrival and the sudden escape of your son Chaco have anything to do with each other."

Bryce took a drag on a cigarette he had lit. "Not at all. We just arrived ourselves. I only had a moment to speak with Chaco, certainly not enough time to plot out how I could let him go."

Blazer dismounted his horse and stepped closer, glaring threateningly at him. "No?" The man moved his eyes from

Bryce to Troy. "I've been told your white son there was very close to Chaco."

Troy met the man's eyes squarely. "Sure we were close. So what?"

Blazer looked around. "Your ... wife here, Troy? That girl who was Chaco's captive at one time? Oh, and how about the baby she had ... prematurely? He here, too?"

Troy stepped off the small porch of the cabin and headed for the man, but Bryce put out his arm, stopping him. "The colonel was just asking about the family, son," he said sarcastically. "I don't think he meant anything insulting." He looked from Blazer to Troy. "When you begin your journals in the national newspapers, you can tell the citizens of Arizona and this country what a *fine* man Colonel Blazer is ..." Bryce looked back at Blazer, "or what an uncouth, insulting, mannerless officer he is, a man who hangs other men without trial and is cruel to poor young women who have had the misfortune of being captives of the Apache."

Blazer's eyes narrowed. "What the hell are you talking about, Edwards?"

"I am talking about the fact that in a couple of months my son will be leaving for the East, to seek a higher education in journalism. He's good, Blazer. Some day a lot of people might be reading his stuff. You wouldn't want him to tell the truth about Colonel Blazer now, would you? Newspaper articles can sway people in a lot of different directions."

Blazer's face reddened. "What the hell happened here, Edwards?"

Bryce looked at Troy, then back at Blazer, taking another drag on his cigarette. "It appears some Apaches snuck up in the night and caused a disturbance, confusing the guards and helping Geronimo and the others to escape."

"Apaches seldom move at night."

"They do when it's someone like Geronimo they want to help. They couldn't very well march up in broad daylight and

260

take him." He threw down his cigarette. "You should have come sooner, Blazer. This reservation is no place to hold prisoners, not the wiley ones like Geronimo. Your soldiers can't be blamed, nor can anyone running this reservation. You know how difficult it is to hold Geronimo. But I'll tell you one thing. He might have stayed this time if he hadn't heard rumors you were coming to hang him. If he had felt truly safe here and could believe we'd keep our promises, there might not have been a problem."

"I never said anything about hanging anyone."

"You said plenty and everybody knows it."

Blazer squeezed his hand over the handle of the pistol he wore at his side. "Are you really going to stay on here, Edwards?"

Bryce folded his arms. "If Washington wants me, which they already told me once they did. I'm waiting for a confirming telegram. I'll stay as long as necessary, and as long as it isn't too hard on my wife and daughter-in-law."

"We can't have reservation agents who favor the Apaches," the man fumed.

"It might be a change for the better," Bryce almost growled in reply. "Up to now we don't seem to have had any who were anything but *against* the Apaches—cheating them, treating them like dirt. I'll tell you one thing, Blazer. From now on, if prisoners are kept here, they'll not be treated the way I saw those men treated when I got here! We'll form our own reservation police. You keep your soldiers out of here. They only make things worse!"

"You can't tell me what to do with soldiers!"

"Try me! The first thing I'll work on is getting full authority to have our own Indian police. It makes things a lot simpler, Blazer, and it helps keep the people calmer. Now I suggest that since there are no prisoners here for you to pick up, you go on back to Fort Bowie, or send out soldiers to find the ones who escaped if you want them so badly."

"You know we can't find those bastards when they're in their own territory!

Bryce grinned. "Good luck, Blazer."

"You're *glad* they escaped," the man snarled. "And I still say you had had something to do with it!"

"Prove it."

Blazer's eyes moved to Mark Hammond. Hammond just shrugged. "Mr. Edwards was right here with me when the shooting started," he spoke up. "We were up late discussing reservation problems."

"You going to accuse a preacher of lying, Blazer?" Bryce asked.

Blazer moved his eyes once more to Troy. "And where were you?"

Troy held his eyes. "In my wagon, with my wife and son."

Blazer nodded, looking back at Bryce. "If those escaped men commit any atrocities against white settlers, I'll hold you to blame, Edwards."

"I am not responsible for any of it, Blazer. But I can tell you that my son is not guilty of any of the things you have accused him of. Raids, yes. Stealing what is needed for survival, yes. But he has never abused a white woman or child. And he is not responsible for what his Apache friends do. Indian men each act of their own accord, Blazer. They have no one leader who orders them to do anything. When raiding or at war, it's each man for himself. You and others like you have a habit of holding all Indian men responsible for what one or a few of them do. It doesn't work that way, any more than it does for white men. When a white man commits a crime, he is tried and punished. He alone, not every man he has ever called friend and his entire family! Now get off this reservation. Your presence will make those who stayed more nervous and I'll lose more yet."

Their eyes held for a long, challenging moment. Bryce knew the man wanted to hit him—to get into a real brawl and try to

262

prove who was the better man. Bryce would have enjoyed such an encounter. He would love nothing more than to have at it with this man. But for now neither of them could act on their desires for fear of losing something more important—Blazer his rank and Bryce his commission as reservation agent.

"My men are tired," Blazer finally spoke up. "I can't move out yet."

"Then set up camp at least a mile from the reservation where you're out of sight of the Apaches."

Blazer whirled and mounted his horse, giving Bryce one last long stare before turning and ordering his men to follow. As soon as they were a good distance away Lisa and Shannon came out of the cabin.

"I could have sworn I saw smoke coming out of his eyes, Pa," Troy spoke up with a grin.

Bryce just stared after Blazer. "That man and I have got to settle something some day. The right time will come."

Lisa walked next to Troy, putting an arm around him gently. "You'd better lie down, Troy."

He winced as he turned and put an arm around her shoulders, walking back inside the cabin. "No argument there," he told her on the way inside. He sat down carefully on a small cot, breathing deeply against the pain. Lisa quickly got him some water and he drank a little before lying back on the cot. "It's so damned hot," he muttered.

Lisa watched him, loving him for what he had done, yet wondering. . . . She moved to sit down beside him, reaching out and stroking his hair. "Troy?"

"Yeah?"

"What you did . . . was it all just to give Chaco his freedom?"

He opened his eyes and looked at her. "What do you mean?"

"I mean . . . he hadn't even got to see Charles."

Their eyes held and he took her hand. "I guess I was a little bit afraid, him being here so close. But if I thought he was completely safe, I wouldn't have done it. I'd have taken my chances. I just couldn't bear the thought of what Blazer might do to him, or how it would affect you to see him die."

"Oh, Troy. It's over. I've told you that."

He smiled sadly. "Maybe. But he was first. And Charles is his son. And I don't think he's as much out of your heart as you say. I saw the way you looked when you saw him, even in the sad condition he was in. And the way you cried that night." He swallowed. "Actually, I was a little bit afraid that if I didn't do something, you might be dumb enough to try something yourself—you or Pa. My mother needs him very much. I couldn't let him take the risk. And you . . . I love you too much and you've already suffered enough shame. If you got caught trying to help Chaco escape, it would be bad for both you and Charles. I was the only answer, and it had to be done quickly."

Lisa leaned down and kissed him lightly. "I love you, Troy. Get well quickly so I can prove it."

He grinned teasingly then, lightly touching a breast with his hand as he let it fall to his side. "That's the best medicine a man can get."

"Lisa." Shannon was at the door then. "The missionaries have found Little Deer for us. They're bringing her now."

Lisa's heart leaped. Little Deer! Chaco had made her his wife, and she was with child. He'd told Bryce so. Lisa struggled with her emotions, a jealousy she had no right feeling, not any more. And Little Deer was a sweet girl, surely a good, devoted wife to Chaco, for no doubt she loved him dearly. And she had once saved Lisa's life.

"Be kind to her," Troy spoke up. "It's what Chaco would want."

She nodded. "I know," she replied in a near whisper. She squeezed his hand and rose, moving to the doorway to see two white women dressed primly in black, leading along a tiny Indian woman with long, shining black hair, her belly much too big for her small frame. Lisa fought the hurt of realizing Chaco

264

had enjoyed someone else in his bed after loving her. But she too had turned to someone new. Life had to go on. One had to be realistic and practical. In this land it seemed that love and romance did not mix well with practical survival. There was little room for the gentler side of life.

Little Deer saw her then. Her eyes widened and she smiled at the sight of someone among these frightening whites that she knew. "Lisa," she exclaimed. Yes. They shared something in common. They both loved the same man. They both had hurt in their own ways. Both had taken his life into their bellies, life that had grown into a living being. Lisa moved off the porch and hurried up to her and they embraced.

"He got away! He got away," Little Deer wept. "I am so happy. I just wish I could go with him!"

"No, you musn't," Lisa warned, patting her shoulder. "The important thing is that you stay well and have his baby, Little Deer. It is what he would want. He asked his white father and mother to find you and take care of you. You must not be afraid of them, Little Deer. They are good, kind people, and his white father will be the agent here. There is nothing to be afraid of."

Little Deer sniffed and pulled away, studying Lisa's exquisite beauty. "Chaco told me you were with child when the soldiers stole you away from him."

"Yes. I have a son. His name is Charles. I am married to Chaco's white brother now. Come inside. I'll show you the baby!"

She turned, leading Little Deer up to Shannon. "This is Little Deer. She and I became friends when I lived with Chaco. She is his wife now. She saved my life once."

Shannon nodded, reaching out and touching the girl's hair. "You have loved my son, and therefore I love you and will love the child you deliver."

Little Deer studied the kind eyes, the remarkably beautiful woman who had given birth to Chaco so many years ago, the white woman who had loved Chaco's father just as Lisa had loved Chaco. She immediately felt the love and genuine concern of this woman called Shannon and she was not afraid. She nodded.

"It is great honor to know Chaco's mother. I am glad you have come here. I was afraid. But now I am not." She turned to Bryce, who had moved closer to Shannon. What a handsome man he was for a white man! "You are the white father Chaco often spoke of?"

Bryce nodded. "I am Bryce."

Her eyes teared. "You are good man. Good man." She patted her stomach. "I will have fine baby for Chaco. Grandchild for you."

Bryce grinned. She was beautiful, but already aging, as so many Apache women did—young but old, their hard life taking its toll early. "We look forward to it. I hope you will have whoever you are staying with move closer to headquarters here. We're building an extra cabin for Troy and Lisa, but Troy will be leaving before long. You can stay with Lisa then, if you like."

She shook her head. "No like hard houses. But I will ask my father to build a wickiup closer to here. I think he will do it, but he is afraid. He does not trust any white man."

Bryce sighed with concern over the pitiful state of affairs on the reservation. "Well, he'll learn to trust me, Little Deer. You tell him that."

She nodded, smiling now. "I will."

"Come inside, Little Deer," Lisa spoke up. "I want you to meet my husband and see the baby. My husband is resting. He was hurt ..." She stopped. Surely Little Deer didn't know. Perhaps it was best she never knew. "He isn't feeling well, but he'll be all right in another day or two."

She led the young girl inside and Shannon stared after them. "What do you think Colonel Blazer will do?" she asked Bryce.

"There is nothing he can do, except maybe try to find Chaco and the others. But that won't be easy."

"Crook is the best. He's the one they'll send. Chaco is still borrowing time."

"I know that. I'm hoping someone else besides Blazer will be in charge by the time he's caught again, that's all. If it weren't for his threats, they might not have left in the first place."

"Bryce, a message is coming in on the telegraph," Lisa called out to him then.

Bryce hurried inside. He had learned Morse code in his army days, and at the moment there was no one else to take the message. He listened, writing down the letters with a quill pen, then tapped out a message in reply and looked at Shannon.

"They want me. Washington wants me to try it."

She smiled, but her emotions were mixed. Bryce Edwards would be the next San Carlos agent.

It did not take long for Bryce to realize his battle would be a difficult one. It was government policy that Indian children should be subjected to an immediate onslaught of white man's ways, that old Indian ways must be weeded out. Bryce objected to this, but treatment of the Indians was becoming standard at all reservations throughout the country. There simply were not enough people in Washington who understood or cared about these things, let alone about the additional problems of unscrupulous men who took advantage of the Indians' ignorance of white man's ways, cheating them at every turn.

Lisa and Shannon both began teaching, as well as campaigning against those back east who set the rules for reservation life, fighting against forcing the little children to have their hair cut, to wear white man's clothing, and to be punished for speaking in their native tongue. Shannon shivered at stories of how some Indian children at other reservations and at special schools were chastised if they spoke anything but English. For those who were sent east, runaways and suicides were rampant.

Shannon opened her own school, finally gaining permission to try teaching some of the children right on the reservation so they would not have to be sent away. Then she and Lisa began visiting the Apache families, urging them to send their children to her own school, surprising them when she spoke to them in their own tongue. She explained that if they at least sent them to the reservation school, they had a chance of staying near their families and would not be forcefully removed and sent away. Most of the Indians did not believe in the white man's schooling and were afraid of it, afraid their children would forget to be Apache or offend some important spirit who would make life bad for them for turning to the white man.

It was an endless, tiring job. A visit to twenty families might bring one or two little children to school, but Shannon began to consider that an accomplishment. And it kept her busy. She needed to be busy, as did Lisa, for both had things to forget, fears that must be ignored in order to stay sane. Their work at the reservation helped.

Soon there were twelve children attending their school, something Shannon considered nothing short of a miracle. She and Lisa became not only teachers but also nurses and midwives, while Bryce found himself surrounded by mountains of paperwork, most of which he was sure was unnecessary. But when one worked with the government, one worked with forms and reports, statistics and surveys, records of supply and demand, births and deaths.

All the work left him little time for what he really wanted to do, which was to police the reservation with Apache men and to start cleaning things up, chase out the whiskey peddlers and do something about local citizens who cheated the Apaches on supplies, or about settlers who continued to nibble away at reservation land. Squatters often moved in on fields already planted by Apaches who were trying to learn to farm. Thousands of acres were lost when the government gave away rights for copper mining to both the east and west of the reservation, and for coal and silver mining to the south.

At times the job seemed an impossible task. Bryce set aside the paperwork and began moving among the thousands of Apaches still at the reservation, acquainting himself with them, letting them know he was there to help, explaining he knew their language and was familiar with their ways, and that he was a stepfather to Chaco. It was not long before the Apaches spread the story among themselves about Shannon Edwards. Some of them remembered. A few of them had known Shannon, remembered the surprising affection between the captured white woman and her captor, Saguaro. That one fact helped them trust her.

Lisa and Shannon both realized quickly how short the attention span of the Indian children was. Shannon said it reminded her so much of Chaco, who had been difficult to teach. These Apache children were free-spirited, delightful young people who were eager to learn but who simply could not sit still long enough to do so. So Shannon kept sessions short, sometimes several short ones a day rather than long, tedious hours at a time. She wanted more than anything else to prove these children could be taught and would be happier left on the reservation.

Troy helped his father with the paperwork, doing some writing and studying in between, planning to leave the reservation within two months. He realized that for the first time he did not truly look forward to going to school in the East. It would mean leaving Lisa, and now he did not want to leave her, but he knew he should go, for his desire to be a good journalist and thereby do what he could to bring more fairness to the treatment of Indians was something that would not go away.

It was not long before more pressing matters took the place of paperwork. Bryce came bounding into the little cabin early in the morning, telling Troy to get his rifle. "We're going to hunt down some skunks," he told his son, "two-legged skunks."

He put on his hat and strapped on a handgun while Shannon watched hesitantly.

"Bryce, will there be trouble?"

"You bet. And I'm going to make it."

"What is it?" Lisa asked in alarm. "Where are you going?"

"You'll know when we get back." He turned to Troy. "I've got several Apache scouts waiting. Let's go."

Troy obeyed, asking no questions, glad for some action. He mounted a horse already saddled for him and they headed into the hills north of the reservation to a cover of mesquite and yucca bushes that overlooked the trail over which cattle were driven into the reservation.

"You see that?" Bryce asked Troy, once they tied their horses and crept up to the bushes to watch below.

"All I see is a bunch of cattle ready to bring in, and a couple of drovers riding up and down in front of them."

"Not just riding up and down in front of them, Troy. Riding *between* the cattle and the river. The bastards are deliberately keeping the cattle from the water. I've had men watching, waiting for just the right moment. They're deliberately keeping the cattle thirsty. In a little while, just before bringing the cattle in to be weighed for slaughter, they'll let those cattle drink from the Gila to their hearts' content. By the time they come in, they'll each be holding an extra twenty or so pounds of water. Come on."

He signaled the Apache scouts and they all moved back down and remounted their horses. Bryce led them over the ridge and down toward the cattle, all of them keeping rifles in hand in case of trouble. Bryce led them into the river and across it, facing one of the drovers squarely. The drover had whirled his horse in surprise at the intrusion, ready to shoot at first until he realized two of those who had come in were white men.

"What the hell—"

"Where's Mace Drucker?" Bryce demanded.

"Who?"

"You know who! Your boss!"

The man eyed the Indian scouts warily, then turned his eyes back to Bryce. "Who the hell are you?"

"I'm Bryce Edwards, new agent at San Carlos. I know Mace Drucker runs this outfit and these cattle are from his ranch. Now where is he?"

The man scowled. "Back at camp. About a mile north."

Bryce turned and said something to the scouts, then turned back to the drover. "I'm leaving three of these Apaches here to watch you. If you make one move to let these cattle drink from that river, they'll shoot you—with my permission. Understood?"

Three of the scouts moved forward, giving the drover warning looks.

"Sure," the man sneered. "Drucker won't like this, mister."

"I don't give a damn what Drucker likes. He's cheating the Indians and the United States government."

Bryce whirled his horse and Troy and the other scouts followed, heading north. In minutes the camp came into sight. Men called out and a few picked up their rifles. Bryce stopped and tied a white cloth to the end of his rifle, then held it up before riding the rest of the way into camp, realizing that the presence of the Apaches might spook the cattle men. They rode in slowly and were met by a line of men with guns, while more stood farther away tending the remuda.

"I'm looking for Mace Drucker," Bryce told them.

"What for?"

"That's my business. I'm Bryce Edwards, agent at San Carlos."

The man who had spoken rubbed his chin, then walked to a covered wagon. After a few moments Drucker appeared, running a hand through his hair as though just rising. He stormed up to Bryce. "What's this all about! Who the hell are you!"

"I told your man I'm the new agent at San Carlos."

"So what! What do you want!"

Bryce studied the older man, whose stomach was protruding from plenty of good food. He could not help envisioning the tired, thin bodies of the Apaches at the reservation. "I came to tell you you're taking your cattle in to San Carlos—right now—and you're going to drive them hard, right through the river, before they can stop and drink too much."

Drucker scowled. "What the hell are you talking about?"

"You know damned good and well what I'm talking about. You've been keeping your cattle from water so they can over-drink before coming in and be nice and heavy with useless water instead of solid meat. Makes for a tidy profit, doesn't it, Drucker?"

"That's nonsense!"

"It's the truth and you know it. I want them brought in now and weighed as-is."

"You can't give me orders."

"I can refuse your cattle all together if I want. Some profit is better than none at all, isn't it?" He slowly lowered his rifle so that it pointed directly at Drucker. "Herd them in now, Drucker, or I'll go back to the reservation and find a hundred Apache men who'll be glad to do it for you. Only thing is, I can't guarantee what they'll do to you when they find out how badly you've been cheating them."

Drucker's bloodshot eyes simmered with hatred. "I'll bring them in," he said sullenly. "But you'll regret this, Edwards! I have connections!"

"I'm sure you do."

"You're a damned fool thinking you can stop everything that goes on around here. There are people who will stop you first! If you had any brains, you'd go along with this and everything else like the others. There could be a lot of money in it for you."

Bryce held himself in check, longing to pull the trigger on his rifle. "I could stand some extra money," he answered. "But that would mean I'd have to associate with scum like you, and

272

I don't care to stoop that low, Drucker. Now clean up this camp and get those cattle moving!"

He pulled back while Drucker gave orders to pull up camp. Drucker walked up to one of his men then, pulling him aside. "You get yourself on to Tucson, Bill. Look up Mister Veck and tell him about what happened here, about this damned new agent. Maybe Veck can figure a way to get rid of him."

"Yes, sir. I'll tell him."

The man saddled his horse and joined the others as they headed out, but he didn't go to the Gila River to help with the cattle. He headed for Tucson.

Chapter Nineteen

"What do you know about this Bryce Edwards?" James Veck paced nervously, an expensive cigar in his mouth.

Bill Drake fumbled with his hat. He was bone tired from his long ride to Tucson, and felt out of place still in his dusty trail clothes, standing in Veck's elegant office, Veck dressed neatly in a well-cut suit.

"Well, sir, he's an army veteran, he's had a lot of experience out here and with the Apaches. They say his wife was once the woman of an Apache warrior. I don't know if she was a captive or what, but she's got a half-breed son who right now is riding with Geronimo and his bunch. They have another son, their own. He's married to a girl who was herself once a captive of the Apache, his own brother, I think. It's sort of a mixed-up situation some folks don't quite understand and don't dare ask Edwards about. He's pretty private about it." The man cleared his throat. "He's a good man at what he does, sir, and I don't think he scares easy."

Veck looked at the man with eyes that were cold, blue slits. "Well, we'll have to find a way to stop him! The last thing we need right now is an honest man running that reservation." He looked Drake up and down haughtily. "You say Drucker had to take the cattle over without watering them?"

"Yes, sir."

"Bastard!" Veck paced again. "Just make sure this Edwards never finds out I have any interest in any of this. The cattle belong to Drucker, understand? Only you and Drucker know I back that ranch. If word gets out, I'll know who to blame, and you'll be looking over your shoulder at the shadows, Drake."

"Yes, sir. I understand. I'd never say anything."

Veck sat down in his chair. "You say he used Indian police?"

"Yes, sir. He's ordered all soldiers out of the area because they make the Indians skittish and make them afraid to come in to the reservation."

Veck smashed out his cigar angrily. "I'll make sure Tucson businessmen hear about that! If this Edwards gets Washington believing we can ease off and that things are more peaceful, they'll pull out some of the soldiers. Removal of soldiers means loss of government contracts, Drake, and loss of business. The papers will scream with this one, and anything else I can use against that man. We might add that he handled Geronimo's imprisonment clumsily and it's his fault the man got away."

"But he wasn't even agent yet then, sir."

Veck looked at him scathingly. "So what? The public doesn't know that." He picked up a quill pen and began writing. "I'll write a note to Drucker. He can keep whatever profit he makes this time, for his trouble and the danger that was involved. There probably won't be enough to split anyway. I want him to keep supplying cattle, but do it on the up and up for a while until I can figure a way to get rid of this Bryce Edwards. He sounds like the kind of man who will do what he can to keep the Apaches from losing any more reservation land, which means an infringement on our ability to buy up more land for mining and for settlers." He scribbled more as he spoke. "Thank God Washington dissolved the reservation once promised to Cochise and his people and sent them all to San Carlos after his death. Now the railroad can go through there with no trouble."

He wrote quietly for a moment, then leaned back, tapping the quill pen on his desk. "Edwards' wife has a half-breed son you say?"

"Yes, sir."

"Hmmm. Interesting. We might be able to use that. I'll get something into the papers about it, reservation agent too prejudiced to serve Washington well, something like that, make it look like he's bound to show favoritism to the Apaches because of the boy, maybe even let them get away with raiding and such." He nodded, grinning then. "Yes. That just might work. The whole Southwest Territory will know Mrs. Edwards is nothing more than a white squaw and that Mr. Edwards is incapable of fairly dealing with the Apaches and Washington. That should set him back a notch or two." He rose. "Of course, no one will know where the stories got started, but just let Edwards deny the fact that his own wife slept with a filthy Apache and has a maggot-infested half-breed son out there raiding and murdering innocent people." He looked at Drake. "What do you think?"

Drake shrugged. "I think it might get Edwards laughed right out of San Carlos, Mr. Veck."

Veck laughed lightly. "You're a good man, Drake." He handed a folded paper to the man. "Take this to Drucker and stay low. I'm going to pay a visit to the newspaper office."

It was a terrible death—a long, drawn out labor no woman should suffer. Lisa and Shannon did all they could, and Little Deer's mother and grandmother made the girl drink special mixtures from boiled herbs and roots. But neither Indian nor white remedies could help poor Little Deer, who struggled to give her Chaco the baby she knew they would have loved if they could have stayed together.

Lisa well understood what was going through the girl's mind. She longed for Chaco as much as Lisa had once longed for him, a longing Lisa told herself was over. Chaco would surely die some day in the not-too-distant future, or live forever as a fugitive—leaving behind two women and two children, all of whom he would have loved with great passion. And if Lisa had not been taken from him, this would not be happening to Little Deer now, for Lisa and Chaco would still be together. It seemed that white intrusion into Indian lands had such far-reaching effects, destroying the lives of those never even seen or directly touched by the whites. Here was a sweet, good Apache girl, dying in childbirth partly because soldiers had taken away her husband's first wife, partly now because her husband could not be with her and much of the girl's spirit had left her soul. She wanted now only to deliver a healthy baby for Chaco and for his kind mother. If she died, it did not matter as long as the child lived.

But the baby was turned. There was finally no choice but to reach inside the mother and get it in the right position. One of the old Indian women would do it. Little Deer's screams could be heard far out on the reservation. Then they stopped. The baby came quickly. The mother bled heavily, never once regaining consciousness after passing out while the baby was turned. She died two hours after her son was born.

He was a healthy boy. He was named Saguaro Cochise Edwards, after the two most important men in Chaco's life. He would be called Sage. Lisa took to him immediately, vowing fiercely to protect him from the hurts Chaco had suffered. She knew she would have help, for Shannon and Bryce would be equally protective. Little Deer's mother agreed to let Lisa take the child, aware that Lisa already had another son by Chaco, and most certainly aware that the boy's best chance for a good life was with the white family that loved him.

Little Deer was given an Indian burial. The women wailed and cried out, cried for much more than Little Deer's death. There were many things to cry about in this land they hated, this place far from what they called home. Little Deer's mother slashed her arms in mourning. So many wept, seeming to use

Little Deer's death as an outlet for all their other sorrows. Their once-great leader, Cochise, was dead, dead at a young age, mostly from a broken heart. Another great leader, Santana, was also dead, of smallpox, the dreaded white man's disease. A few renegades led by Geronimo were all that were left of the once-powerful Apache nation, and they were being hunted. There was one small bit of pride in the fact that thousands of soldiers were now out searching for a handful of Apaches and still coming up with nothing, and that the Apaches were one of the last tribes to hold out. Nearly all other Indian nations were already on reservations, their spirits long ago destroyed.

Lisa clung to little Sage. She prayed her milk would hold up, as she still breast-fed Charles. But he was nearly two now. She would wean him so there would be plenty of milk for Sage. It would not be easy. Charles was at the jealous age, but he would learn. She watched Shannon, standing so stalwart, staring at Little Deer's dead body. Could she be that strong? Now Lisa, too, would have two sons—one more white than Indian, the other more Indian than white. Charles was more fair every day, his hair turning golden like his mother's. Sage would be very dark. Would he have his father's wild spirit that would make him leave her one day? Maybe even Charles would have that certain wanderlust and thirst for total independence. After all, he carried his father's wild blood. But where would they go? By the time they were grown, there would be nothing left of the once-free Apache nation. Perhaps, for their sake, it was just as well. If the Apaches could not live in the way that was natural to them and must now suffer so, she must shelter her sons from that life, educate them as best she could, explain why they must live the white man's way. It would not be easy, but then Lisette Powers Edwards had quickly learned that nothing worth doing was easily done.

Her chest tightened as she suddenly envisioned Chaco lying on the scaffold dead. No! Not Chaco! This must never happen to Chaco! Men like Chaco did not die! She choked in a sob and

Troy put an arm around her while little Charles stood between his father's legs, not sure just what was happening.

"We're all going to make it, Lisa," he assured her.

"Poor Little Deer," she sobbed. "She had so little happiness. I feel like I . . . stole some of it from her."

"You did no such thing."

"How will we tell Chaco?"

"He'll just have to be told, that's all."

"But . . . he has so little left. What a terrible way to live, Troy."

Troy ignored the ache her words brought to his chest. Yes. She still loved him. She would always love him. There was no changing it. He had to accept it.

For the next several days messages were sent out through scouts and runners through the amazing network of communication that the Indians could do so well . . . a messenger . . . a drumbeat . . . a smoke signal. Yes, there were those who could find Geronimo. But they would never lead the white soldiers there. They would go in secret and carry the message. And so they did. Chaco learned Little Deer had given birth to a son, named Saguaro after his own father. And he learned that Little Deer had died.

Much of his spirit left him then. He would never see Little Deer again, and probably he would never see his sons. There was still Lisa, but that was a long time ago and could never be again. He had sacrificed much to live as an Apache. Perhaps he had sacrificed too much. But now it was too late.

It was May 1884. It was time for Troy, now twenty-one, to leave. He had already been putting it off too long, but it was difficult to leave Lisa with two babies, and difficult to leave his father, who needed so much help at the reservation. Things were happening fast now that Bryce Edwards was agent. Every time Troy decided to go something else came up that made him stay. They had rooted out several whiskey peddlers, sometimes in dangerous confrontations. Now a new trouble lurked. Troy actually had his bags packed when the scouts came to see Bryce, interrupting a conversation Bryce and Troy were having.

There were two of them, Apache scouts who helped police the reservation now. And they had come at an odd hour. Bryce rose to greet them as they stood there in uniform, their hair still long, their eyes holding some of the same contempt as the agency Indians who would not cooperate at all with the whites and their new way of life. The scouts were only scouts because by doing so they could realize more freedom than the others on the reservations. But they were at least loyal. Bryce trusted them.

"What is it, White Horse?" he asked.

"War party . . . south of here . . . camped near settlement. We find another ranch already burned, the woman raped before she is killed."

Bryce frowned. "Geronimo?"

White Horse glowered with anger. "No." His eyes narrowed. "White men!"

Bryce's face colored with anger and horror. "Then it's true! My suspicions were true!"

White Horse nodded. "Ai. We spy on them. Five men—all white. They dress like Indian . . . paint up like Indian . . . but they not Indian. They rape and kill their own kind so they can blame Geronimo! They attack next settlement soon! We catch them!"

Bryce moved from behind his desk. "I'll get some men together. Troy, get your rifle."

"Pa!"

Bryce turned to face his son. "What?"

"You know what this means? Arresting white men?"

"I know exactly what it means. But we've got to do it. We have a chance to prove it's white men who are committing a lot of these atrocities, not the Apaches. I've been yelling all along that my reservation Indians have been minding their business. And Geronimo and Chaco and the others are far south of here. They wouldn't take the chance of being caught to come this far north and start raiding again. If we're real lucky, we'll find out who is setting these men up. My bet is somebody bigger is paying them to do this, some fat businessman in Tucson who wants to keep things going so the soldiers don't leave." He strapped on his gun. "Come on. If we're going to catch them in the act, let's get going."

By the time they reached the camp the scouts had told about, it had been abandoned. Bryce searched around for tracks, cursing the fact that one of the men must have smelled trouble.

"This could have been one of the most important arrests this agency has ever made," he grumbled, getting back on his horse. "We've got to stop this or there will never be any peace." Bryce trotted his sturdy Appaloosa a short distance from the camp. "Their tracks lead this way. If we follow them, maybe we can catch them at another raid." He whirled his horse and rode off, and the rest of the Indians with him followed.

Bryce followed the tracks relentlessly until they came to another camp where a fire still smouldered. The scent of the smoke told Bryce and the others that it was more than plain wood that had been burned. Bryce dismounted to find a piece of a feather sticking out of the coals. He quickly yanked it out, but it was too late to salvage anything else.

"Somehow they knew we were coming," he said, looking around at the distant hills. "Damn!" He turned to White Horse. "I think they've burned up their Indian equipment. They don't want to be caught with any evidence on them." He picked up the feather. "But I have this. Maybe there's some way we can use it." He shoved it into his pocket. "Let's keep going."

They rode hard the rest of the day, until they came to a spot where the group of men had apparently split up. Tracks veered off in three directions, one set heading off the reservation, another heading south, probably also intending to get off reservation land. The third set, two horses, turned inward, staying on reservation land.

"Why would they stay?" Troy asked.

Bryce gazed in the direction of the tracks. "I don't know . . . unless they think we've quit following them or perhaps that they aren't being followed at all." He sighed deeply, disappointed that the group of men had split up. "There's no sense in going after the ones who've left the reservation. If they've burned the evidence, there isn't a damned thing we can do." He looked at White Horse, seeing the anger in the man's dark eyes. "You should have arrested them when you first saw them still dressed in Indian gear," he told the man.

White Horse shoved a wad of tobacco in his mouth. He was a big man, a dependable man who wore white man's clothing and always donned a black hat that really didn't look right with his long hair. "Only two of us, five of them. If trouble, we be blamed. White Horse afraid to make arrest without agency permission."

"You always have permission, White Horse. You're agency police, scouts paid by the government. Arrest anyone you think needs arresting. If you're in the wrong, they can always be freed later."

White Horse spit. "No use arresting white men. When it is Indian word against white man word, Indian cannot win. Only makes people angry and makes Indian look like fool."

"We have to keep trying, White Horse. Come on, I'm going to follow these tracks. Joe Youngblood's little farm isn't far from here. Let's go make sure he's all right." He walked his horse slowly, bending over and reading the trail. White Horse and the others followed.

Following the tracks was not easy. They disappeared on hard rock then reappeared again, and Bryce was sure they were headed back into reservation land to possibly raid Joe Youngblood, who was a peaceful farmer, one of the first Apaches to truly settle down at the reservation and try living the white man's way. Bryce's suspicions mounted as they neared Youngblood's spread. To murder a well-liked, peaceful Indian, would be a fine way to stir Apache anger and get the younger men eager for vengeance, goading them into more raiding. Already the raid on the settlers had surely been reported at the nearest fort by neighbors. People would be screaming the Apaches had murdered the white farmer and raped his wife. Now a deliberate raid on peaceful Apaches would only be further harassment, both acts making it look as though the Apaches were making war again, and whites merely retaliating.

It would look good in the newspapers, which would call for more soldiers, stirring things up even more. The government would allow more reservation land to be taken over by whites in order to tighten the ring around the Apaches. Maybe the Apaches would be removed to an even more remote area, opening another vast tract of Indian land to whites.

It was all very obvious to Bryce. Why others could not see it was beyond his understanding. They neared the Youngblood farm, coming up on a rise that overlooked the small spread. A man lay in a field behind a plow.

"Sons of bitches," Bryce growled. "They killed him! We're too late."

An agonizing scream came from the Indian's cabin. Bryce looked at White Horse. "The women," White Horse told him. "Joe has wife, daughter. Maybe the white men are still there, inside with women."

There came another scream. "Let's go," Bryce commanded. They rode hard and fast down the ridge, and just before they reached the cabin two shots were fired inside. Seconds later two men came running out the door, trying to get to their horses.

"Don't move!" Bryce gave the command, reaching them first, his rifle raised. "Touch your guns and I'll blow your heads off!"

The men hesitated, then turned. To Bryce's absolute joy, he recognized Dade Chadwell and Chap Miller. "I'll be damned," he muttered, keeping his rifle site on them. How tempting it was to pull the trigger right then and there. "Move up on the porch, both of you," he commanded, waving the rifle. "And drop those handguns!"

The two men looked at each other, then dropped their weapons. Several of the Indian police went inside, and another went to check on Joe Youngblood. Bryce dismounted, walking closer to Chadwell and Miller. "You two have some explaining to do. We followed your tracks all the way from where you left the others. We know you raided white people, raped and murdered them, disguised as Indians. And we know you tried to burn the evidence. Now we've caught you red-handed murdering Apaches."

Chadwell only smiled. "You have a lot to prove, Edwards. It is Edwards, ain't it? Ain't you the one used to run a tradin' post, the one with a white squaw wife?"

Bryce could not control his anger. He slammed the butt of his gun across the side of Chadwell's face. Miller jumped back, saying nothing, eyeing Troy, who looked just as eager as his father to pull the trigger of his rifle.

"Yeah, I run a trading post," Bryce sneered at the groaning, crumpled Chadwell. "And I have even more charges against you two. You attacked my son, nearly killed him. He named you when it happened, and I recognized the names! You're just damned lucky it wasn't Chaco who found you! And people might be interested to know that not long after you hurt my son, another Indian family was found murdered, the woman mutilated. You were in the area at the time. And I know you both also trade whiskey to the Indians." He kicked at Chadwell's already battered face. "You won't be grinning for a while, you stinking bastard!"

Miller glowered at Bryce. "It's like Dade said, Edwards.

You've got a lot to prove. Do you really think any white court is gonna' find us guilty of anything?"

Bryce backed up. "We'll see."

One of the Apache men came out of the house, his eyes on fire. "Woman and little girl ... raped ... killed." He turned and spit tobacco at Miller. "Chaa!" He spit out the Apache word for manure. Then he turned to Bryce. "We hang them! Now!"

"No! We take them to Tucson and make them stand trial. We show the public what is really going on."

"White man will not harm them! They will tell lies!"

"We have to try, Running Dog. We have to at least make the people start thinking, make them see some of the things that are going on here, even if they let these two go. Believe me, I'd like to hang them myself. They tried to kill Chaco once, humiliated him, beat him. But if we kill them here and now, the citizens will only point their fingers and say the Apache is still hungry for murder, still uncivilized. They'll say the Apache police and those who claim to be peaceful really aren't. They'd turn around and hang you and White Horse and the others, and it wouldn't matter what I said in your defense. But if we bring them in, it will show that we want white man's justice."

The others looked restless, and another returned from the field, shouting that Joe Youngblood was dead also. Heated words were exchanged among them, the Indians' blood hot for revenge. Finally White Horse and Running Dog convinced the others to try it Bryce Edwards' way. Chadwell and Miller were put on their horses, their hands tied tightly behind them and their feet tied with a rope under their horses. Chadwell groaned in agony, a huge blue welt forming on the side of his head. The Indians buried Youngblood and his wife and daughter.

"Let's get these two bastards to the guardhouse at San Carlos," Bryce told Troy. "I'll get some soldiers from Fort Thomas to help me get them to Tucson and I'll testify against them myself."

285

Troy watched with a heavy heart. His father was excited, trying so hard to do his job right. But he had great doubts about his being successful in prosecuting Chadwell and Miller. He wanted very much to kill them himself, just as the other Apaches did, for a great deal of what had happened to Chaco was the fault of these men's attack on him. He could only pray Bryce would be successful in prosecuting them; to fail would be a terrible blow to the man.

Chapter Twenty

Wired messages flew between Tucson and Washington only days after the newspaper story appeared. By the time government representatives visited the reservation from Tucson, everything had happened so fast that Bryce had never even seen the story. Papers did not arrive promptly at the remote reservation, and the latest story in the Tucson papers did not arrive before three men in expensive suits, accompanied by a marshall, all came to San Carlos together in one stagecoach.

Troy looked up from where he sat outside, writing his own version of the arrest of Chadwell and Miller, practicing how he would tell the story if he were a reporter, how he would be unbiased and truthful. Bryce, Shannon and Lisa all came outside the small headquarters when the coach clattered to a stop in front of it, and two-year-old Charles stood beside his mother, clinging to the skirt of the blue print dress she wore with no petticoats because of the heat. Sage, who had been having fits of coughing, slept next to Troy in a wooden cradle shaded by a tarp Troy had put up against the mean Arizona sun.

Bryce wore blue denim pants and a calico shirt; Shannon, a plain gray dress. She and Lisa both wore their hair twisted into neat buns at the base of their necks. All of them were on the defense as soon as the men arrived, and Bryce could not hide the suspicion in his eyes when he greeted them as they climbed out of the coach. The three men in suits looked guilty and uneasy.

"Are you Bryce Edwards?" one of them asked, putting out his hand.

Bryce took it hesitantly but gave the man a firm handshake. "I am."

"We're representatives of the Department of the Interior, appointed to Indian affairs and stationed in Tucson," the man replied.

Troy rose, setting aside his tablet.

"I am Sam Kniebes, and this is Joseph Yale and Robert Just," the man went on, pointing out the other two, who nodded curtly. "This over here is Marshall Hamlin, out of Tucson. You have two prisoners here, we're told?"

Bryce eyed Kniebes as he replied, "I do. I know for a fact they beat and attempted to kill my adopted son, Chaco. That was a while back. But we recently caught them red-handed fresh from an attack on whites—a white woman was raped and murdered and evidence was left to make it look like Indians did it. When we caught up with them, they had murdered an entire Apache family who lived peacefully on the reservation as farmers. The woman and little girl were raped."

Kniebes sighed and looked at the other two.

"You really intend to prosecute these men?" Yale asked him.

Bryce stiffened. "I do."

Kniebes moved his eyes to Shannon. "Is this your wife, Mr. Edwards?"

Bryce frowned. "It is." He turned. "And this is our son, Troy, and his wife, Lisa. Clinging to her skirt is my grandson, Charles. The one over there in the cradle is Sage, Chaco's son."

Kniebes studied little Charles. Was he also Chaco's son, as it was rumored?

"Would you men like something to drink?" Bryce asked.

Kniebes cleared his throat. "That would be nice. It's been a hot, dusty ride."

"I'll get you some lemonade," Shannon told them.

All four men watched her go inside, totally surprised by her beauty. Her slightly southern accent gave her an air of mystery, for she obviously had all the attributes of a woman who was once a true southern belle. Surely the stories about her couldn't be true.

Bryce began rolling a cigarette. "Well? To what do I owe the honor of your visit, gentlemen? Have you come to help me haul in Chadwell and Miller?"

The three government men looked at each other. "If that's what you really want, Edwards," Kniebes spoke up.

"Of course it's what I really want." He sealed and lit his cigarette.

"It could be a very trying experience, Mr. Edwards," Robert Just put in. "We think we should warn you that people in Tucson are very much against this."

"So what? No man should get away with what they did. It's time we showed the Indians there is justice on both sides. And it's also time people realized that there are certain factions who do their best to keep people riled against the Apaches—for their own profit. I intend to bring all that into the open."

Shannon came out with the lemonade, offering glasses of it to the men on a tray. Lisa bent down and picked up Charles. She didn't like these men at all. She glanced at Troy, who moved closer to his father defensively. His heart tightened when he saw the way the men looked at Shannon and Lisa. They thanked Shannon for the lemonade.

"I know your intentions are right and good, Edwards," Kniebes went on after sipping some of the drink, "but you must consider the consequences."

"Consequences?"

The man glanced at Shannon again before going on. "It

289

could be ... detrimental to your family ... even dangerous for you. And it would all be so pointless."

Bryce felt his anger building. He took a long, quiet drag on his cigarette. "What the hell are you trying to tell me?" he asked, his friendly attitude vanishing.

Kniebes glanced at Shannon. "Can we speak without the ladies present?"

Shannon stiffened and Lisa's cheeks colored with rage. "By all means," Shannon said coolly. She looked at Lisa. "Let's get Sage and go for a walk, Lisa. I have a feeling we have better friends among the Apaches here than we do with the men who have just arrived." She moved hastily to the cradle, gently lifting Sage from it and walking off. Lisa hesitated, glancing at Troy.

"Go ahead," he told her. "Maybe it's best."

Her eyes teared and it tore at his heart. She quickly followed Shannon, leading little Charles along beside her. Bryce turned angry eyes to Kniebes.

"What was that for?" he asked. "You might as well get to the point, Kniebes."

Kniebes sighed deeply. Bryce Edwards appeared to him to be a strong, stable man, and he obviously had experience with the Apaches. He didn't see why the newspaper story should change anything, but Arizona citizens were in an outrage. He took a folded newspaper page from his pocket and handed it to Bryce. "I'm afraid we're here about this, Mister Edwards, and to ... uh ... to ask you to step down as agent here. Another man has already been appointed to take your place." Bryce's eyes clouded, and he took the newspaper, opening it and reading the headline: WIFE OF SAN CARLOS AGENT WHITE APACHE SQUAW. "It has been learned that Mrs. Bryce Edwards, wife of San Carlos Agent Bryce Edwards, once lived among the Apache and gave birth to a half-breed son, known as Chaco. The boy now rides with Geronimo." The words began to blur before Bryce's eyes as he stumbled through the rest of the sordid article, which made Shannon look like an Apache whore and Chaco a warring renegade who ought to be hanged. "Is this the kind of man we want running an Indian reservation?" the article read. "Can such a man be capable of running an agency fairly, showing no favoritism to the Apaches? Arizona has enough trouble with its warring, murdering savages without the San Carlos agent being on the side of the Indian.

"Now it is learned Edwards has actually arrested two white men for the murder of Indians. Does he really think any court in the great Territory of Arizona will consider prosecuting white men for something that thousands of other white men have done in the name of defense and justice? Are we really expected to punish our own for doing something that is only helping rid Arizona of its dreaded renegades who commit unspeakable atrocities against our women and children?

"As one of our most prominent citizens, James Veck, points out, 'Let Bryce Edwards come to Tucson, and see who gets hanged!' Mister Veck has long been an advocate for the growth of this great city of Tucson and the civilization of our beautiful Territory of Arizona, to the point that every corner is safe for our brave settlers. 'I will not stand for any defense of these savage killers called Apaches, who continue to thwart progress for our Territory, with all its beauty and natural resources,' quotes Veck. 'Perhaps Bryce Edwards considers the Apaches a natural resource, but I consider them pesty varmints, and varmints are usually exterminated. Considering Mr. Edwards' family status, it is apparent he cannot possibly be objective in his treatment of the Apache Indians, and I, along with the great majority of citizens of Tucson and Arizona Territory, say he is not fit to run San Carlos.'"

Bryce's hand shook and a lump formed in his throat. How could they print such trash against Shannon! He felt sick inside as he handed the article to Troy, whose face darkened as he read. He looked at Kniebes then, his gray eyes spitting fire.

"How dare they say such things about my mother! By God,

291

some day I'll be printing my own articles, mister, and people will know the truth!" He grabbed at Kniebes, but Bryce stepped between, facing Troy. The pain on his face was like nothing Troy had ever seen.

"Don't bother, Troy," he said, his voice gruff with emotion. "They would only use it against you ... and maybe Lisa. At least she wasn't mentioned."

"Not this time," Yale spoke up. "But if you pursue this, Edwards, she will be."

Bryce whirled, his jaw flexing in anger.

"Mr. Edwards," Kniebes spoke up, grasping Bryce's arm. "Believe me, none of us had anything to do with that article. That's the God's truth."

Bryce jerked his arm away and Kniebes stepped back. "We aren't here to condemn," the man continued. "We're only here at the insistence of Washington and the War Department. They've been barraged with telegrams from Tucson demanding a stop be put to what you're trying to do. They're behind you, Edwards. But they can't ignore the demands of the public. You've done a good job here, but they want you to step down. However, you're free to proceed with prosecuting Chadwell and Miller. That's why we brought the marshall with us. But we showed you this newspaper article so you would understand the suffering all of this could cause your family. Surely your wife has suffered enough over the years."

Bryce seemed to wither before their eyes. "Get off this reservation," he groaned, turning away. "Take Chadwell and Miller with you to Tucson. Let them go there." He swallowed, turning back around, looking ready to explode. "You tell them if I ever see their faces again, I'll kill them on sight, and I won't do it quickly!"

Kniebes seemed to breathe a sigh of relief. "We're very sorry, Edwards."

"Sorry?" He forced a sneering smile. "Men like you don't have the least bit of understanding what my wife has suffered, or what life is really like here for the Apache. You have no appreciation for people like me and my wife, people who came here first, fought the first wars, put up with the loneliness and deprivation, those who did what they had to do to survive!" His voice broke and he turned away. "You bastards!" He walked inside the cabin and slammed the door.

Kniebes turned to Troy. "We really are sorry, son. You must believe that."

"My pa was only trying to do what was right. He's done more for this reservation and the Apaches than anybody yet. He's honest and brave. It took guts to do some of the things he did, cleaning up the cheating and whiskey peddling! He's the best man you've ever had for this job. You tell that to Washington." He stepped closer to Kniebes, fists clenched. "And you tell the newspapers in Tucson that some day they'll have some competition—from me! Some day I'll print my own newspaper, and it will print only the truth, not a bunch of unqualified garbage! Now go and get those two men out of the guardhouse fast—real fast—before I walk over there and blow their guts out myself! And while you're at it, you can do the explaining to the Apaches yourselves. Go ahead and explain why those two men won't be prosecuted. And then ask yourselves why they still talk of making war . . . why they still don't trust the white man . . . why they still feel cheated!"

Yale cleared his throat. "We'll . . . uh . . . we'll send someone. Please tell your father he'll be paid through the end of the year, to cover the expenses of his trouble in leaving his trading post to come here. . . ."

"Just leave," Troy hissed, looking ready to land into them again.

"The . . . uh . . . the new agent will be here inside of two weeks," the one called Just spoke up. "But your family is welcome to stay here as long as necessary to clear up paperwork and such, or if there is any other reason you need to stay . . . if your brother should return."

"Return? Why should he come here where they all die! It's things like what you're doing right now that keep my brother and Geronimo and the others clinging to their freedom in the mountains."

He turned and walked to the cabin door, then looked back at them, pointing to a building in the distance. "That's the guardhouse. The Indians who run it speak English. Take your marshall and go tell them why you're here. For now you had better just tell them you're here to take them to Tucson but not why. You might not leave this place in one piece!"

He went inside the cabin, his heart shattering at the sight of Bryce slugging down whiskey, something he had never seen his father do. Practically a third of the bottle was gone already.

"Pa, don't."

Bryce turned red, angry eyes to him. "Why not?" He stumbled over to a wall to lean on it. "How could they ... print that," he groaned.

"It's going to change some day, Pa. I'll make it change."

"Shannon! Shannon," Bryce whispered, his head resting on his wrist against the wall. "My God!"

"Pa, you've been strong all these years. So has Mother. Don't let them bring you down now. You did your best and you should be proud."

Bryce turned, leaning his back against the wall. "James Veck. What do you want to bet he *pays* men like Chadwell and Miller?"

"Wouldn't I love to prove it!"

Bryce drank more whiskey. "Fat chance."

"Pa, you shouldn't drink that."

Bryce closed his eyes. "She'll find out. That paper will come to the reservation and she'll find out. Even if it doesn't, how else can I explain why we have to leave?"

Shannon came rushing inside then with Lisa. "Bryce, they're taking Chadwell and Miller away," she said excitedly. "Are

294

they going to ..." She stopped short, seeing the devastation on his face. "My God, Bryce, what is it? Is it Chaco?" she asked.

Lisa's heart tightened and she looked at Troy, who was staring at his father.

"We're going back home, to Fort Bowie," Bryce groaned. He slugged down more whiskey and Shannon's eyes widened.

"Bryce! Why! And ... why are you drinking?"

He watched her, loving her so much he felt sick. His eyes teared. "Because there are powers greater than justice," he answered, his words starting to slur. "Because there is no justice at all for the Apaches." He closed his eyes and sighed deeply. "I expected physical problems, maybe somebody trying to shoot me." He laughed bitterly. "I could have handled that, fought just about anything they would have tried." He walked closer, reaching out and toying with a piece of her hair, his words choked. "But I can't fight ... you being hurt ... insulted. I won't subject you to that, Shannon. And I don't know how ... to undo what's been done." He suddenly pulled her close, hugging her tightly, quiet tears falling into her hair. "Shannon ... my Shannon. I'm so sorry. I never ... should have taken this job. I thought I could help."

She returned the embrace, feeling his agony, his love. "That's all that matters ... what's in the heart, Bryce. You did your best. You would have been the best agent they've ever had." She leaned back and looked up at his distraught face, her heart breaking at the sorrow in his eyes. "I'm sorry if having to leave is my fault. It's ... it's Saguaro, isn't it ... and Chaco?"

He sniffed. "It doesn't matter."

"Bryce, I don't care what they've done. Whatever it is, it's over now. Please let's stay a little longer ... just a few more months ... to see if Chaco shows up. They keep saying they've almost got Geronimo. Why, Bryce? Why do we have to go? We've been through so much. We can handle whatever this new problem is."

He smiled lovingly. "It's possible. But we have no choice.

They've already appointed a new agent—John Clum. And even if we did stay, life would be hell for you, Shannon. We'll stay long enough for me to show Clum around, and then we're going home."

Their eyes held, and she could see he was determined. Life had been hell at San Carlos, and yet she didn't really want to leave. She felt so attached now to many of the women and children. She loved them. She enjoyed helping them. It was a way of extending her love for Saguaro and a good way to keep busy while waiting for Chaco. But something terrible had happened. Bryce Edwards was not a man easily broken.

"We know the truth—you and I," she told him, smiling for him. "That's all that matters, isn't it?"

He swallowed. "I thought it was," he answered quietly. "But ... now ..." He threw back his head, jerking in a sob, then let go of her and stumbled through the door.

"Bryce," Shannon called after him as he mounted his horse. He turned and rode off. Shannon turned to Troy. "My God, Troy, I've never seen him like this. What is it?"

He blinked back tears, pulling the sheet of newspaper from his back pocket where he had put it. "You might as well know ... so you'll be prepared. I'm sorry, Mother."

Shannon looked at him curiously, taking the paper. Lisa moved beside her, reading over her shoulder, then turned away, wanting to cry. Outside the coach left with the "prisoners" inside, along with the government men and the marshall. Their deed had been accomplished. Men like Bryce Edwards would not get in the way of progress, and progress meant the assimilation, or elimination, of the Apaches. Arizona was becoming civilized now.

Troy rode out to the grove of cottonwoods where he'd seen his father go. They had waited two hours for him to come back, and Shannon wanted to go to him, but Troy insisted she wait until he was sober. He rode out himself, deciding to keep an eye on his father until he was himself again. He found the man lying facedown in the grass, an empty whiskey bottle beside him. This was not Bryce Edwards ... not the Bryce Edwards Troy knew.

"Pa!" He dismounted, hurrying over to him, touching his shoulder. "Pa, you shouldn't have. Mother needs you more than ever, and you go off and get drunk."

Bryce rolled over onto his back. "Thought I'd ... see ... what it was like for Chaco. Those men ... making him drink that whiskey." He grinned. "Not bad. It's the way ... he felt the next day. You know how I'm going ... to feel? Poor ... Chaco." He laughed then, harder and harder until suddenly he was crying.

Troy's eyes teared. "Goddamn it, Pa, why are you doing this to yourself?"

"Myself?" Bryce sniffed, turning back over, burying his face in his arms. "It's ... what I did ... to her," he wept.

Troy frowned. "You? Oh, Pa, I've never heard you talk so stupid." He picked the man up and dragged him to a nearby creek.

"What ... you doing?" Bryce mumbled.

Troy threw him into the creek and Bryce yelled, pulling back. Troy threw him back, this time soaking him entirely. "Damn you! Damn you," he yelled. He jerked his father out and threw him down on his back. He knew he would never be able to throw the man around like this if Bryce Edwards was sober. "You've been through hell for my mother ... loved her even after she stayed with Saguaro ... been proud of her even when other people looked down on her." He grabbed Bryce's shirt and made him sit up. "You've been her strength, made her feel like she can be proud, and she can! She thinks it's because of her ... that you're embarrassed about that article and wish you never would have married her."

"No. No, that's ... not so."

"Then go tell her!"

Bryce pushed at him. "Leave me ... alone. You ... don't understand."

"Don't I? I've lived with you all these years, you know ... and I'm going through almost the same thing with Lisa. Mother ... she loves you so much, Pa. She's always been able to depend on you and now when she needs you most you aren't there."

Bryce rolled away from him, running a hand through his hair. "She was just ... just a little girl ... when I met her," he said sadly, his words still slurred. "Just a little girl ... so innocent. And she loved me...." His voice choked. "God, she loved me. I ... taught her everything. I was ... first. Did I ever tell you that? Back in Virginia.... She was so young, and I ... loved her. And I got orders. I had to ... leave ... and all of a sudden all I could think of was ... making love to Shannon Fitzgerald before I left ... like maybe I'd never see her again. But I did ... see her again ... in a tipi ... having Saguaro's baby!" He almost hissed the words. His voice choked then. "Nobody knows ... how I felt ... when she left with him. I kept it inside." He broke into tears again. "And I felt guilty, Troy, for ... for that short little time that I ... hated her."

He lay down and wept for several minutes. Troy rubbed at his shoulder. "Hell, Pa, that was a natural feeling. You didn't really hate her."

"I've been ... trying to make up for it ... all these years ... by loving Chaco ... doing what I could for Saguaro's people. I really do care, Troy. But sometimes it's to ... to prove to her it's okay ... that I love her in spite of Saguaro. She ... couldn't be blamed. It was just my own jealousy. And I ... I never had family ... grew up in an orphanage. Shannon was ... everything to me. It was like ... like everything was being taken from me."

Troy wiped at his own eyes. Never in his life had he seen his father like this, or realized just how deep the whole incident with Saguaro had left its mark.

"Pa, you're just human. Did you think you weren't? Did being a soldier mean you weren't supposed to have feelings, that you were supposed to endure all things with a straight face and a hard heart? Jesus, it was a bad time for you. And when you finally found her, it was natural to hate her when she chose Saguaro."

"But I killed him. I killed him, Troy. Maybe it wasn't all ... just because he wanted to die. I was glad ... he wanted to die. I *wanted* to kill him ... and yet I didn't. I've never ... got over the guilt ... and I've loved Chaco ... like my own ... tried to do my best with him ... because I killed his father ... not so much because he's Shannon's son ... but because I killed his father." He wiped at his eyes and sat up a little. "You see? I'm not ... the great humanitarian you think I am."

Troy studied the eyes that were like a mirror of his own. "Quit blaming yourself, Pa. You're the greatest man I know. I don't care what you say. Maybe you did some things out of guilt, but you do love Chaco and you love his people, and it took courage to try to straighten things up around here. And there's not a man alive who'd go through what you went through that day Mother left with Saguaro without feeling some kind of hate. You're crazy to let that bother you. Come on back to the house, Pa."

"No. Not ... like this." He ran a hand over his face and through his hair again. "I love her so much, Troy. I ... should have known better than to come here ... should have known something like that might happen. I've hurt her."

"*They* hurt her, not you. I'm glad you told me, Pa ... how you feel and all. You should have told her. She would have understood. She feels guilty, too, you know. She's in the house crying, thinking you hate her because it's her fault you couldn't stay on here and help the Apache, her fault you couldn't prosecute those men. So you see? You both love each other so much you're going around feeling guilty about stupid things. Now come on. I'm not leaving you here all night to catch pneumonia. You've got to come back."

"No, I . . . not yet. Just let me sit here awhile."

Troy sighed. "Just a little while. I'm going back to check on Mother."

Bryce only nodded, turning away. Troy squeezed his arm. "I love you, Pa. I'm damned sorry about those men. But I'm making you a promise right now that somehow, some day, I'll get men like that James Veck. I mean that."

Bryce swallowed. "I know you will, Troy. You're a damned good man . . . a good son." He turned and met the young man's eyes. "It will happen to you, Troy . . . with Lisa. The hurt. Part of her . . . can never belong to you."

Troy hid the hurt and jealousy. "I know that," he answered. "I knew it from the beginning, Pa. We'll be all right."

Bryce just looked away. "Tell her I love her."

"She knows that." Troy rose, going to his horse. "I'm going to tell her you're all right. I'll be back in a while, Pa."

Bryce nodded and Troy turned his horse. Yes, he knew he'd feel the hurt, too. He already had. But it was different for him and Lisa. He had not been her first. Shannon belonged to his father because he had already won her heart and body. In that respect, Lisa could never belong to him. She would always belong to Chaco, and that was the hell of it.

Bryce sat watching the water of the stream rush by, fed by mountain water. Soon it would dry up, as everything did in this land. What had held him here so long? Why did he love this desolate country? It was as though he'd come out here and had been hypnotized. He sat staring at the water for a long time, thinking back across the years, the terrible months during which he thought Shannon was dead.

"Bryce." The name was spoken behind him. He turned to see Shannon standing there. Their eyes held. "I am your wife. I have been your wife since I was practically a child back in Virginia. How long ago has that been? Twenty-four years?

Twenty-five? You've been holding out on me, Bryce Edwards. I thought I knew every side of you, thought *I* was the one who needed *you*. All this time you needed me just as much."

He turned away but she knelt down behind him, putting her hands hesitantly on his shoulders. "Bryce ... my beautiful beloved. You have never let me be the strong one, let me do the comforting. Forgive me for always crying on your shoulder, for not recognizing you are only human. To me you've always been like a god. And I have never, never loved another man more than I have loved you, as God is my witness."

He turned back to her, studying the brilliant green eyes. He pulled her tightly into his arms then, whispering her name. He rolled her over, feeling more like twenty-five than fifty-four, wanting her, always seeing her as he saw her when she was a young southern belle so innocent and trusting. His lips moved over her neck, and he nestled his face against her full breasts.

"I'm drunk," he murmured.

She smiled sadly, winding her fingers into his hair. "Really? I didn't know."

He raised up and met her eyes. "I love you, Shannon. I wish you knew how much."

"My God, Bryce, after all we've been through, how could I not know how much you love me? I just wonder if you know how much I love you."

He studied her eyes. "I'm so sorry ... about the article."

She tried to disguise her pain. "Why? You didn't write it. You were doing the right thing, Bryce. Don't you ever forget it. And don't ever, ever stop doing what you can for Chaco and the Apaches because of me. The day you do that is when I *will* stop loving you. We aren't going to let those men and people like James Veck destroy us, Bryce. Do you understand? Nothing can destroy us. Nothing. We learned that, a long, long time ago."

He bent down, kissing her mouth hungrily, moving to her

neck, her breasts again. "When I'm sober I'll show you," he whispered.

She closed her eyes, cradling him in her bosom. "You've already done that, Bryce Edwards, not just in our bed but in every moment, every look, every touch, every deed. You never had to prove anything to me. And now we've got to stay together and strong. The children will need us. God only knows what will happen to Chaco. The biggest test may still be ahead of us. But we'll survive it, because we have each other." She stroked his hair. "I'll have my Bryce, my handsome, brave soldier who came calling on me once in his uniform and almost made me faint dead away with love."

He lay there quietly for several minutes, and she realized he was asleep. She kept stroking his hair, his shoulders and arms. "I'm so sorry I let you down that day," she said softly. "But I never loved you more than I did then, saying good-bye to my Colonel Edwards."

Chapter Twenty-One

Lisa turned to watch Troy finish polishing new boots. "I hate to leave after what happened with that article and all. I feel like I should stay with Pa until he gets back to the post."

"He has your mother. He'll be all right, Troy. It was just such a blow to all of us. But your father is strong. And you've put off this trip long enough. If you're going to start reporting the stories you know need writing, you've got to get to New York and get a little experience. And the sooner you go, the sooner you can come back."

He looked at her and grinned. They shared the extra little cabin that had been built for them, the cabin she was to have shared with Little Deer once Troy was gone. But Little Deer was dead, and soon she and the rest of the family would be going back to the post. It would be almost two weeks before the new agent came, and Lisa was sure that Bryce, being the conscientious man he was, would stay awhile longer to show the man around.

Troy put a log in the belly of the black wood stove that heated their cabin. "It's a little chilly tonight."

Lisa's heart ached for him. The experience with his father had been traumatic for him and surely made him wonder about his own marriage. Here he was, married to a woman not of his choosing, soon to be supporting two sons that were not his own. This was an example of the extent of his love for Chaco ... to care for his woman and sons. This was the kind of man that Troy was, and she loved him for it.

"I hope Pa will be all right," he spoke up, coming toward the bed then and removing his shirt.

"You've got to stop worrying, Troy. Your parents have been through worse. They love each other very much. You just concentrate on your writing."

He sighed and sat down on the edge of the bed. "Well, some day I'm going to make up for that article about my mother. I'm going to do what Pa couldn't do, through my writing."

Lisa lay back, reaching out and tracing her fingers down his muscular back. "You will, too. I know you will."

He removed his boots and socks, then stood up to undo his pants. "I can't believe I'm really leaving." He met her eyes. "I just hope to God you don't suffer as much as my mother has. With or without me it won't be easy for you, Lisa. I'd hate to see you written about like they wrote about my mother."

"If she can bear it, so can I. We understand what we did. No one else has to."

He climbed onto the bed, still wearing his long johns. He hovered over her, studying the disturbingly beautiful face. "It doesn't seem right, leaving you like this. It will be hard riding out in the morning, then that long, lonely ride on the Butterfield to places I've never been before."

"You'll lose your lonely thoughts once you get to see things and go places you've never been before. Just think—all the way to New York City! I'm from the East, but I've never seen a place like that."

He grinned and kissed her nose. "Well, maybe I'll go back and take you with me next time."

Their eyes held. "I get kind of chill thinking about it, Troy. I mean, so many things are changing—you going away, us going back home, Chaco out there somewhere, and the Apaches losing everything." Her eyes teared. "Why do I get this feeling you won't be the same Troy when you come back?"

He put a hand to the side of her face. "Because I won't be. I'll know more, be more experienced. So what?"

"So your feelings for me might change. You might not like coming back to a woman you never chose in the first place, and to two sons who are not your own. We might seem like just a burden to you."

He kissed her lips lightly. "I could never think of any of you that way."

"But you're still so young, and I'm the only woman you've known." She reddened. "Except for the whores around Fort Bowie."

He chuckled. "You know about them?"

She puckered her lips and pushed at him. "I'm not that ignorant, Troy Edwards."

He laughed harder and kissed at her neck. "Then you know you aren't the only woman I've ever known. You're just the only one I've loved. There's a big difference, you know."

"I know. But you were kind of forced into loving me, Troy, without ever going out into the world and finding a wife on your own. I feel so guilty about it."

"Well, you can quit. I wanted to marry you and I did. So that's that." His lips moved over her neck to her breasts. She lay naked in the bed. This was his last night home. It was understood they should make love.

He pushed the covers to her waist, gently sucking at the full nipples that still nursed Sage, drawing out her own passion, taking his time so as to enjoy every moment, every soft curve, every whimper, every delicious part of her so that he would remember. He hid his own doubts and fears as to what lay ahead for both of them. This was tonight, and this was all they had for at least a year.

She raked her fingers through the thick, blond hair, offering her breasts to him in sweet abandon. He moved his lips over her chest to the other breast, then to her lips, kissing deeply, reaching down to push off his long johns. He left her for just a moment to get them all the way off, then moved in under the covers.

"The lamp is still lit," she said then between hungry kisses.

"I want it lit. I want to see you, remember you, every last curve and hidden place," he told her.

She felt on fire as he moved over her in his special, gentle way, trailing his lips over her breasts again, then over her belly, down and down, pushing the covers back as he went and moving his lips over her thighs, the calves of her legs, kissing her feet. Then he trailed back up, and her desire and passion grew as he moved to that secret place reserved for only the most special of men. Chaco had been that special. He had been the first to teach her this reckless abandon and the joys of turning herself over, body and soul. But now she belonged to another. She was Troy's wife, and she would allow her husband the pleasures he deserved, for in giving them, she enjoyed such ecstasy in return.

She was totally his now, at his command, unable to stop him, not wanting to stop him, for she would be denying herself her own pleasure. She was hardly aware that she cried out his name as the pulsing ecstasy moved through her, making her feel like a wanton woman, making her reach up for him as he moved on top of her, then reach down to guide him into her depths.

Yes. They must do this—over and over. He was going away. Troy was going away and her heart was sad. She must give him this pleasure before he left, remember his own manly build and kind ways. He was beautiful to look at, easy to love, a man who commanded respect by his very being.

They moved with a natural rhythm, ignoring the imminent parting, ignoring the doubts that always plagued their tender marriage, ignoring the outside sorrows that could so easily invade their minds and hearts and spoil this moment. They would not let it happen.

She took him into herself, arching up to him in great waves of desire, yet always, in these deepest moments of ecstasy, Chaco would flash into her mind. Sometimes it would be Chaco hovering over her, Chaco making love to her this way. Oh, but that was so long ago, or at least it seemed that way, and Chaco was gone. For all she knew he might even be dead. She must not think of him. She must not! Not when she was in the arms of Troy, her husband, the man she loved now. This was right. This was what should be. And he was so sweet and beautiful and kind. Troy! Troy! It must only be Troy.

He groaned out her name, grasping her hips and pushing hard as his life flowed into her. This time he did not move away. He lay there a moment, saying nothing, then started kissing her again. When his lips moved to meet hers, she realized his cheeks were wet with tears, and she could not help wondering if they were only tears of having to leave. Perhaps they were tears for himself, for the things he would miss because of the burden of promising his love to her and to Chaco's sons. Would she ever get over the guilt?

He was moving inside of her again, and she could feel him growing within her. He seemed desperate to get all he could of her before he left, as though he would not get this chance again.

They moved together, again lost in one another, while outside an unusually chilly wind moved through the reservation, bringing with it a hard rain. Apaches huddled in their wickiups and rude cabins, wondering why another promised government shipment of supplies was late and mourning over the fact that Bryce Edwards would be leaving as agent. They did not understand this. He was a good man and had helped them. His wife was good, too. Why did he have to go? It seemed the white men always did things backward and did not know what they wanted. It frightened them to have things constantly changing, and angered them to realize the two white men who had murdered and raped not only Apaches but whites would not be prosecuted.

In the hills above a man huddled alone, his heart aching for the woman he could not have and crying for the one he had lost to death. His loneliness had become unbearable, for he also missed his mother and stepfather and his brother. He longed to see his sons. The obsession to see them had become more than he could bear, and for this he had risked leaving Geronimo and coming down from his hiding place in the mountains. Surely he would die soon. He would not die without seeing his blood sons.

He huddled under a blanket against the wind, not daring to build a fire and be seen. Perhaps he was a fool to come, but he must see his boys—and he must see his Lisa again. He wondered if she slept in his brother's arms this night. Of course she did. How could it be otherwise? He put away jealous thoughts. He had no right to any of them now. But just to see her face, touch her hair, speak to her—how wonderful it would be. And to hold his sons in his arms!

He concentrated on the spirits that guided him. He must not be caught. He must not linger too long. He would see Lisa and Troy—see his sons—then go. Go to his death, for that was all that was left for him now.

Breakfast was quiet. Lisa made it at her cabin for everyone. Shannon struggled to keep the tears from coming. It was bad enough not knowing anything about Chaco, thinking perhaps she might never see him again. Now Troy was leaving. It was for a good reason and she was happy for him. But he was her son, the son she had always been able to keep with her. It seemed each child was special in his own way, so special. Wasn't it only yesterday that they were small, running and playing together, one so dark, the other so fair? Now both would be gone. But at least she would have her grandchildren.

Lisa sat down with Charles in her lap, while Sage slept on the bed. They all laughed as Charles picked up a fistful of biscuit with gravy on it and shoved it into his mouth, unable to get quite all of it in.

"Oh, Charles, look at you," Lisa fussed, grabbing for a towel. A knock came at the door and Bryce opened it to let in an Apache scout who looked nervously around the room, eyeing everyone, his eyes lingering on Lisa and little Charles for a moment before turning back to Bryce.

"What is it, Red Dog?" Bryce asked him.

"Me . . . Victor . . . we see someone. He not see us."

"Who? Who did you see?"

Red Dog looked around the room again before answering. "Chaco," he answered quietly.

"Chaco," Shannon gasped. "Here? At San Carlos?"

Red Dog nodded. "We leave him. Come tell you first."

Lisa and Troy looked at each other. Their eyes held. "Why would he take such a chance?" Lisa asked in a near whisper.

Troy sighed, rising from the table. "To see his sons. That's my guess." He looked at his father. "What do you think?"

Bryce ran a hand through his hair. "I don't know what to think, except that he's got to be crazy."

"He's heard about Little Deer," Shannon spoke up. "That's what it is. He's heard she died and that she had a son. He has two sons he hasn't ever seen and it's killing him."

Bryce looked at Red Dog. "Was he alone?"

Red Dog nodded. "Ai. He alone. Geronimo not come here. He far down in Mexico, I think."

"Don't tell anyone," Bryce told him. "Officially, I can't give you orders. I can only ask out of friendship that you not tell anyone you've seen him and that you pass the word to the other scouts to leave him alone if you spot him. If he is around, he'll probably leave soon. It's too dangerous for him here and he knows it."

Red Dog nodded. "You are good friend . . . ," he put a fist to his chest "here. You good friend to Apache. We no hurt Chaco. New agent find out, he tell us get him. We no let him find out. He no come maybe two more weeks. Chaco be gone by then."

Bryce nodded. "Thank you, Red Dog. And thank you for coming to tell us."

Red Dog nodded. "You good friend," he repeated. He left then, and the room was quiet for several long seconds.

"Well," Troy finally spoke up, "Chaco certainly knows how to keep us on our toes, doesn't he?" He looked straight at Lisa, almost longingly. He rose then. "I can't let anything else keep me, Pa. It's best done and over with. I'd stay till we know what this thing is with Chaco, but it seems like there is always something to keep me here." He walked up to his father. "My horse is already packed. White Horse will ride with me to the Butterfield station and bring the horse back with him."

Bryce nodded. It tore at Troy's heart to see the dark circles under his father's eyes. They embraced. "Some day it will all work out, Pa. I'll make it work. You hang on and keep the faith. You'll see."

Bryce said nothing. He patted his son's back and then turned away. Troy went to Shannon. Yes, she was aging, too. These last few months had been too much. She was grayer, thinner. But she was a strong woman. She rose and hugged him, crying quietly.

"Promise you'll come back to us," she whispered.

"You know I will, Mother." His eyes moved to Lisa. "I have a wife and two sons, remember?"

He held Lisa's eyes while he hugged his mother. Lisa saw his thoughts. Chaco was somewhere about. Would he try to see her? Had she really put him out of her heart?

He kissed his mother's cheek, then turned to the babies, picking up each of them and giving them a kiss.

"Me go, Daa," Charles told him, indicating he wanted to go with "Daa," his father.

"Not this time, Charles. You take care of your mommy."

The words tore at Shannon's heart. It seemed only yesterday

that Chaco used to beg to go with Bryce when Bryce served at Fort Bowie. Could her sons really be so grown?

Now Troy and Lisa were embracing—tightly, so tightly. Bryce and Shannon each picked up a baby and went out, and Troy pulled back and studied Lisa's eyes, so blue. "Follow your heart, Lisa. We had an understanding when we got married. I made some promises that I'll keep. All you have to do is tell me what you want."

"Troy, what are you talking about?"

He searched her eyes. "That look is still there in your eyes when someone mentions Chaco's name. And there is still something about you that is missing when I make love to you in the night. It's good and wonderful. I've never felt as good as when I'm making love to you. But in your mind it's still Chaco who holds you."

Her eyes widened and she looked away. "No. It's you. I love you, Troy."

He took her chin and made her face him. "And I love you. We've shared friendship, and we do love each other in a special way. Now we'll be apart with lots of time to think. When I come back, we'll know a lot more."

"I don't want to lose you, Troy. You're the most wonderful man . . ."

He put his fingers to her lips. "You don't owe me, Lisa. You never have. But I do love you and I'll come back to you. And if this marriage is going to work, we will know then. I want you to think real hard. You might even see Chaco again. I don't doubt my brother will try to find a way to see you if he's determined to see his sons. He can't see one without the other, and it's been a long, long time since you got to talk to Chaco alone. I can't wait around to see if he tries to see you, Lisa. I just want you to know . . . to search inside yourself, make some choices. When I come home, I'll ask no questions. We'll either be husband and wife or we won't, but I'll always look after you and the boys."

311

"Troy, how can you talk that way after last night?"

He grinned sadly. "Because I'm no fool, Lisa. I know good and well that you truly do love me, just as I love you. But sometimes our kind of love isn't enough. I want it to be. Maybe we'll learn that it is." He kissed her, a long, hungry kiss as though a kiss of good-bye—not just this temporary good-bye but a longer one. She flung her arms around his neck, returning the kiss with ardent passion, wanting him all over again, loving him so and trying to show him he was all she wanted.

He released his kiss and they embraced tightly. "Oh, Troy, come back," she whispered.

"I will. No matter what. I'll be back." He kissed her hair, and there were tears in his eyes. "I have something to do, Lisa, above and beyond anything that happens in my personal life. I have this ... this mission ... this calling. I'll be back, and I'll make up for what happened to my father and my mother and you. Whatever happens between us, that won't change." He kissed her forehead, then turned and walked her to the door. They went outside and he looked at her once more, almost the look of a lost little boy.

He hugged his father and mother once more, then mounted up. "I'll be back," he assured them all once more. His last look was for Lisa. "Good-bye."

"Good-bye, Troy," she sobbed. "I love you."

He just nodded, turning his horse and riding off. As he left the reservation he felt it—the eyes—someone watching him. Yes. Someone was definitely watching him. He had to grin in spite of the thought of Lisa seeing Chaco again. Chaco used to love to hide when they were small and dare Troy to find him. Troy never could. Even then Chaco had the Apache instinct for literally melting into the rocks. He was doing it now. Troy was sure of it.

Chapter Twenty-Two

Lisa stayed late at the little schoolhouse, to which she had become so attached. She had helped Shannon here more than once, carting both babies with her so that she could watch Charles and breast-feed Sage when necessary. Here she had helped teach little Apache children. Here she had also taught older children who were willing to learn new ways. And here she had helped mothers understand how to help keep their children from getting diseases, how to better care for themselves. She had struggled along with Shannon to show them that not all whites were bad, had promised them that government supplies would surely begin coming in more regularly.

While all this was going on, the preachers and other male help on the reservation were teaching Indian men how to farm, how to survive a new way. But it was an impossible task. The cultures of the Indian and the white man were so different it would surely be a generation, perhaps two, three, or four generations, before the Indians began to live differently. Their restless spirit had been so obvious, and now seemed so broken. If they could not live their old ways, they did not want to live at all.

With Troy gone it all seemed even more depressing. Now they would leave this place. White men in power had dashed

Bryce Edwards' hopes of truly accomplishing something here, and now they must leave. She stared at the empty little benches. Fewer and fewer children had been coming lately, ever since Chadwell and Miller were freed and Bryce was forced out of San Carlos. The Indians were not as ignorant as some wanted to believe. They knew what was going on, that they were being duped and cheated. More and more men turned to the whiskey that was made so readily available for them through the illegal traders, who traded cheap whiskey for valuable government goods, which were resold someplace else. The Indians had no understanding of white man's bargaining, and so it was easy to take them for everything they had.

She sighed, blinking back tears. She had to get home. Shannon had already left, taking the babies. But Lisa was finding it hard to leave the little building. She would miss the wide, brown eyes and bright smiles of the Apache children. And she hated the thought that many of them would now be sent to other schools off the reservation, where many of them would lose their spirits, lose those smiles, aching for home and family. They would cringe when their hair was cut off, and squirm in uncomfortable woolen clothing. Those in power had claimed that teaching them on the reservation simply would not work, that they must be completely removed from their families and familiar surroundings. Shannon and Lisa and others had argued against it. But those with the real power, people without the tiniest bit of understanding about what goes on inside the mind and heart of the Indian—the importance of the Indian spirit and religion—had made up their minds. They were treated like dogs to be trained on a leash.

It was over now. They had been here such a short time, deliberately denied enough time to prove their theories and show the kind of progress they might have made. She put a shawl around her shoulders. It was much warmer again, but chilly at night. It was getting dark, but she was not afraid. She smiled at the thought of what her friends back home in Illinois would think of her now—having worked on an Apache Indian reservation, been lover to an Apache man by whom she bore a son, having married his brother and taken in her Apache man's Indian son by another woman. What strange turns her life had taken! It was as though someone had taken her hand and led her down a totally new path in life.

She blew out the lamp and walked out, closing the door behind her. She hurried down the steps toward home when an old Apache man leaped from behind an out building as she passed it, startling her so that she gasped and halted.

"Witch!" He spat the word at her, stalking straight up to her so that she had to back up. "Teach Apache children hate Apache way! It is bad what you do!"

She swallowed, putting a hand to her chest and telling herself to stay calm. The man held a whip in his hand, rolled up and balanced as though ready to lash out at her. "I ... I don't teach the children bad things," she answered. "I only teach them words." She could smell whiskey, and wondered if he was sober enough to reason at all.

"Teach bad things," he repeated. "White witch! All you witches come here ... take away sons and daughters ... make them be white ... kill spirits! Our God say ... we should not let children come to white school. White man's witches and demons steal the souls of our children!"

"It ... it isn't so. You can come and visit some day. You're welcome ..."

"No come school! You leave children alone!" With that he raised the whip. Lisa screamed and tried to run, but the black cord came around her waist and she felt a sting in her back. The whip caught her like a lasso and she fell. She felt her panic building as she grasped at the weapon and wiggled to get free of it.

The Indian man yanked on it, rolling her body. Before she could rise the whip came down again across her back and she cried out in terror, still struggling to get to her feet. Again the man lashed out, catching her arm.

"Someone help me," she yelled, wondering if the man intended to whip her to death. She barely made it to her feet when the cord came around her neck. The man pulled, choking her with it. She tried to grasp at it to pull it away, but to no avail.

"Witch die! Little children be free," the man growled.

Lisa felt the air and life leaving her, and dusk began to turn to blackness. But she was suddenly released, and she heard grunts and struggling. She thought she heard the sound of punches but she was not certain, her thoughts were too confused, her sight too dizzy from lack of air. She stayed on her knees, gasping for breath, wondering if her windpipe was damaged, for the breath would not come right away. She wanted to scream for help, but no sound would come out of her throat.

Someone was behind her then, embracing her gently. "Stay still and try to relax," a voice told her. "You will start to breathe again naturally. Don't struggle for it, Lisa."

She stayed bent over, held by a strong arm. Was she right in thinking the voice belonged to Chaco? She heard little whimpering sounds coming from her own throat as she began to get her breath back.

"It is all right," the voice told her. "He will not bother you again. He was just drunk." He picked her up in strong arms and she rested her head on his shoulder. Chaco! It was Chaco! She tried to cry out his name, urge him to get away, but his name only came in a whisper as he carried her back inside the little schoolhouse. He set her carefully on her feet and she put a hand to her throat, looking at him wide-eyed as he relit a lamp. He was dressed simply in buckskin leggings and moccasins and a blue calico shirt that was not fully buttoned. A lovely turquoise necklace adorned his throat and chest. The blue and turquoise seemed to accent his dark skin and handsome face. His hair was brushed out plain and long, one feather tied into the side of it. He looked good, healthier than she expected but still a little too thin.

"Hello, Lisa," he said with a smile.

Their eyes held in a moment of sudden passion and old feelings. He looked her over as though she were some precious gem, stepping closer and putting a hand to the side of her face. She stepped back, tears in her eyes.

"Why are you here?" she whispered. "They'll catch you! You shouldn't be here. Troy risked his life to help you escape, and now you're back! You must go, Chaco!"

He shook his head. "Here. Come here. The cuts are bleeding."

She held back, but his dark, gentle eyes commanded her to come forward. How could she not obey? Why was she such putty in his presence? Why did he look so wonderful? But the eyes—they were tired. Dark circles betrayed his sorrows. Chaco. Sweet, beautiful Chaco. She stepped closer and he put a hand on her shoulder, sending fire through her blood as he gently made her turn around. He tore away the back of her dress a little where the whip had cut through the clothing and her skin.

"The bastard," he muttered. "You are bleeding. Does it hurt bad?"

"It ... stings a little. That's all. I think the dress helped keep it from doing much damage."

"I am sorry I did not get to you sooner. I was coming to the school to try to signal you, talk to you. I have come to see my sons. I have been waiting for the right time. Then I saw him beating you. I hesitated, hoping you could get away so I would not have to make my presence known."

He pushed away another piece of her dress where there was another cut on her back.

"Did the old man recognize you?" she asked. "Did anyone else see you?"

"He is too drunk to recognize anyone. If he did, no one

317

would believe him. Men full of whiskey see lots of things. I do not think anyone else saw."

He turned her around to face him. Their eyes locked in old love and desire. "You look so beautiful, Lisa."

Her eyes teared and she reached up and touched his face. "Are you all right? You're too thin, Chaco."

He shrugged. "When you are always running and hiding, there is no time for grand meals."

He grasped her hand and kissed the palm, closing his eyes and trembling. She wanted to pull her hand away, but could not bring herself to do it. "Little Deer," he whispered. "It did not take long for her to die?"

How could she tell him about the long, terrible labor? "No," she lied. "It didn't take long. And there wasn't much pain. There was just too much bleeding afterward."

He opened his eyes, watery with tears. "My son?"

"We named him Saguaro Cochise. We call him Sage. I . . . I've taken him in. I still had milk because of Charles. I'm nursing him. He's a healthy, handsome boy, very dark like his father and mother."

His eyes fell to her full breasts, breasts that nursed two sons he had never even seen. How had he come to this? There was nothing left now but to see his sons before he died. But now . . . now here was Lisa . . . beautiful, precious Lisa, whom he had never stopped loving. The ache of knowing none of it could ever be again. . . . "Lisa," he groaned.

He pulled her into his arms and both of them wept . . . wept for more than each other . . . wept for a people and a way of life that was dying and would never be again . . . wept for the loss of the happiness they could have had if people had left them alone.

"I have never stopped loving you, Lisa," he told her, his tears wetting her hair.

"And I have never stopped loving you," she answered. "Oh,

Chaco, I try to forget those wonderful days we had together, and the nights. I try so hard, but I can't."

His lips were kissing her hair, her temple, her cheek. Her face was turning to him automatically, and then his lips were searching her own. Wrong! So wrong it was now, yet so right. How she needed to kiss him again, hold him again. He had so little left. How could she deny him a last kiss?

But that was all it took, for the fire was still there, deep, deep inside. The wild fire of his spirit burned into her body and soul, finding deep inside the still-hot coals and fanning them into splendid passion long buried. He searched deeply, discovering nothing had changed, knowing still this could and should not be, trying to remind himself she belonged to Troy now. But he could think of her only as his own, and the thought of his brother claiming her only made him want her all the more, want to prove he was still first in her heart, to know at least that much before facing the end of so many other things.

He released the long, hungry kiss, trembling, aching for her, for anyone who had ever truly loved him for himself. "You ... walk home," he told her in a near whisper. "I will follow in the shadows. When it is safe, I will come to the cabin where you stay. I have been watching. I know where you are. You can let me in. I can see my sons."

She forced herself to pull away, wiping at her tears and looking up at him. "This isn't right, Chaco. I ... belong to Troy now. You ... shouldn't have come at all."

He grasped her shoulders. "You are mine. You have always been mine. I was your first man."

"Chaco, don't ..."

"I have little time left, Lisa," he said almost desperately. "If I could change it all, I would. But what is done is done! I am branded, but I do not regret any of it, for I did what I thought I must do to help my people. My only regret is you, that I have hurt you so." He swallowed, holding his jaw rigid for a moment while unwanted tears trickled down his cheeks. "And I do not

319

want to hurt my brother. Yet my love for him, and knowing what is right and wrong, do not seem to matter when I touch you, see you. Troy is gone. There is no one to know we shared one last moment of love before it was over for me."

"My God, Chaco, don't do this to me. It isn't fair!" She broke into bitter sobbing, covering her face with her hands. "I've tried so hard ... to forget you. I've ... given myself to Troy ... told him I love him. He's so good to me. He's given up so much of his own personal life to take care of me and both your sons. He's so ... devoted to you."

She cried for several long, silent seconds, then wiped at her eyes with the sleeve of her dress, looking up to say more, only to see that he was gone! Her heart raced. She had sent him away without really meaning to. Yes, she had wanted him to go, yet now that he had....

"Chaco!" Her eyes darted around the little room. "Chaco!"

Why? Why had she done that? Poor Chaco! He was so lonely, so lost. It was her last chance to tell him she loved him, that they all loved him. Now she had made him go. He had reached out for her and she had turned him away.

She wept more as she blew out the lamp and went outside. "Chaco." She half whispered the name, afraid to shout it lest others might hear. There was no sign of him. It was fully dark now and she hurried through the shadows to her cabin, where Bryce and Shannon both waited with the babies, looking very worried.

"Lisa! Bryce was just going to look for you," Shannon exclaimed. "My God, Lisa, what happened?"

Lisa realized how she must look, dirty and bleeding, her dress torn. She was almost glad for the excuse it all gave her to look upset and to be crying. "An old Indian man ... he ... attacked me," she sobbed. "He said I was ... a witch and taught bad things ... to the children."

"Good God," Bryce fumed. "Where is he!"

Lisa wiped at her eyes with a shaking hand. "He was drunk.

He just ... passed out before he could really hurt me," she lied.

"Oh, Lisa, come and let me help you clean up. Let's get you into your nightgown."

"I'll go check things out," Bryce spoke up. He put a hand on Lisa's arm. "You all right?"

"I ... think so. More shaken than anything else," she answered, averting her eyes from his. He must not know! He must not know she had seen Chaco.

Bryce left and Shannon helped her wash and change, while the babies both slept in a small bed kept in the corner of the main room.

"You poor thing," Shannon fussed. "You shouldn't be alone tonight. I'll stay with you. Or you can come over to our cabin."

"No!" She answered so quickly Shannon looked at her in surprise, then frowned.

"What is it, Lisa?"

Lisa began to redden. This woman was too damned wise. Why had she answered so quickly?

"I just ... I want to be alone, that's all. Troy's been gone such a short while. I like to sit ... and pretend he's here. We'll be leaving soon. I have some memories in this little cabin. I want to be by myself tonight. I'm not afraid. He was just a drunk old man."

Shannon watched her a moment longer. Something else was wrong but she could not be sure what it was. It surely couldn't be Chaco. He wouldn't dare come right into San Carlos ... or would he?

"I don't like leaving you alone, Lisa. You've been hurt."

"I'm all right," Lisa insisted. "Please, I ... I really want to be by myself. Tomorrow we're going home. I want to stay alone tonight."

Shannon sighed, patting her arm. "If you're sure. We're close by if you need us, you know."

"I know."

Bryce was back then, mumbling about the "damned whiskey traders." "I found the old man," he told them. "He's out cold. I just dragged him onto some grass and let him sleep. It's old Juan. He's always drunk and he's a mean old cuss. If I could have stayed longer, I could have possibly controlled the whiskey." He patted Lisa's head. "You all right now?"

"Yes, thank you." She tied her robe around herself. "I think I'd just like to go to sleep."

"Well, Shannon will stay ..."

"She'd rather be alone, Bryce."

He frowned. "Nonsense. Not after what happened."

"It was just one drunk old man and he's passed out," Lisa spoke up. "Really, Bryce, I'd rather be by myself tonight. We're leaving tomorrow. I have so many things to think about. Shannon already agreed."

"Well, if you're sure. I don't like it myself."

"I'm fine. Troy has been gone for three weeks and every night you two have stayed here or I have slept at your cabin. I really would like this one night alone ... to kind of ... say good-bye to this little place. God knows it isn't fancy, but I've called it home. That's why I spent so long at the schoolhouse, thinking about everything, saying good-bye. I'll miss the children so."

"Yes. Won't we all?" Shannon spoke the words sadly.

Bryce walked over to her and urged her toward the door, looking back at Lisa once more. "You sure?"

She gave him a smile. "Yes. I'm sure."

He frowned again, shaking his head before walking out with Shannon. Lisa hurried over and bolted the door, putting her head against it then and breathing deeply. Chaco. She had seen Chaco, been held by him, kissed by him. Should she tell them in the morning? She almost wished ... No. That was wrong. Wrong! Wrong! She wished she'd get a letter from Troy. He had probably not even reached New York yet. He was probably on a train somewhere in Illinois—perhaps Indiana or Ohio. She had seen those places once, oh, so long ago. Was she really from there? Had there ever really been that other Lisette Powers? And what would going east and seeing so many new things and meeting new people do to Troy? He was so talented, so handsome.

She felt so lonely. Why had she sent Chaco away? Because it was the right thing to do, that was why. It was best. She was too weak when she was near him. Still, she could not help feeling she had been cruel to turn him away so quickly. He had risked his life to come and see his sons. Poor Chaco. He had nothing left. Nothing.

She walked over and checked the babies. They were sleeping soundly. She was relieved to see Sage seemed to be breathing steadily. It seemed his coughing was getting worse, and she didn't know what to do about it. She turned down the lamp and lay down on the bed, but sleep would not come. Her mind reeled with a mixture of things—old childhood memories, her parents, the awful ordeal with the outlaws, Chaco, Troy, giving birth to Charles, and the sad life for the Indians at San Carlos. Around and around her thoughts whirled, always ending with Chaco. Her eyes began to droop, but popped open again when she heard a scratching sound at the door.

She sat up straight, her heart pounding. The sound came again. She moved to the doorway, taking down a handgun she kept on a hook high above it. "Who is it?" she asked quietly, in case . . . just in case . . .

"It is I. Chaco," came the words, coarsely whispered.

She hesitated. Should she turn him away again? No. She could not. She put up the gun and unbolted the door, stepping back and letting him inside quickly, then rebolting the door. Their eyes met, and in the next moment he swept her into his arms.

"I could not stay away," he groaned. "I wanted one last time with you, Lisa."

It took only those words to melt her into clay. He pressed

her tightly against himself, searching her mouth, moving his hand to her hips and pressing his hardness against her in terrible longing.

"Oh, Chaco, Chaco," she whimpered when he left her mouth. "I wanted you to go, and yet I didn't. I prayed you'd come back. God forgive me!"

"We will have each other. We will have each other once more, Lisa. I must leave before dawn." He released her slightly. "All this time I have been living and hiding in the hills, afraid every day I would be caught, sleeping at night with no fire. Three days ago I found an old Apache man I once knew. He was hunting far out on the outer edge of the reservation. He recognized me and I asked him if I could have refuge for just a little while. He hid me in his wickiup. That is how I managed to stay a little longer. But every moment I take a chance on being caught. I trust the old man. He is wise and he can hold his tongue. He put my horse among his own, telling others he found it. Before the sun is up I will leave. But I knew I must see you—and my sons. I cleaned myself up before coming to see you at the school, so you would not see how it has really been for me."

"Oh, Chaco." She rested her head against his chest. "What about Bryce and your mother?"

"I long to see them, especially my mother. But it would only upset her more. I do not like doing this to you, either, but I want to see my sons, Lisa. And then when I am near you ..." He kissed her hair, noticing the babies asleep then on the small bed nearby. "Shiye!" He moved away from her, quietly leaning over them. Charles lay sprawled on his back, his dark blond hair a mass of waves, his lips puckered in deep sleep. He was a hefty boy, big for two. Sage lay on his stomach, tangled dark hair so thick it almost hid his face. His arm was stretched out beside Charles', and the contrast of their skin was obvious.

A strange gasp came from Chaco's lips. He groaned something in the Apache tongue and went to his knees, touching each child lightly. He put his head down on the edge of the bed, saying nothing. Lisa's heart shattered. Children were so important to the Apache. Surely it was killing Chaco to not be able to be with his sons. She reached down and stroked his hair.

"They're good boys, Chaco. They give me no trouble at all. And they're very strong and healthy." Why should she burden him by telling him about Sage's cough? "They'll be fine men some day. Troy and I, as well as their grandparents, will see to that."

He stayed there for a long time before turning to her, his face stricken with pain and loneliness. He gathered her into his arms then, and both knew what must be. He rose, picking her up with him, carrying her to her own bed and laying her on it. He untied her robe and pulled it open, then hesitated. She reached up for him. Right or wrong, she was not going to turn away the man she first called husband, the man she still loved, the man who had fathered her son.

He came down and met her lips, and from then on her world was a swirl of ecstasy, a dark, hard-muscled body hovering over her, her gown coming off so easily. Somehow they were both naked. She was so lost in his kisses and his touch and his whispered words of love that she was hardly aware of how it had happened. His fingers were exploring that secret place that he had been the first to touch and invade. Fire ripped through her very soul as his lips and tongue searched her own mouth, traveled over her neck, tasted of the breasts that fed his sons, moved over her belly and to that place he had owned first.

Chaco! His very touch set her aflame. His presence made her lose all sense. His loneliness drew out all her love and her desire to please and comfort him. Now he moved back up over her body. His lips were parting hers again in a fiery, deep kiss; his body moved over hers, skin against skin, his most manly part pressing against her belly, searching for solace and one last moment of ecstasy.

She cried out and wept when he entered her. Chaco! At last! One last time. She would have him one last time. She never dreamed they would have this chance again. For this moment she was not Troy's wife, and in a way she never had been. She gave no thought to right or wrong now, no thought to how she would feel tomorrow or how she would tell Troy. There was no room for such thoughts. There was only room for this man, this beautiful, gentle, spiritual man who took her to heights of ecstasy no one else could bring her.

Everything that had happened since she was taken from him vanished from her mind. She was back in the wickiup in the mountains, alone with Chaco, living a hard but sweet life. And it was good. It was so very good.

They could not get enough of each other. It had been so long! So long! And yet here, in his arms, the months apart disappeared. They refreshed every memory, every touch, every glorious moment of sharing and giving. She arched up to him almost desperately, and he took her the same way, so that when they finished both were spent. He tumbled beside her, pulling the covers over them and holding her close.

"Lisa. My Lisa," he whispered, kissing the thick, golden hair, running his hands over her back. "I have betrayed my brother, and yet I am not sorry."

She kissed his chest. "Somehow I don't think we have," she answered. "He said something before he left. We'd heard someone had spotted you and you might be around. And the day Troy left, he said ... he said I should follow my heart—think about our marriage—what we will do when he returns. He acted so strangely, Chaco, as though he knew."

Chaco closed his eyes and sighed. "Do you love him?"

She snuggled closer. "Yes. Troy is easy to love. He's a good man. But I don't love him in the way I love you. We're almost like ... like good friends. But I ... I've been a wife to him, Chaco. He loves me. He wanted me that way and he's given up so much for me. I thought there was no hope for us, and I needed a real home for Charles."

He shuddered with jealousy. But he could not blame Troy. "You do not need to explain, Lisa. You are a woman with needs and he is a man with the same needs. He is your legal husband."

"It's all so strange, so confusing." She looked up at him then. "I'm in love with two men." She touched his lips. "But you are most special. You are the father of my child ... my first love."

He kissed her fingers. "There is so little time to talk, to say all the things that should be said." He stroked her hair. "I am so sorry, Lisa. So sorry I hurt you so. If there was a way we could have a life together, I would take it. But I see no hope. Anyplace I go, they will seek me out. Even if I could get away, start someplace new, it would be hopeless. There is too much hatred and prejudice. The white man would not sell me land or give me a job. It is no life for someone as beautiful and gracious as you. And no life for my sons. Troy will be a successful man some day. With him you have a future. With me it would always be stolen moments like this."

Their eyes held. Oh, if only time could be stopped! He met her lips again, his handsome, beautifully etched face coming close to her own, claiming her mouth with his, his body pressing against hers again. Yes, he would take her again, and she would let him.

Chapter Twenty-Three

Lisa awoke to the sound of Sage crying. She reached out, in her sleepy state envisioning both Troy and Chaco, then was suddenly fully awake. Chaco! Little Sage was squirming on the bed, and now Charles was waking up.

"Potty, Mommy," he whimpered, climbing off his bed.

Lisa sat up, wondering what time it was. Memories of the night before swirled before her—Chaco making love to her, holding each of the babies in their sleep, kissing each of them, crying. And then he was gone. Gone! She stared at little Charles. He'd never known his real father had held him. He would never know Chaco at all.

She choked back tears. Had last night really happened? She moved on stiff legs to a wash bowl and quickly washed, then pulled on a plain gray dress and brushed her hair.

"Just a minute, darling," she told Charles.

She set down the brush, then glanced at the bed. It was a tumble of blankets, the remains of her heated lovemaking only hours ago with Chaco. Now it seemed as though she had been visited by a ghost. She put a hand to her belly. It ached from taking him almost violently. She looked around the room, half expecting to see him standing there. But she knew better. In a way it was almost a relief. They both had needed that one last moment. It was the night, the chance for goody-bye, that they had been cheated out of when the soldiers came for her.

It had been a fulfilling, beautiful night. She should regret it but she did not. But she did have to decide whether to tell Troy. She hurried over to the door and opened it for Charles. It was a warm day. He ran outside in his little nightshirt and around the side of the cabin, where he pulled up the nightshirt and relieved himself in the sand. Bryce was walking over, already dressed. Surely he and Shannon had been up for a long time, preparing to leave. Why had they let her sleep so late?

She put on a smile, wondering how she looked. She was suddenly nervous and self-conscious. He took a cigarette from his mouth and threw it down as Charles ran to him. "Gampa," the boy shouted. Bryce swept him up into his arms and carried the boy inside.

"You slept later than usual," he told her. "We were about to come over here and break the door down if you didn't open it soon."

She put a hand to her hair. "I ... I guess I was just extra tired. The strain of the last few weeks ..."

Bryce set Charles down and picked up a still-crying Sage. He jostled the boy in his arms until he quieted, watching Lisa fidgit with a pot of cold coffee. He walked closer. "Lisa."

She turned, reddening. He had that look that told her he knew something. "What?"

"The old man who beat you. This morning he carried on about seeing Chaco last night. Said Chaco hit him and kept him from beating the white witch."

She turned away. "Drunk men see a lot of things."

Bryce glanced at the tumbled bed. He was experienced enough to recognize the sweet scent of lovemaking that still hung in the air of the tiny cabin. "My God, Lisa, was Chaco here?"

She began to shake. "No. No, he wasn't here."

"What the hell are you going to tell Troy?"

329

"Nothing!" She literally screamed the word, walking away from him and clinging to the back of a chair. "I mean, I don't know yet. There's nothing to tell." Her shoulders suddenly shook. "My God, don't hate me! I love you both. I need you. And I need Troy. But he he just came in the middle of the night to see Charles and Sage. He was here and so ... so pitifully sad and lonely. How could I not steal that one last moment?"

She wept bitterly. Bryce came closer, keeping Sage in one arm while he reached out with the other to touch her shoulder. "Don't cry, Lisa. You knew earlier, didn't you? That's why you wanted to be alone. You knew he might come."

She only nodded. Charles ran to the table, grabbing a piece of stale bread and darting back outside to feed it to a stray dog that often came around.

"Is he all right?" Bryce asked her.

She nodded again. "For now. But he's ... so broken. It was like ... like the last good-bye we never got to have when the soldiers took me away from him."

For a moment he saw Shannon standing there. He remembered the day she had been forced to choose between himself and the father of her child. She had chosen Saguaro. Yet he knew how much she loved him. He would not forget the agony of that day for the rest of his life.

"I'm ... I'm sorry, Bryce," she sniffed, still turned away. "I never meant to hurt Troy. I love him."

"I know that." He came around in front of her, handing her the baby. "Sage needs changing and feeding. Take care of him and we'll be over soon to help you get ready to go."

She took the baby from him, finally looking up to meet his eyes. It was like looking at Troy. Yes, she could understand how Shannon could bear Saguaro's death. She had had Bryce Edwards. "Will he hate me?"

Bryce sighed deeply. "I don't know. I don't think so. Not if I know Troy. But it will hurt. I know that kind of hurt, Lisa."

330

She looked down at the baby, cuddling it close then. "God knows it isn't your fault or Chaco's or Troy's," he groaned. "It's the fault of this damned society, of people who won't let others live the way they want to live, love who they want to love. I tried, Lisa. But one man alone can't fight it." He moved to the doorway. "I'll take Charles over with us for a while."

He walked out, and Lisa quickly changed Sage, then sat down on the edge of the bed and opened her dress. The baby found its nourishment, and she thought of how only hours earlier Chaco had tasted of the same breasts, offered to him in a far different way than she offered sustenance to this baby now, offered in heated desire and painful love. Now his son fed at her breast. His sons. She had two of them. She had something of Chaco that could never be taken from her.

Moments later Shannon came to the doorway. Their eyes met and held as Shannon came closer, looking upset. "You should have told us, Lisa."

"I couldn't. There wasn't much time. He wanted to see his sons. But he wanted to see you, too, very much. He was afraid to take the chance. He almost didn't even come here, but the temptation to see Charles and Sage was too great." She bent down and kissed Sage. "He said to tell you he loves you so and misses you very much." She met the woman's eyes again. "Please don't hate me. I . . . I know I've hurt Troy. But he was here and . . ." She swallowed. "Oh, Shannon, what would you have done? What if Saguaro had come after you returned to Bryce, and you had one last chance to share his arms again, knowing this would truly be the last time? What would you have done?"

The woman trembled, and one tear slipped down her cheek. She turned away, and the room was suddenly too quiet. Lisa's heart ached for the woman. She had never had that last chance. Saguaro had died. "I . . . I would have . . ." She did not finish. Bryce was approaching from outside. "Shannon, where are those old boots I like? These things are killing my feet already. I've never had a pair of boots that bother me like these do."

He came closer and she suddenly embraced him.

Dade Chadwell and Chap Miller sat enjoying a fresh-killed rabbit. An Apache woman they'd stolen and raped lay shivering nearby, her hands tied behind her now, her body naked and beaten. She watched them in terror, wondering what they would do to her next, wondering if she would be mutilated in the way that other Indian women had been by white men, dying some slow, horrible death.

"What do you think about that Veck," Chadwell told his friend. "That man did us right good getting us off. Imagine, having a party for us at that fancy place of his, even lettin' us at his whores for nothin'. My friend, we're nothin' short of heroes for killin' them Apaches."

The both laughed. Their rifles rested nearby and ready. They were in Apache country, on their way from a meeting with Veck in Tucson to another meeting with cattleman Mace Drucker. As usual, they took their time, skulking after lone Indian families to terrify. They weren't in too much danger, for most of the Apaches were at San Carlos, and Geronimo was supposed to be in Mexico.

"That Indian-lovin' son of a bitch Edwards sure got a kick in the ass, didn't he," Chap Miller returned. "I wouldn't mind humpin' that white squaw of his, and that perty little gal that married his son. How much you want to bet she's hot for Apaches, too."

Dade Chapwell just chuckled. "At least we're back in business now. We've made Veck a happy man, which means even better pay. All we have to do is carry messages and help with some of the raiding. Maybe when Veck gets his hands on more Indian land, he'll put us in charge of somethin' important. We've worked for him for a long time."

"If you can call raidin' and stealin' and rapin' work," Chap added.

Dade burst into loud laugher that made the Indian woman jump. Both men finished their meal, licking their fingers and wiping their mouths on their shirtsleeves.

"What do you want to do with the woman?" Dade asked Miller.

Chap stood up, walking over to her, rubbing at his full stomach. "Well, what do you do with an old horse that's served its purpose."

"Shoot it."

Chap removed his handgun, bending down and pressing the barrel against the terrified woman's forehead. "That's right." He cocked the hammer, but at the same moment he heard a war cry behind him. He whirled, startled.

"What the hell ... ?" Dade went for his rifle, but an arrow pierced his shoulder and he screamed out and fell. A party of eight or ten Apache men descended upon them, yipping and calling in their short, piercing cries of war. Chap aimed his handgun and shot, but his bullet hit nothing, and the Apaches kept coming. He fired several more times before running for his horse, but something screamed into his right thigh and he slumped in agony, the head of a barbed arrow showing through the front of his leg, flesh and skin hanging from it. In moments several warriors were dragging him away from his horse, while he screamed and fought at them to no avail.

"God, no! No!" Tears of terror spilled from Chap's eyes as his clothes were ripped from his body. Someone ripped the arrow back through his leg with immense strength, and he wondered if his screams could be heard in Tucson. He was raised up then, held by two strong Apache men. Nearby Dade was also held, both men stripped naked. A handsome young Apache warrior stepped closer to them, his face painted, his dark eyes brimming with a thirst for revenge.

"Finally," he hissed. "I have found you!" He whipped out

a knife and stepped closer to Chap, laying the blade under his eye. Chap had never known such horror, for he recognized the Indian. Chaco—the half-breed he and Dade had ambushed several years earlier. He was much older now, but still familiar. He couldn't find his voice. He could only shake his head and tremble, and his tears were plentiful. Chaco ran the tip of his knife down the man's cheek, drawing blood. "I have scouts who talk to me," he sneered. "I know about what happened with Bryce Edwards ... what you did to those Apaches ... that you went free. But your freedom is over now, white man! I have a long memory! When I am through with you, you will wish the people in Tucson had hanged you! It would have been a much easier death!"

Chaco backed away then, shouting orders to the others, who immediately shoved the two men to the ground and began tying hands and legs spread-eagled to stakes they pounded into the ground. Chaco walked over to the humiliated, tortured Apache woman, cutting the rope from her wrists and handing her a blanket to cover herself. "They will die for this," he told her. He handed her his knife. "You may have the first cut, but cut only a little. They must die slowly."

She took the knife, walking over to look down at the ugly, white, dirty bodies of the two men who had beaten and shamed her. She knelt beside Chap first, enjoying his loud weeping. She reached for his penis, smiling as he screamed and begged her not to hurt him. The cutting began.

Chaco just grinned, the screaming and begging music to his ears. He rummaged through their belongings as each Apache man took a turn then letting blood in special ways that brought great pain but did not bring death. Death would be reserved for Chaco's pleasure. Chaco handed out rifles and guns, then searched through their clothing, finding quite a lot of money, a couple of pocket knives—and an envelope.

He studied the envelope, which had nothing written on the outside of it. It was something the average Apache would cast aside as worthless, but Chaco had had enough education and was wise enough in the white man's ways to know it could be something useful. He carefully opened it, unfolding a note inside.

"Agent at San Carlos will give you no trouble. Accepted the money. Water the cattle at the Gila just before taking to reservation, as previously planned. You will be paid well." It was signed simply "Veck."

Chaco folded the note and shoved it into his parfleche. He wasn't quite sure how he could use it yet, but these two men had connections with someone name Veck. As an Indian, there wasn't much he could do about it. But perhaps his white father could make something of it, perhaps use it as some kind of evidence to prove certain people were deliberately cheating the reservation Indians and accepting bribes to do so. Whatever the note meant, the person who wrote it had been foolish enough to sign it. Chaco would keep it and think about how to use it.

He turned his attention then to Dade and Chap, whose tortured and bloodied bodies were becoming unrecognizable. He bent over Dade, knife in hand. "Now, my friend," he told the man. "I want to be sure you see everything that is done to you. I do not want you to close your eyes against it, so first I will cut off your eyelids. You will see much better then. And if you tell me what I want to know—about a man called Veck and why you carry his letter, I will end your life more quickly after that—or I can keep you alive all night, whichever you prefer."

A year of raiding passed. Geronimo and several others finally surrendered to General Crook, but not Chaco. Rumors that promises would not be kept and that Geronimo would be hanged again stirred the hostile Apaches enough to cause them to make yet another break, embarrassing General Crook and forcing his dismissal. Again the Edwards breathed a sigh of relief, but it was getting to the point that it was hard to determine if it was more of a relief having Chaco caught than having him free. Surely life was becoming extremely difficult for the few sorry refugees—refugees in their own country. It all seemed so ridiculous and pitiful.

The Tucson newspapers screamed with headlines about the "hostiles" and the "atrocities" they continued to commit, including the "sad and vicious murders" of Dade Chadwell and Chap Miller, whose bodies were found mutilated beyond recognition, with only their clothing and identifying papers left to tell who they were.

"Do you think it could have been Chaco?" Shannon asked Bryce as she laid the paper down.

His eyes gleamed. "I hope to hell it was," he answered. "I only wish I could have been there to help!"

In all the stories about the "savages" and the "heroic" soldiers who pursued them, no one mentioned that Geronimo had with him only some eighteen warriors, while Naiche, son of Cochise, and another few men rode with Mangus. Bryce fumed over the way the size and ferocity of Geronimo and his followers were grossly exaggerated, while the thousands of soldiers now being gathered under Crook's replacement, Brigadier General Nelson A. Miles, were being heralded as true heroes. The prisoners under Crook who had not escaped were sent to Fort Marion in Florida, with no hearings, no trials, no attempt to discern who might be more guilty than the next. Among those seventy-seven prisoners were only fifteen men, the rest were women and children, including two wives and three children of Geronimo and two wives and two children and the mother of Naiche.

For the Apache, Fort Marion was a living hell. Many others sent there before them had already died of disease and shattered spirits. It was a pitiful way for the once-proud and free people to live, in a land far different from the dry mountains to which they were accustomed. The hardest part for them was to be separated from their homeland. Some would never see Arizona or New Mexico again. Many would be buried in a land totally foreign to them, many others would be shipped to Oklahoma when released, never to be allowed to go home. Lisa's biggest fear was that if caught, Chaco would also go to Fort Marion. What a horrible existence that would be for him! To know he was there would be almost worse than knowing he was dead.

Now five thousand soldiers were gathered under General Miles, five thousand soldiers to hunt down perhaps thirty Indians. Lisa had written to Troy to tell him about it, and she knew by his reply he thought it utterly comical. "Such brave men they must be," he said of the soldiers. "Such courage it takes to go out against an enemy when you outnumber him a hundred and sixty to one. How proud they must be. I can't wait to write my own column about this one."

And write it he did. His article was accepted by a major eastern newspaper and printed. Sympathy for the Indians was growing in the East, and the article was widely accepted. Troy brought it with him in May, 1886, almost two years since he'd left. He was on his way home....

The train rattled over its tracks. Troy sat reading the latest sensation stories about the Apache fugitives. He had to smile when he read about Chaco and Geronimo and the others again eluding the soldiers, escaping from General Crook. But he bristled at the thought of those that remained being sent to Fort Marion. What a humiliating end to their proud way of life. No doubt some of them had been promised that if they gave up, they could at least stay at San Carlos. But already San Carlos was being broken up and sold off to whites. A few of the Chiricahuas were sent to join the Mescaleros at Chilocco in Oklahoma. But most, for no reason at all, were sent to Fort Marion.

He closed his eyes and put his head back. He could not envision Chaco at Fort Marion. He'd been studying about the place—a hideous prison in Florida, where the weather was hot and humid and the mosquitoes were abundant. Indians sent there were already dying like flies. Many, he was sure, after having children taken from them and sent off to special Indian schools, did not even want to live. To be torn from them was torture. Malaria and tuberculosis were rampant at Fort Marion. The situation for plains Indians sent to Oklahoma was not a lot better. Perhaps if their spirits were lighter they could withstand the sicknesses that plagued them. But with no hope left, how was one supposed to want to live at all?

Three days later he was on the Butterfield, now moving into old, familiar country. His thoughts had been on the Apaches all the way home, and he continued to scribble notes as he considered how they were now being treated. What had they originally done wrong? Fight for their homeland? Fight to live the way they chose to live? Where was the awful crime? Yes, they had committed some atrocities against whites—out of fear and desperation and an attempt to make them leave. But what about the way in which the whites had treated them? What about the rapes, the hangings, the uncalled-for raids on villages and the slaughter of little babies and women? What about the uncounted broken treaties, the rape of Indian land, the lies and the cheating? No one seemed to ever mention those things. But he would. He would mention them in his newspaper articles. He would start his own paper in Tucson, and people would know the truth.

But there was one other thing on his mind now, too. He stared out at the passing red rocks and scattered cacti. Joanna. He never dreamed it could happen. Lisa had been right when she said he hadn't been out in the world enough to know what he really wanted. And what he really wanted was Joanna. She was from New York—only eighteen years old. He had met her in journalism school—a woman in journalism school! She was just starting. It fascinated him to see her there, and excited him to get to know a woman who was a good writer and with whom he shared so many of the same likes and interests. She was beautiful, though perhaps not as beautiful as Lisa, few women were. But she was beautiful in an elegant, eastern way, a society girl who was not spoiled or wishy-washy. Her eagerness to know all about Arizona and his half-breed brother and his knowledge of the Apaches made him feel important.

Joanna. He had fallen in love quite by accident. But he could not have her. He had made promises to Lisa. Now it was up to Lisa to decide the fate of their marriage. He would not push her. He would not tell her about Joanna, not now, perhaps not ever. If Lisa wanted to stay married, he would say nothing. But he would have to write the letter. He'd told Joanna all about Lisa, about the odd situation of his marriage. It hurt him to think of the look on her face then. Yes. She loved him. She'd told him so. She'd be more than willing to come to Arizona and live with the successful Tucson newspaper man, for that was what he intended to be. He would be successful. He would build her a fine home in Tucson.

He bent his head and rubbed at his eyes. No. He would never do those things. He had been a fool to let himself become interested in someone else. He had been very wrong. And he did love Lisa, but not like he loved Joanna. Perhaps that was the way it was for Lisa. He understood better now her love for Chaco, understood that it was possible to love more than one person. Joanna would be waiting for a letter from him. He could not write it yet. He had to wait until he got home to Lisa.

He wondered why Lisa had never mentioned Chaco in her letters. When he left San Carlos, the scouts said they had spotted him. He had expected to hear something more about that, but Lisa had never written anything about it.

The coach lurched, bouncing him back to the present. He gazed out the window again. It seemed so strange going home now. He was a different person. He wondered what Chaco would think of a place like New York. Troy had never dreamed there could be so many people in one place, with brick streets and tall buildings and a rush of carriages and people. And they had electric lights! He wondered how long it would take remote places like Fort Bowie to get electricity. He'd like Chaco to see an electric light bulb. And what would the Apaches think of things like the grand theaters he had seen, horse-drawn trolly cars, factories, and the great ships that came into the New York harbor?

He brushed at his new suit. It would be a fine, dusty mess by the time he arrived. Six to ten more days, they had told him. He'd wire Fort Bowie when he arrived at the nearest stage station and have someone send for Bryce. He had only given them an approximate time of arrival. How would Lisa look? More important, how would she feel? He had been gone nearly two years. He had told her in his letters all the wonderful things he had seen, and she had written back the latest news of the Apaches, and how the boys were growing.

Yes. They were so different—their interests so far apart. He had written that he loved her and missed her, and she had replied the same. She had not mentioned Chaco, and he had not mentioned Joanna. Why should he? Even if he told her, it was something that had to be done in person, not in a letter. There had been nothing intimate between them. But he'd hated leaving Joanna behind, had wished he could go back for her, and felt jealous at the very thought of her becoming interested in someone else.

Dust rolled into the window then and he pulled down the canvas cover. It made the coach dark, but the dust was choking him. What a different world this west was. It seemed incredible there could be places like New York City and Arizona on the same planet. . . .

Suddenly he heard yips and war whoops. His heart raced, and he lifted the canvas, sticking his head out the window to see several painted warriors coming up from behind, shooting and shouting, riding hard.

"My God," he mumbled. He was the only passenger this day. More were to be picked up at Lordsburg in New Mexico, but

340

none had gotten on. Now it appeared they had been wise in not traveling this day. Troy ducked back inside, fumbling in his duffle bag for his handgun. The coach lurched forward as the horses were whipped into a dead run. There had not been Indian trouble along this particular route in quite some time, and the station master at the last stop had assured Troy there should be no problem. All he could think of now was Geronimo. He supposedly was the only true renegade still raiding and killing, and most of his victims' lives were not spared.

The coach jolted wildly, leaning first one way, then another, and Troy had to grab a hand strap to keep from being tossed about. He heard a scream from above and knew a driver had been hit. The shouts came closer, and Troy peeked out of the canvas to see a painted pony fly by. An Indian jumped off it and grabbed the luggage rack above, one of his legs swinging inside the window.

Troy shot his gun, and a hole opened up in the Indian's thigh. He screamed and fell from the careening coach, but by then two more Apaches were jumping aboard. The second driver screamed, and Troy saw his body tumble, after which the coach began slowing.

Now war whoops and doglike yipping surrounded the coach, as at least ten warriors circled it. Troy's first thought was that he would never see his parents and Lisa and the boys again, not to mention Joanna, unless he could muster up the names of some of the Apache he knew and convince these men he was not their enemy. But these last holdouts were surely full of vengeance. Many of their families had been shipped off to Fort Marion and their children taken from them and sent to white schools where many of them died. They had nothing left in them but hatred, and Troy could only pray he would not be tortured by these renegades before being put to death. He cocked his pistol and waited.

The coach finally came to a halt. A moment later the door swung open. Troy raised the pistol, holding it steady, warning the intruder quickly in the Apache tongue that he was a friend and that his brother was Apache. But he did not finish his words. His eyes widened and he slowly lowered the gun. "Chaco!"

For a moment they stared at each other in equal surprise. Chaco squinted. "Troy?"

Troy nodded, and Chaco looked at him strangely, moving his eyes from his brother's face to the gun and back again, as though he thought Troy might use it.

"I'll be goddamned," Troy exclaimed, putting aside the gun. "You don't know how good it is to see you, Chaco, to know you're all right and you haven't been caught yet."

Chaco grinned then, quickly ducking inside and hugging him for a moment, then backing out again. "Come! Come with me," he told Troy. "I will take you to our camp where we can talk. My friends will not harm you. It has been many years, my brother, since we could truly talk. I have much to tell you."

"And I have a hell of a lot to tell you."

Troy grabbed his carpetbag and briefcase, climbing out of the coach and brushing himself off. The other warriors pranced their horses nervously, shouting something to Chaco in Apache. One rode up and grabbed Troy's hat from his head, putting it on his own while the others laughed and shouted about what a fine scalp the white man's golden hair would be.

"We might as well take it," one yelled. "The white man always says we scalp our victims."

Chaco barked something to them and they quieted, looking at Troy as though he were some kind of freak. Chaco turned to Troy. "I have told them you are my brother. They do not understand how it could be possible." A trace of a grin passed over his lips, then he turned. "Come with me."

Troy followed him to a horse while the others looted the stagecoach and ransacked the bodies of the dead drivers for money and weapons. Troy watched a moment. So, this was how wild his brother had become. He faced Chaco. "You can't expect to get fair treatment when you do things like this, Chaco."

Chaco shrugged. "What is fair, my brother? The Indian never got fair treatment when he tried to do things right. So what does it matter? There is no fairness left in this world." He reached up and grasped his horse's mane. "Not in life . . . or war . . . or love."

Their eyes held for a moment, in a near challenge. Both had made love to the same woman. Deep jealousy tried to break the brotherly love, but it could not. Chaco smiled sadly then, turning and leaping up onto the back of the horse. He reached out his hand. "Come. We have a camp not far from here. In four days we go to meet Geronimo again. We stay scattered. Thousands of soldiers search for us now. Have you heard?"

"Oh, I've heard a lot of things. I'll tell you about it."

Chaco nodded. Troy took hold of his arm and Chaco helped him climb up onto the horse behind him. They rode off. Troy had no idea where he was going.

Chapter Twenty-Four

Troy hung on as Chaco headed into the hills, moving through rocks and crevices that looked impassable. Troy soon lost track of where they might be. The coach had been waylaid somewhere east of Fort Bowie, but Chaco headed south. They climbed dangerously steep paths into the nearby mountains, half sliding down stony escarpments, moving through a deep canyon and then another seemingly impassable crevice until they came into an opening surrounded by high rock walls. The area was almost like a giant outdoor room. In it were perched a few wickiups, while it was evident some of the renegade Apaches had been camping in caves nearby.

There was a smattering of women and children in the tiny village, their faces gaunt and almost lifeless as they stared at Troy. Their arms too were thin, and the bellies of some of the children were swollen. Chaco rode up to a wickiup and halted his horse. "Climb down," he told Troy.

Troy obeyed, a little apprehensive as the rest of the warriors came riding in shouting and yipping, holding up the clothing, weapons and ammunition they had found. One carried a box that had food packed in it for the drivers. He dismounted and set it down, then stood back, letting the women and children partake of the precious contents. Troy was touched when he saw that the men did not touch the food, and the starving women and children did not grab for it like animals. They began sorting it out, making sure everyone got something, even if a sandwich had to be broken in quarters.

Chaco touched Troy's arm. "It is sad watching them die this way," he told his brother, bitterness in his voice. "But it is sadder to watch them die far from home in a place like that prison where we are told many were sent. And these women would rather let their children die of hunger in their arms than to have them taken away to a school in the East, never to see them again."

Troy met his eyes. "How long can this go on, Chaco?"

Their eyes held. "I do not know. For as long as we hang on to life, I suppose."

Troy turned away. "Damn! For God's sake there has to be a way to make it all work, Chaco. Maybe ... maybe somehow the Indian can live the way the white man expects without losing himself as an Indian." He faced his brother again. "Why can't we have both ... both cultures ... living together?"

Chaco's lips curled into a sneer. "Because the white man will not let it be so. He wants the Indian to forget his blood, his beliefs, his dress, his customs, his religion, his language—everything! On the reservation they take the children away, make them cut their hair and wear white man's clothes. They beat them if they speak their own tongue! And most of them die there because their spirits have been killed. Without the spirit, the body cannot endure."

He whirled and walked a short distance away. He was tall and still well-built, in spite of his own obvious loss of weight. To Troy he was as much or more Indian than ever, as wild as the rest of them. But he was still Chaco, still his brother.

"If they would let us cling to our old ways, we would consider going to the reservation. But now even the reservation is gone. We know now that if we surrender, we will go to that place where they send all Indians, east of here, far from our home-

345

land. And many of us will go to that prison in Florida." He turned back to face Troy. "Yes. We know about that place where men die every day! Some of us will not get even that much. Geronimo fears being hanged and so do I! We cannot talk to them at all. No one wants to hear our side!"

A horse thundered past them, then whirled and came close. A painted warrior leaped off the animal, coming close to Troy and looking him over, reaching out and removing a gold watch chain from Troy's vest pocket. He looked at Chaco and said something in the Apache tongue. Chaco barked something back to him, and the warrior shoved the watch back at Troy, looking him over as though he were something comical. Chaco spoke to him some more, and the man's eyes softened somewhat.

"This is Coyotero," Chaco told Troy. "He is a good friend. He taught me many things when I first came to the Apache. He says you are pretty fancy to be a brother of mine."

Troy met the man's eyes challengingly, but saw that Coyotero was grinning. He could not help but grin back. "Tell Coyotero the fancy clothes don't mean I can't fight as well as the next man."

Chaco laughed and spoke up to Coyotero, who said something back, grasping Troy's hair in his hand and yanking on it slightly. The man turned and left then, and Troy rubbed his head while Chaco kept laughing. "Coyotero says it is very sad that you are my brother. He would like to be wearing that blond hair on his belt, or to tie it into his horse's mane. The white men always talk of our scalping our victims when we do not scalp at all. But we are thinking of doing so, just for spite."

"Well, save mine, will you?" Troy removed his suit jacket and shook some of the dust out of it. "I should have known better than to wear these things out here."

Chaco looked him over. He was more handsome than ever, a replica of Bryce Edwards, a tall, strong young man. Jealousy pierced his heart like a sword when he thought of Troy making love to Lisa. "Why were you on that coach, my brother?" he asked.

"I'm on my way home from New York. I took a short journalism course there, worked for a big newspaper for a few months." He laid the jacket carefully over his carpetbag and began removing his vest.

"Then ... you have not been home yet. You have not seen Lisa," Chaco replied, speaking the words warily.

Troy removed his tie and began unbuttoning his shirt. "No." He hesitated, studying his brother closely. "Why?"

Their eyes held, Chaco's almost sad. "Come into the wickiup," he told Troy. "It is cooler. I will give you some water. We will smoke and talk." He ducked inside and Troy followed, feeling apprehensive again, this time about Lisa. He picked up his bag and briefcase and clothes and set them inside. "Is something wrong, Chaco? Has something happened to Lisa?"

Chaco eyed him strangely, picking up a white man's pipe he had stolen. "No," he said quietly. "They are all fine ... as far as I know. I am not exactly able to keep track of any of them any more." He looked from the empty pipe to Troy. "Do you have tobacco? We cannot get such things any more unless we steal them. I ache for some good tobacco."

Troy nodded, removing his shirt and sitting down on a blanket opposite his brother. He opened his carpetbag and rummaged in it to find a can of tobacco, pulling out his own pipe. "Here you go," he said, handing the can to Chaco. "Have a good smoke, brother."

Chaco stuffed the pipe, studying his brother's fine, strong build. They were so much alike in many ways, yet so different. He handed the can back to Troy, whose eyes were beginning to fill with a mixture of suspicion and sadness. He stuffed his own pipe, while a strange silence hung in the air. The world of wild savagery outside had left them. They were brothers now, alone together for the first time in years.

"I was never able to thank you, my brother, for helping me

escape San Carlos. When daylight came, there was blood on my clothes and it was not mine. I worried you had been badly hurt, but later my spies told me you were well. I was glad."

Troy puffed his pipe. "I couldn't let you stay there," he answered. "I couldn't let my brother be penned up like a pig. That Blazer came just a couple of days later, so it's a good thing you got away when you did. I hear Blazer might retire soon. That might help if you're ever caught."

"It would only keep me from being hanged—maybe. Instead, I would go to that prison, and that would be worse for me." He puffed his own pipe. "But I always wondered, Troy, if part of the reason you freed me was so that I would not have the chance to see Lisa again."

Their eyes met, and Troy's face colored slightly. "It might have been. But Lisa or no Lisa, I'd have done it, Chaco. You know that."

Chaco nodded. "I know. That is why I feel . . ." He stopped, his eyes tearing. He looked away, cursing under his breath in the Apache tongue.

Troy struggled with his emotions. Here was his brother, whom he loved so very much yet sometimes hated for being first in Lisa's life. "Chaco, when I left San Carlos, the scouts had told us they thought they'd spotted you hanging around there. When Lisa wrote me, she never did mention if it was true, if anybody ever saw you again, nothing. Should she have told me something?"

Chaco puffed his pipe quietly, then set it aside and stood up. He removed his weapons belt and and a quiver of arrows, throwing them aside. He stood there shirtless but wearing deerskin leggings and moccasins. He turned to Troy, his eyes red and watery. "Yes. There is something she should have told you. And perhaps it is best I let you go home and let her do the telling."

Troy held his eyes. "No. Perhaps you should tell me so I'll be prepared when I go home."

Chaco turned away, saying nothing.

"Chaco, when I left Lisa I left her free to do some thinking and choosing and to decide just what she wants to do about our marriage. I love her, and she loves me. It's possible to love in different ways. You know that from being married to Little Deer."

Chaco nodded. "Ai. How well I know it." He flung back his head and breathed deeply. "I had to see my sons, Troy. I . . . I could not bear knowing I might die without ever seeing them. I had to take the chance! I had to go there. I went . . . only once. It was almost two years ago. I have not seen any of them since."

"Did Pa or Mother see you?"

He shook his head. "No. I . . . had to go deep in the night . . . when it is easier to hide. I went only . . . to Lisa's cabin. And I meant only to see my sons."

Troy knew what his brother was saying. He wanted to hate him. How he wanted to hate him! But all he could think about was Joanna. And he thought about how it must have been for Chaco and Lisa in the beginning—to love someone so much and not be able to have them. That was how it was now for him and Joanna, except that he had never even had the privilege of bedding the girl. He struggled with an urge to shout and call his brother names. He laid aside his own pipe, considering calling his brother out for a fight to the finish. But given the way Chaco had been living, he had no doubt who would probably win such a fight. Chaco had spent most of his life fighting.

This was no one's fault. It was the fault of circumstances that had forced Chaco and Lisa to be apart in the first place. Love drew no lines. It had been wrong for Chaco to love her, knowing it could never last. But there was no reasoning when it came to love. His own love for Joanna was wrong, but it was there, nonetheless.

He cleared his throat, swallowing to stay in control. "Well. I

349

guess you and I must have a pretty good idea how Pa and your Indian father must have felt at one time, don't we?"

Chaco slowly turned, his eyes deep, dark pits of sorrow. "Their sorrow was surely great indeed. I understand now why my father wanted to die. He died bravely fighting. He might have killed Bryce Edwards that day if his spirit had not left him. He let Bryce kill him instead. He wanted to die. In the same way, perhaps, I should fight you. But Saguaro and Bryce were not brothers. We are. It cannot end that way for us. I cannot raise my hand against you, Troy."

Troy rose, his jaw flexing in a mixture of anger and love, jealousy and sorrow. "And you know I can't raise my hand against you," he answered, his voice hoarse with emotion.

Chaco swallowed. "It is done. There will never be another chance for me, my brother. And even if there were, I would never betray you again."

"Betray me?" He let out a quick gasp to keep the tears from coming. He smiled sadly. "I don't call it betrayal." How could he explain Joanna? He decided not to bother trying. "I guess all men betray someone they love at one time or another, Chaco. Most of the time they don't mean to do it. The one you betrayed was Lisa ... because you refreshed her memory and brought it all back for her again."

Chaco nodded. "Ai. But when I am near her ... I am a weak fool."

Troy sighed and turned away.

"Troy." The name was spoken almost in agony. "Forgive me before I die. I do not want to go to my grave with my brother hating me."

Troy swallowed and quickly wiped at his eyes. "Don't be silly. There's nothing to forgive. Not really. I never set any rules for Lisa. I knew what I was getting into when I married her, the chance I was taking. At first it was just to give the baby a father. There was nothing between us, Chaco. Then after a while ... I don't know ... she's so good and so beautiful ...

350

and she's suffered so much. I wanted to be a real husband to her . . . and she could see there was no hope for you and her. So it just . . . seemed natural to start living like a husband and wife ought to live. We were already good friends." He thought about Joanna. How cruel and strange and twisted everything was. Chaco should be with Lisa. He should be with Joanna. He turned and faced Chaco. "I'll stay with her if she wants, Chaco. You have my promise I'll always take care of her and your sons, and I'll love her, be a husband to her if she still wants me that way."

Chaco nodded. "She will want you that way. And she will need you. There are dark days ahead. You cannot hold this over her. The day the soldiers came and took her from me . . . we never had a chance to say good-bye. Many things were left undone. Now it is finished."

"Yes, too may things are finished, Chaco. Too many things." He reached out his hand and Chaco took it. "For my father's sake, and for our mother's, let us remain friends."

Chaco squeezed his hand and then suddenly embraced him. "Agreed, my brother," he whispered.

They hugged each other for a quiet moment, then Chaco let go and turned away. "We have a lot of other things to talk about, Chaco. I want you to listen to me," Troy told him then. "I have ideas and I need your help."

"*My* help?" Chaco turned in surprise.

"Yes." Troy sat down. "But for now the sun is setting and I'm damned tired. Sometimes I think it's more comfortable riding a horse than riding in one of those damned coaches. The dust about kills a person."

Chaco grinned. "I will give you a horse to ride to Fort Bowie and point you in the right direction . . . when you are ready to leave."

Troy nodded and their eyes held again. "I'd like to stay a few days, Chaco. Is that possible?"

Chaco smiled warmly, happiness in his eyes. "Ai. Stay as long as you like, my brother. It will be the last time. . . ." His eyes teared. "The spirits were smiling upon me when they led me to the coach you rode in. There are few happy moments left in my life now, Troy. This is one of them. This is a memory I will keep."

Troy nodded. "I'll treasure it also, Chaco . . . forever."

Colonel Blazer rode to the trading post with two men. His duty with the army would end in two days. He was fifty-five and had had his fill of Arizona and Indians. But he had some last duties to perform. This one could easily have been handled by men of lesser rank—by anyone, in fact. But Blazer wanted the pleasure himself. He would enjoy telling the Indian-loving Bryce Edwards that his own cherished son had been murdered by Apaches.

He approached the trading post with a smile on his face. A woman came out, a beautiful woman with reddish hair. How was it that Edwards' wife seemed to age so slowly and gracefully? It wasn't fair for a man to have a woman like that. Still, it was beyond the colonel's imagination how Edwards could actually have married her after she had lived with an Apache man and had borne him a son. All the beauty in the world couldn't make up for that.

A younger woman came out to stand beside the older one. That would be the one called Lisa Powers, the girl from the wagon train. Every time he looked at her he wanted to hit her for insisting it was not Chaco who had killed her mother. What kind of woman would protect a filthy Apache? Only the worst kind. And they actually claimed her baby was Troy's.

He grunted to himself. He knew perfectly well whose baby it was. The two women made a fine pair indeed. If he could have kept Lisa Powers a little longer, he'd have got a confession out of her, and he'd have set her straight about Indians and got her mind to thinking right again. How would both women feel about the Apaches now, once he told them the dirty savages had killed the older woman's son, the younger woman's husband? What an ironic and absolutely wonderful twist!

He and his two men halted their horses in front of the cabin where Lisa and Shannon stood. Bryce came running from a barn, frowning as he came closer to see Colonel Blazer nodding and tipping his hat to the women. Lisa glared at him. She hated him and always would. Looking at him gave her a chill. Blazer only smiled at her.

"Afternoon, little lady."

She said nothing.

"What are you doing here?" Shannon asked.

"Well, now, that's not much of a greeting."

"You wanted to hang my son once. Why should I be friendly to you?"

"What is it, Blazer?" Bryce spoke up, moving up onto the porch. "You've come a long way on a hot day. What's so important that a colonel has to come out here to tell us?"

The colonel dismounted, handing his reins to a sergeant who grinned knowingly at him. Blazer approached Bryce, frowning. "Well, for one thing, you'll probably be glad to know I am retiring in two days. You can argue with some other colonel after this."

Bryce folded his arms, looking down at Blazer, who stood two steps below him. "I suppose I should wish you well. I know your job isn't an easy one. I remember well."

"Oh, yes, you never failed to remind me of when you were colonel at Fort Bowie, Edwards, or to tell me all the things I was doing wrong."

Bryce eyed him narrowly. "I never told you what you were doing wrong. All I ever did was argue with you about my son." His arms came down then, his face paling. "Is it Chaco? Has he been caught?"

Shannon grasped Lisa's hand.

Blazer smiled smugly. "No, Edwards, although maybe you'll wish he and Geronimo and all the others *had* been caught."

"What are you talking about?"

Blazer removed his hat. "Edwards, I'm afraid I've come to give you some bad news."

Shannon's heart tightened, and Lisa swallowed. Chaco! Was he dead?

"It looks like your other son, Troy, is most likely dead. And you should know that he died at Apache hands."

Shannon gasped.

"No," Lisa squeaked, leaving Shannon and moving closer to Bryce. "You're lying!"

Blazer's eyes cut into her like a knife. "Now, little girl, maybe you won't be so high and mighty about sticking up for that filth! They killed your husband, and we all know how Apaches kill—slowly, through torture!"

"That's enough, Blazer," Bryce shouted to him, putting his arm out and gently pushing away Lisa, who paled and felt weak. Her mind screamed. It couldn't be! It couldn't be! Troy! "How do you know all this?" Bryce was asking. "What do you mean it *looks* like he's dead? Do you have proof? Where is his body?"

"We haven't found it yet. Your son was a passenger on a Butterfield stage that was attacked yesterday. We just got word by telegraph. Both drivers were killed. Their bodies and the coach were looted and the coach was burned. There was no sign of your son, which most likely means the devils took him with them. You know what that means. He might even still be alive, but he's probably as good as dead. Apaches can take a week to kill a man if they want to, every moment of it filled with excruciating pain for the victim! I expect that blond hair . . ."

The man did not get to finish the sentence. Bryce backhanded him so hard that he fell backward to the ground. Instantly the other two soldiers drew their revolvers on Bryce.

Shannon pulled Lisa back, her heart beating wildly. Troy! It couldn't be! It couldn't!

"Put your guns away," Blazer ordered. "I can take care of myself," he growled.

Bryce came down off the porch, fists clenched. "You've got no right telling the women that way," he snarled, "and you don't even know if it's true!"

Blazer was struggling to his feet, his face beet-red. The two men were almost evenly matched, both in their mid-fifties, both still well built and strong, both toned by rugged living in the West.

Bryce bent over threateningly, fists still clenched. "I've wanted to do this for a long time, Blazer. You're almost a civilian. You might as well start now!" He landed into the man and this time both of them went down.

"Bryce," Shannon screamed. "Bryce, don't!"

They rolled on the ground, and Bryce got in two good punches before Blazer managed to grasp his hair and pull, gouging at one of Bryce's eyes at the corner with his thumb. Bryce cried out and threw out his arms, knocking his hand away, and quickly got up, bending over and holding his eye. Instantly Blazer barreled into him, jolting Bryce in the midsection with his head and shoulders and sending him backward to the ground.

In spite of his pain, and hardly able to see, Bryce quickly scrambled up again. He saw the blur of Blazer heading for him, and he kicked up, catching the man under the chin. Blazer sprawled backward with a grunt. Bryce shook his head and blinked, trying to see better, while Blazer groaned and rolled to his knees, then grasped a hitching post and got to his feet, panting heavily. Bryce managed to watch him with his good eye, his other eye burning fiercely and totally blurred. He came for Blazer, who in the last minute threw a fistful of sand and gravel in his face. Bryce made a light grunting noise, again blinded. He bent over, shaking his head again, and Lisa and

355

Shannon watched in horror as Blazer ripped off his weapons belt and went for Bryce again. He kicked Bryce hard in the side with a booted foot, and Shannon was sure she heard a rib crack.

"Bryce!" She ran to help him, but one of the other soldiers moved his horse to cut her off.

"Stay put, lady."

Blazer kicked Bryce twice more in the back. Then Bryce's anger overtook his pain, anger that Blazer could be so callous toward the women, anger over Blazer's attitude toward the Apaches. His eyes had partially cleared. He rose up, ignoring the vicious blows, and waited until Blazer came close to kick him again. He rammed a fist hard into Blazer's face, hearing the nose crack. Blood poured from it as Blazer stumbled backward. But Bryce did not let him fall. He grasped him by the front of his uniform and held him, hitting him several more times in the face until one of the other soldiers pulled a gun again.

"Put it away, mister," Lisa shouted, pointing a rifle at him. When she had run inside to get the gun, no one even noticed. The startled soldier looked at her in surprise, then just grinned. Lisa fired the rifle. A bullet whizzed past him and he dropped his gun in astonishment and backed his mount. Lisa held the rifle on the second soldier then, telling him to back away from Shannon. The man obeyed.

"Bryce, stop!" Shannon screamed at him. He was pummeling Blazer's face into mush, his eyes wild, his teeth gritted. His eye was bleeding, as was his lip, but Blazer looked in much worse condition. Bryce hesitated when Shannon screamed at him, standing there panting, still holding on to Blazer.

"Bryce, you'll kill him," she pleaded.

He stared at Blazer's bloodied face. "Wouldn't I love to," he snarled. He shoved Blazer, letting him fall to the ground, then turned and looked up at the other two soldiers. "When he comes to . . . you tell him if he tries to do something about this,

I'll make sure his superiors know how he behaved in his last couple of days of duty. I don't think they'll take kindly to a colonel brawling with a civilian, nor to the manner in which he came here to tell us our son is dead at Apache hands! Now get off my land!" He stumbled up onto the porch, snatching the rifle from Lisa and aiming it at them. "Hurry it up!"

One of the soldiers jumped down, picking up his dropped pistol and then trying to pick up the colonel. "Help me out, Jakes," he spoke up to the other man. The second soldier dismounted and helped pick the man up. They managed to hoist the colonel over his horse, then mounted their own.

Bryce cocked his rifle. "In all my years running Fort Bowie, I never knew an officer who conducted himself like Blazer has," he growled. "You tell him he'll be goddamned lucky if I never say anything about this! Maybe General Miles would be interested in knowing."

"I wouldn't tell him, Edwards," one of them spoke up.

"I'll tell him whatever I like. I have a good army record behind me, mister, and I know most of the top men. And if you were under my command, you would be sitting in the fort prison right now. You get off my land and don't you ever come on it again."

The two men gave him a sour look, then turned and rode off.

"Bryce," Shannon groaned, moving closer and touching his arm. "Bryce, you're hurt."

He lowered the rifle, glaring out at the men. "I'll live." He looked down at her, then pulled her into his arms, looking over at a stricken Lisa. "Don't either one of you think Troy is dead. A man isn't dead until his body is found. He can speak some Apache. Maybe he talked his way out of something. If we're lucky, it was Chaco and his bunch who attacked that stage. Who else could it be? Geronimo, Chaco, Naiche, and Mangus—they and the few with them are the only ones loose doing any raiding. Blazer just thought he could get us all upset before he retired, he just wanted to get in one more dig at me because I side with the Apaches. Troy isn't dead, you hear me? I don't believe it and don't you believe it either."

"Oh, Bryce, when will we know? Where is he?" Shannon wept.

"He'll show up. One day soon he'll show up."

Lisa turned away. Chaco! What if it *was* Chaco? It was their only hope. And yet if it was Chaco, would Chaco tell him? Her heart tightened with a mixture of hope and sorrow.

Chapter Twenty-Five

Breakfast consisted of boiled potatoes and coffee, both stolen in a raid on a ranch a few days earlier and carefully used now. Nothing was wasted.

"Since so many whites have come to settle here, and with all the miners crawling around the mountains, the game has fled," Chaco told Troy. "There was a day when we could ride out and find enough meat for a week ... two weeks. No more." He handed Troy a tin plate of plain potatoes. "I am sorry. This is all there is."

Troy took it, his stomach growling with hunger for much more. "This is fine," he answered.

Chaco sat back and ate nothing.

"Did you already eat?" Troy asked.

Chaco shook his head. "I am not hungry. I have trained myself to eat once a day and very little. It leaves more for the others."

Troy frowned, setting down his plate. "Then give mine to somebody else."

Chaco smiled sadly. "You are a guest. Eat. I will be offended if you do not."

Troy sighed, picking up the plate and putting a piece of the bland potato into his mouth, wishing he had gravy for it. "You should see New York, Chaco. You would never believe there could be such places. Hundreds of buildings made of board and brick—probably thousands of them. Hundreds of brick streets, thousands of people and carriages, buildings many stories high. There are stores there where you can buy anything imaginable, and grand theaters and restaurants that serve foods of other countries like France and Spain and Germany and Italy. There are people of all different nationalities. And every day more come in great sailing ships from other countries, coming to America to work in the factories or build their own farms. They all have some kind of dream, I guess, and they think they'll find it here."

He saw the sadness in Chaco's eyes, and he set his plate down again, drinking some stiff, black coffee from a tin cup.

"It seems there is an endless supply of white men," Chaco answered. "Already there are too many here, and yet the great ships you told me about bring more . . . and more. A man cannot win a battle when he is outnumbered ten thousand to one, can he, my brother?"

Their eyes held. "No. He can't. I just wish you'd have realized that a long time ago, Chaco—before you left."

Chaco leaned forward, picking up a stick of kindling and tracing it around on the dirt floor. "I did not leave to make war," he answered quietly. "I left because I could no longer live among the whites. I could no longer bear the insults, Troy— the looks, the whispers. After those men beat me and shot me and made me drink that whiskey . . ." He met Troy's eyes. "I found them, Troy. I found those men. They had killed an Indian family, and they were torturing and raping the woman." His dark eyes lit with hatred. "They died . . . and they died slowly," he hissed.

Troy felt a chill, realizing his brother could be as ruthless as any Apache when it came to his enemies.

"Pa wrote and told me they'd been found. We always wondered if it was you. Do the soldiers or anyone know it was you?"

Chaco shrugged. "I do not think so. But they will accuse all of us together. That is the way it is for the Indian. All are punished for what a few do." He rested his elbows on his knees. "Tell me about your writing, Troy. Did you learn something at that place?"

"Enough to know I want to start my own newspaper—in Tucson. And I had an article I wrote about the Apaches published in a big eastern newspaper." He reached over eagerly for his briefcase, opening it and taking out the article. "Here. You read it and tell me what you think."

Chaco took it hesitantly. "I know only what our mother taught us in reading. I did not go on to school like you."

"You can read it. If there's a word you don't know, tell me."

Chaco frowned, concentrating on the article then while Troy ate more potatoes. It took him several minutes to read it. He swallowed then, clearing his throat before speaking. "This is ... very good," he spoke up. He met his brother's eyes, his own watery. "I did not know you cared this much. It is dangerous for a white man to speak out like this."

Troy shrugged. "So what? Somebody has to do it." His eyes lit up and he set his plate aside again. "Chaco, I want to help through my writing."

Chaco eyed him carefully. "How?"

"By things like what you just read. Maybe somehow I can get the public's attention when I start my own newspaper, and I can explain the Indian spirit, the Indian religion, how easy it would be to have peace if they would just try to understand what it is you're fighting for."

Chaco started to hand back the article.

"No. You keep it," Troy told him. "I have more."

Chaco folded it carefully, obviously deeply touched. He cleared his throat again before speaking. "If you write about the Apache ... you must tell the truth. To do it right, you must first think like an Apache, be an Apache inside. That is not easy for a white man to do, even one who is brother to an Indian."

"I know that. But you could help me, Chaco. Talk to me. Tell me all of it—what goes on inside your soul, their souls. God knows how much time we have, and after I leave here we might never see each other again. I don't want this opportunity to slip away. When I was a boy, I never tried to truly understand it. Now I realize how important it is to understand ... how important it is to loving and accepting you—and how important to my writing. I want to do it right, Chaco. Teach me to forget that I am a white man. Teach me the soul of the Indian."

Chaco smiled, love in his eyes. "I am not so sure it can be done."

"Try me!" Troy's excitement was almost boyish. "Let me be your eyes, your voice. Let me explain things through the Apache point of view, Apache reasoning. How many men in my position have an Apache brother, someone right in the thick of things who can explain what's happening in your hearts? I can help, Chaco! I know I can."

Chaco returned to tracing the ground with the stick. "It would not be easy, making you understand." He sat up straighter, putting a fist to his heart then. "To understand ... how we feel about the land, the water, the trees, the animals. All are sacred. The white man holds nothing sacred but money and power."

"I'll explain those feelings through my writing. I know I can do it."

Chaco slowly nodded. "Perhaps you can, my brother. We may have only a day, perhaps a week. We never know when we must move on. But in a week we go no matter what ... to meet up with Geronimo. Then you must leave us."

Troy's eyes saddened. "Where will you go then?"

"Perhaps the Sierra Madre. Mexico."

"The soldiers will keep searching. They're determined this time, Chaco."

362

A deep sadness passed through Chaco's dark eyes. "I know. We all know."

Troy's eyes teared then. "Chaco, I hope somehow . . . somehow this all ends well. I don't see how it can right now. But if it does . . . God, Chaco, you and I . . . we could work together on writing this. Maybe you could help me write a book!"

Chaco laughed lightly. "A book? How could I help you write a book?"

"A book about the Apaches, their whole way of life, maybe what your life has been like, battles from the Apache point of view." He sighed. "I don't know. It's just an idea right now. But you remember it. You come to me if you can, if you ever get out of this mess."

Chaco studied him lovingly. "I will remember." He turned and carefully put away the newspaper article in his parfleche. Then he took out an envelope and held it up. "You really want to help?"

Troy looked curiously at the envelope. "You know I do."

"You are a good man, my brother. I believe your writing will be a great thing. But maybe there is another way you can help—right now." He handed over the envelope. "I found that on the white men I killed—the men who beat me and made me drink the whiskey. I found my vengeance. And I found that on one of them. When I read it, I thought perhaps it could be used some day to help us, to show the white people it is not always us who do the bad things. I am not sure how it can be used, but I did not want to throw it away. I have been wondering what to do with it. Now that you are here, I can give it to you."

Troy frowned, opening the envelope and taking out the note inside.

"I forced one of the men to tell me who that man Veck is. He is James Veck, a very wealthy man in Tucson. He paid men like Chadwell and Miller to dress like Indians and raid ranchers, paid them to handle whiskey traders, supplied guns and whiskey to Apaches—many bad things in the eyes of the white man."

Troy read the note. "Agent at San Carlos will give you no trouble." he read aloud. "Accepted the money. Water the cattle at the Gila just before taking to reservation, as previously planned. You will be paid well. Veck."

He looked up at Chaco, his eyes wide with surprise.

"What do you think?" Chaco asked.

Troy folded the note, putting it back into the envelope and then slipping it into his briefcase. "I think it's a pretty damned incriminating note! And Pa hates this man James Veck. He had bad things printed in a Tucson newspaper about our mother, and he's mostly responsible for Pa being let go at San Carlos and for those two men getting off free. Pa would give the world to have something on that man. Veck could be in a lot of trouble over this if it's handled right." He leaned closer, his eyes excited. "It was damned smart of you to save that, Chaco. I'll show it to Pa. The note could be to the man we caught once on the reservation trying to water his cattle before bringing them in. If we could at least get some suspicion going—get the government to do some investigating. . . ." He slapped his knee. "Damn! This is great! Just great! We finally have some evidence!"

Chaco nodded. "It is good then?"

'It's damned good!" He turned and threw open the briefcase again, taking out a tablet of paper, a quill pen and a bottle of ink. "Let's get started, Chaco. Let's start with religion—or customs, if you want—why the Apaches are so warlike, how the women are treated. . . ."

Chaco laughed lightly. "You might not have enough ink."

"Then what I can't write, I'll remember."

Their eyes held and Chaco sobered. "How can I make you stop thinking like a white man," he said almost sadly. "That is the first step. You must go to the inside, Troy. The white man tries to be like all the others, follows others. He is not an individual. For the Indian, it is important to be true only to oneself. This is why I chose to come to be with my people. The white man judges people by race, color, education, wealth. He uses no other form of judgment. It matters little to him what is in the soul, how good a man is. The Indian does not see man in that way. He allows each man to be what he chooses, believe what he chooses. Each Indian man seeks his puha, his personal medicine, usually through visions. To get the vision he must suffer, through things like the Sun Dance ritual of the Cheyenne—through fasting and prayer, through terrible suffering. If each man does not suffer, then he has made no sacrifice. He has not earned his place in life. He will never find his inner spirit. This is why we die so quickly when we are put on reservations and in prisons and told we must not practice any of our old ways any longer. To take these things from us is to say we can never know ourselves, never be men. This is why the young men now kill themselves. They have lost something vital to their life, to their soul and spirit. They do not see the truth, because the white man tells them they cannot seek the truth any longer. A man must have a vision, seek the spirit that will be his guardian for life. Without this, he stumbles in darkness and is weak. With it, he is very strong, very brave."

Troy wrote rapidly, wondering what "spirit" guided his brother but afraid to ask. He remembered hearing once that an Indian man usually told no other man his personal vision and spirit. Who had told him? His mother? His father? Someone on the reservation? So many things had happened to him in his short life through living in this wild land.

Chaco went on, now getting excited himself. The day passed into night, with occasional breaks while Chaco sat quietly with his eyes closed and Troy said nothing, afraid of breaking his concentration. By the next morning Troy had over a hundred pages of scrawled notes, red eyes, and a sore writing hand. He fell asleep in the early dawn. Only two hours had passed when Chaco nudged him awake.

"Wake up, my brother! Soldiers come! We must flee!"

Troy sat up straight, instantly wide-eyed but aching all over.

Chaco was scrambling, gathering his blankets and parfleche, shoving what little food he had into it. He grabbed his rifle and weapon belt and quiver of arrows, turning to face Troy, who was just getting to his feet.

"You stay," he told Troy. "The soldiers will help you get to Fort Bowie and the trading post. Our mother and father and Lisa must know by now you were taken and will be worried."

"But, Chaco, we have so much more to talk about. You haven't even told me about all your experiences with the Apache—the wars, the raids. . . ."

"There is no time, my brother. We must go quickly! Scouts have spotted soldiers only two or three miles away!"

Their eyes held and Troy's teared. "I don't want to leave you, Chaco." His heart raced desperately. This could be it! This could be the last time he saw his brother again! He felt as though he'd just gotten to truly know him. He'd just begun to feel the old closeness from when they were boys, yet it was much better than that, for he was beginning to understand Chaco's spirit.

"We have no choice, my brother," Chaco said quietly. "But there is something special between us now, more special than before. We are more than brothers. We are one in spirit and we have loved the same woman. Go in peace. Write your articles. Help us all that you can. There may be no help for me . . . those of us who live now. But perhaps your writing can help our children and grandchildren."

"I'll do all I can, Chaco."

Chaco nodded. "I know you will. You are a white man only on the outside, my brother. On the inside, you are Indian."

Troy could not stop a tear from slipping down his cheek. He stepped closer and quickly hugged his brother, "God be with you, Chaco."

He backed away and their eyes held once more. "And with you . . . and Lisa. Tell her . . ." He looked away. "Tell her . . . I am sorry . . . for all of it," he said brokenly. He ducked outside then. Troy stood and waited. He did not want to watch his brother ride away. He heard the horses then, amazed at how quickly Indians could gather up their things and flee.

After several long, quiet minutes he picked up his own things and stepped outside. The little camp was empty. The morning hung quiet, a huge, red sun rising in the east. Then came the faint sounds of horses at a light gallop, sabers rattling, saddles squeaking. The soldiers were coming. He waited in the middle of camp. It was several minutes before the men finally showed up, moving up through two huge, overhanging rocks, then halting, their leader looking startled at seeing the Indian village. He ordered rifles readied.

"There's no one here," Troy shouted, stepping forward and laughing inside at how easily the soldiers could have ridden into a trap. "They're gone, been gone a couple of days. You'll never find them now." He walked up to the apparent leader, a lieutenant. "I was beginning to wonder if anyone would find me," he told the man. "I wondered if I should try to walk out of here and find civilization, but I wasn't sure I'd make it in this heat. God only knows where there's water besides the little stream near this village."

"Who the hell are you?" the lieutenant asked in surprise. The others just stared in wide-eyed shock at finding a white man in the village of Apache renegades.

"I'm Troy Edwards."

"Edwards! We thought you'd be dead—tortured to death, scalped! What the hell are you doing here?"

Troy grinned. "I had the luck of being attacked by my own brother. What do you think of that? Must have an angel on my shoulder."

The lieutenant frowned. "Chaco and his renegades camped here?"

Troy nodded. "They're long gone now."

The lieutenant eyed the camp carefully, seeing no fresh fires. Troy was glad Chaco had ordered none be built that night, suspecting soldiers were close. Fresh fires would tell the soldiers they had not left that long ago.

"Why didn't your brother give you a horse so you could get out of here?" the lieutenant asked Troy.

Troy frowned. "They had barely enough mounts for themselves. Many of them had to walk. I know this country. I told him I could make it out of here if I had to. But I figured soldiers might come searching and that I'd wait around a day or two and find out. Makes things a lot easier on me."

The lieutenant eyed him narrowly. "You're lying. Your brother is nearby, isn't he?"

Troy's face darkened with anger. "Look around. I told you they're gone. Now I'm pretty damned tired and dirty and I'd like to get home to my wife and folks at the trading post. You going to take me, or do I have to report that the soldiers wouldn't help a stranded civilian?"

The lieutenant hesitated, then turned to his men, singling out three of them. "You three take him back. I'm going on with the others to try to track Chaco. Get a message to General Miles that we've found a renegade camp and will see if we can track them."

"Yes, sir."

The lieutenant glared at Troy once more, then ordered his men to follow as he rode through the camp. Troy watched after them, praying that Chaco and the others would get away once more.

Lisa watched the horse approaching. She sat on the porch of the cabin rocking Sage, now two years old. She was worried about him. He didn't seem to be growing much physically, and his cough persisted, but the doctor at Fort Bowie insisted the boy was fine. Four-year-old Charles, healthy and active, ran around chasing chickens.

Lisa's heart quickened when she saw who the rider was, as one of the men who helped out at the trading post stopped him. "Troy," the man shouted. "How the hell are you! Goddamn, the soldiers tried to tell us you were dead! But Bryce wouldn't believe it."

"I just saw my father and mother, at Fort Bowie," she heard Troy answer. They had gone in to Fort Bowie that morning to see if there had been any word. So, they had already seen him. But they were not with him now. They had let him come ahead alone.

She felt flushed and confused—overjoyed to see him, unsure how he felt about her. She rose and hurried inside with Sage, while Charles went running. "Daddy," the boy yelled, his sun-burned face upraised to the only father he'd known.

"Hey, Charlie, you remembered, huh?" Lisa listened to the joy in his voice at seeing Charles, greeting the boy as if he were his own. Her eyes teared. Troy! She hurried to a mirror, glad she had for some reason been inclined to put on one of her nicer dresses and do her hair. She wore a blue cotton print dress. He like blue on her. Her golden hair was swept up at the sides with pretty combs in it. She was glad that at least Sage was asleep.

She hurried to the door to see Troy swinging Charles around and hugging him. His clothes were wrinkled and disheveled, and when he turned she could see the start of a beard. He caught her eyes and stopped whirling and laughing. He knew! He'd been with Chaco, and he knew! She wanted to go to him, run to him. But her legs would not move. She turned away from the screen door. She heard Troy saying something to the help about taking Charles and keeping him occupied for a while.

"Sure thing, Troy. I understand," the man told him with a chuckle. "I'll keep the little devil out of your hair for a while. Sure is good to see you're all right."

Lisa waited nervously. His footsteps were on the porch. The screen door squeaked open.

"Aren't you glad to see me, Lisa?"

She turned, her eyes watery. "My God, Troy, you know I am! We thought you might be dead."

He studied her eyes. Yes. She was very beautiful. If she still wanted to be married to him, he would have to force himself to forget Joanna. He opened his arms. "Well, here I am ... alive and well ... a little dirty and wrinkled and bearded, though. I've been riding two days straight ... right from Chaco's camp to the fort and home." He wanted to hate her, hit her. But he'd come to understand too many things.

"Then you were with Chaco!"

He nodded. "He was fine when I left him. He said to tell you ... he was sorry for all of it. I guess you know what that means."

Her face colored. "It's ... been so many years. ..."

"Lisa, I know everything," he interrupted.

She swallowed, her eyes tearing more. She turned around, hanging on to the back of a chair. What had she done! She had slept with Chaco!

"You look mighty good," he told her. "Did I come all this way and go through all that hell just to find out I can't even get a hug from you?"

She looked at him in surprise. Was he telling her it was all right? Did he actually understand? To what lengths did his compassion go? "Troy, I ..."

"The look on your face sure resembles the look on Chaco's when he tried to tell me. I expect the three of us couldn't love each other more ..." His own eyes teared. "And I expect it will boil down to you and me, won't it? The soldiers are hot on his trail, Lisa. And he's starving. It can't last much longer. If they cross the border, the Mexican soldiers will be after them. And I'm told the Mexicans are making a pact with Americans to allow our soldiers to cross the border in pursuit of Apaches if they're on a good trail."

She pressed her lips together, nodding in a sort of resignation. She walked up to him hesitantly, then flew into his arms. "My God, Troy, I'm so sorry," she sobbed. "I never meant for it to happen. I love you, truly I do."

He hugged her tightly. She felt good against him. Surely he was not the only person denied the chance to be with the one he really loved. Saguaro could not keep Shannon. Chaco could not keep Lisa. And Lisa could not have Chaco. But there could still be love. It came in so many different forms. They could still satisfy needs and desires, support each other, be good friends.

"It's all right," he told her. "I'm home now. We're going to Tucson. I'll have a nice house built for us and I'm opening my own newspaper. We'll live like a real married couple, like we've never really had a chance to live." He kissed her hair. "You got your last good-bye. It's over now, Lisa. We'll start out brand new, maybe have a baby of our own."

She turned her face up to his and their lips met. His whiskers scratched at her chin, but it didn't seem to matter at the moment. He would shave and clean up, and she would show him she loved him, give him a proper wife's welcome after the sun set and the children were asleep.

"Oh, Troy, you should hate me," she said once he released the kiss.

"I know you too well for that, Lisa Edwards." He pulled away slightly, studying the blue eyes. "Just tell me ... right here ... right now. Tell me what you've decided about us, and we won't mention anything about what has happened while I've been gone." He was tempted to tell her about Joanna, but decided against it.

She swallowed. Why should she have any more lingering hopes about ever being able to be with Chaco? "I want to stay married, Troy. I want to go to Tucson with you."

He touched her cheek with the back of his hand, leaning forward and kissing her forehead. "Then, it's done. From now on it's just you and me. The past is past."

She nodded. Then she looked him over, touching his face, his chest. "Are you all right? What happened?"

He led her over to the table to sit down. "My coach was attacked by renegades. I was damned scared until the door opened ... and there he was ... Chaco himself looking right at me."

"Oh, Troy! Thank God he was with them."

"You bet. They were in a killing mood. I saw what they did to the drivers and it wasn't pretty." He reached over and took her hand. "He's so wild now, Lisa. But the love between us hasn't changed. He took me back to his camp, and we had some time to talk."

She reddened again, looking down. He squeezed her hand.

"We learned a lot about each other, Lisa. As far as you and Chaco ... I saw the loneliness in his eyes, the sorrow. I couldn't hate either one of you. For more reasons than you know I could understand." Again he thought of Joanna. "I guess we both knew then how Saguaro and Bryce must have felt about my mother." He sighed, squeezing her hand again. "At any rate, we had some time to talk. And I'm ready, Lisa. I took all kinds of notes—really got inside of Chaco, inside the Apache mind, you know? I understand so many things so much better!"

She met his eyes and saw the pure excitement there. "You're ready? Ready for what?"

"To go to Tucson! I'm going to start my own newspaper, Lisa, and I'm going to print unbiased news about the Indians. I'll have all the regular news, too, but I'm going to run special articles on the Apaches. I might even write about other tribes eventually. But for now I'll concentrate on the Apaches. People are going to understand them for once. I'll make them appreciate the Indian culture, understand their religion...."

"Troy! It's suicide!"

He just grinned. "Maybe so. Maybe not. If I do it right, people will listen and start to think a little."

"But they hate the Apaches. Every white man in Arizona and New Mexico hates them!"

"That's the whole point. What is hatred, Lisa? It's nothing more than misunderstanding. I'm going to make them understand."

Her eyes teared "Troy, you're so brave to do such a thing."

He grinned almost bashfully. "I don't know about that part of it. I'm probably more crazy than brave."

"No. You're brave. And I love you for it."

He searched her eyes. "You aren't afraid to go with me, then? It might not be easy for you. People will try to find things out. They'll talk."

"We've been through all that. Maybe you could come out with the plain truth about me and Chaco and Charles, if you have to—explain your love for your brother. I don't know. You're a good writer, Troy. I think you can make a name for yourself with this."

He grinned. "Can you think of a better way to get attention for your work than to walk right into the lion's den with a juicy steak in your hand? I'll either tame the lion or get eaten alive."

"I'll be with you ... whatever happens."

"I'm going to go even farther than writing about Indians, Lisa. Chaco gave me something, a note he found on two white men he killed." He went for his briefcase. "It was those two men Pa tried to prosecute, the ones who hurt Chaco that time. Chaco got his vengeance and I'm glad. At any rate, you remember that James Veck, the businessman in Tucson who published that trash about Mother?"

"I remember."

He came back to the table. "Look at this." He handed her the note. She put her hand to her throat as she read.

"Troy! This is proof he's cheating the government."

"Enough proof to have him investigated, which is what I am going to do."

She handed back the note and stood up. They embraced

again. "Oh, Troy, I pray you can get him convicted and that your newspaper will be successful."

"We'll do it, you and I together." He pulled away. "Let's go over to our own cabin. I'd like to take a bath and I need a shave. I'm sorry I'm such a mess."

"It doesn't matter. I'm so happy you're home and you're all right . . . and that you . . . forgive me."

He ran a thumb over her lips. "There isn't anything to forgive. Now let me have a look at Sage while you go fix a tub for me. Then I'll have somebody watch Sage."

Desires swept through her that she kept buried since being with Chaco. Troy was home now. And she had made her final decision. She left him, going to their own cabin and preparing a large iron washtub they kept in the corner, mixing cold and heated water. Minutes later he came inside and closed the door, bolting it.

"It's good to come back here to the old home rather than back to San Carlos," he told her. "I think San Carlos was too hard on you and Mother both. It's hell watching what's happening there."

He turned away and he began undressing. "It doesn't matter much any more," she answered. "They're breaking up San Carlos, sending some of them to Indian territory to the east, most of them to that horrible prison in Florida."

"I know about that."

She heard his clothes dropping to the floor, heard the water splashing. She walked through the curtained doorway to their bedroom. It was time to look to the future. It had been a long time for him. He would want his woman. She undressed and put on just a robe, then walked back into the main room. He sat in the tub with a mirror in one hand and a razor in the other. He glanced at her, his eyes moving over her. Then he smiled. He finished shaving, secretly wondering what Joanna would be like in bed. He would never know. He finished washing and stood up, taking a towel from the table to dry off.

Lisa watched him. He was magnificent—bronze skin, blond hair, deep gray eyes. And he was different—more worldly, more manly than ever. He was twenty-three now, but had been through so much he seemed older. She was twenty-three herself. Chaco was twenty-six. Where had the five years gone since first he fled with her to his hidden village?

But this was not time to think of Chaco. It was truly over now. Her blood raced at the sight of Troy, for he was already swelling with manly needs. He walked up to her, untying the robe and pulling it open. He pushed it over her shoulders and she let it fall to the floor. He fingered the full breasts.

"Welcome home, Troy," she whispered.

He picked her up in his arms and carried her to their bed, laying her gently on it. She was glad this was their old cabin and not San Carlos, not the cabin and the bed in which she had made love with Chaco. He moved over her then, but did not take his usual time readying her. His need was too great. In moments he was inside of her, groaning with pent-up needs.

He grasped her hips, surging almost violently inside of her, filing her with his abundant manliness, bringing out all the old, buried desires, making her a woman again. A moment ago he was almost like a stranger. It had been so long. But it had taken only these short moments to rekindle the old friendship, the old love, the reawakening to the fact they were husband and wife. His beautiful spirit, his bravery, his dreams, all made her love him dearly and want to please him.

She took him just as desperately as he took her, wanting his forgiveness, wanting to erase Chaco forever, little knowing that Troy, too, had someone to forget.

Chapter Twenty-Six

The Butterfield rattled along its route with a soldier escort. Until Geronimo and the others were captured, no one was safe, or so the public thought. But the passengers in the coach were not afraid. Troy and Lisa Edwards were headed for Tucson. The word Apache brought no fear to their hearts. Little Sage slept on the seat opposite them, although how he managed to sleep at all Lisa could not understand. Charles moved constantly from one seat to the other, looking out the window first on one side and then the other. He was an active child, terribly curious and not easy to manage. Lisa could see Chaco—the restless spirit, the daring attitude. The boy did not seem to know the meaning of fear and he was already riding ponies. But Sage seemed to want to do nothing but sleep.

"We should have a house that isn't right in town, Troy," Lisa told him. "The boys need space. And I'd like to get a pony for Charles."

"I wouldn't want to be right in town anyway. Tucson is not exactly tamed yet." He grabbed Charles and plunked him in the seat between them. "Now you stay put, young man, or you'll feel my hand on your behind, understand?"

The boy pouted but finally obeyed. Lisa watched Troy as he bent over to take a look at Sage. Such responsibilities he had taken—a wife and two sons, neither of them his. He seemed withdrawn from her at times, his mind on something far away. Perhaps it was only his plans for a newspaper that kept his mind so occupied.

"It was good of Pa to lend me the money to get started," he told her, leaning back again. "I'll need all kinds of equipment. I telegraphed St. Louis from Fort Bowie and they're shipping most of it out by train and wagon, so it shouldn't be too long before it arrives. I'll pay back Pa as soon as I can." He looked at her then. His eyes looked tired and lonely. "I'm afraid you'll have to stay in a hotel for a few days till I find us a place. But people move in and out of the city all the time. It shouldn't take long to find us a place to live. The most important thing is to find a building for an office and get started advertising. I'll spend a lot of time roaming the streets, interviewing people, trying to drum up subscriptions. I'll be gone a lot, Lisa, at least at first."

"That's to be expected. I'll be all right. I have the children."

"I may have to work an extra job just to make ends meet until money starts coming in from the paper. I guess I'll write and print out the paper nights."

"You'd better be careful or you'll work yourself to death."

"No I won't. I like to be busy anyway. I have a lot to do, Lisa."

They hit a bump and Sage squirmed but still slept. Lisa reached over and patted him. "He sleeps much more than Charles did at this age," she said. "I hope he's all right."

"He's Chaco's son, isn't he? He's bound to be healthy and strong."

She sighed and sat back, looking at Troy. She wanted to ask him why he felt he needed to be so busy. Was it all just the writing, or was it a way to bear the responsibilities he had agreed to take? "Maybe the boys and I should have stayed with Bryce and Shannon until you were more settled. We'll be in your way."

377

He reached around Charles and patted her shoulder. "Don't be silly. I need you with me. This is the first chance we've had to be family, truly be family, since we were married."

Married. What a strange marriage it had been, she thought inwardly. From near strangers to dear friends to lovers. And all of it seemed so precarious. Perhaps if she could get over her own guilt she would worry less about their future.

Charles's head nodded and Shannon pulled him down so that his head rested in her lap. He had finally drifted off to sleep. She stroked the sandy hair. "Troy," she spoke up then.

"Hmmm?" He tried to stuff some tobacco into a pipe, but the jostling carriage made it difficult.

"Who is Joanna?"

He froze for a moment, her question so startling him that he could not think at first, nor could he keep his face from coloring slightly. He turned surprised gray eyes to meet her penetrating blue ones. He slowly lowered his pipe. "What on earth made you ask that?"

"You spoke her name in your sleep last night—twice."

His eyebrows arched as he struggled to feign surprise and innocence. "I did?"

She searched his eyes. "Who is she, Troy?"

He smiled nervously. "She's just a friend, someone I met in journalism school. She was quite an unusual girl. One doesn't see many women in such a profession. She's very nice and quite brilliant, I might add." He laughed lightly. "But I can't imagine why I would have spoken her name in my sleep!"

She closed her eyes and turned away. "Oh, Troy," she whispered. "What are we doing? What am I doing to you?"

He grasped her shoulders and turned her to face him. "You aren't doing anything to me, Lisa Edwards," he said sternly. "Joanna is no one special, believe me. How can a man control what he does or says in his sleep, for God's sake! Now we've both been free to speak our minds and make our decisions, and we love each other and want to stay together. There is nothing

378

more to it. We're husband and wife, and here we are on our way to a new home in Tucson. I need you, Lisa, and I love you. So no more talk about this Joanna, understand?"

He leaned over and kissed her lightly, but the coach jolted, knocking them closer together and knocking his hat off. Troy broke into laughter then, moving over and putting his hat back on. "Welcome to Arizona," he chuckled. "Land of brick-laid roads and lush, green gardens."

Lisa laughed herself, deciding Joanna surely was no one important to him after all. "This is certainly nothing like New York, is it," she spoke up.

He sat there quietly then, eyes closed. "No," he answered, suddenly sobering. "It's nothing like New York."

Her own smile faded and she looked out the window then at endless red-rock canyons and blooming cacti. In the distance the mountains loomed. Somewhere out there Chaco roamed— alone, destitute, hunted. The old familiar pain pierced her heart so that it actually hurt, and she wondered if it would ever, ever go away.

They settled into a two-story white frame house on the outskirts of Tucson. The neighboring women were a grand mixture of kind and cruel, some shunning Lisa because of her "mysteriously dark" son, a son not even of her own blood. But they fully accepted Charles, who was fair and who, they believed, was her "true son" by Troy Edwards. Lisa explained nothing. It was not their business. She simply referred to both Sage and Charles as her sons, and to Troy as their father. She almost enjoyed the looks she sometimes got, and the rumor quickly spread that Troy Edwards must surely be part Indian, even though he didn't look it. After all, he was going around town speaking on behalf of the detestable red men whom everyone else would be glad to see dead or imprisoned.

But Troy carefully explained that he was not Indian, that it was his brother who was Indian. It seemed important that they know a man who was all white was supporting the Apaches. If they thought him part Indian they would not listen to anything he had to say.

Out of curiosity, several people promised subscriptions. It would be interesting having another newspaper to read, especially if it was going to be supportive of the Indians. What an odd sort of paper to write! Other newspapers began printing stories about Troy, stories to try to keep people from subscribing to a paper not even being printed yet. Troy was branded as an "Indian lover," and people were reminded it was Troy Edwards and his father Bryce who tried to convict two innocent white men of atrocious crimes, not only against Indians, but against whites!

Troy worked hard that summer. By day he worked at odd jobs for a supply store. By night he sat up writing to the light of a lantern, pouring onto paper everything he had learned from Chaco. He had already decided his newspaper would be called *The Voice,* and he had enough subscriptions to get started. All he needed was his equipment, and it arrived six weeks after his own arrival in Tucson. He worked harder than ever then, anxious to get going on his project. Week by week he would inform them. Week by week he would print articles about the Apaches, starting with all the information he had been able to gather about their origins and history to the current period. He would explain every last detail. He would carefully design each article to teach his readers a little more about the Indians every day. At first perhaps they would not listen, but one by one they would begin to understand. There would be at least a little bit more respect and understanding for those who were first in this land.

Finally he found a small vacated building that would become the home for *The Voice.* But the day he took Lisa into town to show it to her, they both discovered how deep the hatred was running. "Go home, Indian lover," was written across the front of it in white paint.

Lisa gasped, her heart aching for Troy.

"Take your white squaw with you," was written in smaller letters on the door.

Several men were gathered near the building, standing behind a handsome older man dressed in the finest suit one could buy in Tucson. James Veck puffed a cigar, looking Lisa over appreciatively. Whatever the mystery about her, it couldn't take away from her utter beauty.

"I thought I was through with the Edwards bunch a couple of years ago," Veck sneered, the cigar still in his mouth. "Don't you ever learn?"

Troy stepped closer to him, fists clenched. "It's you who's going to learn, Veck," he sneered. "Get away from my building!"

Veck's eyebrows arched and he stepped away, signaling the others to follow. "No problem, Edwards. No problem yet, that is. Just as long as you don't use it for that excuse of a newspaper you plan to publish."

"I'll do what I want with my building. And it won't be long before some people around here begin wondering just who the enemy is, Veck." Troy eyed the man squarely, standing only a couple of feet from him, unafraid.

Veck frowned. "Now what is that supposed to mean?" he sneered.

"It means I know something I think everybody else should know, Veck . . . about you."

The man's face darkened with anger. "What would you know . . . as if there is anything for you to know at all."

"You'll find out . . . when the time is right."

Veck eyed him narrowly. This young man was dangerous. Perhaps he should have him killed. But then he liked challenges. Through challenges he could make fools out of others and show his own power. He would rather make a fool out of

381

this one than to kill him. His bright blue eyes moved to Lisa and the two little boys on either side of her holding her hands.

"Fine sons you have there, Mrs. Edwards," he spoke up. The men behind him laughed.

Lisa clung to little Sage, who began coughing again.

"Tell us, Mrs. Edwards," one of the other men shouted. "Which is better? A white man or an Indian?"

Lisa screamed Troy's name as he dived into the man who had made the remark. She pulled Sage and Charles back. Sage began to cry as Troy and the man who had made the insulting remark rolled in the street, exchanging punches until Troy had the definite upper hand, landing four devastating blows to his opponent before other men pulled him off, a few of them punching him hard in the middle while others held him helplessly at their mercy. Sage cried harder and Charles yanked his hand out of Lisa's and ran toward his father. One of the men pushed him down, but instead of crying, Charles got right back up and began pummeling the man with little fists.

"Charles, no," Lisa yelled frantically, running up and half dragging Sage with her to get to Charles. She yanked him out of the way while the men who had beaten Troy dropped him at her feet. Some of them picked up the man he had knocked unconscious. Lisa knelt over Troy, shaking with horror, reaching down to touch his hair. "Troy," she whispered.

"Tell him to forget this newspaper thing," a voice came.

She looked up at James Veck. "You'll regret this," she hissed. "You'll end up leaving this town with hardly more than the shirt on your back!"

"Oh?" He took the cigar from his mouth. "And how will that be, my beautiful Mrs. Edwards?"

"You'll find out soon enough!" She surprised him when she rose and pulled a small gun from her handbag. "Now you get away from me, or by God, I'll kill you here and now!"

He broke into a light, nervous laugh but stepped back. "Well now. Looks like those wild Apaches got to you. You are the young woman the Apaches attacked a while back, aren't you? Of course you are. Wasn't it Troy Edwards' own Indian brother who . . . took you?"

The words were spoken with dirty overtones and she held the gun steady on him, not flinching.

"Get away from us, Mr. Veck," she warned again.

He only grinned, bowing lightly. "At your service, Mrs. Edwards. But you really should put the gun away. I'd hate to see a pretty thing like you arrested and sitting in jail. Think of the children."

Sage clung to her now, coughing and crying. Charles threw dirt at Veck and the man flinched. He glared at the boy, then back at Lisa. "You really should teach your child better manners, Mrs. Edwards."

"And you should have better manners yourself for a refined businessman. But we all know what you really are, don't we, Mr. Veck? Such an honest, respectable man."

He eyed her closely, then only nodded. "Good day, Mrs. Edwards."

He turned, rejoining the others. They all walked away laughing, except the man Troy had knocked unconscious. A couple of men picked him up, and a crowd of onlookers stared as Lisa put her gun back into her handbag. Could it be true the light-haired son was fathered by the infamous Chaco and not by Troy Edwards? And where did the second child come from?

Lisa bent over Troy, who was getting to his knees, holding his stomach. "Troy, we were going to take Sage to the doctor. You'd better see him, too, now."

"I don't . . . need a doctor."

"Don't be silly. You did that one man in good, but you can't expect to outdo twenty more." She helped him up, beginning to tremble now over the entire confrontation. "Oh, Troy, I thought they were going to kill you," she squeaked.

He held his ribs, panting, but he managed to get an arm around her shoulders, partly to comfort her and partly for support. "They won't go that far, honey. I'm just sorry I brought you here to find those filthy words scrawled on my building."

"I don't care about that. I'm coming down here and help you paint the whole building white. We'll get the rest of the paint off the windows, and you'll have your newspaper." She put an arm around his waist, then ordered Charles to take Sage's hand and follow them. "The first thing we'll do is hint that James Veck is the instigator of all our problems, so if anything happens, he'll be the first one blamed. That will keep him from bothering you as much. And before long we'll have some real stories to print about James Veck. Did you contact that government man?"

"I did." He stopped walking and faced her. "You're awfully pretty when you're riled, Lisa Edwards."

She blushed then. "My God, I held a gun on him!"

He grinned. "You sure did." Their eyes held. "Thank you, Lisa," he said more seriously. "Thank you for taking the risk coming here with me, for supporting my cause."

"It's my cause too."

Again the pain of realizing she still loved Chaco stabbed at him, the renewed realization she had slept with him. Again he thought of Joanna, and how wrong and twisted everything was. Yet they needed each other right now, even though they were both in love with someone else. "Yes," he answered. He kissed her forehead and turned to walk again, leaning on her as the pain in his ribs grew worse. They reached the doctor's office, but the man seemed reluctant to help Troy. He finally consented, declaring Troy had a couple of cracked ribs and badly bruised knuckles. He wrapped his middle and Troy grimaced with the pain. When he was finished he got down from the doctor's table and nodded toward Sage, now in Lisa's arms looking sleepy but coughing too much to truly fall asleep.

"I'd like you to look at the boy, doc," he told the man. "He coughs all the time and he's getting weaker. He was born good and strong, and up to a few months ago seemed happy and playful. Now he's kind of listless."

The doctor glanced at Sage. The boy's skin was dark, obviously containing a great share of Indian blood. "Is that boy Apache?" he asked.

Troy was putting on his shirt. "Yeah. He's Apache. He's the son of my bother Chaco and his dead wife, Little Deer. We took him in."

The doctor shook his head. "I'm sorry. I don't work on Indians, especially Apaches."

Troy stared at him dumbfounded and Lisa's eyes widened. "But he's just a baby and he needs your attention," she blurted out.

"Sorry. I don't work on Indians." The doctor met her horrified eyes and shook his head. "Look. A lot of Indians, especially the little ones, die of tuberculosis. It starts with a bad cough. Even if I did check him over, there would be nothing I could do. It's hard to treat even in white men. But with Indians . . ." He shook his head. "They seldom survive. I can tell by looking at him that's what he's got. The best thing you can do is to take him home and love him for the time he's got left. I'll give you a little medicine for the cough. I just hope he hasn't given it to anyone else. The rest of you seem fine." He turned to take out the medicine, and Lisa stood there staring at him in near shock. He was callously telling her little Sage was going to die, as though he were speaking of her pet dog. "Here you go," he told her, handing out a bottle of the medicine.

"There . . . must be something," she choked out. Chaco! How could she ever tell Chaco his little son had died, died without ever seeing his father again or knowing him at all!

"I'm afraid not," he replied. "Especially not with Indians. It hits them extra hard. All of you had better go on home now and get some rest."

Lisa stared at him. "You hypocrite," she hissed, tears coming to her eyes.

"Come on, Lisa," Troy said gently. "Take the damned medicine and let's get out of here."

She turned her eyes to meet his. "They won't stop us," she told him, holding her chin up proudly. "We won't let them."

"That's right. Come on now." He took the medicine from the doctor and picked up his jacket, reaching into the pocket and handing some coins to the doctor. "Thanks for all your help," he said sarcastically. "You're a real dedicated man."

They walked out together, Troy leading Charles by the hand, Lisa carrying a sleepy Sage's damp, tired body.

"One cannot help but admire the courage and skill of that most famous remaining Apache—Geronimo," read the article in Troy's first paper. "General Miles, for all his five thousand men, all his equipment, his fresh horses and army fighting skills, has still not managed to find this most elusive Apache. I have no doubts that in the pages of history books in generations to come, it is Geronimo who will stand out on the pages, with little to be said about General Miles other than that he was perhaps the soldier who was made the biggest fool of by the Indians. But then, of course, I suppose he would have to take the second place to George Armstrong Custer."

People began buying. While other papers carried on about the "fleeing savage" still being pursued by "our heroic men in blue," Troy's articles gave more truthful accounts. Then came reports that Miles was uprooting approximately four hundred very peaceful Apaches who remained at what was left of San Carlos. They were causing no trouble and were making a living at farming. But Arizona citizens hated the sight of any Apache and were crying out for the removal of all of them from the Territory.

"In an effort to cover his bungling of his commission, it appears General Miles has 'captured' several hundred peaceful Apaches at San Carlos, claiming they are constantly drunk and disorderly and that their young men are planning a new war. Nothing could be farther from the truth. When will a promise be kept? We ask when the Apaches will let us live in peace. I ask, when will we let the *Apaches* live in peace? These reservation Indians bring us no harm. To remove them now will totally destroy any remaining trust they might have in the white man."

But there were not enough people like Troy Edwards to prevent the inevitable. Delegations from these peaceful Apaches were sent to Washington to state their case and to plead to be allowed to remain on the land left to them. The government's original plan was to send them to Fort Sill, where they would be near the Comanches and Kiowas, a ridiculous scheme, as the Apaches and Comanches had always been enemies. The Oklahoma panhandle was considered, but the land was too barren. Whites surrounding Oklahoma were screaming to be allowed to settle in that territory and pleading that no more Indians be sent there. They objected to adding the displaced Apaches to any other area in that territory. And so the Apaches were to be kicked out of Arizona completely, yet there was literally no place to send them. Troy did not fail to point out the ridiculousness of the unnecessary move, nor to let it be known that Chatto, one of the leaders of the delegation to Washington, had pleaded that his wife and children, held in captivity in Mexico, be returned to him, as well as pleading to be allowed to stay on the land he now farmed in Arizona.

I wonder if whites understand that Apaches have the same feelings about their children as we do," Troy wrote. "Chatto has a wife and two children in Mexico, and he loves them dearly and wants to hold his children to his heart again. He has said so in his own words. He has asked the government to get these people out of Mexico (and our government knows exactly where they are, living with a family in Chihuahua) and return them to him. It

387

is well known Mexicans often use Apache women and children as slaves. We object to slavery, but our hearts are hardened when it comes to Apaches.

I urge Arizona citizens to allow the four hundred or so peaceful Apaches left here to live in peace and farm their land, and to allow the return of Chatto's family. But I have doubts what will happen. The government will make Chatto and others believe they can stay on their land, and they will promise to "try" to find Chatto's family and bring them back. But none of those promises will be kept. The wheels are in motion now to rid Arizona of its original citizens—the Apaches. There is no stopping what has been started. These are sad times, and we will live to regret out treatment of these native Americans.

Troy could not have come closer to the truth. Every time General Miles suggested a place where these Apaches could be sent, Washington turned him down for one reason or another. It had been agreed they must leave Arizona, but no one could agree on where they should be sent. Telegrams flew like a blizzard, until, to the horror of the Apaches and to their few sympathizers, Washington began to discuss Fort Marion as the destination of the "prisoners of war."

"What war?" Troy printed in his paper. "These people were never at war with us. They had settled into peaceful farming, obeying the peace treaty. Suddenly we call them hostiles and say they are our prisoners. Is General Miles this desperate to claim he has 'captured' some Apaches? Let General Miles go find Geronimo and do what he is supposed to be doing."

In other newspapers Miles was heralded as the "savior" of Arizona. But all he had done so far was to displace several hundred peaceful Apaches. Now they were considering sending them to Fort Marion, but the commander there advised he could take no more than eighty, stressing that the living conditions there were not "agreeable" to Indians and that he was already overcrowded. The old Spanish fort was in disrepair and its roof leaked. The sanitary conditions were very poor, and few prisoners could ever be allowed outside because the prison was surrounded by the town of St. Augustine. The swampy, humid area was a hotbed of disease for Indians accustomed to the arid mountains and deserts of Arizona.

Troy explained these matters in his newspaper, ignoring continued threats from his opponents:

> Where once the Apaches were beneficial to the economy of Arizona in that our businessmen, people like James Veck, made their money from army contracts; now we hear that Florida is actually asking for Apache prisoners, offering them a home at Fort Pickens near Pensacola, where they will become a "tourist attraction" and bring more money into that state. Isn't it interesting how "humanitarian" we become where money is involved? There are times when I am embarrassed and ashamed to be a white man.

Fort Marion continued, however, to be the targeted destination of the peaceful Indians. But Miles knew they must be handled carefully and not told where they would ultimately be taken, so that they would not flee to the mountains. Many were detained at Fort Leavenworth, held there until their fate would be decided, while Apache runners were sent to find Geronimo and urge him to surrender. Those sent to find him were convinced Miles wanted only peace and that no harm would come to Geronimo and those with him. They would all be given a new home (yet no one knew where) and they would be reunited with their scattered families. A Lieutenant Gatewood was sent with two Apaches Miles knew Geronimo trusted— Kayihtah and his cousin Nednai. An interpreter, George Wratten, would also go. Miles knew that the only way to hope to approach Geronimo was to send a small party of trusted men to seek him out.

"We shall see what kind of promises are made to Geronimo," Troy wrote in his paper. "And we shall see how they are kept. For my part, I consider this the last treachery. Geronimo will walk into a trap, and those who welcome him will have smiles on their faces and outstretched hands—and they will lead Geronimo straight to the gallows or to prison. My prayers are not for the soldiers. They are for Geronimo."

"And for Chaco," Lisa spoke up that night after reading the article.

Troy hoisted Charles onto his lap. He was making barely enough money to support them with the newspaper now. He had quit his extra job and was spending a rare evening at home.

"And for Chaco," he replied. "I'm just trying not to mention his name. I don't want to draw too much attention to him."

"I know."

Sage began coughing in his sleep. Lisa hurried to his room, bending over him and rubbing his back until he quieted. A moment later Troy was beside her.

"I'm so worried about him, Troy. He's thinner and weaker. How could I ever tell Chaco. . . ." Her voice choked. "I love him . . . like my own," she sobbed.

Troy took her into his arms. "I know, Lisa," he whispered. "Why don't you try to get some sleep? Every night you're up half the night with Sage. He's sleeping pretty good. Put Charles to bed and get some rest."

She turned away. She needed him but lately he seemed remote. They had not made love for several days, closer to two weeks. She knew his work was taking him from her. But it was more than that. Something more.

She took Charles to his room and Troy returned to his desk and took out a tablet. "Dear Joanna," he wrote. "You may continue to write me in care of the post office. But I urge you not to do so. I have told you in two other letters that I have no choice now but to stay in Tucson with my family. They all need me very much, and now it appears that little Sage is dying. I will never forget you, Joanna, and I love you. But some things simply cannot be. This thing with my brother . . . the Apaches . . . well, I hope you can understand. If there were any way we could be together, I would use it. But it would be at the cost of people too dear to me. I have made my choice, and I urge you to forget about me and go on with life."

He put down the pen and put his head on his desk, where he fell asleep.

Chapter Twenty-Seven

Troy awoke with a start, sensing someone near. He raised his head to see Lisa hurrying down the hall. "Lisa?" He rubbed his eyes, trying to get his senses straight, to remember the time and where he was. He had fallen asleep at his desk, apparently. He looked down at what he had been writing and a chill swept through him. "Lisa," he whispered.

He quickly rose, hurrying down the hall after her, going into the bedroom to find her lying on the bed weeping. He cursed his stupidity in falling asleep. Hesitantly he approached the bed and climbed on beside her.

"Don't cry, Lisa. It isn't nearly what you think."

She curled away from him. "It doesn't matter. We're ... even now ... aren't we?" She wept harder.

He put a hand on her shoulder. "It's got nothing to do with getting even. When I became friends with Joanna, I knew nothing about Chaco. Lisa, there was never even anything between us, not sexually."

"You love her." She pulled a pillow to her to hug it. "You love someone else ... and I'm making your life miserable. I was afraid ... once you went away ... and met other women...."

"Jesus, Lisa, there weren't 'other women.' I never went with

392

that in mind. We just happened to meet ... to be in the same class. She was interesting. We were assigned to the same newspaper together. It just sort of happened by accident. Living in New York was like a whole different world. It was like Arizona didn't even exist."

"My God, my God," she wept.

"Lisa, don't hate me. I couldn't bear for you to hate me."

She turned, lying on her back and facing his. "Hate you? I could never hate you. It's me I hate. It's the lies, the pretending." She sat up. "Troy, don't you see? We can never last, even if Chaco should die. I can never be sure ... if you truly love me ... or if you stay with me out of duty. Shannon and Bryce warned us this could happen. We weren't ... supposed to care in the beginning." She jerked in a sob and wiped at her eyes. "But we did care ... and yet somehow ... it isn't enough. We love each other ... and we make love ... but something is missing."

"No! No, it isn't."

"Troy, I love Chaco. And you love Joanna." She turned away. "If another man married me ... wanting me from the beginning ... I could learn to accept someone else. But hard as I try ... I cannot get over the terrible guilt I carry ... being married to you ... because of the way we got married. You've been so distant lately. I thought it was just your work. But it's been more than that, hasn't it? You've been thinking about this Joanna ever since you returned. That's why you spoke her name in your sleep."

He sighed, lying down on his side, reaching up and pulling her down beside him. "All right," he told her, holding her arm firmly. "Yes, I think about her ... but in the same way you think about Chaco ... as someone I can't have."

"But yours is by choice, not by circumstance. You could be with her if not for me."

He studied the beautiful blue eyes. "Lisa, you said it was by

393

choice and I made my choice. Just let it rest. We have each other ... this home ... the children and the paper...."

"That isn't enough. Not for you. You deserve more, Troy. Much more."

"I already have the best."

She closed her eyes. "Not what's best for you. I saw the letter, Troy. You wouldn't have written it if you didn't have deep affection for her." Another tear slipped out of one eye and down the side of her face. "What is she like, Troy?"

He didn't answer at first. She opened her eyes to see pain in his own. "It's all right. You can tell me about her. We might as well get it out in the open."

He lay back beside her. "Her name is Joanna Gale. She's eighteen ... very bright and well educated. She also likes to write. She comes from good family in New York ... one of six children. She says she's always been very independent. Her folks didn't want her to try her hand at journalism, said there was no future in it for a woman. That made her mad and she set out to prove otherwise. She's about your size but has dark hair and eyes." He carefully took her hand. "She's not as pretty as you. She's just ... different. We found we liked a lot of the same things, and she was attracted to me because I was from a place she'd never been." He smiled sadly. "You wouldn't believe the picture they have back east of the Wild West and the Indians. We got to talking after class one day and she peppered me with questions till I almost got a sore throat from talking so much. She was fascinated to learn I had a half brother who was part Apache Indian and lived and rode with Geronimo."

He raised up on one elbow, looking down at her. "Lisa, do you know back east they have dime novels about the West— wild stories about Indians and mountain men, pictures of buffalo big as mountains, mountain men fighting bare-handed with grizzly bears. It's the craziest thing you ever saw. You'd think everybody out here was superhuman. I swear that's how Joanna thought of me."

She studied the handsome face, the kind gray eyes. What young eastern girl wouldn't fall in love with a rugged, handsome man from the West? She wondered if that was how it had been for Shannon when she met Troy's father. Surely Bryce looked very much then like Troy did now—and in full uniform, full of tales of fighting wild Indians. No wonder Shannon fell in love with him, especially if he was as kind and strong and brave as Troy.

He leaned closer. "There was nothing that much to it, Lisa." He met her lips, searching her mouth, trying to reassure her, but the letter was too vivid in her mind. She turned her face away.

"It isn't right, Troy. I want so much for it to be right, but it isn't and we have to face that." She sat up wearily. "It might not show now. You might not even feel too much resentment now. But it will come. Some day it will come and you'll hate me. I love you too much and value our friendship too much to let that happen. I'd rather ... part now ... before we have children of our own and things get any more complicated than they already are."

He sat up, too, touching her arm. "Part? You mean ... divorce?"

She met the eyes again, her heart feeling so torn. "Yes. We agreed in the very beginning the marriage was just for looks, until Charles was born." She touched his face. "Let's end it, Troy, before the hurt just gets bigger and bigger. Don't mail that letter to Joanna. Tell her you're free."

He looked away from her, getting off the bed and running a hand through his hair. "No. I ... I love you, Lisa."

"And I love you. But it's not going to be enough. Troy, I want to part friends, not bitter enemies."

He looked at her with concern. "But ... what would happen to you ... to Charles and Sage? I love them like my own, Lisa."

She swallowed back a new urge to weep. Sage! Little Sage, always so sick now. "I'm sure that between you and your father,

I'll be all right. I can go back and live with them. Perhaps another man will ... come along...." She sniffed and swallowed. "But there can never be ... another Chaco," she whispered.

He walked closer and knelt in front of her, taking her hands. "Lisa, I don't want you to be alone."

She forced a smile through her tears. "Oh, I won't be. I'll have your parents ... and Charles and Sage. I won't be alone, Troy. Some women have gone through much worse. And I'd be so much happier knowing you have what you really want."

They could hear Sage coughing again. Their eyes held, both thinking the same thing. Little Sage was dying. He squeezed her hands.

"Let's think this out, Lisa. Maybe you should go back to the post with my folks. Maybe we should be apart again for a while. But for now, just tell them you've come back because of Sage. If he is ... if he is dying ... they should be near him. He's their grandchild. And he should be taken out and buried high in the mountains." His eyes teared more. "Chaco ... would want that. Pa would do it for him."

She nodded, her body jerking in a sob.

"We're not giving up yet, Lisa. Understand? Not quite yet. Let's make each other a promise right now that we won't do anything about this till Sage is ... till we know what will happen to Sage. And even then not until we know for sure about Chaco. Agreed?"

She sniffed. "All right." She took one hand from his and touched his face. "You're so good, Troy. I married ... a stranger ... and gained the best friend I will ever have. Promise me we can always be friends, Troy, even if ... if your Joanna should come here and marry you. Make her understand."

He took her hand, kissing the palm. "I'd never marry a woman who wouldn't understand. And I'd not live in peace if I couldn't see all I wanted of Charles and Sage." He squeezed her hand. "I've always wanted this to work, Lisa. It still might.

396

Don't give it up yet. Don't say anything to my folks. They have so much on their minds already."

"We all do. Surely you've wanted to tell us all about Joanna. Troy, I have to give it up, when I see how your eyes light up when you talk about her. What on earth did you tell her about us?"

He sighed and stood up. "The truth. And I told her more than once I would never leave you as long as you and the boys need me. I meant that."

"Of course you meant it. But you will never be happy, Troy."

"I have been happy. You're beautiful, wonderful."

"But I'm not the one you would choose. I can't live with that constant guilt, Troy, the constant knowledge that I am your responsibility but not your true love. I would be happier alone than living with a man I am making miserable."

He smiled sadly, coming back to sit beside her. "I've never been miserable, Lisa."

She leaned forward and kissed his forehead. "You were miserable when you wrote that letter. I could tell by the words." She ran her fingers through the thick, blond hair. "We tried, Troy. We tried very hard, and there is nothing wrong in that. I've been through so much, it's made me stronger. I'll be all right."

Someone knocked on the door. Troy frowned, jumping up and hurrying to the outer hall, going to the parlor and taking his rifle down from over the fireplace mantel. Lately they had been plagued with constant threats from Indian haters. Anyone who came this late at night could be someone who meant them harm. Lisa darted out into the hallway.

"Stay back," Troy ordered, cocking the rifle. He stepped close to the front door. "Who's there?"

"It's me ... David."

David Truman was one of two men Troy had hired to dig up news for him and to write articles of their own for his paper. The other was Arnold Spring. Both were from the East, men who were not so prejudiced against the Apaches. Troy opened the door to David, a tall, skinny young man not much older than Troy. Both David and Arnold slept in a back room of the printing office to help guard it.

"What do you want this time of night?" Troy asked. "Somebody vandalize the office?"

"No. Some soldiers are in town on leave, and I loosened them up with some whiskey. They told me it's been quiet, but it looks like Geronimo is about to surrender. Special scouts and a representative for Miles were sent out to find him. We already know about that. They say he's been found and is talking about coming in. He's holding out in the Torres Mountains in Mexico."

Troy turned to Lisa. "They'll trick him," he said quietly. He closed his eyes and sighed, turning back to David. "Any mention of my brother, Chaco?"

"No. I don't know if he's with Geronimo or not. I'll bet you any money the Indians they sent to Geronimo don't even know themselves that the government is thinking of sending them to Fort Marion. They probably think they'll get to go back to their land at San Carlos and return to their farming. There's no way Geronimo would consider coming in if he wasn't assured he could join his own people at San Carlos and live there peacefully. If any mention was made of Fort Marion, they'd all run so fast they wouldn't even leave dust."

Troy nodded. "The ultimate treachery. Miles couldn't capture him by force. He'll take him by lying through his teeth, making promises that won't be kept. One thing is for sure. If they get their hands on Geronimo this time, it will be all over. There will be no more escaping. He'll be so chained and guarded he won't be able to take a piss without soldiers around. And you can bet he'll either be hanged, or sent so far away from here . . ."

Lisa made a whimpering sound and turned away. David felt

398

suddenly like an intruder. "I'll leave now. Maybe I shouldn't have come to tell you this so late at night. I'm sorry, Troy."

"It's all right. Thanks for the information. Keep your ears open, and check with the telegraph office in the morning. I think I'll send a wire myself to my pa and see what he can find out at Fort Bowie. Besides, I have to tell him Lisa is leaving Tucson and going back to the post."

David frowned curiously.

"It's Sage," Troy quickly explained. "He's pretty sick. I think it would be better for Lisa to get out of here right now, what with things getting so thick about the Indians. And my folks should be with Sage." He sighed deeply. "The doctor doesn't think he'll live much longer."

Genuine concern filled David's brown eyes. "Damn. I'm sorry, Troy."

Troy glanced at Lisa again. "Yeah. We're all sorry about a lot of things."

It was early September of 1886 when the news hit Tucson. Geronimo had indeed surrendered.

"Geronimo has seen his Chiricahua Mountains for the last time," one newspaper read. "If we are lucky, he will soon see Arizona for the last time."

People laughed and cheered in the streets. The saloons were overflowing with both men and whiskey. Bands played and guns were fired wildly all night.

"Geronimo has surrendered upon the promise that he and those with him will be reunited with their families," Troy wrote out that night, preparing for his own version of the surrender. "Now let us watch and see how many promises are kept. The Apaches, indeed all Indians, take the pledges they make in treaties very seriously. They are made with every intention of never breaking those promises. But the whites break them at every turn. This is the cause of the constant wars and the anger of the Indians. They believe promises should be kept. Can we prove for once that we are capable of doing so?"

Lisa came over to his side. "Was there any word of Chaco?"

He sighed, rubbing his eyes. "None."

"If you're going to take me back to the post, take me now, Troy. I want to go to Fort Bowie. Perhaps we can get there before they ship Geronimo off to Florida and see if Chaco is with the prisoners."

He looked up at her, taking her hand. "Are you sure you want to go there? If he is with them, it might be best not to see him at all."

She clung to his hand. "I have to know."

He rose, putting an arm around her. "And you're sure about going back to my folks?"

"I'm sure. We both know it's best, especially with Sage's condition. Maybe the fort doctor will give him more attention than the doctor here will."

"Maybe. But it won't do him much good, Lisa. The only problem is I can't be with him too. I can't be two places at once, and things are just getting going with the newspaper. This work is so important, Lisa. . . ."

"You don't have to explain. And there is nothing you can do about Sage but stand and watch. If he gets worse we can wire you."

He nodded and their eyes held, loving but knowing their marriage could not go on. "God, I'm so sorry, Lisa," he whispered. "I want so much . . ."

She put her fingers to his lips. "You're my best friend in the whole world, Troy Edwards. Right now that friendship is all I need. It's vital. I don't ever want it to go bad. I need you too much. I need your strength and your understanding, and you need mine."

He embraced her, wondering at the strange turns people's lives took at the hands of fate. What would have happened to Lisa if she never would have come west, or if it had not been

Chaco who captured her? How much control did one really have over his life?

"Sometimes when the wind howls, Lisa, I hear them crying," he whispered. His throat tightened. "I hear them all ... crying."

Geronimo, Naiche (son of Cochise), and the other leaders of those last warriors waited proudly at Fort Bowie for promises to be kept. They were to be given a place to live and to be reunited with their families. Even if sent to Florida, they were to be with their families and be allowed to return one day. They truly believed they were safe now, unaware that Washington was urging that the hostiles be tried and punished by civil authorities for their atrocities against whites. Even General Miles objected to this, aware that no civil court in Arizona or New Mexico would give any Apache a fair trial.

While Miles hurried the "captured" Indians to Fort Bowie, Troy and Lisa made their way back to the Edwards trading post. By the time they arrived little Sage was coughing so hard he was spitting up blood. Lisa decided it was impossible to accompany Troy and Bryce to Fort Bowie, and considering Sage's condition, even Shannon could not bring herself to leave Lisa alone with Sage, especially when Charles was such a handful.

"Maybe it's better neither of you is there anyway," Bryce told them.

The men left. Shannon took Sage from Lisa's arms and Lisa sank into a rocking chair, breaking into tears. "So many things are over, Shannon," she groaned.

Shannon studied Sage's thin face. "Gamma," he said, reaching up to touch her cheek. She knew Sage was not well, but she had not expected this. No one needed to tell her her grandson was dying. She sat down in a chair across from Lisa, pulling the boy close to her bosom.

"It's more than this thing with Geronimo, and more than Sage, isn't it? Your wire said you would stay with us for a while."

Lisa met her eyes. Shannon Fitzgerald Edwards was such a perceptive, sensitive woman. "We ... promised each other not to say anything ... until we knew about Chaco ... and Sage."

"You aren't going to stay together after all."

Lisa sighed deeply, putting her head in her hands. "I found a letter he had written ... to a girl back east he met while he was there. Her name is Joanna." She sniffed. "He loves her, Shannon. He was telling her to never contact him again, that he'd made up his mind to keep his brother's family. But I can't live with him that way." She met Shannon's eyes again. "I can't stand the guilt, Shannon. He never had a chance to have what he really wanted, and he turned down a young woman he truly loved just to stay with me and the boys. Do you see how impossible that is? It might work for a while, but ... some day he'd end up hating me, Shannon. I don't ever want that to happen. I value his friendship too much."

Shannon nodded. "I see."

"You told me once ... to never hurt him. But we've ended up hurting each other. The hurting has to stop quickly, Shannon. It's not like ... like you and Bryce. You loved Bryce first. You were already in love with him. Troy and I had to ... to struggle to make love happen. If it can't come naturally, there is no hope. We love each other ... as dear friends. I'll always love and cherish him as the finest man I know. But I don't love him the way a woman should love her husband. I just hope ... you will forgive me and allow me to stay with you. Somehow I'll find a way to be on my own. Troy will always help support us...."

"Lisa, you have been wife to both my sons. Why would I not welcome you back with us and give you a home here for as long as you need one. We love you. We will help however we can. The important thing for now is Sage. Bryce will bring the fort doctor back with him.''

Lisa put her head in her hands again. Maybe there was some hope for Sage. She had to think there was, just as she had to think there was hope for Chaco.

"Lisa, you should keep busy," Shannon told her. "We have a long wait ahead of us. Why don't you steam some water? We'll treat Sage the way we treat croup. I'll sit under a blanket with him and perhaps the steam will relieve the coughing.''

Lisa nodded. "Yes. Yes, I'll do that.'' She jumped up, seeming to be almost glad to have something to occupy her time. She glanced at the mantle clock. Not only would the men most likely not be back today, but it might be several days, for they would wait at Fort Bowie to discover the fate of Geronimo. Whatever his fate, Chaco's would surely be the same ... if he was with Geronimo at all.

It was eight days before Bryce and Troy returned. "Chaco wasn't with them,'' Troy told the women.

"Oh, thank God,'' Shannon breathed.

Troy looked at Lisa, seeing the relief mixed with worry in her eyes. "According to some of the other captives, Chaco and Coyotero escaped and are still holding out. But it's dangerous. They can't stay in Mexico. The Mexicans are killing every Apache in sight. That's why Geronimo gave himself up to American troops rather than Mexican. They'd have shot him for certain.''

She turned away and Bryce rubbed at his eyes, then the back of his neck, tired from the past days that were grueling emotionally. "I spoke with Geronimo, and shook hands with him,'' he spoke up, turning to look out a window. "I had never met him. He was just coming into his own when I quit the army, but he was impressed to realize I'd known Cochise well ... and Saguaro. I can see why he's a leader. Even at his age, he's strong and sharp, with a keen, dark eye that sees right through a man and gauges his honesty and truthfulness. He isn't a tall or extremely big man, but there is a certain power and energy about him that radiates from his very being. I've never met a man quite like him." He turned to the women. "They gave themselves up in complete trust and honor. They believed General Miles. He promised them a reservation of their own, said they would be reunited with their families and have horses and wagons of their own and would be left alone. But it was just a stall to keep Geronimo from bolting. He and Naiche and the others were herded to Bowie Station and loaded onto a train like a bunch of cattle, to take them to Fort Marion and imprisonment."

He swallowed and turned away, breathing deeply to stay in control. "When they were . . . herding the Indians from the fort, the post band started playing 'Auld Land Syne.' And the soldiers . . . laughed at them." His voice broke. "They laughed." He swallowed again and took a deep breath. Troy sat down wearily in a chair. "They don't have . . . the slightest idea what this has all meant . . . to the Apache," Bryce finished in a near whisper.

"They brought in the rest of the reservation Indians," Troy added. "They were living peacefully, harming no one. But they brought them in anyway and disarmed them, loading them on a train, too. Even the scouts, the men who believed the promises of freedom and land if they helped the soldiers, men who risked turning on their own people. The soldiers turned around and disarmed them and threw them on the train with the rest. Some of them . . ." He clenched his fists. "Some of those Apaches had never even seen a train before. Children ran from it in terror and had to be herded back. Some of them were literally thrown on." He stood up." My God, Mother, it was so hot! So hot! And they closed all the doors and air vents to the cars. Do you know what it will be like inside there, all of them stuffed in there like they are? Women, children . . . all going to prison!

People accustomed to fresh air and mountains and sunshine stuffed into a dark, stinking cattle car and taken to a hellhole where most of them will die!"

Shannon grasped her stomach and turned around.

"Free! Yes, what a free country this is," Troy growled. "We free the slaves and we take our own native Americans and ship them off to death as though they were some kind of animal to be rid of!" He turned watery eyes to Lisa. "I'm going back, Lisa. I'm going back right away. I have some writing to do, and I'll not stop with my little newspaper in Tucson. I'm sending some articles back east to the bigger papers! People are going to know what happened here!"

She turned and held his eyes proudly. "They should know. And you can tell them. You do it, Troy. If Sage gets worse, we'll wire you."

He nodded. "I'll go pack my carpetbag." He started past her and she reached out to him. They embraced, saying good-bye in more ways than one.

Chapter Twenty-Eight

Geronimo and the others were not even to be reunited with their families. Women and children were separated from the warriors and sent on to Fort Marion. But President Cleveland ordered that the men be sent to Fort Pickens in Florida. Every promise made to Geronimo had been broken. He had surrendered on the word of General Miles that he and the others could again be with their families and that they would be given land of their own. None of this was to come true.

One high army official even tried to get one Apache who had saved his life freed. The Indian was Ahnandia, one of the reservation Indians who had been living peacefully, an industrious Apache who was even learning to read. The army official explained to the War Department the worthiness of Ahnandia, and that the man was "very much attached" to his wife. But even that appeal was denied. Ahnandia would go to Fort Pickens, his wife to Fort Marion, even though neither of them had done anything wrong. Their crime was to be Apache.

The "capture" of Geronimo had been nothing more than Geronimo's own consent to give himself up to Miles in return for certain promises. If he had not given up willingly, he might never have been caught at all. Yet in General Miles's annual report to the secretary of war, he stated: "The hostiles fought until the bulk of their ammunition was exhausted, pursued for more than two thousand miles over the most rugged and sterile districts of the Rocky and Sierra Madre mountain regions, beneath the burning heat of midsummer, until worn down and disheartened, they find no place of safety in our country or Mexico, and finally lay down their arms and sue for mercy from the gallant officers and soldiers, who, despite every hardship and adverse circumstance, have achieved the success their endurance and fortitude so richly deserved."[1]

Troy Edwards did not waste any time printing his version of that "endurance and fortitude." His articles about the Apaches were so well done that he actually began to win a sympathetic audience. Circulation grew, and Troy Edwards rapidly gained recognition as a journalist who sought the truth; his articles were reprinted widely in eastern newspapers. He worked hard at digging up some remnant of sympathy for the "last remaining people who represented the original Americans who have, after all, only fought for what once belonged to them."

"We must not forget," he wrote, "what a grave error it would be for us to destroy the Indian culture and bury it forever. This must never happen, for in spite of the hard feelings, the terrible crimes committed by our native Indians, such crimes were committed in an effort to protect and preserve their own loved ones. We must remember that these people were the first true Americans, and they are important to our history and heritage. We must protect and love the land as they would have, and regard the land and its precious gifts as sacred treasures, to be honored, as its original people should also be treasured and honored."

Although a great majority of people still did not fully sympathize, he was at least making them consider alternatives to a complete annihilation of Indians and their customs and language. Through his efforts he was also building a name for himself, enough so that he began to gain some respect even in Tucson. His office was no longer vandalized and his life not threatened so often. It was then, when he was sure he had enough interest to make people want to get rid of those who had profited from Indian deprivations and were getting rich off the government, that he made his move against James Veck. He had already secretly discussed the letter from James Veck with government officials, who were investigating the incident. Then he made his move, coming out with headlines like, "ASK JAMES VECK" and "I CHALLENGE JAMES VECK." He continued with articles about evidence that James Veck conspired to cheat the Apaches and therefore the government and the American people, at San Carlos. "Whenever such unscrupulous cheating went on, it only prolonged the Indian problem, undermining their faith in the white man and causing new outbreaks and anger in the hearts of the red men who had believed we would help them."

Charges were soon brought against James Veck, and the people of Tucson began to murmur against him. It was in the middle of this latest challenge that Troy got the telegram:

"Come home. Sage died this June 2. Taking to mountains."

Their little party was somber. Even Charles, now five, sensed the seriousness of what was happening, although he could not quite understand what death was. His three-year-old brother was not coming back. It seemed impossible. Surely he would wake up one day and Sage would be running to him wanting to play. He rode quietly in front of his mother, whose horse pulled the travois that carried little Sage's body.

Lisa had no tears left. She had loved the boy like her own son, for he was Chaco's blood. Chaco! Where was Chaco? Was he even alive? Perhaps he was lying dead somewhere in Mexico, buzzards eating away his flesh. Troy rode beside her. He would hold her tonight, comfort her. But they would not make love, not just because of Sage's death, but also because they simply would never make love again. It was over and they both knew it. So many, many things were over.

Shannon rode in front of Bryce on Bryce's horse, lines beginning to show around her eyes, her hair a little grayer. She had suffered too much. Bryce kept a strong arm around her. He was a robust man for his age, his hair still thick, his features handsome. But the gray eyes betrayed the many sorrows he also had suffered. And no sorrow could be greater than watching a small child die, especially when that child was a son, a grandson. It seemed that everything that had truly linked Chaco to the Apaches was gone—his friends and leader imprisoned, his Apache wife dead, and now his Apache son.

They reached a spot about three miles from the post, a place in the lower mountains where Chaco and Troy used to ride and play. Bryce dismounted, helping Shannon down. Troy also dismounted, walking over to Lisa and reaching up for Charles, lifting him down and then helping Lisa down. She moved to the travois, bending over the little bundled body and touching it lightly. She straightened and looked at Bryce.

"Maybe it was for the best," she spoke up. "He looked Indian. Life and choices would have been as hard for him as it was for Chaco. Maybe this is God's way of relieving him of the misery he would have known."

Bryce looked back at her with bloodshot eyes. "Maybe." He looked at Troy. "Help me build a platform. We'll not put him in the ground."

Troy nodded. They removed poles they had brought along, and Shannon and Lisa both just sat staring at the distant, higher mountains while the men worked. Lisa's throat hurt so much that she wondered if she would be able to keep breathing.

The platform was built, and Bryce carefully lifted Sage's small body from the travois, raising it symbolically toward the sun, then laid it on the wooden, blanket-covered bed of the platform. He and Troy then began securing the body. Lisa could not help the new tears that finally came as she laid an arrow next to him, an arrow that Chaco had made by hand when he was younger; then she covered the baby with a shirt that had been his father's.

Troy read some scripture, and little Charles's lips puckered and his eyes teared. Why were they putting Sage way up there on that thing? Were they going to leave him there all alone? Now everyone was crying. Troy could not go on. Bryce had started to say a prayer for Chaco. That was when they heard it . . . a long, piercing cry that filled the air and seemed to echo from one canyon wall to another, almost like the cry of a wolf, full of chilling sorrow.

They all turned, Lisa's heart pounding wildly when she saw a figure at the top of a rise to their left—an Indian on a horse, silhouetted against a sunrise.

"Chaco," she whispered.

Troy came up behind her, putting an arm around her. "Do you think it's him?"

"I'm sure it is," Bryce answered before Lisa could.

"He knows! Somehow he knows," Lisa spoke up. "He knows Sage is dead. That was a cry of sorrow."

The figure began to descend the ridge and Lisa's hand tightened on Troy's. Shannon stepped forward slightly, and little Charles stared. Was a wild Indian coming to kill them? Troy turned and quickly picked up the boy.

"You might as well know that's your father coming," he told the boy. "It's time you knew the truth, Charles."

The boy frowned, looking at Troy. "You daddy."

"I'm your uncle, and I love you very much, Charles. But that man coming there . . . he's your real daddy. But he's Indian, and some men are hunting for him, so he had to hide. He's my brother, and I have agreed to take care of you until he can be with you."

Charles frowned in total confusion. The figure came close enough to see him better. Lisa gasped at blood that ran down both of Chaco's arms from self-inflicted wounds out of sorrow.

410

His hair was loose and long and an ammunition belt hung across his chest. His face was haggard, and he turned wild, dark eyes to Charles, sucking in his breath with pride at the sight of the strong, handsome boy. He rode closer, and Charles stared in awe as this fierce-looking man Troy had said was his daddy reached out and touched his thick, sandy hair. Chaco's skin was much darker than Charles's. He was wild and mean looking, but for some reason Charles felt no fear. The man's eyes turned to Lisa then.

"So, it was Sage."

"Chaco," she whispered, stepping forward and grasping his horse's mane, resting her head against his leg.

Chaco moved his eyes to Troy. "I did not know for certain. I have been watching. I saw you leave with the travois and a small bundle tied to the back. I saw my mother and my woman weeping."

He said "my woman" as though Lisa had never belonged to anyone else.

"It was tuberculosis," Troy told him. "It seems a lot ... it seems to be a common disease to Indians."

Chaco smiled in almost a sneer. "Yes. So it seems. And what the white man's diseases do not kill, the soldiers and Mexicans do. The Mexicans have killed Coyotero. I am the only one left."

Troy closed his eyes and turned away, setting Charles down. "I'm damned sorry, Chaco," he spoke up. Charles stood transfixed, still staring at this strange Indian who was supposed to be his father.

Shannon walked up to him, reaching up and taking his hand. He squeezed it. "I came not just because of my son. You were all together and away from the post. It was a good way to see all of you once more before I ...." He hesitated. "Before I am gone from you."

"But ... where would you go, Chaco? There is no place left."

He held her eyes, then glanced at Bryce. "My father found a way. So will I."

411

Shannon's eyes widened. "No, Chaco! There are other ways."

"What other ways? Prison in Florida? I know about that place. Death would be better!"

"That's crazy talk," Lisa said desperately. "I don't want to hear any more...."

A shot rang out and her body jerked. Chaco's horse lurched and Chaco's eyes widened as Lisa slumped to the ground. His horse's sudden movement caused his mother to fall down.

"Lisa," Troy shouted.

"Mommy! Mommy!" Charles ran to her but Troy grabbed him and tumbled him to the ground, throwing his body over Lisa and Charles both.

"Snipers," Bryce had shouted already. "Stay down, Shannon."

"They are only after me," Chaco yelled, whirling his horse. "I will lure the shots away from you!"

"Chaco," Shannon screamed. She started to get to her feet as Chaco rode off, but Bryce knocked her down.

"Goddamn it, don't get up!" He scrambled to his horse and managed to get a rifle out, then took his handgun and belt from his saddle horn, throwing it over to Troy. "Can you see any of them?"

"No, I ..." He raised up slightly. "Jesus, we're surrounded! Chaco's coming back this way. They're coming at him from another direction."

"Get behind some rocks! I'll get Charles!" Bryce ran hard, grabbing Charles and ordering Shannon to follow, while Troy picked up Lisa's limp body in his arms and ran with her behind a large boulder, praying she was not dead. Charles began to cry and Shannon held him close, trying to soothe him.

Chaco came thundering toward them, hanging off the side of his horse as bullets whizzed by him. Troy and the others backed up against a cliff above which the other snipers were poised. Chaco was yipping like the warrior he was; suddenly he sat upright on his horse and whirled straight for his pursuers.

"My God," Troy murmered. "He's asking for it!"

There were only two of them. "Take the one on your left," Bryce shouted over to Troy. Troy took careful aim. Bryce's rifle rang out and the man on the right flew from his horse. Then Troy shot. The one on the left yelled and fell from his horse, his foot catching in the stirrup. The horse thundered past them, dragging its rider with it.

Chaco whirled again, riding toward them. He dismounted quickly and ran to Lisa.

"Lisa," he groaned her name, bending over her and pulling her into his arms, rocking her. "Lisa! Lisa!" He murmured something in the Apache tongue. "It is . . . my fault," he spoke up then. "Everything is my fault. Look what I have done to her."

"Damn it, Chaco, it's not what you've done. It's what *they've* done!"

"What is the difference?" He held her in the crook of his arm while Bryce watched carefully from his own hiding place, watching for the remaining snipers, who would surely come for them. It was Chaco they wanted, but they would not get him. Not if he had anything to do with it.

"Chaco," Lisa groaned. She opened her eyes, studying the dark, handsome face through blurred vision. Blood seeped in dangerous amounts from a wound just above her right breast. The bullet had entered her back, just under the right shoulder blade, and had exited in front, leaving the largest hole there. It had passed right through her and part way into Chaco's horse, but not deep enough to harm the animal, which stood nearby now, its eyes wide and wild.

"I am right here, Lisa," Chaco told her soothingly. "Do not die, Lisa! Do not die! My agony will know no bounds if you die!"

"Stay . . . with me. Don't . . . go away . . . this time."

"I will stay. I will not leave you." His eyes filled with tears

413

and he drew her close, whispering in her ear. "Forgive me, Lisa. It was me they were after. I should not have come!"

"Nothing ... to forgive. Sage. You ... had a right," she mumbled.

"Sons of bitches," Troy muttered. "How did they know!" They could hear horses then. "Get ready!"

Chaco gently laid Lisa down, then crouched beside Troy. "You and father keep them busy. I will get behind them." The words were growled. "I will show them what happens to men who attack an Apache man at his own son's burial site!"

He was gone so quickly there was no time for Troy to object. Bryce caught Chaco's quick movement and in an instant he was gone, melting into the rocks in the mysterious way Apaches had of doing so. He knew without asking what Chaco would do. He began firing at the six men approaching, while Shannon crouched over Charles, wincing at the loud shots. Nearby Troy fired also, hitting one man before running out of bullets.

The other five kept coming. Bryce took careful aim and hit another before the remaining four were upon them, whooping and shouting like Indians themselves. It was obvious they were nothing short of white trash out to get a name by capturing the infamous Chaco, and Bryce had no doubt what would happen to the women if any of them succeeded. He knew Troy was out of bullets. They had not come prepared for such an attack. Now the men were upon them. One aimed at Bryce, his gun going off the same time as Bryce's. The shot grazed Bryce's arm, but not before Bryce's bullet hit the man solidly in the chest, knocking him from his horse.

Troy dived into another, literally reaching up and yanking the man from his horse, wrestling with him on the ground. Bryce ducked another bullet, rolling on the ground and coming up to swing his rifle into the back of yet another before the man could reload his own empty gun. The man cried out in pain and fell forward, clinging to his horse's mane.

The remaining man cocked and aimed his pistol at Bryce,

but an instant later a huge knife was thrust through his chest from behind. Chaco yipped and howled when he saw his knife meet its mark. Bryce whirled, realizing Chaco had just saved his life. The man went down in wide-eyed surprise, and in the next moment Chaco leaped down from the rocks above, darting about so quickly no one could possibly shoot him, trying to lure out any snipers that might be left.

Troy still wrestled with his own man, managing to push the man's gun hand down to his chest and hold it there while he gouged at his eyes. "You stinking son of a bitch," he growled. "How dare you try to kill a man in mourning over his own son!"

The gun went off and the man jolted. The bullet had gone into his chest at close range, opening a hole that spurted blood all over Troy. Troy sat there frozen for a moment, then yanked the gun from the man's hand and aimed it directly between his eyes. The man groaned and Troy fired. After that Troy's hand shook and his eyes teared. Yes! Now he understood more than ever! How easy it was to kill a man when he was your enemy out to get you first! Of course it was easy for Chaco to kill. Why shouldn't he kill, when he knows what they would do to him if he did not. You kill the enemy before he kills you. It was the law of survival.

He slowly crawled off his opponent's dead body, turning to see Chaco yanking the man off the horse that Bryce had whacked with his rifle. The man hit the ground with a thud and Chaco grasped his hair, taking a small tomahawk from his side. Shannon gasped as he held it up.

"Chaco, wait," Troy shouted, stumbling over to him. "Don't kill him! I want to know how they found us, how they knew you'd be with us."

The man screamed when Chaco yanked back his head. Lisa heard it all as though in a dream.

"You heard him," Chaco growled. "How did you know to come here! Who sent you!"

The man gasped, staring at Chaco fearfully, for he truly looked the savage murderer at that moment. The man had heard so many tales of Apache cruelty he literally shook.

"We heard ... the kid died. We've been watchin' the post. . . ."

Troy leaned over him then. "It's more than that! You look too stupid to have figured it out. Somebody sent you, didn't they? Maybe somebody in Tucson heard why I'd left and decided to follow."

"N ... no," the man answered. Troy's eyes narrowed. "And you're a stinking liar," he growled.

Chaco placed the hatchet directly under the man's nose, pressing enough to nick the skin and making the man whimper. "Get him off me!"

"I will get up when you tell us how you got here," Chaco sneered. "Speak quickly, my friend, or I will quickly move this tomahawk up and you will have no nose left on your face!"

The man looked up then with begging eyes at Bryce. He'd heard Edwards was a kind-hearted man. Maybe he would help. After all, he was white. But Bryce looked down at the man in disgust. "You'll tell the truth or get no help from us, mister. I've got no sympathy for a man who'd go after another man who's grieving for his dead son!" He stepped back. "Chaco is free to do what he wants."

Chaco pressed more and the man whined. "Veck! James Veck," he literally squeaked.

Troy's eyes widened. "Veck! What are you talking about?"

"He ... hired us. He heard you was goin' back home ... that you'd got a telegram to return right away. Veck paid off the telegrapher to tell him the contents of the envelope and then ... then he hired us to follow you ... figured if it was Chaco's kid, Chaco would show. Everybody knows the kid was his."

"You piece of trash," Bryce growled. "If Lisa Edwards dies, you'll hang! You might get away with killing an Indian, but by

416

God you won't get away with killing a white woman ... especially when her husband is Troy Edwards! Everybody in the country will know about this, mister, and you won't be safe anyplace you go." He looked at Troy. "See to Lisa. Get her on the travois. We've got to get her back quickly."

The only attacker left alive looked up at the vicious-looking Chaco, who slowly drew the tomahawk across under his nose, leaving a stinging cut. "What about me?" the man squeaked.

"Let him up, Chaco," Bryce sneered. "We need this one alive."

Chaco got up reluctantly. "The Apache has a thousand ways to make a man die slowly," he hissed. "I would choose the worst one for you!"

The man put a hand to his badly bleeding nose. "What did he do to me?" he almost screamed. "Stinking savage!"

Bryce grasped the man by the shirt front and yanked. "If you don't cooperate I'll let him do anything he wants with you! You're going to jail at Fort Bowie, mister, and then you're going to be escorted to Tucson, where charges are already being brought against Mr. James Veck. You're going to tell your story to the public—how Veck hired you to follow and kill Troy Edwards and his Apache brother, Chaco, how you ambushed them at a small baby's funeral! You're going to tell the whole world the kind of man Veck is, you understand? Because if you don't, by God I'll find a way to get you. I fought Apaches for a lot of years when I was in the army. I know all their methods of torture and I'll use them on you if you don't do what I tell you."

He turned to Chaco. "Keep an eye on him." He went to his horse and took off some rope, coming back and tying it about the man's waist, then his wrists so that his arms were able to move only a few inches in front of him. He tied the wrists together, then tied the rope to the pommel of his saddle. "You're walking back, mister, and you'd better be able to walk fast or you'll be dragged!"

Shannon watched in horror, holding Charles close. Chaco only grinned. "That is too good for him, Father."

"I know. But I want him alive," Bryce answered. He mounted up, and Chaco walked over to his mother.

"I would like to take Charles with me. I want to hold my son in my arms one last time."

"You're . . . going with us?"

He watched her sadly. "I promised Lisa I would not leave her. I will not break that promise this time. She will need my presence to want to live."

Her eyes teared. "But . . . we'll probably have to get the army doctor. We'll have to report this. Soldiers will come for you."

He blinked back tears. "I know," he said softly. "What is the use, Mother? If I die in that place, I will die among my friends."

She choked in a sob. "Chaco . . ."

He touched her face. "Do not cry, my mother. You have always known how it must end."

She slowly handed Charles over. At five, he was an armful. The boy reached out and touched Chaco's cheek curiously, as though to wonder if the dark skin rubbed off. Chaco forced a smile, although a tear ran down his cheek. "You are a fine son," he told Charles. "A fine son."

"Sage go away," Charles pouted. "He's not coming back?"

Chaco swallowed and shook his head. "No. He's not coming back."

Charles looked down at the bleeding arms and the blood now on his clothes. "You hurt?"

Chaco shrugged. "A little. Come with me. It is your mother who is most hurt. She will need us. You must be a very good and quiet boy around her."

"Mommy go away, too? Like Sage?"

Chaco breathed deeply. "No. We will not let her go away like Sage."

He turned and plopped the boy on his painted horse, easing

418

himself up gracefully behind the boy while Shannon climbed up onto Troy's horse. Troy would ride Lisa's horse, pulling the travois carefully behind it. Bryce would follow all of them, pulling the sniper along and not waiting to see if he would walk or be dragged. It made no difference to Bryce.

Chaco turned and took a last look at little Sage's bundled body on the scaffold. A pain moved through him as he remembered not just Sage but poor Little Deer, who had loved him faithfully and had died giving birth to the boy. Perhaps now they were together. He turned and looked down at Lisa as the travois was dragged past him.

"I love you, Lisa," he said loudly, hoping the words would help. But she looked pale . . . too pale.

"We'll send soldiers to get the damned bodies," Bryce told Chaco. "I don't want those bastards buried near my grandson."

Chaco nodded. They rode carefully for home. Inside Lisa screamed for Chaco to run. He didn't have to stay with her. Staying would surely mean surrender and imprisonment. After all these months and years he had eluded the soldiers, now he would be caught, and it would be because of her. It would always be because of her. Chaco! Chaco! She tried to speak the name but could not. What would happen to him now? Her precious Chaco. He could not go to that place! He must not!

Chapter Twenty-Nine

Bryce greeted the doctor and the several soldiers with him on the front steps of his cabin, rifle in hand. Troy stood beside him also holding a gun. Both were still disheveled from the encounter with the civilians who had tried to kill them. A black bruise was spreading across Troy's right cheek and there was a cut over his left eye.

"What is this?" the doctor spoke up. "Your man came to me saying your daughter-in-law needed help, Mr. Edwards."

"That's right," Bryce spoke up. "And you also know Chaco is here or you wouldn't have brought all these men along."

"I am Colonel Whit, sir, new commander at Fort Bowie. I have orders from General Sheridan and General Miles to arrest Chaco and see that he is sent to Florida with the other prisoners."

"Not until we know if Lisa will be all right. Chaco's presence could be the very thing that keeps her alive."

The colonel frowned. "I don't understand."

"You don't have to. Chaco will go with you ... after the doctor has looked at Lisa. And when he does go, I'm going along to be sure he gets fair treatment. I've seen too many Indians killed while trying to 'escape.' Murdered is usually the word for it."

"I assure you Mr. Edwards, no harm will come to him . . . if he cooperates."

"Just the same, I'm coming along." He waved the rifle at the doctor. "Go on in. She's lost a lot of blood. She needs some sewing up and we need something to give her for pain."

The doctor dismounted rather reluctantly, unhooking his bag from his saddle. He hesitated at the steps. "Is that wild Indian inside?"

Bryce grinned wryly. "He is. He is with Lisa. So is my wife. Don't worry, he won't scalp you."

The man frowned and brushed past him. Bryce turned his attention to the soldiers then. "You can either go on back and trust me to bring Chaco in, or you can camp here on my land and wait. It could be all night, it could be two nights . . . however long it takes to be sure Lisa will be all right."

"You can't do this, Edwards," Whit spoke up.

"This is my land and I'll do what I want."

The colonel's eyes narrowed. "Then I'll stay and wait! Do you really think I'd trust you to bring him in?"

"You can trust my word as good or better than any man's, and as good as a colonel in the army for a lot of years. I was in your shoes once."

The colonel scowled. "Yes, I know all about that. But trusting your word has little to do with it. The first chance he gets Chaco will bolt again. I do not intend to lose him this time. You'd better warn him he'll be shot if he tries to run."

"He won't run. He's a man of his word and so am I. Now you're welcome to camp down there by that corral," he added, pointing to a place several hundred yards distant from the house.

"I want to post two men inside to keep an eye on Chaco."

"He's with Lisa and the doctor. I'm not going to let two strangers stand there and watch. Now get going."

The colonel hesitated, his jaw flexing in a desire to shoot Bryce Edwards. But the last commander at Fort Bowie had had his run-ins with this man, and from what he could gather, Colonel Blazer had always come out on the losing end. There was an honesty about Bryce Edwards' gray eyes that made him decide to trust him, and a sadness there that made itself evident. Colonel Whit softened, sighing and removing his hat.

"I am sorry, Mr. Edwards, about your grandson."

Bryce's grip eased on the rifle, and his eyes teared. "Thank you. Now get going."

The colonel turned his horse and ordered his men to follow him out toward the corral Bryce had indicated. "They say, sir, that the other grandson, Charles, is really Chaco's child," a lieutenant told the colonel when they got farther away. "The girl Lisa was once Chaco's captive."

The colonel nodded. "I'd heard that. But the white brother married her. It's a strange story, Lieutenant, but there might be something to it if the girl wants Chaco with her now. Just keep a close watch on that cabin. If he tries to escape, you know what to do. A prisoner is still a prisoner."

"Yes, sir."

Inside the cabin Lisa lay shivering from shock and loss of blood.

"Part of the shoulder blade is surely broken off," the doctor told Shannon. "I'm going to have to get in there and try to remove the pieces. From the location of the wound, I don't think any vital organs have been hit. If there is no damage to her right lung, she should be fine once we get this bleeding to stop."

He glanced up at Chaco, who stood threateningly on the other side of the bed, arms folded, his dark eyes boring into the doctor as though to warn he'd better save the girl's life. 'So,' he thought, 'this is Chaco. He's more handsome than I had pictured. Could it be true—about this wild, vicious-looking Indian and this beautiful young woman?'

Lisa groaned Chaco's name and he came closer, bending

422

over her and putting a hand to the side of her face. "I am here."

"Don't ... run away again."

"I told you I would not. The doctor is going to fix you so you get well. And I will stay right here."

"It ... hurts."

"I know. I have felt the hurt of a bullet wound. But you will get better." He looked over at the doctor, who was taking some instruments from his bag. "You have something for pain?"

The man frowned and nodded. "I have something. She won't feel too much. She'll be mighty sore when she wakes up, though." He looked at Shannon. "Get some water boiling good and hard, will you?"

"Certainly."

She left the room and the doctor turned to see Chaco holding Lisa's hand, bent over talking softly near her ear. "I will always love you, Lisa," he heard. Chaco gently kissed her cheek, her forehead. "Do not die. It will all be for nothing if you die."

The doctor was amazed at the young man's gentleness, his apparent true concern for the woman. But hadn't she been his captive? Was it possible for an Apache to have feelings? To understand gentleness? And was it possible for a white woman to actually love one? He shrugged. The only explanation could be that this one was half white. Surely no full-blooded Apache could have human feelings.

Chaco looked up from his chair beside the bed as Troy entered the room. Their eyes held for a moment before Troy went to Lisa's bed, leaning over and touching her forehead. "The doctor says she'll be all right," he said quietly. "She'll sleep a while yet."

A dark hand reached over and touched her cheek. "It is my fault," Chaco said, pain in his voice. "So many things are my fault."

Troy sighed, rising and walking around to quietly pick up another wooden chair and set it closer to the bed, and on the same side as Chaco and facing him. He sat down wearily. "Chaco, you never asked for any of this. We both started out the same, remember? We were raised the same, loved the same. But you looked Indian. People wouldn't let you live among us in peace. It's not your fault, Chaco."

Chaco took his hand from Lisa, leaning forward with his elbows on his knees, flexing his hands nervously. To Troy he seemed too big and wild for the room, and it sickened him to think of his brother in prison. It would be the worst torture.

"Chaco, I helped you escape once. I'll do it again if you want to try it."

Chaco closed his eyes and shook his head. "I am through running," he answered dejectedly. He met Troy's eyes with his own tired ones. "The battle cannot be won by one man."

Troy leaned closer. "Chaco, listen to me. Maybe there is a way for you and Lisa to be together."

Chaco frowned. "Together?" He looked Troy over. "She is your wife now."

Troy's eyes saddened. "It isn't working, Chaco. We wanted very much for it to work, but we didn't get married for the right reasons. Her heart is too full of you, and I ... I ... met someone ... while I was in New York. I had determined to let it go, and I would have. But Lisa found out, and she refuses to stay married to me. She thinks she's cheating me out of what I really want and she wants to part while we're friends, not wait until I might become bitter and resentful." He sighed and rested his head in his hands. "I argued against it, but she might be right. I love her, Chaco, but not like you love her and not like I love Joanna. Lisa and I ..." He raised his head and met Chaco's eyes, full of concern and surprise. "We're just damned good friends, Chaco. We tried to make it more than that ... wanted it to be more than that. But it just isn't working. I'll

424

always love her, and Charles is just like a son to me. I'll always help take care of them."

Chaco's eyes showed his sorrow. "You are ... divorcing her?"

Troy turned away, then stood up. "Yes. It's a mutual agreement. We were only waiting to see what would happen with Sage ... and with you."

"But I ... I would not want any other man to touch her. You are my brother. You I could trust. She is young. Other men will want her. ..."

Troy turned, sitting back down and leaning close. "Chaco, I'm going to do everything in my power to make it possible for *you* to take care of her, to be with her, free, and her legal husband."

Chaco's eyes darkened and a sneer moved across his face. "That is foolish talk. It can never be so!"

"Yes it can, Chaco!"

Chaco got up then, walking to a window and looking out at the soldiers who stood guard there. "There ... out there is what awaits me, my brother," he said angrily, keeping his voice low for Lisa's sake. "Soldiers! Perhaps death, and most certainly imprisonment in Florida where I will be lucky to live two years. I am better off ending my life ... diving through this window right now and running and letting them shoot me down!"

"Goddamn it, Chaco, listen to me," Troy growled, walking over to him and grabbing his arm, yanking him around. A flame of defensiveness flashed through Chaco's eyes as he jerked away. Troy did not flinch. Yes, his brother was wild. But he had not always been wild, and he could surely be tamed again.

"What is this foolish thought you have?" he sneered at Troy. "It is easy for you to dream. You are white, you are educated."

"I'm just a man, and so are you!" Troy's face colored with anger. "Some day people are going to understand that, Chaco. And you're going to help me make them understand!"

"Me?" He grinned sarcastically and turned away. "Are you still going to write that silly book about the Apache?"

"Perhaps. If I do, it won't be silly. But that's not what I'm talking about now. Will you please ignore that damned, stubborn pride of yours and listen to me? Don't fall into the trap of hopelessness the rest of the Apaches have fallen into, Chaco! Don't you see? It's what they want. It's the best victory— destroy the pride, the spirit! That can only happen if you *let* it happen! But you were the last holdout, Chaco, and you can continue to be the last holdout by not letting anything they do to you destroy Chaco, the man."

Chaco turned around, frowning. "You are talking in circles."

Troy stepped closer. "To begin with, don't you think it's about time you stopped destroying Mother? That's what you're doing, you know, slowly but surely. For years she has worried over you, suffered sleepless nights and untold anxiety. And what of Lisa? She hasn't had a happy day since she was taken from you."

"I cannot change that."

"Yes, you can," Troy almost hissed. "That's the attitude I want you to get rid of, Chaco. You *can* change it!"

Chaco turned away again. "I do not understand you."

"Chaco, I'm an important person now and getting more well known every day. People read and pay attention to my articles. I am winning more and more sympathy for the plight of the Indian. It's just a dent now, but it will get bigger. It might take years. But in the meantime, at least some people are paying attention. And if I write fast enough and campaign hard enough, I think I can bring enough pressure to get you out of Fort Marion. And once you've gone there and served some time and been set free, then it's over, Chaco! Don't you see? You'd be a free man. And since you're half white, you could come home. You know Pa would let you run the trading post. He's getting tired of it, and he wants to take Mother back to Virginia to see the graves of her parents and brother while she's still young

426

and well enough to make the trip. And *I* need you, too! I want you to help me with my writing. Once I get you out ..."

"You cannot get me out," Chaco growled, whirling to face him. "It is impossible!"

"No, it isn't. And Pa knows some important people in Washington. He could pull a few strings. ..."

"And what of my brothers left behind? Why should I be able to go free and not they?"

Troy just stared at him, then sighed and turned away. "I know how it would make you feel. But I think it's about time you at least tried our way again, Chaco—for Mother's sake, and for Lisa's. Don't keep putting Mother through this. And you have a son. Do you want him to grow up never knowing his father? Do you want some other man to marry Lisa?"

Chaco actually flinched and Troy knew he had hit a nerve. He stepped closer. "Damn it, Chaco, isn't being free to be with Lisa and Charles enough incentive for you to at least try? What good does it do them to have you sitting in prison in Florida?" He walked to the window himself then. "There is no going back, Chaco. You can never live the free life with the Apaches again. They're all removed, and Arizona is becoming more and more settled. We don't like what is happening, but we can't really stop it and we have to be realistic about the future." He turned and met his brother's eyes. "Chaco, once you go to prison and are let out again, you will be freer than you have ever been. You would have a whole family waiting for you, and a means of making a living. You grew up that way. It isn't totally foreign to you. And some attitudes are changing. People can't get away with the cruelty they once did. And you were always good with horses. If you don't like the trading post business, or if it fades out, you've got the ranch. I don't need it. I've got my paper in Tucson now, and that's where I intend to live with Joanna."

His eyes lit up with hope as he continued, seeing that Chaco was at least beginning to listen. "Chaco, I'm even having James

Veck prosecuted. Everyone knows now that the note you gave me that he had signed was found on the same two men Pa tried to prosecute a few years ago, men who were suspected of raping and murdering their own kind and blaming it on Indians just to keep the war going so men like Veck could get rich! Now we have one man alive who attacked us and who admits James Veck sent him. Things are slowly going to get better, Chaco. If I didn't believe that I'd be giving up myself, but I refuse to do so and so should you!" He came closer and grasped Chaco's arms. "For God's sake, Chaco, at least try it, for Lisa's sake! For your son! You don't have to give up being Apache, just give up the running and thoughts of death. Think about life, Chaco, and Charles and Lisa and our mother. Think about what a fine, strong, intelligent human being you are, and the family you have who loves you and wants to help."

Chaco smiled sadly. "I will think about it. But you have forgotten two things, my brother, that could keep any of it from happening." He turned away, looking out at the soldiers again. "First, I have to get to Fort Marion without one of them finding a reason to shoot me. And once I am there, you have to get me out. The freedom you speak of is far away, and perhaps just a dream after all. I feel in my heart that Geronimo and all my Apache brothers and sisters will never see their homeland again."

"Maybe not. But I'm going to make sure they are not forgotten, Chaco. Not ever! And some day they will return. It might be their sons and grandsons who get to come back, but they *will* come back."

Chaco turned to meet his eyes, his own red and watery. "You really believe this."

Troy nodded. "I do."

Chaco took a deep breath, reaching out his hand. Troy grasped his wrist, and Chaco's hand folded around Troy's wrist. "I will try to believe it also," he told Troy. "I will go to that place and I will try not to lose hope, but even if I am freed. . . ."

He glanced over at Lisa. "Perhaps it is best for her I do not return. Being with me will only bring her more sorrow and troubles. Perhaps once I am gone, it would be best if she never saw me again. I love her too much to keep hurting her."

Troy squeezed his arm. "No, Chaco. The biggest hurt would be to know you are alive and she can't be with you. Do you think the risk matters to her, any more than it mattered to our mother?"

"Saguaro died. They could not be together. She married a white man."

"She still suffered because of her life with Saguaro. Why not let there be a happy ending this time, Chaco? Mother could never have Saguaro. But Lisa can have you. I think Mother would be a very happy woman to see that happen."

Chaco released his grip, turning back to the window and putting his hands on the center sash, hanging his head between his arms. "I do not know. I must think long and hard about it." He looked at the soldiers again. "And I have not yet made it to Florida, nor do I see a lot of hope of ever getting out of there again."

Troy put a hand on his shoulder. "I'll get you out if I die doing it."

Chaco turned again, and this time they embraced. "Some day we're going to race again, Chaco—you and me—out on the desert like the old days when life was easy and we didn't have a care in the world."

Chaco gritted his teeth and squeezed his eyes shut against tears. He made no answer.

Lisa lay in pain through a restless night, aware of only one thing that eased the pain. Chaco. Never did she wake without seeing him sitting there, his hand in hers, his dark eyes watching her lovingly. In sleep her mind whirled with dreams—Chaco, holding her,—Chaco fighting for her, Chaco running from soldiers. Soldiers! Soldiers everywhere. She could hear them giving orders, sabers clanking.

She jerked awake. The morning sun was shining through the bedroom window and again she heard the voices, but they were real, not a dream. "Chaco," she whimpered, trying to sit up.

Quickly he was there, making her lie back down. "Do not move. You will bleed again."

"Soldiers! I . . . heard them. Run away, Chaco!"

He leaned closer, smoothing the hair back from her face. "I cannot run anymore, Lisa. I have to tell you good-bye now. This time I go with the soldiers."

Her eyes widened. "No," she said louder, bringing Shannon into the room.

He returned her look sadly. "Ai."

"Shannon, don't let the soldiers take him," Lisa said frantically, the tears coming.

"You stay calm, Lisa. We have no choice now. Bryce will go along to make sure Chaco is well treated."

"No! No! I'll . . . never see him again!" She looked back at Chaco. "Don't go with them!"

Shannon turned away to hide her own tears and panic. Chaco! Her son! Going to that horrible place! He could die there.

"It is all right, Lisa," Chaco tried to reassure her. He leaned down and kissed her cheek.

"Why are you here? Why didn't you run away?"

He kissed at her tears. "I could not leave you, not again, not when you were hurt. We had to get the doctor from the fort to help you. And so the soldiers found out I was here. There was no other way, and in a way I am glad, for I am tired of running, Lisa. It is over now."

"But . . . they might kill you . . . or you might die. You'll go to that prison. . . ."

He put his fingers to her lips, his own eyes tearing at the sight of the devastation on her face. "Lisa, my Lisa. You must be strong. I am so sorry for all the hurt I have caused you."

430

"It ... wasn't you," she wept. "Oh, Chaco, I don't want to live. ..."

"No, Lisa, do not talk that way." He studied her lovingly, his own tears coming now. "One so young and beautiful should never talk that way. You must live ... for me ... for my son. Promise me you will always be here for my son."

"Oh, Chaco, how can I go on?"

"Because you are strong, like my mother. And Bryce and my brother will work to get me out of that place so that I will be a free man."

"But what if they don't let you go?"

One of his own tears fell on her cheek. "Lisa, I want you to ... promise me you will go on with life ... that if it looks hopeless and I may be gone for many years ... you will not waste your life waiting. I know about you and Troy. But he will be your good friend, and you will always have my mother and father. Yet what you will need most is a man ... a good man who will look after you and let you be a woman ... and who will help you raise Charles."

"I don't want anyone but you ... not ever!"

"Promise me, Lisa, that you will not waste your life, and that in choosing a man, you will choose the finest ... one who will be kind to my son and to you."

"No! No," she wept. "You can run away, Chaco. You can take me with you."

His body shivered in his own sorrow. He bent his head down, crying into her hair. "No. I cannot run away now. Even if I could, I could never take you with me. It ... has to be the right way, Lisa, or it ... cannot be at all. Please promise me you will be strong, not just for me but for Charles."

She stroked his hair with her left hand, for it hurt her whole right side to use the other arm. Her pain was only accented by her sorrow. "Stay ... another day ... a week," she begged.

"If only I could," he whispered.

In the next moment Troy walked in, an old pain of possession stabbing at him when he saw them together. But she was not his. She had never been his. Even if Chaco died, it was best they parted. He swallowed. "Pa says he can't hold them off much longer, Chaco. The colonel is getting angry and Pa's afraid to get him too upset. It's best they have good feelings toward you, and they think they've waited long enough. Whit has orders to get you back to Fort Bowie."

Chaco tried to rise, but Lisa, crying, clung to his hair, refusing to let him go. He quickly wiped at his own tears, then grasped her hand, pulling her fingers open. Troy turned away from the pitiful sight.

"Promise me, Lisa," Chaco told her. "My son is my life. You must hang on and teach him about the Apaches ... tell him about me and why it is I cannot be with him. Make him understand so that he does not hate me."

"He would never hate you," she wept. "He will ... love you ... like I do and ... like all of us do."

He forced a smile for her. "To the end of my days I will love you, Lisa. If I go to my death, I will take your memory and love with me. My only regret is hurting you as I have. If I could do any of it differently, I would. But it was not to be so." More tears slipped down his face as he leaned down once more to kiss her lips. "I am not truly worthy of you, and I am honored to have called you my own, even if it was just for a while."

"Don't say that," she wept. "Don't say ... you aren't worthy. You're ... as worthy as any man ... and I love you, Chaco."

He raised up kissing her hand. "And I love you. Good-bye, Lisa. You will get well now. I thank the spirits for that."

He got up from the bed. So little time! Always so little time! "Chaco," she whimpered. But he turned away deliberately, looking past Troy, tears on his face. He walked out, facing his mother while in the other room Lisa sobbed.

"Good-bye, my mother. I am sorry. You are a good white woman, and I see why my father loved you."

She held herself stiffly, struggling to be strong for him.

432

"Good-bye, son." She picked up a bag from the table. "Fresh biscuits. When you were small and ... liked to go off riding ... you always took fresh biscuits. Sometimes you ..." Her voice broke. "Sometimes you would steal them."

He grinned almost bashfully. It seemed almost a joke now, stealing biscuits from his mother to stealing supplies for survival from settlers. "I was practicing for the day I would become a renegade," he told her.

He stepped closer and embraced her, holding her tightly as she wept.

"You women ... so much crying," he told her, trying to smile through his own tears.

Colonel Whit came inside then with Bryce, stopping short at the sight of tears on Chaco's face. It seemed incredible an Indian could have such deep feelings. There was a closeness to this family that surprised him, for he had already formed his own opinion upon hearing Shannon Edwards had a half-breed son. But the woman was beautiful, and her love for the young man was as great as any mother's love for a son. Was it possible this Chaco was not as bad as some said?

Chaco gently pushed her away, taking the sack of biscuits and forcing himself to smile for her. He stood erect, again wiping at his eyes. He turned to Troy. "We have said our good-byes. I wish happiness for you, my brother. But you must promise to always look after her."

"You know I will. You just remember what I told you. You're coming home, Chaco."

Hopelessness came into Chaco's eyes. "It is a nice thought." He turned to Bryce. "There are no words for a man such as you. Few men in this world would love a woman's half-breed son as you have loved me. May the spirits always smile upon you, my father. I know that Saguaro watches, and is pleased with the way you kept your promises to him."

Bryce swallowed, moving beside him. "I wish there were a

way out of this, Chaco. But I'm going with you and staying with you for part of the trip."

Chaco nodded. "Good. It is good." He walked out, past Colonel Whit, without even looking at the man. He stepped outside into a circle of twenty soldiers who all eyed him warily, their hands on their rifles. Chaco looked around at them with a sneer. "It takes only one bullet," he commented. "Am I so feared?" He smiled sadly. Colonel Whit came out and took wrist irons from his belt, grabbing Chaco's arm. Chaco jerked it away and the rest of the soldiers stiffened, one of them cocking his rifle.

"Chaco, you've got to cooperate," Bryce warned him. "Please. Your mother is watching. Do what they say. We're going to get you out of this."

Their eyes held, and Bryce felt his heart breaking when he reached out to take the sack of biscuits from Chaco while the colonel snapped the wrist irons on him. Here stood Chaco, the feared Apache renegade, a grown man. But Bryce Edwards saw only the chubby little Indian boy he'd taken into his heart because he was the son of the woman he loved. Where had that bright, happy innocent boy gone? Happiness had been stolen from him by hatred and prejudice.

Chaco turned and mounted his own Indian horse, which would be led by soldiers. Bryce mounted his own steed, riding directly behind Chaco. One thing was sure. He'd kill the first man who tried to bring harm to Saguaro's son. They rode out, leading the last warrior. The mountains were empty and lonely now.

Chapter Thirty

The wheels turned quickly against James Veck, as did many of his former friends in Tucson. The investigation of Veck drew many other prominent businessmen into the picture, and the general public was outraged that these men would deliberately do things to prolong the Apache wars for their own profit.

Stuart Morse, Cleve Newsome and Howard Smith were also brought up on charges of conspiracy against the government and the people of Arizona. Names and accusations flew following Troy's original suggestive articles, and it was not until James Veck was prosecuted that Troy produced the letter his brother had found on two white men who had been raping an Indian woman—the same two men Bryce Edwards had tried to prosecute for killing another Indian family and for atrocities committed against other whites in the effort to frame Indians. Then came the prosecution's surprise witness, the man Bryce and Troy had quietly kept imprisoned at Fort Bowie, waiting until he could testify against Veck, the man who was part of those who had been paid by Veck to kill Troy Edwards and Chaco.

One uncovered plot led to another, until the public was pounding at the jail door to hang James Veck. But Veck was whisked away to serve time in prison in California, his vast fortune crumbling without his guidance, and some of his money used to pay large fines set by the government. Along with Veck went several other businessmen and a few less prominent citizens. But it seemed ironic to Bryce and Troy that only now, after getting rid of all of its Indians, did Arizona finally do something about the depredations against them, the false accusations. It was too late to be of any benefit to the Apaches. But it was at least a small victory for Bryce Edwards, after suffering the humiliating setback he'd incurred when he originally arrested Chadwell and Miller.

Then came Troy's stepped-up campaign to get his brother released. First came articles printed in his own paper and sent to eastern papers, telling his brother's story—how Chaco was raised among white men but never had a chance because of hatred and prejudice. His writing was so eloquent that he even had people sympathizing with Chaco's "white" wife and accepting the relationship, feeling sorry for the son left behind and for the loss of an Apache wife and son. The hideous living conditions at Fort Marion, and the fact that Indians there were dying rapidly, far from their beloved homelands, were revealed. Geronimo and the other last warriors had not been taken to Fort Marion after all, but to Fort Pickens, where the public could come and stare at them and see the infamous Apache leader. Neither place was healthy for an Indian.

It was months before Bryce and Troy could discover just which place Chaco had been taken to. It was Fort Marion, the worse of the two prisons. Troy stressed in his articles that the old fort, with its dungeons below, was no place for Indians accustomed to clean, mountain air and arid climate. At Fort Marion they were forced to pitch tents on cold, concrete slabs, and that was how they lived, becoming even hungrier when the government cut their rations drastically, leaving the commander at the prison barely enough food to feed his overflow of Indians—three hundred and more when there was only room for perhaps seventy-five. Troy's readers were quick to sympathize with Chaco, and letters began pouring in to the President and the War Department, urging that Chaco, Geronimo, Naiche, and the rest be released and given the land promised to them when they were tricked into surrendering.

"Malaria is common," Troy wrote. "And now the children are being taken from the women prisoners. There are fewer things sadder than taking a child from an Apache. Sometimes the women manage to hide them under their full skirts, and they find other ways to hide them, trying desperately to keep them from being taken away. The children are lined up and picked out like so many cattle for slaughter, and to the Indian it is just as bad as slaughter. They are usually sent to the special Indian school at Carlisle, but it is a death trap. Turberculosis infects most of the children there and many have already died. Those who live have their precious and sacred long hair shorn, and they are given white man's clothing and white man's names. They are punished for speaking in their own tongue.

"Is this what we call freedom and democracy? Some say I am disloyal to my country when I write these things. On the contrary, I write them to urge our government and the War Department to live up to what this country is supposed to stand for."

In addition to his articles, Troy wrote a letter daily to the President of the United States, determined to pester the man until he gave up. "Are Geronimo and the others who are imprisoned at Fort Pickens aware of what is happening at Fort Marion?" he asked. "Have they been kept informed? Do they know anything about their families? General Miles promised them they would be reunited, but this has never happened."

Soon, citizens aroused the attention of the Indian Rights Association of Philadelphia, stirring investigations into the fact that many innocent Apaches were incarcerated at Fort Marion and that none of the promises made upon Geronimo's surrender had been kept.

Troy took advantage of the stir. "These Apaches are treated as nothing more than sideshow freaks. It is well known that on

437

their journey by train to Florida crowds gathered at every stop, pushing and shoving to get a view of the 'wild' Indians. Geronimo and the other leaders imprisoned at Fort Pickens cannot even be escorted outside the walls for fresh air without crowds of people swarming around them."

The families of those warriors at Fort Pickens were allowed to leave Fort Marion and were sent to join their husbands and fathers at Fort Pickens. The rest of the Apaches, who caused so much overcrowding at Fort Marion, were sent to Mount Vernon Barracks in Alabama, near Mobile. Thus, the last holdouts were kept separated. Again, it was months before Bryce and Troy found out what had happened to Chaco. Having no family at Fort Pickens, he had been sent to Alabama with the others. At Mount Vernon the prisoners slept in crude, two-room cabins with dirt floors and no furniture, sleeping on boards or on the ground, a far less clean and habitable environment than any wickiup or a tipí, cold and damp in winter and hot and stuffy in summer.

"The prisoners at Mount Vernon struggle to live a clean and ordered life with what little is given them," Troy wrote. "Those who visit there are surprised at the extreme love and devotion given the little children. Children are so loved that their parents keep all letters sent to them from children who have been forced to go to Carlisle, and they keep these letters wrapped in pieces of cloth for protection, the cloth being beautifully embroidered. I have told before of this intense love, and urge that my own brother, whose mother is white, be released so that he can be reunited with his own wife and child, where we know he will be a productive, peaceful citizen. We fear it is only a matter of time before he, too, contracts the dreaded tuberculosis that kills so many in these places and that killed his own little Apache son."

Sympathy became widespread, except in Arizona. Arizona citizens remained hateful. They wanted no Apaches returned there. However, upon the appeal of Mescalero Apaches who still had a small reservation in New Mexico, several Mescaleros who had been involved in a roundup of the peaceful reservation Chiricahuas, including Geronimo's Mescalero wife, Ihtedda, and their daughter, Lenna, were removed from prison and sent to New Mexico.

It was late summer, 1889, after two years of imprisonment, that the telegram came to Bryce's trading post. How the bureacratic red tape had been bypassed, no one would know. Perhaps it was simply in answer to the well-publicized writings of Troy Edwards, who was being acclaimed as a brilliant writer. "Some of the most enlightening information on the American Indian ever written," one New York critic declared. Or perhaps it was because some high official in Washington remembered the dedicated service of Bryce Edwards during the years of the heated Apache wars with Cochise and the infamous Saguaro. Whatever the reason, Chaco had been sent to New Mexico with the Mescaleros.

Lisa took hope. For two years she had waited, wanting to go on with life as she had promised Chaco, but unable to consider a life without him. Her letters to him had been faithful and full of hope. But they went unanswered. It was obvious Chaco was trying to make her forget him, sure that he would never be freed. She had been a long time recovering from her bullet wound, for some of the life went out of her when Chaco was taken away.

"Surely if he's come this far we can get him home," she told Bryce.

Bryce studied the telegram. "I'll wire Troy and tell him. We owe a lot of this to him."

Lisa felt the old pain in her heart. Troy Edwards had given so much for his brother. He had almost given up his own happiness. In spite of her own loneliness, she was glad she had sued for divorce. They were still friends. But Troy was married to Joanna now, and they lived in a fine house in Tucson, where

Troy was well known and well liked, and where he now worked nights on a book he had always wanted to write.

"This is no guarantee, Lisa. We might still run into a lot of problems. Maybe we shouldn't even draw attention to the fact that Chaco is in New Mexico. They might ship him back to prison."

"We have to take the chance," she answered.

He nodded, looking at Shannon. "Agreed?"

Her eyes lit up with hope. "Agreed."

"There is one last problem," he warned. "Chaco has to want to come. You know how stubborn he can be. He might decide we're all better off without him. He might decide to stay with the Mescaleros."

"He won't," Lisa answered quickly. "He'll come! I know he'll come!"

Bryce sighed with doubts. "I hope you're right. And I hope he's well."

Letters and telegrams flew again, with the result that Chaco, because of his white blood and promises from his white family that he would "behave," could at last come home a free man. But then came the telegram that Chaco had chosen to stay in New Mexico. Lisa sent three pleading letters, as did Shannon, but they were not answered. Chaco still refused to return. Lisa's hope grew dim, and she proposed that she go to New Mexico herself to convince Chaco to come home.

"No," Troy answered. He was visiting with Joanna, and they sat in a family conference discussing the matter. "You don't know what you'll find. Maybe there is some reason we don't know about. My guess is he's just being stubborn. Either way, I'll go myself. I'll get that bull-headed Apache back here where he belongs."

They all had to laugh at the remark. "I must say I look

forward to meeting this mysterious brother of yours," Joanna spoke up. "I think!"

Troy patted her stomach, swollen with his child. He was a happy man, happier than Lisa had ever known him, except for the absence of his brother. That would make his life complete. She studied Joanna, a pretty, dark girl whose brown eyes sparkled with love for Troy Edwards, whom she all but worshiped. After the initial uncomfortable meeting, the two women had grown to like each other very much, and the addition of another grandchild to the family would help ease the pain of the past several years. Charles was seven now, and asking incessant questions about his real father, always wanting to know when he was coming home.

"So, it's decided then," Troy spoke up. "I'm going to New Mexico."

It was February 12, 1890. Lisa, now twenty-seven, waited at Bowie Station. The rest of the family waited inside while she stood on the platform. It had been agreed she would be first to greet him, if he came at all. Chaco was thirty now. Their son was nearly eight. If ever they were to be a family, it must be now or never. She must keep the promise she had made to Chaco.

They had received the letter from Troy, sent by special messenger to reach them quickly.

"I am returning February 12. Meet me at Bowie Station. Cannot promise Chaco will come. He was beaten by a guard on his train trip to Fort Marion, shot in the right leg. The leg was not well treated and got infected. It was cut off below the knee. He walks on a wooden peg and uses a cane. This is the reason he did not reply to our letters and why he refused to come home. He feels he is not fully a man. Pardon my boldness, but I told him if he came home to Lisa, he would find out how much of a man he still was. She would show him." The remark helped ease the horror of the news, and Lisa reddened when the letter was first read.

"I told him it is what is on the inside that makes the man. Those were once his very words to me. I reminded him of that. I think I have him convinced to come home but cannot promise. Either way, I am coming February 12, for I miss Joanna and worry about her condition. Chaco understands this and knows he must decide. I will do my best. Love, Troy."

Part of his leg cut off! What a demeaning thing for an Apache warrior! Lisa did not doubt it would have no effect on his manliness. It could not change his handsomeness, his muscular build, the way he sat a horse. It could not affect his ability to make love to her. It changed nothing. It tore at her heart to think of his awful pain and suffering, alone, in prison, with no one to comfort him.

Shannon's tears had been bitter after hearing the letter, but somehow Lisa could not cry. Somehow she only felt stronger. She had a mission now, her mission was to bring love to one who had lived too long without it. Life must change for him. She would help him. Yes, she most certainly would show him he was still a man.

She heard a train whistle then, saw the great black engine looming in the distance, coming in from the east. Her heart raced, and she prayed with all her faith and diligence. She squeezed her hands together to stay in control. Chaco! He had to be on it.

It seemed to take forever for the train to get to the station. Finally it was there, rumbling to a halt, steam hissing from its sides. Conductors jumped down and lowered the steps, and people began disembarking. There weren't many passengers today.

Finally she spotted Troy, disembarking from the last car. He was alone! Her heart froze and she felt faint. No! Chaco had to be with him! He had to! She felt her legs going weak. Her eyes teared and her throat hurt.

Then Troy reached up, taking two bags from someone—his

own large suitcase and a smaller carpetbag. Then someone handed out a cane. She let out a whimper, unaware of anyone beside her, her eyes glued to the last car while she managed to get her legs to carry her farther down the platform closer to the last car.

A tall, dark, handsome man stepped down then, holding on to the step railing, the left pantleg rolled up and tucked around just under his knee, revealing a carved oak peg leg. He took the cane from Troy and turned, spotting Lisa immediately.

Their eyes held and neither seemed able to walk. His face was thin, but handsome ... Oh, so handsome! This time it was plain, not painted for war. He had a serious look of maturity about him she had never seen before, a determination in his dark eyes. He held his chin erect in that arrogant manner the Indian had of signaling his fierce pride, and she could see he had decided he would not let the missing leg bring him down. His look was almost challenging.

Lisa found her legs, walking closer. He wore denim pants and a lovely blue cotton shirt, open at the neck to reveal a beautiful turquoise necklace. His long, black hair was pulled back into one thick braid down his back. The challenge in his eyes changed almost to fear as she came even closer. Troy squeezed Chaco's arm, picking up the bags and walking up to Lisa.

"I've done my best," he said quietly. "The rest is up to you." He took her hand and squeezed it lovingly, then left her standing there, facing Chaco, who seemed unable to move.

"Always, you look so beautiful," he finally spoke up. "You do not change."

Her eyes glittered with love. "Nor do you," she answered.

He could see by her eyes that she truly meant it, that the missing leg went somehow unnoticed.

"I was so afraid ... you wouldn't come," she squeaked.

He studied the vivid blue eyes. "I almost didn't. But then I remembered my vow not to hurt my mother any further ... my

443

duty to my son ... and my desire to see you again ... to touch you again. How many years has it been since the night we spent together? Four? Five? I have lost count."

She came closer, unable to hold back the tears then. "You won't ... ever leave this time, will you? Promise me ... you'll never run away again."

He shook with old sorrows, grabbing her and holding her close then, weeping quietly into her hair for several seconds before he could find his voice. "Help me, Lisa," he whispered.

"Oh, Chaco, I love you so. For so many years I thought this moment was impossible."

"It will still not be easy."

"It doesn't matter. I'll have you beside me! My Chaco! My love!"

Shannon Edwards stepped out of the station and watched them, remembering another Apache warrior, now long buried somewhere in the mountains. Some still spoke his name in awe. Saguaro. But that way of life for the Apache was ended. There would be no more Saguaros, no more Chacos and Geronimos and Cochises. They must all find a new way of life. For many of them there would be no coming back to their beloved homeland. Little known to her then, the greatest one, the one called Geronimo, in spite of pleadings by many pro-Indian groups, would be one of those never to return.

"Miles talked very friendly to us, and we believed him as we would God. I looked in vain for Gereral Miles to send me to that land of which he had spoken; I longed in vain for the implements, house and stock that General Miles had promised me."

Geronimo, after nineteen years as a prisoner.[1]

Geronimo lived out his life at Fort Sill, Oklahoma, making and selling bows and arrows, and peddling autographed pictures of himself. He died a very old man and was quietly buried there, far from his homeland, never to see his beloved mountains again.

1. *Geronimo, The Man, His Time, His Place*, Angie Debo, University of Oklahoma Press, 1976, page 295, footnote 27: Senate Executive Doc. 117, 49 Cong. sess., pp. 22,30; Barrett, *Geronimo's Story of His Life*, pp. 144–47, 178.

2. *Geronimo's Story of His Life*, Stephen Melvil Barrett, Duffield & Co., New York, pp. 113-114.

Author's Note

I hope you have enjoyed my story. For those of you who have never read *Arizona Bride,* and want to read the story of Shannon and Bryce Edwards, and the Apache warrior, Saguaro, you can order it from Zebra or look for it in your book stores.

I hope you will also look for my several other novels, including *Lawless Love, Rapture's Gold, Prairie Embrace, Heart's Surrender* and other historical romances, as well as my Indian series, *Savage Destiny.*

Feel free to write me at 6013-A North Road, Coloma, Michigan 49038. Include a letter-size, self-addressed, stamped envelope, and I will send you my latest newsletter and add you to my mailing list.

Thank you!

F. Rosanne Bittner